# PROSECCO & PAPARAZZI

## BOOK ONE, THE PASSPORT SERIES

CELIA KENNEDY

Booktrope Editions
Seattle, WA 2015

Cover Design by Michelle Fairbanks
Edited by Kathryn Galan

Previously self-published as *Charlotte's Restrained, The Accidental Stalker, 2011*

*This is a work of fiction. Names, characters, places, brands, media, and incidents are either the product of the author's imagination or are used fictitiously. Any resemblance to similarly named places or to persons living or deceased is unintentional.*

PRINT ISBN: 978-1-5137-0166-0
EPUB ISBN: 978-1-5137-0188-2
Library of Congress Control Number: 2015913666

# Acknowledgments

When I was writing *Prosecco and Paparazzi*, my children asked me repeatedly to whom I was going to dedicate my book. My answer was, "Myself! I did all the hard work." Initially they looked shocked, but, when the surprise wore off, they had a good laugh. The truth of the matter is that there are many people to thank, most of them unknowing contributors.

First, my family, because they are ultimately important. They make you laugh, make you think, they are the people who you develop your emotional bank with. From that, all things are possible.

I want to thank my lovely husband, Paul, who dreams with me. I was going to say he is my ballast, but the dictionary defines ballast as *"a heavy substance placed in such a way as to improve stability and control."* While he provides stability, he makes me weightless and gives me wings.

To Claire and Shane, in addition to my loving you for exactly who you are, you inspire me by watching you try to do new things on a daily basis. I would not have tapped into the gift almost all children possess and most adults forget: *the unwavering belief that trying to do new things is normal.*

Then, my friends who talked me off the ledge: Thea, Lisa, Marie, Victoria, Carol, and the Crusher Ladies. I am blessed a thousand times over.

To the authors extraordinaire at Chick Lit Chat and Author's Cave—you are indispensable. I would particularly like to thank authors Kathryn Biel, Gina Henning, Whitney Dineen, Maggie Le Page, and Tess Woods. Alongside being brilliant authors, you are fabulous friends. Thank you for a most fruitful and hilarious summer afternoon. I am in your debt.

I would also like to thank my dream team at Booktrope. Samantha March, Brenda Kissko, Kathryn Galán and Michelle Fairbanks: I am forever indebted for your support, guidance, and hard work. Thank you also to Jennifer Gilbert for bringing me into the fold.

*As Always,*
*Thanks for reading!*
*Celia Kennedy*
www.celiakennedy.weebly.com

# A Tasty Cocktail to Drink Along

## *Lemon and Elderflower Fizz*

<u>Ingredients</u>

75 ml gin
Juice ½ lemon
2 t. caster sugar
50 ml elderflower cordial
750 ml bottle prosecco
4 T. lemon sorbet

<u>To decorate</u>

2 T. caster sugar
Juice and strips of zest from ½ lemon

*Method*

To decorate the glasses with a sugar rim, tip the sugar onto a flat plate and the lemon juice into a bowl. Dip the rim of each glass in the juice then twist on the plate of sugar to stick.

Put the gin, lemon juice, sugar, and elderflower cordial into a large jug. Stir until the sugar has dissolved. Add the prosecco then the sorbet, and give it a good stir.

Pour into the prepared glasses and pop in a few strips of lemon zest.

*This is my favorite prosecco cocktail… but, I've been known to enjoy an ice cold glass of the lively sparkling wine all by itself!* —Celia

Recipe from: http://www.bbcgoodfood.com/recipes/lemon-elderflower-fizz

# Chapter One

*May 2012*

**"DES BANNERMAN'S LAWYERS** are on the phone!" Taylor, my roommate, held the phone out to me so I could read the Caller ID and see their names myself. "Do I need to remind you how much we have riding on this week? We do not need this! Not now!" She punctuated her thoughts by stabbing the air with her index finger.

Trying to remain calm, I decided that answering the phone call from Mead, Jameson, and Kelly was not the best course of action. There was only one thing to do. Call the King of Romantic Comedies himself and ask what was happening.

I tapped my teeth with a freshly manicured fingertip. For the trillionth time I wondered what had been misinterpreted so gigantically.

Heading down the short hallway toward the bathroom, I called over my shoulder, "I'm going to take a shower." A preemptive strike to alleviate my soon-to-be-overwhelming headache.

"What? How can you take a shower?" Taylor squawked as she looked around the apartment wildly. "Shouldn't you finish packing and get the hell out of here?"

"Listen, I'm going to take a shower and think of a way to get ahold of him. Then everything will be fine! Remember, Gemma promised," I said, wanting to allay her fears as well as my own.

*It was simple enough*, I thought as I washed my hair. The day before, I'd seen Des having lunch at The Volstead, a midtown bar. As I was leaving, there had been no option but to walk past his table, so I'd taken a deep breath and stopped to say hello. We'd exchanged stilted pleasantries and, when the short conversation came to an end, I'd said goodbye and left.

Technically, I did violate the restraining order by coming within five hundred feet of him. Technically, I did violate the restraining order by talking to him. But he hadn't seemed any more frightened or perturbed than the last several times our paths had crossed.

I stood under the hottest water my skin could stand for a full five minutes, the scent of lavender body wash floating in the mist, before I suddenly remembered something Gemma had said that made me regret not answering the phone.

Pulling back the shower curtain and reaching for a towel to wrap around my hair, I called out to Taylor, "Did they call again?"

"No, you still have a chance to get out of here before the police arrive!" she yelled anxiously from the living room.

I muttered to myself, "If I haven't been arrested yet, I doubt today is the day," then rushed through my routine of lotions, potions, spritzes, and sprays.

My earlier bravado had been replaced with total confusion.

While I was rooting around the closet for clothes, Taylor entered the room, emitting an aura of panic. Sitting on the foot of my bed, she patted it. "Charlotte, come sit down. We really need to talk about your situation with Des Bannerman."

With more confidence than I felt, I said, "Hang on a second. I know it's bad timing, and, if your mother finds out, we could both get fired or worse! But listen, while I was in the shower, I remembered something Gemma said when I was in London. I need to get ahold of her. She might know what's going on. But first, I need to get dressed, find her phone number, and *then* just maybe I'll get to the bottom of all of this so I can get my life back!"

She remained silent throughout my declaration, but her blue eyes expressed all her uncertainty. "Charlotte, you've finally lost it."

Twenty minutes later, and after a thorough search of my briefcase, I found Gemma's business card, sat on the edge of the sofa that dominated our living room, and dialed her number. While listening to the ring of the telephone, I gnawed my knuckle.

I was startled when a voice on the other end of the phone said, "Creative Artists Agency, Mr. Allen's office. How may I direct your call?"

"Yes, I was given Mr. Allen's phone number by Gemma Newley. My name is Charlotte Young of Faith Clarkson International. If possible, I would like to speak with her."

"Just one moment, please." Silence filled the airwaves. No elevator music, just silence.

I knew from Gemma that Mr. Allen also represented Des Bannerman. The silence abruptly ended when the same woman's voice said, "I'm sorry, but Mr. Allen is unavailable. May I direct your call elsewhere or take a message?"

Through misdirection, exaggeration, and name-dropping, I somehow managed to bungle my way into obtaining the phone number for Des Bannerman's personal assistant. Feeling very excited, I could see the finish line when my call was put through to her.

Taylor, who had been pacing the carpet while I bluffed my way through the maze, motioned for me to hang up. I turned my back on her so that her panic wouldn't escalate the fear I already felt. Just as I was about to give up, a very squeaky, high-pitched voice answered the telephone. "Ms. Smith answering for Mr. Bannerman."

My thoughts scattered, and the clarity I'd had earlier evaporated. As I felt all the things I wanted to say to him bubble up inside me, I panicked. "Ms. Taylor Clarkson on the line, one minute please."

I thrust the phone at Taylor and hoped with all my heart that she would take mercy on me. "What do you want me to say?" she hissed, her hand covering the phone.

My brain whirred, wondering what the best option might be. "Mention the party tonight. Let her know there's a private showing of *The Block* by Romare Bearden at the Met beforehand. Faith Clarkson will send a car. Go!"

Speaking quickly into the phone, Taylor calmly stated, "This is Taylor Clarkson of Faith Clarkson International speaking…"

When I first met Taylor, I couldn't imagine that we'd have anything in common. First of all, she came from a very wealthy family, each generation having added to the coffers already overflowing with gold. Really successful people—you know the sort, the kind that "summer in the Hamptons." She always wore designer clothes and had the latest trendy accessories mixed in with family heirlooms. Second, and most importantly, she was the daughter of the owner of the PR company that I worked for, Faith Clarkson International.

We became roommates out of necessity. We met my first day on the job. She was just ahead of me in line, waiting to order a bagel and Diet Coke from a street vendor. She told me that, after grad school, she had been determined to stand on her own two feet and not use the family name as a stepping-stone. She took my ribbing over her taking a job at the family's business in stride. "Well, I'm not stupid," she'd said with a smile.

She'd found a great apartment but couldn't afford it on her salary. I'd immediately asked what the rent was and, later that day, gave her my half of the deposit. That was five years ago. We were still roommates but more due to friendship than finances...

"...Fabulous! We'll send a car to drive Mr. Bannerman to the private showing at the Metropolitan and then escort him to the London NYC opening we're hosting for Gordon Ramsey." There was a brief pause where she nodded her head. In her sycophant professional voice, she ended the conversation, "I'll send an email with the details. Thank you so much!"

While she dazzled Ms. Smith with the details, all I could think was, *Taylor was brilliant! Better than brilliant.* She'd changed the situation from one where I'd possibly be arrested and lose my job into a coup for the company, instead. I doubted that even Carl Lewis was that fast on his feet.

Before my eyes, the cordless phone landed in its cradle, and Taylor collapsed on a straight-back chair in a gooey heap. Taking advantage of her vulnerable state, I begged for the details. "What did Ms. Smith say? Is he going to be there?"

"Charlotte, do you have any idea what just happened? I just lied to Des Bannerman's secretary so that *you* can meet him in front of some obscure painting that no one has ever heard of! My mother is going to fire you and disown me. And may I ask how exactly we're going to set up a private viewing for later today without her finding out?"

I changed tactics quickly. "First of all, you were fabulous! Don't worry about the rest, I'll handle it. What I need to know is, is he going to meet me at the Met or not?"

"I'm emailing her the specifics. She said that she'd ask him once he's available. She'll call me this afternoon at some point. You're just going to have to wait. I really can't believe what I just did." Taylor's voice cycled through a wide range of emotions, while her French-tipped fingers twiddled with her Christian Louboutin ankle strap.

Taking me by the hand, she dragged me to the sofa. "Look, Charlotte, this could either be the best thing for both of us or the worst. You cannot mess this up! If we do this right, you just might not go to prison, and I might be able to find a way to convince my mother that I'm more than her daughter."

I barely listened to her. My real focus was on the relatively immediate possibility that I might move out from under the cloud I'd been living under since I'd met Des Bannerman last winter.

Taylor must have seen my eyes glaze over, because, the next thing I knew, she demanded, "Have you heard a word I've said?"

"Sort of."

"Okay, it's 9:30. We have to figure out what you're going to say and what you're *not* going to say," she said anxiously. The crease between her eyebrows marred her otherwise flawless skin.

"Yes, but who's going to help you?"

Craziness, or the perception of it, feels contagious. A person innocently gets in a pickle and then, forever after, when something odd happens, people get a look in their eyes that tells you they're wondering *Is there any truth to that rumor?*

Unfortunately for me, photos and misunderstood quotes were what had given me trouble.

\* \* \*

Finally making it to work, I found myself sitting in my office, trying to look busy, which I was, if you considered reading *Page Six* articles about Des Bannerman to be a professional task.

There were some photos of him at various New York City events. The camera loved his blue-eyes, dimpled chin, and thick brown hair. I stared at his pictures, trying to find flaws. To my regret, there weren't any faults to be found, from his square jaw to his sculpted body. One didn't have to look hard to see the muscle beneath his form-fitting garments. Fortunately, the women in the photos whom he towered over didn't resemble his ex-girlfriend, Brynn Roberts, which left me hopeful. While I couldn't say that it was her who had convinced Des to enlist the help of his lawyers, I was completely convinced that she hadn't taken a liking to me.

My office door whipped open, and Taylor rushed in. I'd never seen her look so stressed, so I powered down my computer screen. If she saw what I'd been reading, she'd have gone ballistic.

"Have you been writing down what you're going to say to him? Did you include all the things we talked about earlier?" she asked at the same time as I asked, "Has Ms. Smith called?"

"No," we answered simultaneously. We both sighed.

On our way to work, Taylor had given me a list of topics that she wanted me to discuss with Des, primarily the many services Faith Clarkson International could provide. I led her to believe that I was more than willing to give the business pitch. However, what Taylor had yet to fully understand was that Des and I were way past idle conversations about a business relationship. We had a personal relationship of sorts, and he'd be even more confused if I tried to pull off some sort of pitch.

Initially, she'd wanted to meet with him; I was to casually join them later. Eventually, I'd managed to convince her that I should meet with Des on my own. All it took was mentioning that she could be charged for assisting me in violating the restraining order. After all, the phone call did come from our apartment, and if it came down to it, she could always claim innocence. She'd come to the conclusion that it would be best for me to meet him alone.

"Taylor, have faith. I know that it's best to be as professional as possible," I said, my voice ringing with optimism.

Taylor looked anxious. "I know. I'm just worried."

While scrounging through my desk drawer for a much-needed breath mint, I avoided lying. "I know things look bad. It will all work out. Gemma promised."

Taylor pulled my office door open and said, as she left, "For all our sakes, I hope so."

The afternoon drifted by slowly. Between reviewing the latest financials for the company and the lack of a return call from Ms. Smith, my stomach churned.

Just as I was becoming disgusted with myself, my telephone rang. As I quickly snatched up the phone before my assistant could answer, I managed to chip a nail. "Damn! Hello?"

Taylor, with a voice full of trepidation, told me that our plan was a go. I would meet Des Bannerman in front of the painting *The Block* just as the museum closed.

It was 4:45. I quickly checked the website and found out that the Metropolitan Museum of Fine Art closed at 9:00 on Fridays. I had four hours.

With a plan of action in place, I managed to settle down and focus on the work. After everything Taylor had done for me today, I didn't want to let her down. The easiest way to thank her was to make us both look good and not give Faith Clarkson ammunition. It was as I climbed into the back of the black town car, hired by Faith Clarkson International to take me to the museum, that I thought, *How did it come to this?*

# Chapter Two

**SITTING IN BLEATING TRAFFIC**, I stared out the window and thought about my current situation. Starting at the very beginning. All the way back to when I met the group of women who now hovered at my epicenter and who were knee-deep in my dilemma...

*   *   *

Marian, Hillary, Kathleen, Tiziana and I had met at Oxford. We were all at varying points on the same path, graduate students at the Said Business School.

I met Kathleen first. Her blonde hair glistened in the late summer sun as she taped posters on a lamppost for a pub crawl for American students studying abroad. It wasn't her I noticed so much as all the guys ogling her wiggling backside as she smoothed down the tape. I pushed through the crowd of surging testosterone and introduced myself. Excited to meet a fellow American, I invited her to go out for a drink at the nearest pub. With perhaps a few too many beers in us, we found ourselves standing in the restroom. While repairing our makeup in front of the mirror, I noticed that we were polar opposites. She was tall, lithe, and blonde, while I was (quite) short, curvy, and dark—my mother's Mediterranean ancestors mingled throughout my features, while Kathleen looked like a Viking. Our only common feature, besides being female, was that we both had ridiculously long hair.

Three days later, at the pub The Bear, we met Marian. She was there spying on a groom at the behest of her good friend, the bride. Her job: to make sure he didn't get out of line.

We were young, easily influenced, and really drunk. We had been in and out of four pubs in about two hours. While ordering a round of drinks, we heard chanting, "Stripper! Stripper!" The next thing I knew, Kathleen's elbow collided with my kidney as she pointed at Tiziana.

Tiziana! Every woman's nemesis. Think of Sophia Loren wearing a man's white dress shirt with a long string of pearls and a pair of flashy stilettos. To be fair, Tiziana appeared shocked when she realized the stripper comments were directed at her. You'd think a girl who oozed that much sexuality and dressed that skimpily would get used to being the object of every male's fantasies. She looked more than a little nervous when a couple of guys drinking with the groom became a little too friendly and suggested Tiziana show the soon-to-be-married man a little mercy.

Marian reminded me of a bull when she was angry: snorting nose, steam out of the ears, crazy eyes. A smart person would back away, slowly. So, when Marian dragged Tiziana outside before anything could happen, we were worried for Tiziana. None of us knew her, but still, I didn't think she'd done anything worthy of dismemberment. When Kathleen and I followed them out to where they stood on the narrow sidewalk, Marian was swearing away at Tiziana, and Tiziana was shouting back in Italian.

Just when things had calmed down a bit, a very regal-looking woman opened the pub door and took in the situation. "Oh! What luck. I found your… purse?" She handed Tiziana a bedazzled black clutch.

Why we all burst into laughter, I wasn't quite sure. I didn't even know if we were laughing together or at one another. After we controlled our laughing, Hillary, the regal one who had smirked a bit, invited us to go back in for a glass of wine.

Hillary couldn't apologize fast enough. "The groom's my brother! I'm here to make sure he doesn't overdo it. Sorry his friends are such cretins…"

*  *  *

We'd been close friends ever since.

Looking out the car window, I saw that we'd made very little progress. Glancing at my watch, I saw that there was plenty of time,

Taylor having insisted that I leave an hour ahead of time. There were still forty-five minutes until I was set to meet with Des Bannerman.

My thoughts drifted back to a little less than a year ago...

* * *

Over the winter holidays, we met up to do a little skiing in Chamonix, France, which is a cluster of villages in the French Alps that caters to the famous and very wealthy. Rumors and sightings of famous people floated through the village night and day.

Kathleen, who was living in France, was infatuated with all things royal. For her, the entire vacation was deemed "perfect, simply perfect" when we saw the entourage of Monaco. She hadn't admitted it, but I think she spent many a pleasurable moment dreaming of princes, white horses, and what Grace Kelly's jewelry collection might be like.

We even saw the back of Heidi Klum's head and a few other celebs whose identities were less than certain—one doesn't want to claim to have seen Justin Timberlake if it was really the bartender at the local discotheque.

Living in New York City and working for a PR firm had jaded me as regards celebrity. Our firm managed the publicity for many accomplished public figures.

However, my jaw hit the glacier when we heard Des Bannerman was in town. When that news reached our group's ears, all heads swiveled in my direction. I felt my knees go weak and my heart race. I had openly adored and gushed about Des Bannerman for years. Juvenile, for sure. But still, I had fantasized about being the object of his desire since I first laid eyes on him. We had both attended an event at Oxford, where he had initially gone to school before finding great fame in romantic comedies. But, as did all famous people (I assumed), he vaguely made eye contact with me, smiled, and then moved on.

In Chamonix, every event became an all-out effort to find him. We tried to ascertain his whereabouts, to determine which places he might go, and we skied black diamond slopes we had no business skiing on (since he was an excellent skier). Every outfit, tube of lipstick, and dollar was spent in pursuit of Des Bannerman.

To that end, we decided to search the Casino de Chamonix. None of us were truly gamblers, but we had all read *Blackjack for Dummies* that afternoon while sipping Chardonnay at a local hotspot. So, armed with fists full of dollars and accessorized in the latest fashion trends, off to the casino we went looking for Lady Luck... and the previously mentioned Des Bannerman.

Early in the evening, most of my cohorts had lost all the money they were willing to lose and had been swept off their feet by handsome foreigners. Oddly enough, I had amazing luck. And since I had never won so much as a penny before, the fact that I was up seven hundred dollars was close to a miracle.

I told the woman sitting next to me that, if this kept up, we should look for sightings of the Virgin Mary. (No laugh, not even a roll of the eyes; she clearly took her blackjack too seriously.) At some point she lost her last chip, and I was left at the table with a mobster-looking fellow— okay, he had no neck, which, in my books, made him a mobster.

I felt a gust as Hillary suddenly arrived. She carefully turned her refined shoulder to the mobster and said, "Charlotte!" She was practically vibrating on the spot. "We've just spotted Des Bannerman!"

Instantly I jumped off my stool, keeping my hands on my chips, of course, and scanned the casino. As there weren't many places to hide, I sighed and told her, "It was probably that guy we saw on the chairlift yesterday... You know, the one with the Brad Pitt hairstyle from *Burn After Reading* but with brown eyes."

"Well, at least come have a look. You've been searching for days. I can't believe after all this you would prefer to sit here rather than do a full sweep. I'll go get the girls." Hillary was off in what, for her, was a flash.

As I stood there contemplating what to do, the dealer asked if I was going to place a bet. One more couldn't hurt. After placing my bet, I was sizing up my hand when I felt someone standing next to me. I doubled my bet before looking at the newcomer. The most gorgeous woman in the world stood next to me. I knew who it was: Des Bannerman's girlfriend. My luck was extending beyond the cards; fate, destiny, cosmic karma were all on my side.

Hillary came sauntering over full of excitement. "I'm sure it's him. You have to come. Who cares about blackjack! This is Des Bannerman we're talking about."

The whole time she was talking, I was doing my best to get her to be quiet. Not even putting my fingers over her lips and shaking my head managed to calm her down. My only hope was that people blamed her distorted speech on alcohol.

Discreetly, I glanced to my side to see if the object of Des Bannerman's affections had understood any of this. While she continued to look at her hand, an amused smirk played about her trout-pout lips.

Looking back at Hillary, I tried a subtle nod of my head toward my non-mobster gambling companion. It was hopeless, however, because Hillary knew next to nothing about Des Bannerman.

"What? What are you doing? Come on..." She was now yanking my arm out of its socket. Deciding to retain a little dignity, I picked up my chips and let myself be dragged off.

"Hillary, do you have any idea who was sitting next to me? Do you not read *Hello* or *People* or watch *Showbiz Tonight*? That was Brynn Roberts, Des Bannerman's girlfriend, and Golden Globe winner last year for best actress in that movie with George Clooney. The one about a war somewhere," I hissed at her back.

Switching direction abruptly, she said, "I knew she looked familiar! We have to go back!"

"No! I can't possibly go back now. She's bound to tell him that I'm stalking him. Then, when he meets me, he'll be frightened," I pointed out.

"We need a plan. What should we do?" Hillary finally asked.

"Let's go scout around and see if we can find him at another table or the girls. Maybe they know something," I offered in frustration.

We strolled around the casino for a quarter of an hour. We saw someone who we thought was Kevin Bacon, but it turned out to be some German guy, and then we saw someone who very well could have been Margaret Thatcher, except she was smiling. Then, as if all the worlds collided, as if the sun came bursting from behind the grayest cloud ever, as if time had slowed down, there was Des Bannerman! Coming out of the men's room, adjusting his shirt, with a little tiny bit of white showing from, you know, *down there*. Oh my god! I could see Des Bannerman's underwear! My heart pounded, and there, in the darkest corner of Casino de Chamonix, I met my destiny.

Hillary giggled from behind her hand. "Oh my god! Can you believe it? He wears tighty-whities. I would have thought that he'd have custom underwear sewn by Armani himself!"

We howled with laughter. Of all the things that I had fantasized about, I never had managed to work tighty-whities into the scenario. Silk boxers, bath towels, low-rise jeans, tuxedos, but never, ever your standard everyday white underwear.

I could hear Hillary asking me what my plan was as I watched Des Bannerman approach, walk past, and continue on his way. Not even a glance. I mean, while I might not have Brynn Roberts breathtaking, fragile beauty, plenty of men had affirmed what I knew about myself, my curves and curls had plenty of appeal.

"Look at me. What do you see?" I beseeched Hillary.

"Well, what do you mean?"

"He didn't even register my existence. It's a good thing my ego's not that fragile." Then, in a blinding flash, it all fell before me. I announced, "I've got it!" I grabbed Hillary's hand for support, both physical and psychological, and walked to where I thought I would find my destiny.

Sure enough, there he was, standing beside Brynn, his finger trailing patterns on her bare, well-sculpted shoulder and whispering in her ear. It must have been juicy, because Brynn looked up at him with absolute lust in her eyes. She gazed into his so intently that she didn't notice the white flash coming from his crotch.

"Okay, here's my plan! I need to tell him that his fly is down!"

"Are you crazy? You're going to walk up to Des Bannerman, introduce yourself, shake his hand, and say, 'By the way, your fly is down'?"

"That's my plan exactly. Who doesn't wish that someone had told them in that situation?"

"I see your point, but remember he's English. Be dignified," she implored.

She quickly assessed me, making sure that my lips were glossed, my dress was plunging, my hair was fluffed, and my teeth were free of food matter. Then she gave me a quick spritz of perfume.

I looked at my friend and couldn't truly believe that I was on the verge of meeting the man I had dreamt of for over a decade. "Okay, take a deep breath, be calm, be intelligent, and be brief," were her words of wisdom.

As I turned back to the table, I was thrilled to see they were still there. Des's hand was elsewhere entertained, but I was determined not to lose my chance.

I walked straight up to the table. I cleared my throat, took a deep breath, and promptly placed a bet. All the while, my ears were ringing so much that I could barely understand a word the dealer was saying. I blatantly stared at Des, taking in his face's classic features. His brow bone, jaw, and nose were rugged and refined at the same time—and his carefully crafted body was begging to be caressed. Seeing his perfection up close, my body heat radiated off of me in visible waves, and I started to feel drips running down my back. My hair started to stick to my forehead.

I lost count, but the dealer made pay-outs and collected losses and dealt a few more rounds before Hillary shoved an ice-cold unidentifiable beverage in my hand. I made a horrible squelching noise as I slid off my stool. The dealer smirked and reminded me to take my chips.

"What happened?" she cried.

"What happened? What happened?" I panicked. "How am I supposed to walk up to him and get his attention? Have you seen her? Have you seen him? My god! He's even more gorgeous up close. How can she stand herself? She gets to sleep with him. I want to pee myself just contemplating it."

All the while, Hillary was steering us toward the women's bathroom, where I immediately looked in the mirror. Gone was the confident woman; gone was the lipstick (which now appeared to be all over my teeth, since I had apparently gnawed my lips off at the blackjack table). All that was left was a sweaty mass of human existence.

"Okay, we're going to wipe you down, freshen you up, and start over. Can you do it? Think you can? I think you can!" She had become part rugby coach, part cheerleader.

Taking deep breaths and silently chanting, "I can do this, I can do this," I refreshed myself with strategic splashes of cold water, reapplied my makeup, and swept my long, curly hair up into a stack that cascaded down my back.

"Very sexy."

Off we went, out of the bathroom and into the pinging smoke-hazed world of the casino.

I breathed in and out, and, while walking back to the table, I chanted my mantra. "I can do this, I can do this." But they were gone.

"Oh no! Where did they go?" I wailed.

Experiencing a whole different physical reaction, I was consumed by instant remorse. I was deeply regretful of my cowardice. Then I went into overdrive. My need to find him was visceral.

We wound our way through gaming tables, clusters of humanity, and slot machines, and finally found our friends. We pried them free of their newfound lovers and pleaded with them to go search the casino and report any sightings of Brynn or Des.

I was thrilled to no end when our newly-made friends offered to help. Feeling confident that there would be no table left unsearched, no corner left unlooked, we ventured forth.

After half an hour passed, all seemed hopeless.

I posted myself near the women's bathroom because I felt faint. I continued to berate myself for not taking advantage of my earlier opportunity while trying to remain positive. (Very tricky.)

Then Hillary came dashing over. "We've got him! You can do this! Tidy your lipstick, and off you go!"

En masse, we all casually yet purposefully approached Des and Brynn. They were at a table together, playing blackjack. I was close enough to hear them arguing about whether she should take another card from the dealer.

"Take one," I sagely suggested. Suddenly, I was an expert at the game.

The bluest eyes I'd ever seen looked up at me, and that carefully constructed smile that I'd seen in so many movies was directed at me. My heart almost stopped, but my brain kicked in at the last moment and reminded it to beat.

"Excellent! Tell us, are you an authority on blackjack? On whose word should we accept such an opinion? Do you make a habit of giving advice to perfect strangers? And, if you're decided to be said expert, why only take one card instead of doubling our bets, or perhaps even playing two hands?" He fired questions at me in much the same way that Tom Cruise cross-examined Jack Nicholson in *A Few Good Men*. *Could I handle the truth..? Maybe not.*

"Actually, I'm not, but I did stay at a Holiday Inn Express last night!" He looked at me in utter confusion.

"Clearly you don't watch much American television," I added.

"Ah, that's the explanation. You're an American." Des's blue eyes glinted with superiority when he zinged back at me, poking the air with his finger.

While I had been playful, the superior tone of his voice instantly put me off. "I hope that not all people buy into stereotypes. For example, should we assume that, because you're English, your teeth need straightening, capping, or whitening?" I inwardly cursed myself for my temper.

At this point, I received a genuine smile and chuckle from Des that evaporated my anger.

"Darling, it's time to go!" Brynn stood up and possessively placed her hand on Des's shoulder. Clearly, his sharing a laugh with someone else was not on Ms. Roberts's agenda.

"Well, it was charming to receive such useful advice from such a learned traveler! Good evening. Enjoy your stay at the Holiday Inn Express." With that, Des Bannerman departed from the table, taking his companion with him.

The universe reconfigured, the clouds re-gathered, the sun faded, and with them went my hopes.

Hillary, Kathleen, and the rest came thundering over. "How'd it go? What'd he say?" they asked in unison.

It was a bit embarrassing, considering that Des and Brynn were only about two feet away. "For the love of God and all that is holy, could you at least wait for them to be out of hearing range?" I whispered loudly.

The flash of white passing by at waist level reminded me of "The Grand Plan." I had forgotten to tell him about his fly. I still had a way into the sphere of Des Bannerman's world. All hope was not lost, and Brynn's agenda be damned: I was going in for another play.

"I'll be back!" I said with the same determination as the Terminator.

I returned immediately. They'd disappeared, again. "What is it with these people? They disappear instantly! I need help finding him! Go! Find him!" I felt like a general sending her troops into battle.

Thankfully, the troops returned unscathed, and quickly. Des and Brynn had made it only as far as the bar. That seemed like an exceptionally reasonable place to reacquaint myself with him. Not too over the top at all.

Again, en masse we trooped to the bar. Hovering on the boundary of personal space, we chatted about skiing, the hot spots we had ventured into, the spa we were visiting the next day—anything we could think of to keep us there, hoping beyond all measure of hope that Des would turn around and provide an opportunity to speak to him.

Nothing happened. We talked, but he didn't turn around.

"Move closer," I whispered. En masse, we took a step backwards. Considering there were now nine of us, fortunately we did so without too much incident. "Ask me about my luck at the blackjack table," I whispered to Kathleen.

"So, Charlotte, how was your luck at the tables? Did you lose a bundle?" she dutifully enquired.

I tried to sound confident, affluent, and knowledgeable. "I'm up seven."

"Oh!" the masses replied, as if I was a blackjack genius.

Nonchalantly, I scanned the room, my gaze pausing at my target on the bar stool. *Nope, still no notice from him.* "Take another step back!" I commanded.

With great courage and verve, the group took another step backward.

"Bloody hell! Watch it, mate! You've gone and stepped on her foot!" growled Des. Brynn was grimacing in pain and rubbing her offended foot.

"Oh, we're so sorry, we were just trying to get the bartender's attention," Kathleen spoke up.

"Quick on your feet, Kathleen! Well done!" I complimented while Des attended to his battle-wounded beauty.

I stepped forward and asked the couple, "May we buy you a drink to help dull the pain?"

After a lingering glare that managed to convey where her pain really lay, Brynn refused and announced that she was returning to "the chalet" since her foot was finished for the evening.

"Coming, darling?" she purred, perched on one foot like a gorgeous flamingo.

Pinching at his bottom lip, he looked up at her through his eyelashes, boyishly charming. "If your foot doesn't require me for the evening, would you mind? I promised Ted that I would meet him. I haven't seen him in ages. Darling, do you mind?"

Myriad emotions crossed her beautiful face but finally arrived at acceptance. "Fine! Could you call the car for me? I'll see myself back and have a soak in that marvelous bath." Brynn simpered up next to Des and said just loud enough, "For God's sake, be careful. This group is just on the verge of throwing themselves at you. And I do mean that literally!"

Quietly, he soothed her. "Don't worry. I'll have Stan watch a little bit closer. It'll be fine. Just go have a soak and look after your foot. We need you well enough to go skiing tomorrow. The weather is supposed to be perfect at the summit. A lovely day of skiing, just you and me." He spoke melodically, his blue eyes laser-focused on her.

It wasn't until then that I realized that another neckless fellow wasn't too far from the lovebirds. He was talking on the phone and no sooner did he finish the call than he leaned over and whispered into Des's ear.

"The car is out front. I'll walk you out. Pierre, Andre, or whatever the hell his name is, will get you safely back. Have Miranda call me and let me know you've made it safely."

With that, Des, Brynn, and two muscle-bound, neck-free individuals proceeded toward the casino doors. Brynn, carefully bundled up in furs, gloves, and glasses, gave Des a quick peck on the cheek, and then she was out the door with Mr. NoNeck Number One, leaving Mr. NoNeck Number Two to protect Des.

My opportunity just improved one hundred percent. I would be able to execute "The Grand Plan" and then some. "Tiziana! Please, please, please, would you be willing to distract Ted?"

Tiziana was my closest friend. Without any jealousy, we all acknowledged her as the true beauty among us. It's quite disgusting, actually. Tiziana had many things in common with Sophia Loren; she was Italian, gorgeous, and intelligent. And they both oozed "Look at me!" upon entering a room.

She couldn't help it. God had given her all the right things in all the right places, jiggling at all the right times.

"Of course I'll help you, so long as my Gianni doesn't hear of this!" she purred.

She wasn't practicing; she always purred. I thought it was an Italian woman thing. Every answer was given in a sing-song, catch-me-if-you-can kind of voice. I spent a fair amount of time just listening to her speak. From time to time, I'd tried to duplicate her sultry style, but I ended up feeling ridiculous.

We all discreetly watched Des and Mr. NoNeck wander the casino. After finding a quiet table off to the side and placing a bet, Des settled in to play a hand of blackjack.

"Okay, what's the plan?" the girls wanted to know.

"Well, I think I'll hang back for a while and watch him. I don't want him to get frightened. Maybe after Ted has arrived and they've chatted a bit, Tiziana and I will wander over. What do you think?"

In agreement, we made our way to the bar and found a table to sit at. The waiting was excruciating, for me at least. The girls were having a great time. Tiziana, as usual, had drawn a group of men into her sphere. Our earlier cohorts had wandered off when they heard Tiziana agreeing to help me with Des. Now new males were vying for her attention, drinks were being passed around, compliments were being passed out, and I was avoiding all things alcohol. I didn't want to make any mistakes.

Fifteen minutes into playing blackjack alone, an elegant, well-dressed man walked toward Des. Des stood up and gave the man a half-hug, half-handshake. They proceeded to sit down, order drinks, and play cards. In between placing bets and loosely watching the game, the two men appeared to be giving each other a good ribbing. It was amazing to be sitting here in Chamonix watching Des Bannerman laugh his head off. I'd had dreams of moments like these, but never in my wildest fantasies did I think I would spend actual minutes just observing the man.

After another twenty minutes of staking out the table, I thought it was time Tiziana and I meandered back to the blackjack tables.

I gently but firmly extracted a male hand from Tiziana's waist. "Tiziana, it's time to go," I whispered into her ear. Without pause, she put her hand on the cheek of the male trying to win her favor and said a few kind words. We were off.

I am a fairly smart woman, at least smart enough to allow Tiziana in her resplendent jiggling and oozing fashion to clear a path through the casino. As she did, I issued instructions to her from behind, telling her to find out from Ted how much longer Des would be in town, where he was staying, and, above all else, to be sure not mention that I was trying to meet Des. After a circuitous path through the blackjack tables, we eventually arrived at the desired table.

I was not surprised that Tiziana had already captured Ted and Des's attention. Well, to be fair, every male's attention. Those two continued to stare just south of eye level, while the dealer asked if we'd like to place a bet.

I was certain the dealer had no idea what words were coming out of his mouth, because it was something like, "Mademoiselle, are you available? To place a bet, I hope. I mean, would you like to sit down? May I get you a cocktail? That is, the casino would happily offer you a drink!" Stumble, stumble, stumble. I had to say that I genuinely enjoyed these occasions.

Once Tiziana had been carefully escorted onto her stool, I plunked down beside her.

"Darling, of course I'd love something. Champagne for two!" she purred.

"I can't drink while working but perhaps afterwards. I could think of nothing I would enjoy more," the dealer replied, stunned by his good fortune.

"Darling, while that might be wonderful, I was ordering for myself and my friend." Her letdown was gentle.

Only then did a hundred pairs of eyes register my existence. The only pair that I cared about locked onto me and registered recognition. I could vaguely hear chuckling in the background. I seemed to have only one functioning sense whenever in the direct presence of Des.

"Ted, best be careful. Our charming table companions are undisputed blackjack experts. I've heard from reliable sources that one in particular is brilliant at the game. I heard it said that she was up seven. By the way, do you know what 'up seven' means?" Des asked while the champagne was served, the dealer's face burning with embarrassment. Ted got up to sit beside Tiziana.

Bingo! Desired effect! Des stood up and moved over one seat. While he hadn't sat down next to me, he was in close range. We now appeared to be a group as opposed to perfect strangers.

Tiziana was looking at her cards and determining her strategy when Ted leaned into her and said, "I would be most grateful if you would give me the benefit of your expertise. I'm on a terrible losing streak and will end up giving this chap quite a bit of money if it continues. Please, change my luck for me!"

Turning her head so that she and Ted were nose to nose, Tiziana trilled in a low, throaty voice, "I would love to, darling, but you see, I'm not the expert. I leave that to my dear friend, Charlotte. I'm afraid my skills are outside the game of blackjack." Several jaws dropped. "Would you care to recount your skills? I'm dying to know. But first, please, tell me your name," Ted persisted. "My name, darling, is Tiziana. What's yours?" Ted looked a little startled. "I'm sorry, could you say your name again?"

I jumped in because this certainly wasn't the first time someone had been startled upon hearing her name. I leaned forward and said, "Her name is pronounced Teet-zee-awwn-na. With an 'August'-type 'a' on the 'anna' part."

"Well, Teet-Z-Awna, I'm very pleased to meet you. My name is Ted. Not at all as exotic as yours."

And so the game began. Tiziana reeled Ted in breath by breath, carefully including me in the conversation at first and then gradually allowing the conversation to drift away from everyone but the two of them.

As was so often the case when in Tiziana's presence, I got the left-over guy. But what a guy! After a few more glasses of liquid courage and several hands of blackjack, Des got up and came to sit beside me. I assume it was because Ted hadn't spoken to him in quite some time.

You can tell a lot about a movie star when they get up close and personal. For example, not only were Des's eyes blue, they were azure; not only were his teeth white and straight, they were identically shaped and spaced; not only did he have dimples, but his dimples had dimples. Struggling to think of something to say instead of just gaping at the man, I placed a bet and nonchalantly said, "Nice hair! New look?"

"You think? The director wants me to grow it longer for a movie I start shooting in a few months, but I think it makes me look ridiculous," he said, flicking his golden locks over his shoulder.

Smirking, I said, "No, what makes you look ridiculous is when you flick it over your shoulder."

Fortunately, he had enough of a sense of humor to laugh at the comment. All those perfect teeth and dimples just a few inches away were almost too much to take. I decided to occupy my hands by placing another bet. "So, is that what all the muscle is about?"

"No. I'm always this ripped." He laughed as a flush ran up his neck and across his cheeks.

"Really? That must take a lot of time." I noted that his biceps were bulging inside his fitted long-sleeved shirt.

"I'm kidding. I detest working out. I'm to play a roman warrior, so I've been with my trainer four hours a day for several months. When he's finished with squeezing every last drop of sweat from me, I spend a few hours a day being chased by a sword while I wear armor. I'm meant to be learning how to be heroic." He laughed.

"Sounds like fun. Well, in case you're curious, the training is working out, but I think the blond hair might have to go."

"I'll let the director know," he replied, as he drained his glass of amber liquid. He signaled for another and motioned toward my now-empty glass of champagne.

With beverages refreshed, my luck with blackjack continued, and soon I was instructing him in the fine art of when to split, when to double, and when to raise his bet. In between our scholarly pursuits, we made catty comments about the people in the casino, laughed when two men ran into each other after laying eyes on Tiziana, and counted how long it took people to realize he really was Des Bannerman once they sat down at the table.

"Personally, I really don't see what the big deal is. I'm just another bloke," he would tell them and then order drinks for the table.

It wasn't lost on me that there hadn't been a single mention of anything personal nor had there been any action to lead me to believe that he found me attractive. We were just pals. Other than the lack of lingering kisses and wandering hands, it was just as I'd imagined spending an evening with him would be: entertaining, relaxed, and surreal. It felt perfect.

"Hey, I'm up five!" Des cheered. Ted looked up long enough to laugh at Des's good fortune. He and Tiziana had quit placing bets but continued to talk quietly beside us.

"Charlotte, I must say that I've truly enjoyed the knowledge I've acquired this evening, not to mention the opportunity to enjoy such charming company. However, I fear it has come time for me to get myself and Ted out of here and to some place where we can sober up and get some rest," Des announced after asking the dealer for the time. It was 4 a.m.

Though I was disappointed to have the evening end, I knew it must. This wasn't a fairy tale. There was no point in saying anything other than a cheerful goodbye.

As Tiziana and I stood up to say goodnight, Ted gallantly suggested that they drive us home. Considering we had no idea where the rest of the girls had disappeared to, we took them up on their offer.

On our way to the entrance of the casino, Des looked down at me. "You're a tiny little thing. How tall are you?"

"Didn't your mother tell you not to ask a lady a question like that? Let's just say, I wouldn't mind being a full foot taller. I feel a bit ridiculous at times. Maybe your trainer has some steroids or something."

"Are you suggesting something?" He raised an eyebrow, a silent challenge.

"No, not at all! I'm sure that's all you." I swept a hand gesturing from my head to toe. "And this is all of me."

"You should go into show business. A lot of celebrities are short. Have you ever seen Robert Downey, Jr. or Reese Witherspoon?"

"In real life? Oddly, no. Our paths haven't crossed," I answered sarcastically.

Mr. NoNeck called for the car while we gathered our things from the coat check. While we were bundling up into our coats and hats, Tiziana murmured discreetly, "Darling, how did it go? Did he profess his undying love?"

"Yeah, right! He's charming, unexpectedly friendly, and he made it clear, without words, that he feels nothing more. Quick, let's get home so I can dream about this!" I sighed, mostly satisfied with how the evening had gone. Just then we were joined by Ted, Des, and NoNeck to be escorted out of the casino.

I noticed that none of the three men had put on their coats. "Won't you get cold?"

"No, the cold air will do me good. Bracing wind, no better way to sober up. A little hypothermia never did anyone harm," was Des's reply.

As we walked through the door and headed for the steps, I suddenly remembered the critical part of "The Grand Plan."

I leaned over to Des. "Hey, I've been meaning to tell you all night that your fly is down. You've been flashing your tighty-whities." I pointed to his white patch of fabric.

He looked up with a sheepish grin, embarrassed. "Now she tells me! A little hypothermia in some places could do a lot of harm," he replied in a high-pitched yelp. I giggled.

It was then that the sun rose. *Then* I realized that it wasn't the sun rising, it was about a million flashbulbs. Quickly, Mr. NoNeck guided us toward an open car door while politely shouting at the paparazzi to let Mr. Bannerman pass through.

"Bollocks!" muttered Des.

\* \* \*

The inside of the car was luxurious. The soft leather seats that were warm to the touch; the golden glow of low lights; and the smell of heavenly aftershave. I settled myself into my seat and leaned back into the cozy cocoon. I noticed a bottle of champagne in an ice bucket.

Soothing music filled the car, and Des leaned toward me. "Would you care for a glass?" He placed his hand on my thigh and moved toward me more intimately. "You have the loveliest eyes. I hate to be so cliché, but a man truly could lose himself in them," he murmured as he leaned in to kiss me. I felt my heart pound, and all sense of time stopped. Des Bannerman was kissing me…!

\* \* \*

"Charlotte, are you in there?" came a shout while a hand battered the door. My head was fuzzy, the room was too bright, my heart was pounding, and parts of my body were excessively warm… I emerged from my dream completely disoriented.

"Come in," I called. "What's going on?" As Marian entered the room, I asked, "Where did you get to last night?" I propped myself up and pushed hanks of hair out of my eyes.

Marian was by far the most outgoing of us all. She was from County Cork, Ireland and possessed the charm that the rest of the world associated with the Irish. "I have something for you to see!"

Pulling on my glasses, reserved only for the first thing in the morning, I picked up the newspaper she'd tossed onto the bed. "Oh my god! How can this be?"

On the cover of the local newspaper was a picture of Des and me looking very much together, with my finger pointed at his crotch. Though my French was poor, I inferred from the subtitle, *Des Bannerman Caught with His Zipper Down.*

"Oh, this is awful!" I said to no one in particular. "Can you believe this?" It was so surreal that I started to laugh.

"What's all the commotion? Where were you last night, Marian?" Hillary asked as she opened the door to her room. After crawling into my bed and reclining against the pillows, she took the paper from my fingers and read the headline, bolting upright. "What did you do last night?"

"Nothing, darling. Our dear Charlotte was the perfect lady. I must say that I think he was quite taken by her." Tiziana oozed into the room. "Move over," she continued.

The four of us lounged against the headboard to read the article. It took all four of us to get through it, since our French was so atrocious. After many failed attempts, I pleaded with Marian to go get Kathleen. "She lives in Paris. She reads and writes in French every day!"

The rest of us continued to struggle through the article while muffled pleas to Kathleen were sent down the hall. Once the predicament was conveyed, she sleepily stumbled to our room to join in the excitement.

With all five of us piled on the bed, Kathleen grabbed the newspaper and read it, gasping every few seconds.

"Oh, for god's sake, read the article!" I shouted. I was out of patience, and my heart was palpitating.

"Okay, the article says, *Des Bannerman's evening ends very differently from how it began. He exchanged one beauty for another! Originally Mr. Bannerman arrived by private car with his longtime companion, actress Ms. Brynn Roberts. During an evening of drinking and gambling, Ms. Roberts became annoyed with Mr. Bannerman's attentions to another young lady. Ms. Roberts was seen leaving the casino alone. After her departure, Mr. Bannerman was joined by billionaire Ted Blackwell from Great Britain. Mr. Blackwell made his fortune in the computer industry and is now semi-retired to focus on philanthropic interests. Perhaps the two young ladies who joined Mr. Bannerman and Mr. Blackwell were looking for charitable donations. Mr. Bannerman emerged from the casino with his new companion on his arm and his zipper down. The foursome made a quick getaway in Mr. Bannerman's private car for places unknown."*

My face couldn't get any redder or hotter. "Oh my god!" I was so lost in my horror that it took a while to register that eight eyes were burning holes into me.

"Darling, what if Gianni sees this?" Tiziana demanded, for once not purring.

"How would Gianni see this? It's in the local paper," I replied, not caring about Gianni. But what would Brynn Roberts make of this?

"Charlotte, every online tabloid and celebrity rag in the world is going to have this for a front page by the end of the day," was Hillary's helpful reply.

"Oh my god!" I said again.

The remainder of the morning was spent with the five of us sipping cups of tea and reeling from shock. I simply couldn't believe I'd ended up on the cover of a tabloid (or two).

Fortunately, the focus switched from me when Hillary and Kathleen began to give Marian a dressing down for taking off in a car with a man she'd met at the bar. In her good-natured way, Marian returned fire and did not take Hillary and Kathleen too seriously. "His name is David, he's from Chicago. He's traveling with a group of friends, too. We're all leaving in a few days. What's the harm in having a little fun?" After assurances that she would run at the first sign he was a lunatic, we all drifted into quiet contemplation.

"Well, I'm afraid I must face the music," interrupted Tiziana. "I'm going to call Gianni and explain this silly situation." With a little roll of the shoulders, as if to carry her breasts more purposefully, Tiziana glided from the room in search of a private place to make her plea.

We all grinned as she left. The drama of an Italian love life wasn't new to us. We knew that there would be confessions, ultimatums, passionate pleas, and eventual declarations of undying love. Secretly, we all wished for more passion in our lives, but none of us could sustain the energy it required.

I quietly worried and wondered until it was time to get ready to go to the spa. If I was a fly on the wall of Brynn and Des's bedroom, would they be talking about last night? Laughing it off? For a moment, I allowed myself to fantasize about her throwing something at him, yelling, "What do you mean you love her?" Then I shook off the ridiculousness of that thought and started to get ready.

We were spending the day at a local spa that catered to the corps d'élite. Hillary had booked us all the "Pampered Woman's Package." This meant that there would be no point to a shower or fancy clothes. I dressed myself in a warm white track suit, pulled my hair up into a bulging bun, slipped on my fleecy snow boots, and was ready to go. We waited for Tiziana, Marian shouting up the wooden staircase dutifully every thirty seconds to notify her of our impending departure. Finally, she tromped down the stairs, looking somewhat miserable. "Men! They think everything is so simple!" she muttered while shrugging on a black form-fitting down coat with fur-trimmed hood. Flipping up the hood, her doe-brown eyes stared out at me, and her dark red lips pouted.

I threw my arm around her shoulders and squeezed her tightly, offering comfort. Assuming she was at odds with Gianni, I found myself, for the millionth time, wondering if Tiziana really knew what struggling was like. Marian materialized the car keys from her parka, and I left all negative thoughts behind. I didn't want to be in a bad mood.

Stepping out into the cold but sunny day, I heard Marian say, "Jaysus!"

Looking up, I said, "Oh my god!" again. On the small knoll where the chalet stood, the only area not heavily landscaped by snow-covered evergreen trees, was a sea of photographers, all ready to take pictures, shouting, "Which one of you is the other woman?"

"Quick, into the car," called Marian.

Kathleen grabbed my elbow and propelled me toward the white four-wheel drive vehicle that Hillary had rented. It wasn't often that she was commanding, but she said just loud enough, "Everyone, duck your heads, stay in a group, Charlotte in the middle, don't say a word."

"How am I going to keep explaining this to Gianni?" Tiziana muttered once we were safely locked inside the car.

I lost it! I flopped down, lying across Kathleen and Tiziana's laps in the backseat, and laughed my head off. "This is so fucking ridiculous!"

"Bloody hell! How the feck am I supposed to drive through this lot?" Marian muttered, while Hillary directed her to drive more quickly. Marian carefully maneuvered the car through the crowd so as not to hurt anyone, while the rest of us continued to avoid having our pictures taken.

"Girls, what did you *do* last night?" asked Hillary.

"Absolutely nothing," I muttered from beneath my hood. "Can you believe this? I wonder what this is like when you're an *actual* celebrity. I'm not sure how long I can stand this!" I complained.

"Well, I wouldn't worry. A few days from now they'll have forgotten all about you and will be on to the next innocent fool," Kathleen said to console me. "Unless, of course, Des Bannerman declares his undying love for you. Then you're pretty much screwed for the next several years."

I was about to respond to her uplifting comment when Marian said in disbelief, "You're not going to believe this, but a bunch of them are following us. Do you still want to go to the spa?"

"Well, unless they all have reservations, it's probably the safest place for us to go, other than home," Hillary calmly pointed out.

"Excellent point! Oh, well, if I have to keep doing this, I'd better get the super deluxe facial." I laughed.

Kathleen pulled her cell phone out of her purse and spoke a quick fire of French into it. After hanging up, she gave Marian instructions to drive around to the back of the spa.

"Why would I do that?"

"I explained to the receptionist that a car with celebrities is on its way and that we're being chased by the paparazzi. They said to come around back, and we can enter through another door."

We all laughed hysterically, none of us quite able to absorb what had happened. Yesterday we were successful businesswomen, and today we were celebrities.

When we pulled around to the back door of the spa, we were pleased to see a gate swinging shut to block the way of unwanted paparazzi. Marian quickly pulled our rented Audi Q7 up to the door, leaving the keys inside for the valet, and we all dashed into the spa. Carefully composed faces looked up as we made our entrance. A look of confusion trickled down the hall behind us as the staff began to realize we weren't Madonna, Gwyneth, J.Lo, or Angelina.

"May I help you?" came a heavily accented voice from a well-groomed woman of petite stature. Kathleen spoke another rapid-fire of French, and soon we were all escorted into a private waiting room. A fire crackled in one corner and a pool of calm water reflected the perfect serenity of the room; the soothing scent of lavender and eucalyptus hung in the air. We waited only moments before we were each led into a private chamber and handed luxurious, warm toweling robes. After returning to the chaise in front of the fire, I felt my shoulders settling down to where they were supposed to be.

Throughout an itinerary of mud wraps, facials, waxes, massages, scrubs, and plucks, all I could think of was what would happen next. Beyond the paparazzi, newspaper articles, and misunderstandings, I wondered once again how Brynn and Des were handling this.

# Chapter Three

**THE PAPARAZZI WERE GONE** when we left the spa. We didn't have enough celebrity power to warrant their waiting around for the better part of a day. It seemed best for us to return to the chalet rather than venture into the village for a late dinner. Only the trampled snow and shrubs provided evidence of our fifteen minutes of fame.

Tiziana whipped up a dinner of pasta, wine, and salad. Afterwards, while munching on chocolate and sipping more wine, we laughed at the day's earlier events.

"Just think, we thought it would take a few days to leave the spotlight. It took less than one afternoon. I don't know about you, but it makes me wonder what's happening in town that we're so forgettable!" Marian spoke into her wine glass. "It isn't too flattering to go from femme fatale to just another bugger, is it?"

"I have to admit that I've been wondering all day what Brynn and Des have made of all of this," I said.

"Oh, I'm sure she grabbed him by the willy and reminded him who was in charge of the relationship," Marian continued in her colorful way. I loved her banter. The most awful event in the world could have just occurred, and Marian would soon have us all in stitches.

"Do we need anything in town?" I asked as I stood up and started to drift toward the stairs.

Looking up in unison, Hillary, Kathleen, and Marian demanded, "Where are you going?" The only thing Tiziana did was shake her head emphatically.

"You just said you wondered what's happening in town. Let's find out. It's late! We'll be like spies and hang out in the background and see what's happening."

Marian, Hillary, and Kathleen looked at me like I was mad for a minute, and then they hot-footed it up the stairs to get themselves ready.

I was just scrubbing down in the shower with a lemon and ginger-scented bath bar when there was banging on the door.

"Really, are you taking a shower? Some of us are almost ready," called Kathleen.

"They didn't get all the mud out of my hair. I had to wash it again. I'll be out in a minute." With curtain closed, I ran a comb through my hair, tugging mud, shampoo, and tangles free. A glass of white wine was passed through the curtain, and the evening's party was underway.

"To fortitude, strength, and courage!" came Hillary's toast. I felt like I was off to war, and for all of ten seconds, I wondered if I should stay home.

Kathleen, somewhere in the background, was teasing Marian about her one-night stand. "Better to have loved and lost than never to have loved at all—unless, of course, you get a nasty disease!" With much shouting, laughing, and begging for forgiveness, I rinsed off other missed bits of mud and kelp. Damn the torpedoes, full speed ahead, I was going in. Or out, in this case.

The chances of finding Des were infinitesimal, but a girl had to try. While no part of me believed that Des Bannerman was searching Chamonix for me, I admitted to myself that I would love to run into him and find out what he (and Brynn) had made of all the commotion. So I continued to adorn myself with creams, perfume, and makeup. After carefully styling my hair and finally getting some control of it, I addressed my wardrobe. I chose to wear snug jeans with rhinestones up the sides, a white cashmere sweater, a white knee-length down jacket with fur trim, and very high-heeled black boots.

Everyone but Tiziana was waiting downstairs, dressed to go dancing: dresses, high heels, and spangles.

"What are you wearing? You look more like someone who's going to a party than spying," I said, quizzically.

"Everyone will be dressed for a party. You'll stand out like a sore thumb! Go change your clothes!" Marian harangued me.

After thinking it over for a moment, I suggested, "You go cover the clubs and discos. I'm going to try to figure out where a celebrity might go if he was trying to escape the press, reassure his girlfriend, and avoid the public in general. There have to be a few quiet, out-of-the-way places. We'll figure somewhere to meet up. How does that sound?"

Just at that moment, Tiziana descended the stairs in the same clothes as earlier. "Really? You aren't going? I need you! What if Ted's with him? Who will clear the way?"

"I'm going to spend the evening by myself in front of this lovely fire. You don't need me. I'm certain Ted won't be with Des tonight. Would you want to be the third in that threesome? No, darling! Your Des is definitely alone with whatever-her-name-is tonight. If you want his attention, and he wants to give it, you need to be by yourself."

I weighed her advice for a second and then whined, "I need backup! Please, please come!"

"Darling, you don't! I'm sure you can handle this," she said with finality.

Unhappy, but knowing that Tiziana just couldn't understand that mere mortal women didn't possess her charisma and charms, I accepted that I would have to go alone.

In town, Marian pulled off rue Joseph Vallot and headed a short distance down the side road. There, a horde of people dressed to kill were standing out in front of La Cantina. It was one of the many nightclubs in town and currently one of the favorites. Sitting in the warm car, I asked where they were headed. After a few minutes of heavy debate, the decision was to go to the casino. I argued that it was completely unlikely that Des and Brynn would return to the scene of the crime. In the end, I surrendered, realizing they were probably hoping to meet up with the men they'd met the previous evening.

Once there, I told them I was going to look elsewhere and would take a cab back to the chalet. Before going our separate ways, I admonished Marian about going off with a stranger and leaving the others stranded.

"He wasn't strange. He was quite lovely, actually!" She waggled her brows.

"Well, just be careful. Remember to call me if you see Des!" My nerves were clearly getting to me.

"Actually, I was thinking of having a go with him tonight, since you were such a dismal failure last night," Marian teased.

"Not even you can handle two men, Marian," I retorted.

"I believe that's why God gave me two hands," she shouted out the window as she pulled the car into traffic.

I was alone on the streets of Chamonix, which teemed with couples, groups of friends, and the odd individual carrying shopping bags. I supposed it was too much to hope that Des would be standing there waiting for me.

I made my way across the slushy, snowy street in my impractical boots to a newspaper shop. I was about to open the door when I spied a magazine stand just outside the door. "Oh my god!" I said to myself. Every tabloid magazine and a few newspapers had pictures of Des and me on the cover. *Des Gets a Hand!* was one headline. *Heads or Tails?* was another.

*Gross! Thank god Mom wasn't here to read any of it. She'd be mortified,* I thought. The image of my mother holding a hand in front of her eyes as she said, over and over, "You used to be such a good girl, Charlotte!"

I carefully entered the shop and kept my head down, wanting to go unrecognized. I pretended to look at everything from the knee down. Considering how short I was, that was pretty tricky. My options were limited to more tabloids, adult magazines, candy, and random household products. After being in there for five minutes and not having anyone shout my name (my name had somehow been made known to the paparazzi; by the coat check girl at the casino was my guess), I approached the man behind the counter. In very poor French, I asked where a person looking for a quiet evening might go. He regarded me curiously and shrugged his shoulders. *So much for that,* I thought.

I went back out into the cold night air and contemplated where to go. Making the random decision to head back down rue Joseph Vallot, I turned around and barreled into a man whose arms were full of packages. After apologizing, half in English and half in French, I offered up my biggest smile. He just stared at me quizzically.

Taking a deep breath, I inquired in very broken French where one could spend a quiet evening. As only the French could, with a leer and a sneer, in heavily accented English, I was informed that in a resort town there weren't many choices for a woman alone, but there was a cinema. However, he told me, there would be little point in attending, since I wouldn't possibly understand a word—the movies were French.

I thanked him for his evaluation of my linguistic skills and risked asking for directions. He walked me outside and pointed at the cupola atop the only church in town. Quickly, I set off in the direction he had pointed to, wondering why we hadn't gone to Germany instead.

After inquiring with a few English-speaking tourists along the way, I finally found the cinema. I stepped inside and escaped the sounds of the surrounding nightlife. After a quick glance, I concluded that Des wasn't waiting for me with a box of popcorn.

It took me about ten seconds alone in the lobby to realize that what I was endeavoring was based on the fluff of teenage girls' fantasies. "What the hell," I mumbled under my breath. I bought a ticket for a movie that I had never heard of and wouldn't be able to understand called *The Holiday*, starring Cameron Diaz and Kate Winslet. Entering the theatre, which was decorated in crushed red velvet, I immediately breathed in the smell of cigarettes and perfume. They lingered in the air, instead of the scent of popcorn. I quite liked it. "Maybe the French aren't so bad after all," I quietly declared.

I sat down, took off my jacket, and settled in for my two-hour French lesson.

Hollywood had once again manufactured the perfect balance of conflict, resolution, true love, and friendship.

*If only I could do that* I thought, as I wandered back into the lobby, pulling on my jacket and gloves. Who would I start with? Kathleen and her Prince? Hillary and her polo-playing millionaire? Or Marian and her rugby-playing... rugby player? Tiziana would never need help.

In the foyer after it ended, I was thinking of whether to call it a night or go elsewhere when I was confronted by a horrific sight. Brynn Roberts was blocking my exit path, and her lips were curved into a smile that didn't reach her eyes. Instead, they bore the look of utter irritation.

"I have no idea how you knew we would be here, but this is going to stop. Des has explained to me what didn't happen last night. He truly believes that you're just being friendly. But I know! Every simple-minded girl out there looking for a free ride would be stupid not to pursue him. I'm giving you this last chance, and if you don't go now, I'll call the police! Have I made myself clear?" She shot her angry words at me so quickly that I barely had time to absorb them.

I was trying to formulate a response when Des himself stepped out from behind a door. His warm smile met his eyes, and he seemed genuinely pleased to see me.

"Ah, Charlotte, lovely to see you again. Listen, I'm dreadfully sorry if last night's events proved stressful. I know the first few hundred times it happened to me, it was overwhelming. I heard the paparazzi surrounded your home and followed you to a spa. I trust you didn't let it ruin your day. Brynn insisted on staying home. Ted and I skied up at the top. An excellent day, as the snow was perfect, and the paparazzi were helplessly left behind." He paused, and his voice switched to one more conspiratorial. In a whisper, he continued, "Just so you know, I've double-checked, and my zipper is definitely up! So, we shouldn't have that issue tonight."

At this, Brynn's eyebrows shot up, and she gave me a look that completely expressed her lack of appreciation for what had happened the evening before.

Noting this himself, Des quickly changed the subject. "Did you enjoy the film?"

Deciding not to be intimidated by Brynn and make it clear that I wasn't a simple-minded groupie, I jokingly said, "Don't worry about the paparazzi! We rarely find ourselves being pursued relentlessly, so we enjoyed our fifteen minutes of fame. By the time we headed home, the paparazzi were gone."

"They probably left you in search of Des," Brynn replied quickly. "They don't give up that easily. Des and I would appreciate it if you would just distance yourself. Let the paparazzi find other fodder," she demanded boldly, wearing another smile that didn't reach her eyes.

Draping an arm around Brynn's shoulders, Des gave her a concerned look and quietly rebuked her. "Charlotte has been quite gracious about the whole thing, really. It was my oversight that got us into this, but it's her name and face being bandied about. Let's not forget those vulgar headlines. Try to imagine how you would feel if your friends and family saw that!" Brynn turned a deep shade of purple, her anger at his rebuke palpable.

Ignoring his girlfriend's irritation, he went on, "Cameron Diaz is in remarkable shape. Did you see her run in those heels? I'm not ashamed to admit that when I found out she was to be the leading lady in *Love What We Have*, I got in great shape. Those scenes where she throws a punch, she really knows how!" We talked about the movie briefly before he sensed Brynn hadn't joined in.

He withdrew his arm from around her shoulders, kindly took my hand, and said, "Charlotte, it was indeed a pleasure. We're off to find a quiet drink somewhere obscure. Thanks for being so understanding about all of this. We hope that the rest of your holiday is enjoyable. Goodnight."

"Night," I replied. Des nodded while gently ushering the lovely Ms. Roberts out a side door and into the night.

I turned and walked out the front doors, feeling, well, sad. My girlish dreams had led me down a ridiculous path, and now, the woman in me felt foolish for my behavior.

"Impulse control, Charlotte," I said to myself. Just then, a car passed through the intersection. From the backseat, Des Bannerman smiled and waved, and then he winked. My eyes followed the taillights of his car until they disappeared from view.

*What did the wink mean?*

\* \* \*

When I returned to the chalet, Tiziana was indeed curled up in front of the fire with a dreamy look on her face. She was talking on the telephone. "Gianni?" I mouthed to her. She smiled and waved, so I disappeared upstairs to get ready for bed.

As I was changing into warm pajamas and removing my makeup, I continued to lecture myself on appropriate behavior. It was one thing to daydream and quite another to take action. "Some kind of silly Cinderella complex or something," I said, as I heaved a sigh and made my way downstairs.

As I entered the living room, Tiziana was ending her phone call. "Ciao, bello." With a giggle into the phone, she was finished. "So, tell me, did you find your man?"

I told her about the tabloids, the movie, and running into Brynn and Des. She quietly listened while I recounted all the details.

"Odd, though, as I was about to cross the road, his car passed me, and he smiled and winked at me. What do you think?"

"He winked? Darling, he's flirting with you!" Forgetting the lecture I'd just given myself, I allowed her to pull me into fantasies of a romance with Des. We concocted future trips to luxurious places on private planes, drifting on yachts, parading at the BAFTAs.

Fantasyland returned to reality when Kathleen, Marian, and Hillary returned. "Why so early?" I asked.

"It turns out that David isn't as good-looking or interesting when I'm sober," Marian began.

"I didn't meet anyone interesting either. My heart isn't in it," Kathleen replied.

"It just seemed easier to come back and have a glass of wine here! Anyway, how did it go? Did you find him?" Hillary asked.

I gave them the details. They were supportive in their immediate dislike of Brynn Roberts. "Who does she think she is?" Kathleen asked, the rest nodding in support.

We veered into, "He doesn't know what he's missing" statements. All in all, I had very supportive friends.

"Well, are we on for a day of skiing tomorrow? We only have a few days left, and I'd like to ski at least once more," I asked, surveying the group. The scantily-clad, sleepy women with wine slowly raised their hands to vote. "Okay, off to bed, everyone! We'll be on the slopes right after breakfast." I took their wine glasses to the kitchen and myself to bed.

In the morning, I woke up with a headache, feeling completely tired. I had dreamt of Ms. Roberts's unfriendly eyes and people mocking me while I wore a Cinderella gown. I stared at the ceiling and berated myself for last night's fantasy session with Tiziana. "Des Bannerman barely knows you're alive. Grow up!" I admonished myself.

After getting dressed, I went to the kitchen to get some coffee. I overheard Marian say, "Well, it was just a bit of fun, a laugh."

"We all dream of knights in shining armor! I'm sure Charlotte didn't really think he was going to leave his girlfriend for her. She's sensible," Hillary added.

I heard Kathleen sigh at the mention of a knight. "Well, at least she went for it."

"True. Someday, when she's old and grey and a granny, she can say she once was on the covers of magazines all over the world. Her grandchildren will be the envy of everyone. Who else will have a granny publicly accused of giving Des Bannerman a hand job?" Marian threw in.

"They're jealous *they* didn't meet someone," Tiziana purred over my shoulder. She, too, had eavesdropped on the conversation. Nudging me forward, we entered the kitchen with a loud "Buon Giorno" from her. Immediately, talk switched to breakfast and skiing.

The weather over the last few days had produced a crusty layer of ice over powdery snow. Skiing was a bit hazardous and hard work. By lunch, we were all exhausted. We made our way into a restaurant and ordered a hearty lunch and sipped cups of coffee while waiting for our order. We gave each other a good ribbing over our respective wipeouts.

"I swear to god, I didn't see that flag! My bum still smarts!" Marian grimaced, rubbing her posterior.

"Well, I'm sure it's not as bad as your forehead," Kathleen taunted. Marian had missed a danger flag and skied outside of the safe area. The next thing we knew, she'd become a human snowball and was rolling down the hill toward a large rock. She'd put her feet down to stop herself, her skis somewhere behind her. Unfortunately, all she'd done was flip herself around; she'd managed to hit the rock with her head. How her bum got tortured was anyone's guess.

"Well, I think it's a good thing you lost your poles early on. Who knows, you might have harpooned someone or yourself," Kathleen teased.

"I don't resemble a whale of any form," Marian answered good-naturedly.

Toward the end of our meal, we saw people pointing fingers at a crowd as it moved toward us. Heads bobbed up and down as people tried to see what was going on. The hum and pointing gathered in volume.

"Look, it's him!" Kathleen shrieked. A very swarthy male who exuded elegance held her rapt attention.

"Who is he?" I asked, absolutely clueless.

With Kathleen's attention riveted elsewhere, Hillary answered, "It is Miguel Alfonso Montefeltro della Rovere. He is Spain's Prince of Belmonte." Her British blue-blood was showing.

"So, it's okay for you to get giddy about a prince?" I teased them. "Next thing you know, we'll be traipsing all over Spain, France and Monaco searching for royalty."

Three faces turned toward me. "You heard all that?" Kathleen asked.

"Yes, I did. But don't worry, I understand. I'm not taking it seriously. But let me ask you, if you had the chance to meet someone you had a crush on, what would you do? If the prince over there sat down beside you and talked to you, would you be able to walk away without any thoughts of 'what if'?"

Gracefully, they all acknowledged that there would be some lingering fantasies.

It was only when I suggested, "Does anyone want to try skiing up at the top? I heard someone in the lift line say that the sun is shining up there. The map shows that there are a few easy runs," that everyone returned to the present. With trepidation, they agreed to go with me to the top of the mountain.

"Come on! Let's go get some more skiing in before Marian's ass gets too stiff," I said with a smile.

As we were gathering our clothing and skis, I saw Kathleen look wistfully over toward the Prince of Belmonte; his entourage had settled down not too far from us. Quietly, she asked me, "I wonder what he would do if I were to walk up to him and ask if I could join him for a drink?"

"I know! That's the problem. You wouldn't think twice with an average guy. Hell, he would be flattered and happy to have a beautiful, confident woman approach him for a change. It's amazing how being famous removes all the normal rules."

Eventually, we found the correct line to wait in, and talk turned to what everyone would be doing once our holiday came to an end. All our lives had become complex with responsibilities. Between talking about jobs, biological clocks, finding Mr. Right, finances, and other friends, we reached the mountaintop quickly.

Instead of sun, we found that a heavy fog had set in, making it challenging to see even just a few feet ahead. "Look, there's the map." Hillary pointed toward a large sign with skiers gathered around.

We skied over to try to determine which way to go. Upon deciding which run to take, Marian suggested, "Promise you'll stay close to me! I might need one of you to get the ski patrol!"

Though there was general laughter at the comment, I could see a bit of fear in her eyes and slid up next to her. "I got a good look at a few of the guys on patrol. You might want to fake an injury! It might not lead to love, but it might lead to getting laid."

"True!" I could see the wheels in Marian's head grinding. "Well then, if I shout the words, 'Holy Christ,' just stay away, and let me work my magic."

Kathleen, having overheard us, remarked, "More likely she'll be hitting him over the head with her ski pole."

After a little more ribbing as we slid ever so slowly down the mountain, we found ourselves in fog thick as pea soup.

Kathleen, who was in the lead, came to a stop. "Wow, I can barely see a thing," she said when we skied off to the side to join her.

Breathless, I took the map out and looked at it for a minute before calmly stating, "Nobody panic, but I think we're on a Black Diamond. We must have gone the wrong way."

After a minute of worried whining, Marian got everyone to regroup. "Where are your balls? We can manage, we're women! We'll just take it slow. Charlotte, since you're the best skier, why don't you go up front and lead the way?"

Agreeing, we made our way at a snail's pace. I could hear the gals chatting behind me, telling ghost stories of skiers lost in the mountains and having to forage for berries. The fog got thicker, and the conversation gradually dropped off as everyone concentrated on what was directly ahead of them. I pulled off to the side of the run so that we could all catch our breath.

I waited for a minute, then two. I called out their names and wondered what was taking so long. After another minute, I realized that they weren't behind me. Hard skiing and fear had kept me warm, but now a chill began to set in. I decided to head down the hill and hoped to meet them at the bottom or get help.

Trying to calm my nerves, I focused on the first thing that came to my mind. *Des Bannerman*. He really was a nice man. His girlfriend was a piece of work, that was for sure. It must be tough, though, being followed every moment. I supposed I would be bitchy if, every time I turned around, someone was throwing herself at my boyfriend. I talked quietly to myself for a minute or two, weighing the pros and cons of being famous. Taking a break, I stopped again and consulted my map. It was useless, since I didn't have any points of reference. I could only hope I was close to the bottom. Looking around me and seeing blobs of grey, I started to get freaked out. "Come on, woman, you can't let your imagination get to you now. You're almost there."

"Just a quiet word among friends?" asked Des Bannerman, his voice mocking me.

I promptly fell into a heap in the snow. In amazement, I pushed back my hood and goggles. "Where did you come from?" Had he heard any of the conversation I'd been having with myself? Total panic set in. Trying to calm myself, I focused on the situation at hand and tried to get back on my feet. Instead, I entertained Des by sliding around in the snow for a while. After getting a few laughs at my expense, he finally offered to help me to my feet.

Taking his hand, I hauled myself up out of the snow. By then I was sweaty from exertion and wet from melting snow. "I saw your friend, Tiziana, up the mountain, and she told me that you had become separated. I offered to look for you. Fortunately for me, you're the only one down here. Well, actually, you would have been easy to spot in a crowd, as you're the only one down here with a gold jacket. You're a veritable beacon in the mist."

"Thanks for the hand!" I hoped he would understand my reference to the tabloid headlines.

"It's the least I can do, since you've been so helpful." He clearly understood.

"So, where did you see Tiziana? Was she with the rest of my friends? Are they all right? Should I wait for them?" I rushed through my list of questions, still somewhat exhausted from flailing in the snow.

"They're fine. We thought they might know you when we heard your name being yodeled across the French Alps. I'm quite certain people in Geneva, possibly even Zurich, are wondering where Charlotte is. I'm surprised you didn't hear them. They were certain you'd skied off a cliff, by the way. I assured them you would see civilization again. As we speak, Ted is escorting them down to the bottom, where we're to meet up." When he finished speaking, his blue eyes were crinkled up at the edges. I couldn't help but notice that his speech pattern in real life was very much like in his movies, as was his inclination toward monologues.

He continued to smile broadly, reliving a memory.

"What?" The crinkly, blue eyes made me wonder.

"Oh, just thinking about your friend Marian! I'm glad I'm not you. You're in for quite a lecture when we get to the bottom. Not sure I've ever heard anyone, male or female, string the litany of curses together that she did."

I cleared my throat. "I can only imagine. Sorry about that. It's her way of letting you know she cares."

"Yes, well, she threatened my reproductive organs if I took advantage of you. Then she threatened them if I didn't take advantage of you."

Mortified, my cheeks were flaming. I gasped, "She didn't. Please say she didn't."

Clearing his throat, as if he were uncomfortable, he said, "Well, I think it might have been fear speaking, but she mentioned that you had a bit of crush on me. For fourteen years, apparently. That, if you were dying, it would be gentlemanly of me to send you off with a smile on your face. But if you were intact, I was to leave you alone because you were in a fragile state."

Promising myself that I would kill Marian later, I tried to find enough composure to speak. "Well, Marian's just upset. We've been friends forever, and she's protective. Not to mention all those older brothers. She can be pretty unfiltered." I completely skipped over the subject of my crush.

"Not for the reasons Marian mentioned, I'm quite glad to have a few minutes alone with you. I couldn't help but notice last night that Brynn was rather cold with you. She's generally quite sweet, not prone to bursts of anger. Let's just say that life has been challenging lately, and our commitments have plotted against us. The paparazzi have been particularly annoying. This holiday has been months in the making and was meant to be relaxing. Unfortunately, it has been anything but. I know it shouldn't matter, but I would rather you have a more pleasant opinion of her. She is quite lovely."

Saying the first thing that came to my mind, I said, "Okey doke." I nudged my skis downhill. He took the hint and followed behind me.

We skied in silence. I wanted to appear focused on skiing through the fog, but mostly I was caught up in my thoughts. Finally, I decided to seize the moment and came to a stop. He stopped, looking at me curiously.

"I can appreciate that she's fed up, and I'm genuinely sorry that I added to the problem. I can't deny that I enjoyed talking with you the other night. If she's as wonderful as you say, I'm sure, under different circumstances, I would have enjoyed talking with her, as well. But let's be honest. Under what normal circumstances would I be sitting around and hanging out with two of the world's most famous movie stars?"

"Thanks, Charlotte. If it makes you feel any better, I rarely get invited anywhere for a chat. You think, when you're watching the Golden Globes or what have you, that we're enjoying ourselves. Really what's happening is one bloke walks over to another and says with a smile, "You were fucking terrible in that role." Or, "They asked me, but I knew the film would tank!" And the women! They're even more brutal!" he joked. Or at least I thought he was joking.

Not being satisfied to leave well enough alone, I said, "You know, you both chose a way of life that puts you in the public eye. People are curious, and it's that curiosity that helps pay for your twelve houses, fancy holidays, and whatever else. You weren't born royal or wealthy. Don't you remember imagining how wonderful someone's life might be?"

Not knowing what to expect, I was surprised when he answered forthrightly, "You're right. But then, so is Brynn. If people would be content with a smile or even a hello, it would be fine. The problem is that many of the people and paparazzi we encounter want something from us, and they aren't particularly concerned with being reasonable or polite. As for you, at the casino, you were persistent but not rude."

Inwardly, I felt hypocritical. He hadn't caught on to the fact that Tiziana had been part of the plan or that I had been searching for him before the night we met.

"Well, I was a bit rude. To be fair, I can't imagine how you stand all of it. Everyone wanting your attention. You wouldn't remember, but a few years back, you and I were at an event at Oxford. You were speaking about taking charge of your life, not waiting for things to happen to you. Anyway, afterwards I was standing about two feet from you. You smiled, but I didn't know if it was at me. Very deflating to a girl's ego, I'll add. If you or Brynn want reassurance, I have enjoyed your company, I know you love your girlfriend, and I never thought you were interested in me." The last bit rushed out of my mouth and left me embarrassed and breathless.

I was rewarded by a genuine chuckle. "I must say, your frankness is refreshing. You're quite right, you know. Too many questionable people, and, undoubtedly, I've become jaded. I'll endeavor to look at people less suspiciously," he said and then added, "You appear to be quite unique, Charlotte."

I was thinking of how to respond when I saw skiers descending. "It looks like we have company." He looked over his shoulder and up the hill toward them. No sooner had he done that than the cameras appeared from nowhere, and the skiers turned into paparazzi. "My god! They really are everywhere."

He quickly reacted. "We'd better go before they get too close and figure out you're the woman from the casino. Do you think you can make a run for it? I know the fog is bad, but I'll stay in front, and you can follow me."

"I'll do my best." And we were away.

I had never skied at such a breakneck pace. Essentially, we pointed our skies downhill and accelerated at an alarming rate. I kept chanting to myself, "You can do it, nice and easy, you can do it." All the while, I could hear the sounds of skis and cameras clicking behind us. People were shouting, "Des," "Mr. Bannerman," "Brynn"—anything they thought might get our attention. Fortunately, they seemed to be losing ground from the sound of things, which added to my confidence. Occasionally, Des threw looks at me over his shoulder and then focused on the mountain.

I could see the sun beginning to break through the fog and hoped we were close to the bottom. My legs were starting to burn from the effort, and I really needed to go to the bathroom. "Keep going and think of something else," I said out loud.

We burst through the fog and could see the chairlifts not too far off. People were milling around, and a few looked up as we emerged from the clouds. I quickly scanned the distance for Tiziana, Hillary, Kathleen, Marian, and Ted. I couldn't see them and was hoping that they had made it safely down.

I was so busy looking around that I hadn't noticed Des had slowed down. I plowed into him and knocked him over. We bounced around, sending ski equipment flying everywhere. By the time the world quit spinning, the paparazzi had caught up. "Oh, bugger," my companion said between puffs of breath. I opened my eyes to see his beautiful blue eyes between me and the sky. I became aware of our limbs being entangled and his weight on top of me. Quickly fluttering through my mind was the realization that it had been some time since I had enjoyed that particular sensation.

Suddenly, several unknown heads came into view, all with cameras disguising their faces. "Oh, bugger is right," I muttered, quickly covering my face with my arms. The noise was horrific as people shouted at us, asking my name, calling for Des to look their way.

"I'm sorry!" I shouted. I never got a response. Des hauled me up and led the way to a deluxe chalet, leaving our ski equipment scattered to the four corners of the world.

\* \* \*

I woke up the next day with the certainty of several things. My body hurt like hell from my tumble at the end of the run; I had caught a cold; I was probably on the cover of the tabloids again; and Des Bannerman would be staying well away from me and anyone linked to me.

After lying in bed pondering the events of the last week, I heard a light rap on the door of my bedroom. "Come in," I called. The door opened and four concerned faces peered in at me.

"We thought we ought to bring the papers up, so you could get it over and done with," Hillary explained, her voice apologetic.

With a grimace, Kathleen added, "It would also seem that your fifteen minutes of fame aren't over. We can't see the forest for the paparazzi."

I took the papers and scanned the headlines. Through the grayish light of the gloomy sky, I made out one picture of Des and me entwined intimately. Another shot was a close-up of a very distraught Brynn. The worst was a photo of Des and Brynn boarding a private plane late last night, both looking very weary.

I handed them to Kathleen and asked her to translate. The headline and photo captions inferred that we were so overcome with lust that we couldn't take the time to return to our hotel room. Many articles pondered the state of the famous couple's relationship, while others queried how long Des had been having the affair.

I took a deep breath and slowly blew it out while I shoved my hair out of my eyes. "What a mess. I wonder what she's thinking."

They all looked at me with concern. "You're the one with problems. Des and Ms. Roberts have fled the scene, and you've been left behind to handle the whole thing. You need to figure out what you want to do," Marian said as she sat down on the bed beside me.

"That just occurred to me!" I said to no one in particular while chewing my lip. We all sat in silence for a minute or two, absorbing how this vacation had taken on a surreal quality.

"Come on! Let's have breakfast and coffee. Maybe they'll all go away again, and we won't have to figure out what to do," Kathleen said as she pulled me out of bed.

The others were working in the kitchen when I arrived. I had used the excuse of needing to use the bathroom when, in reality, all I needed was a good cry. They ignored my puffy red eyes, and, over breakfast, we devised plans for the remaining few days of our time together.

"We could pack up and go to Saint Gervais Les Bains," Hillary suggested. "They have fabulous skiing."

"How about taking the train to Monaco?" Kathleen inquired. A newspaper had reported that Prince Miguel Alfonso Monte- whatever had left, as well. I shot her a look that told her how pathetic I thought she was.

"I really appreciate the support, but we'd spend all our time packing, rearranging our flights, and traveling. I think we should just take a stand and enjoy the rest our time here." All four of them looked at me dubiously but seemed to accept my opinion as the decision.

A few chocolate croissants and several cups of coffee later, we had decided how to ride out the storm in Chamonix. I went upstairs and began to pull myself together. While washing my hair, I found a nice-sized lump on the back of my head. No wonder I had a headache. While drying myself off with a big, fluffy white towel, I made a mental note to buy a better helmet. I then gently rubbed some cream into my skin and took a few aspirin.

Every once in a while during my toilette, a paparazzi report was called up the stairs. I finally arrived downstairs to find my friends dressed in jackets and boots.

"Are you ready?" Tiziana asked.

"Are you sure you want to do this?" Kathleen inquired.

"I'm not sure this is a good idea. Lambs to the slaughter come to mind," Hillary remarked.

Pulling on my coat and boots, I looked at them. "Do I look ready?"

"Well, actually, you look like you did the day of our final exams at school," Marian offered.

"Well, that doesn't make me feel great! I was a bundle of nerves that day. I thought I was going to be sick. Just leave a clear path to the door, don't let me ramble, and, if at all possible, don't say a word," I instructed the group. "If there's trouble, I'd rather take the blame."

With that, we opened the doors and presented a unified front to the paparazzi. Instantly, the cameras started to click, people started to shout, and I felt the urge to both vomit and wet my pants.

I took one step further forward than my friends, to separate myself from them. I pulled some notes out of my pocket that I had made at the breakfast table and addressed the crowd.

"Rumors that Mr. Bannerman and I have an intimate relationship are completely false. We met purely by chance twice. I would like to apologize to Ms. Roberts directly for causing her any discomfort."

"My friends and I would like to enjoy the remainder of our vacation. We ask that you respect all those involved in this incident and give us privacy. Thank you."

More shouting and camera-clicking continued as I turned and walked back into the chalet. Once inside, I raced to the bathroom. While I didn't get sick, I had almost wet my pants. I pressed a cold cloth to my flushed cheeks and wondered how celebrities, politicians, and other public figures survived having their lives scrutinized.

"Are you okay in there?" Hillary called from the other side of the door.

I opened the bathroom door. "I am now!"

We spent the day avoiding the paparazzi pretty lazily. Blankets, books, a roaring fire, and plenty of chatting provided entertainment. Fortunately, there was enough food in the house to survive the day.

After eating leftover pasta for dinner, Marian turned on the television with the hope that there might be some program that we could understand. "Oh, look, there are cable channels with movies in English!" she said excitedly.

"What's on?" I asked, ready to be mindlessly entertained.

Marian, in charge of the remote control, said, "Our choices are *Casino Royale*, *The Queen*, *Lady Chatterley*, *Little Miss Sunshine*, *The Bourne Supremacy*, and *Bridget Jones's Diary*."

Deciding to go with my request for an ass-kicking movie, we set about collecting food to nibble on before watching *The Bourne Supremacy*.

Kathleen, having become completely Frenchified, unwrapped a room-temperature wedge of Camembert and another very smooth cheese made of sheep's milk. Tiziana placed sliced fruit on a plate, while Marian and I brought an assortment of chocolate to the party. Hillary was content to sip a glass of white Bordeaux.

Just as the movie began, Tiziana's phone rang, and she quietly answered and left the room. We were so engrossed by the chase scenes, people beating each other to a pulp, and how good Matt Damon was that we didn't notice she hadn't returned. It was when the credits were rolling that she sauntered back into the room looking like a cat that had drunk a bowl of cream.

"How's Gianni?" we inquired. She looked a little dazed, gave a little shimmy, and reported that the world was a wonderful place.

Marian, who had spent the day peeking out the window to check on the paparazzi, got up and pulled the curtains back slightly. "Looks like the last few have finally given up."

"Thank god for that," Kathleen replied. "We would have had to tunnel into town for food tomorrow."

The following morning, I stumbled down the stairs and made a pot of coffee. Then I sat in silence, holding a mug, and watched snowflakes fall. Eventually the others joined me, and we all talked about what the day's plan ought to be.

I stretched my legs out in front of me and straightened my spine. "You know what? I'm through with hiding. I didn't do anything wrong. I say we fluff ourselves up, go shopping, have lunch, and get back to normal."

In support of my decision, we leisurely readied ourselves, collectively took a deep breath, walked out the door, and had our photographs taken by a plethora of paparazzi. The noise wasn't nearly as deafening as the day before. We did our best to ignore all of it and drove off in our SUV without running anyone over.

"Bloody hell! They're following us," Marian reported.

"Of course they are. We have Des Bannerman's lover in our car," Kathleen teased.

"I suggest we treat them like annoying children. Ignore them and they'll go away," Hillary suggested.

Hillary's comment made me wonder if it was going to be possible to wander the streets of Chamonix. I thought I might have taken an overly simplistic outlook on this. The image of a bull in a china shop flitted through my mind. Looking around the car, I could tell the girls were happy to get out of the chalet, so I decided not to give in to cowardice. I would follow Hillary's lead and apply the "annoying children" concept.

Eventually, we found a place to park the car then spent a few hours wandering the shops to find gifts for family and friends. Eventually, starving, we sat down to eat.

After flouncing down in her chair, Kathleen jokingly asked, "Has anyone been counting? I wonder how many photographs have been taken today. The newspapers tomorrow will undoubtedly have an itemized list of all purchases we made, leaving readers to wonder if you're buying bric-a-brac for Des's house."

"Don't even say it, because it's probably true," I replied, unable to find the humor in it. "Could we change the subject? When are you and Gianni getting married?" I asked Tiziana, changing the subject.

After she recovered from choking on a bite of warm, crusty bread she asked, "Do you know something I don't? Gianni hasn't mentioned marriage!"

I sensed she wasn't unhappy about the lack of a proposal.

My assumption had always been that this was the direction they were heading. They'd been together forever, they were Italian Catholics, and I assumed one or both would want children soon.

"Well, after all the phone calls and dreamy looks, I just assumed that the next time we'd all be getting together, you would be getting married," Kathleen said.

"I'll be sure to let you know," Tiziana answered, appearing more interested in the menu than anything else.

Lunch was an oddly silent affair. Generally, we have a lot more to talk about. To be fair, I spent most of lunch locked in my own thoughts. It was only when we were sipping coffee that I realized my friends were preoccupied, as well.

Grabbing Kathleen and Hillary's hands, since they were within reach, I said to the group, "I'm really sorry! I'm responsible for all the bedlam. Do you just want to go back to the chalet?"

After pishposhing my concerns, there was no choice but to gracefully and gratefully accept reassurances. We paid the bill and resumed the day's events with a little more enthusiasm than before. A few hours later, we schlepped our bags down the sidewalk in the direction of the car.

Some photographers offered to help Tiziana with her bags.
"Figures," Marian said. "My arms could be dragging behind me,
leaving a trail of blood, and no one would notice. Especially with her
around."

"It's truly amazing, isn't it? The paparazzi have been following us
around because I'm the reported 'other woman' in Des Bannerman's
life, yet when they come in contact with her, they wouldn't care if Des
Bannerman and I were naked in the snow in front of them," I added,
reassuring Marian it wasn't only her.

The rest laughed. "True, so true," Kathleen and Hillary agreed, while
Tiziana was oblivious as she gazed in shop windows.

Either the trip back was less eventful, or we'd become accustomed to
having cars and motorcycles swerve around us and people call out our
names. My favorite was a big German guy on a motorcycle two sizes too
small for him booming, "Charlotta!" That fella was intimidating.

That all changed as we unloaded the trunk of the car. The normal,
tedious task was made much more challenging since there was a
gauntlet of people stepping in our way, cameras flashing, and shouting.
Eventually, we carried our purchases into the house.

"Thank the good Lord that's over. I thought I was going to pee my
pants, I have to go so bad," Kathleen shouted as she dashed up the stairs
to the bathroom.

"Could someone explain to me why she feels the need to inform
us of her bodily functions?" Hillary said to Kathleen's retreating back.

Marian laughed, "I can just picture the tabloids tomorrow, a picture
of Kathleen running through the snow leaving behind a yellow trail.
The title would be, 'Charlotte Flees, Friend Pees!'" Everyone laughed;
well, everyone but Hillary. She only raised an eyebrow and gave us a
disparaging glare.

Returning to the previous day's guard duty, Marian walked to the
window and peeked out.

Kathleen had returned and was doling out glasses of white
Bordeaux to everyone. Marian had just taken a sip from her glass when
she gasped, "Oh my god, one of the paparazzi is coming to the front
door. The nerve!"

"Well, don't open it! All I want to do is enjoy this glass of wine and
probably a few more," I said.

I took a big gulp from my glass and headed to the kitchen to get the bottle of wine. Rejoining them, I continued, "I propose that next year we meet at the bottom of the Grand Canyon. Not too much can happen there."

Whomever Marian had seen approaching now tapped on the door. "Who is it?" she called out in a tone that asked, "Who the fuck do you think you are?"

"My name is Daniel LaRivière, I'm from the law firm of Chapdelaine & Dussault," came the reply.

"Oh god," I said for the thousandth time in the last three days. All eyes in the room quickly swiveled from the door to me.

"What do we do?" Kathleen whispered after a few moments of silence.

"Well, darling, there's only one thing to do. Open the door. We'll take it one step at a time," Tiziana replied, freakishly calmly.

There was a certain amount of logic there. After all, how long could we stay hidden inside?

Marian looked back at me, questioningly. I gave her a tentative nod and let out the breath I'd been holding. She carefully opened the door, leaving her foot behind it just in case the paparazzi made a rush and we had to shut it quickly. By now we were all standing up, gazing through the narrow gap, trying to size up our visitor.

"Well, he looks like a lawyer. I don't see any cameras or tape recorders. Should she let him in?" Hillary asked.

I walked over to the door, taking deep breaths along the way. "Monsieur LaRivière, given everything that has happened, I'm sure you would understand our asking you for identification, to take off your coat and turn your remaining pockets inside out."

"As you request, mademoiselle." He entered, a business card in one hand, his black cashmere coat in the other. He placed his coat over the back of a chair and then deposited the contents of his pockets on the table. Hillary, Kathleen, Marian, Tiziana, and I watched him carefully.

"Should we pat him down to see if he's wired?" Marian asked with a glint in her eye as she handed me his embossed business card.

My brain sent a message causing me to recognize he was pretty hot, while my nervous system encouraged me to flee.

That question was answered by Monsieur LaRivière. "Ladies, I can assure you that I'm not with the paparazzi or any other group associated with the media. If you allow me to open my briefcase, I believe I can answer all your questions suitably."

It was only then we noticed the briefcase. So much for our detective skills! As he was looking at me, I uncertainly said, "Certainly." Feeling the need to fill the quiet while he made a show of unlocking the leather case, I continued, "No one here has anything to hide." I prayed I was correct.

"Interesting choice of words," Monsieur LaRivière replied. "If I may explain why I'm here." He paused briefly to make sure the documents were organized correctly and then continued, "I'm here to deliver documents." This seemed quite ominous. The urge to flee grew bigger. Still looking at me, he said, "Could Ms. Charlotte Young please identify herself and provide me with a piece of legal identification?"

I felt five pairs of eyes on me, four pairs waiting with concern, one pair disinterested.

I stepped forward and took my passport from my purse, which was hanging on a hook beside my jacket. I briefly debated making a break for it but handed it over instead. After looking my passport and me over, Monsieur LaRivière handed it back with an envelope.

The stationery was quite heavy, indicating its high quality. My name was printed in an elegant font and the letterhead was from Meade, Jameson, and Kelly.

"Give us just a minute," I requested.

"I think that would be best, mademoiselle. It would make certain that all your questions are answered."

Feeling my friends peering over my shoulder, I turned the envelope over and carefully opened it. I unfolded the document and several important words leapt out at me. "Restraining Order," "Charlotte Young," "Mead, Jameson, and Kelly," "Des Bannerman," and "Benoît Durand."

I folded onto the nearest chair. "I can't believe this. I haven't done anything." The situation was continuing to take turns for the worse.

A week before, I had been an average person flying to France for a ski vacation. Three days before, the world thought I was Des Bannerman's mistress, and today, I was a stalker being told to stay away from him.

Seeing my face turn from pasty white to green, Kathleen guided me to a bathroom. I could hear Tiziana talking to Monsieur LaRivière in the distance. Kathleen placed a glass of cold water in my hands and then draped a cold cloth on the back of my neck.

"The balls on that man. You didn't do anything wrong," she whispered. Then, even more quietly, "You didn't, did you?" I snatched the cloth away from my neck. "Of course not!" I replied angrily.

I stormed back to the living room, Kathleen rushing to keep up with me. I overheard LaRivière and Tiziana in a heated discussion with her calling into question Des Bannerman's legitimacy.

Upon seeing me, Monsieur LaRivière politely asked if I was all right. "I'm fine." I tugged my sweater down and folded my arms across my chest. "Who are all these people?" I slapped the packet of documents on the table.

"They are the law firm representing Mr. Bannerman," LaRivière replied. My last hope that Mead, Jameson, and Kelly were his friends faded altogether. No possibilities that this was a practical joke.

"Please explain to me why it was deemed necessary for Mr. Bannerman to have a restraining order filed against *me*?" Confusion resonated in my voice.

Monsieur LaRivière went on to explain that the individual filing the request listed "order of protection" as the explanation. The judge, in this case Benoît Durand, believed there to be sufficient evidence to warrant the restraining order. "In addition, I was instructed to draw your attention to the paragraph that states that if you hold any more press conferences regarding your acquaintance with Mr. Bannerman, he is prepared to take further legal action." Mr. LaRivière finished his explanation less vigorously, starting to sweat a bit under the glare of five angry women.

Standing with my feet spread wide, my hands clenched in fists at my side, I snarled with anger. "Given the fact that we live on two different continents and that we don't share the same circle of friends, I can assure you that it would have been extremely unlikely that we would have ended up in the same place at the same time, anyway. You may inform the necessary persons that I am not in the habit of foisting myself onto anyone. So, other than Mr. Bannerman coming to his senses and my giving a damn, I can assure you that I will stay the required distance away from him." I finished at a much higher pitch than I had started.

Without a word, I handed Monsieur LaRivière his cashmere coat. With equal quietness, he placed the items on the table back into his pockets and snapped his briefcase shut. He slipped on his coat, made eye contact with me, and nodded.

"Anything else?" I dared him.

"No, mademoiselle. That is all. Once you read through the document carefully, you may call me with any questions," he said quietly.

"I will call my own lawyer, thank you." I glared with angry eyes at him, at which point he turned and left.

Not another sound was made for a full minute. I stood in the middle of the room, looking at nothing.

I felt warm hands on mine. "Oh, honey, I don't even know what to say." Kathleen spoke in a quiet, whispery voice.

"What is there to say? Meeting him was supposed to be impossible. It was all supposed to be fun. Fun and impossible! What in the world am I going to say to people when they find out that I have a restraining order against me? It was bad enough trying to figure out how to explain to people that Des Bannerman and I barely met. This is serious. Now I have to worry about police records, harassment charges…" My voice trailed off as I returned to my thoughts for a few moments. "What happened…?" My question was left hanging in the air, my eyes filled with tears.

Soon, I was wrapped in Tiziana's arms as she whispered in my ear, "Darling, I'm so sorry."

# Chapter Four

**MY HOPE WAS THAT**, when I returned home to New York City, all this bizarreness would be left behind in Chamonix. The interest of the paparazzi had quickly dropped off upon Des's departure. I waited for the tabloids to find out about the restraining order, but I was spared that humiliation, which made the last few days somewhat enjoyable.

A serious cold front descended on the mountains, so we left the slopes to the more intrepid explorers. With only a few days left, we spent time enjoying the village's eateries, festivities, and nightlife.

One night, Marian was trying to get the barman's attention and became desperate enough that I thought she might take her bra off and raise it like a flag. Just as I was about to intervene, a nearby voice said, "Aren't you the girl who was having a roll in the snow with Des Bannerman?"

Looking through the cigarette fog, I returned my focus to within five feet of myself and gazed at the fellow. His clothes were nondescript, and his voice and body language made it clear he wasn't trying to pick me up.

"Probably paparazzi," Hillary whispered in my ear. "You have the wrong girl, we've only just arrived. We saw the articles in the magazines. Is she still here? We heard she left town right after Des Bannerman," she lied boldly. The guy just shrugged his non-descript shoulders and left to troll the bar.

After that, my fifteen minutes of fame appeared to be well and truly over. We were enormously relieved when the attention returned to Tiziana, leaving us only the simple challenge of allowing one male at a time to vie for her attention.

Finally, the day arrived for me to fly home. My flight was scheduled for the evening before everyone else's. Packed and teary-eyed, with my coat on and a taxi waiting for me, I confessed to my friends, "I really couldn't have done it without you. Get the restraining order, I mean! You really should consider yourselves responsible. Not only did you help me find and meet Des Bannerman, you did bugger all to protect me from him. But don't worry, I forgive you! Well, I'll only truly forgive you if the next time we meet up, one of you has his balls in your hand!"

"Now, that's the spirit! I'm glad you didn't let it get you too down," Marian said while giving me another hug.

Hillary pushed Marian aside. "I'm glad you finally met him, though. Perhaps now you'll quit mooning over him. Move on to someone more worthy, like George Clooney."

Kathleen moaned. "Next time we come here, I expect you to help me meet Prince Harry. He doesn't seem to mind mixing with the riff-raff."

"Don't worry, darling, we'll never let that horrible man hurt you again. We'll be certain he knows how terribly he's treated you. We'll talk soon, bella!" Tiziana reassured me as she embraced me and gave me a peck on each cheek.

"Be good to yourself!" the girls called as I stepped into the taxi.

*Famous last words,* I thought a few days later when I stepped through the etched glass doors that divided our offices from the corridor.

For reasons unimaginable, every wall and bulletin board was covered with photographs and articles about my tryst with Des Bannerman. Des and me at the casino, Des and me at the theatre, Des and me getting in the car, Des and me standing in the fog, Des and me entwined in the snow, Des and me looking shocked. It was overwhelming and over the top.

"I'm going to find out who the hell is behind this and sue their ass off!" I muttered under my breath as I tugged one of the most offensive magazine covers off the wall.

As I was about to turn around and leave, I heard my name called out. "Charlotte!" It was Faith Clarkson, the owner of the PR firm that I worked for.

My stomach clenched, sweat broke out on my forehead, and I willed myself to be calm. I turned around on an elegantly-shod foot, tugged down my suit jacket, and forced a relaxed smile on my face. "Ms. Clarkson?"

"Charlotte, I see you've enjoyed your vacation. Would you please join me in my office?" Her face was deadpan, and her invitation was really only a veiled demand.

"I'll be right there. I'll just go put my coat and briefcase away," I said with an enthusiasm I didn't feel.

I hurried to my office, trying to prepare myself for the upcoming assault. My secretary was sitting at her desk when I walked through the door.

"Hello, Evelle. How have you been?" I asked perfunctorily, as I crossed the room to my office. As I hung up my coat and put my briefcase on my desk, I called over my shoulder, "Could you please bring in my messages and anything that I need to review?"

I looked up to see Evelle standing in the doorway with everything I'd just requested. Her eyes had a bit of a weird look about them, and she just stared at me.

"Thank you, Evelle. Is there anything else?" I broke her out of her stupor.

"Ms. Clarkson would like to see you as soon as possible," she conveyed, the weird looks not having disappeared.

"Yes, I know. I'll be on my way as soon as I manage to get myself a little organized." I took the stack from her hands and placed it all on my desk. It was a large pile, and I thanked the gods for having given me enough to do that I wouldn't be able to leave my office for weeks.

She was still standing there. "Is there anything else, Evelle?" I asked with an annoyed tone.

"Oh, no! Sorry!"

"Do you know who's behind all the photographs and magazine articles?"

"I think you should talk to Ms. Clarkson about that," she said and closed my office door behind her.

I took a quick moment to settle myself. "You knew you'd have to face this, you didn't do anything wrong. Just be honest," I whispered. It was my new mantra, replacing my old mantra, "You can do anything you want."

Smoothing the creases of my black wool Pollini suit, I left the sanctuary of my office and passed Evelle's desk, where she gave me yet another odd look. As I walked down the hallways of Faith Clarkson & Company, I felt like I was in a nightmare... or a freak show. In addition to the walls blazing with images that I was trying to forget, people poked their heads out from behind doors, and a buzz of chatter followed behind me.

"You can do it, just keep walking..." I muttered under my breath. If this kept up, I was going to need therapy.

Eventually I walked the gauntlet and arrived at the office of Faith Clarkson. I asked one of her secretaries if she was available. "She's waiting for you!" the bitchy one snapped. I was escorted into the inner sanctum of the company.

"Ah, Charlotte, you've made it at last. I hope it wasn't too treacherous a journey," she said from behind her large desk, never looking up, continuing to review the document in front of her.

Faith Clarkson, who was reported to be in her late fifties, could pass for a thirty-five-year-old. She had a gorgeous figure, flawless skin, her hair was never out of style or out of place, and she had a wardrobe tailored by the most notable names in the fashion world.

Above all, Faith Clarkson was a vicious businesswoman.

"So, Charlotte, tell me what happened, and I'll tell you what we'll do." She continued to look down and sign a document with a flourish. Only then did she finally look up and gesture toward a hideous chair designed by some Swedish guy, folding her arms in front of her so that her red talons rested on her Burberry-clad biceps.

I sat on the edge of the orange-stained ergonomically-approved chair from the showrooms of Sweden, and, with the remaining shreds of my dignity, I briefly outlined the events of my vacation. I made it as clear as possible that nothing other than the early stages of a friendship had developed. She silently listened while I ended my monologue with a final denial of anything that the paparazzi had reported or inferred from the photographs.

"Let's be blunt. Not only is Des Bannerman an international celebrity, he's dating one of the most beautiful women in the world. I believe you met Brynn Roberts! In addition to being very beautiful and a highly successful actress, she's a Goodwill Ambassador for the United Nations. I knew, of course, that the media had it all wrong!" my employer replied with disdain.

I forced my eyebrows to stay in place and not react to such a cold comment. However, she was oblivious, having swiveled her chair to focus her attention on some distant cloud floating outside her office window. For a minute or two there was silence while I focused on the back of her designer hair and designer chair, hoping that this painful interview would be over soon.

Swiveling around to face me, there was an energy in her eyes that terrified me. "That doesn't mean we can't take advantage of your situation. It hasn't been announced, but it has been a long-term goal to set up a European division of Faith Clarkson. You've provided the Golden Ticket. We'll use your newfound connections to jumpstart the clientele. I'm certain that, with Des Bannerman and Brynn Roberts as our first clients, the office, which will be in London, will be thriving within the year."

She took in a deep breath as she finished, glory and power glistening in her eyes. Looking at her, I saw what had made her so successful. I dreaded what had to follow.

"Ms. Clarkson, may I ask who authorized the photographs and magazines wallpapering our usually elegant and minimalistic halls?" I asked, feeling anger rise inside me. Of course, I couched the question within the flattering words she'd want to hear.

"I did," she replied, and apparently that was all the information she felt obliged to give me.

"Why would you suggest such a thing?"

"To make clear to everyone who works here that everything they do, everywhere they go, there's an opportunity to be taken. You ought to be flattered, Ms. Young." Her voice was flat, with not so much as a hint of contrition or humanity.

"Well, I'm afraid that I'll be of no use to you!"

Not listening to what I had to say, she interrupted, "Our people will set up a meeting. You can provide introductions, and I'll handle the rest."

"I'm afraid that can't happen." I took a deep breath. "There is a bit more to the story." I then filled her in on the meeting with Daniel LaRivière from Meade, Jameson, and Kelly and the restraining order. As I spoke, I could feel the energy in the room being sucked away. In its place came a coolness that quickly devolved into iciness.

After staring at me with emotionless eyes for a very long minute, she spoke. "Well, Ms. Young, not only have you landed into a bit of trouble for yourself, you've made yourself useless in helping us attain clients and connections," Ms. Clarkson said as she pushed her chair back and stood up.

Calmly, she pushed the chair in and menacingly walked around to the front of her desk until she stood just in front of me.

I held my breath as I waited to be fired.

I was burning with anger. If this was going to be the result of an innocent encounter with Des Bannerman, then he and I would face off in court, even if I had to spend my last penny. Just because he had an uncomfortable moment or two with his girlfriend didn't entitle him to ruin my career and reputation and make me the laughing stock of New York City. I had visions of Des Bannerman cowering at my anger and of Brynn Roberts looking contrite.

"Ms. Young, can you please come back to the present?" Ms. Clarkson's voice was filled with impatience.

"I'm sorry, Ms. Clarkson. I understand that this ridiculous situation has affected my reputation and my credibility. It was my hope that people would be able to see this situation for what it is, a mere mortal getting screwed by the gods of celebrity once again," I stated angrily.

With iciness in her voice, Faith Clarkson responded, "Clearly you weren't listening, so make sure you are now!" She drew in a deep breath and spoke clearly and concisely. "I don't know how, but you'll do all that is necessary to ensure that your complication doesn't reflect negatively on our company. In two days, I'll announce the opening of the London office in the fall. Fortunately for you, you have other skills that are quite useful to me. So you're going to be part of the team developing the London office. You'll bring your credentials and contacts from Oxford University to the table and make amends. You'll make this situation beneficial to Faith Clarkson & Company." She finished, "Dazzle me!"

My head bobbed up and down. While I understood her disappointment and was relieved by the knowledge that I still had a job, I couldn't see how it was my responsibility to make the London office successful. However, I would keep those thoughts to myself. "If there's nothing else, I'll head back to my office and begin working on that right away." I spoke in a submissive voice, which I hated.

"I think that is most advisable," she answered. Her tone conveyed that she had tired of me and my problems. With that, I stood up and wiped the perspiration off my hands as I smoothed my skirt and quickly exited her domain.

I hurried back to my desk, walked past Evelle, and closed my office door with the intention of not leaving my office anytime soon. Before losing contact with the outside world, I conference-called my friends.

They all had quite a giggle when I told them varying versions of my first day back at work. "It was like walking through the halls of hell! Then, if that weren't bad enough, I was hauled before Satan. She was greedily rubbing her hands at the thought of all the new clients I could bring her… Lambs to the slaughter was more like it. Then I had to tell her about the restraining order." True friends that they were, each followed this recounting with soothing words for me and scathing critiques of my employer.

*    *    *

As promised, the development of a European branch of Faith Clarkson & Company was all-consuming. Those of us involved gave our lives to it. Some moments were exciting, but most days, I felt like Atlas holding up the sky on my shoulders. One wrong move and it all toppled into one horrific mess.

Using my credentials, a master's degree in law and finance, I spent copious hours scouring the U.K. to find a team who could meet the needs of Faith Clarkson & Company.

A month later, during one of the weekly meetings, Faith Clarkson declared that I would be joining the European office. No, "How would you like to?" or "Would you be interested in?" Just, "You're going." I couldn't tell if I was being banished, bullied, or praised.

Communication with the world outside of work had almost screeched to a halt, having become limited to cryptic emails. Well, except for my parents, for whom I was able to allocate five minutes, once a week. However, this news was too big to limit to email. So I calendared in time to make phone calls.

I started with Tiziana, and then, after talking with Marian and Kathleen, I put in a call to Hillary.

In any event, they were all happy to hear that I would be closer to them after the move to London. It was only Hillary who brought up the fact that I would be closer to Des.

"Well, what can I do? I either take this opportunity or I look for a new job. I'll just have to stay out of his way. I can't believe she actually expects me to go scouting for clients." I answered her concern with more confidence than I felt. If Faith Clarkson was true to her word, and she very well might be, I could find myself trying to land clients alongside the rest of the employees. Faith Clarkson had no concern for my problems.

"If you like, you can stay with me when you first get to London," she offered. "I have plenty of room, and it would be great fun to have someone around! I can help you find a place."

"That would be great, Hillary! I would love that."

When I mentioned Tiziana wanting all of us to gather more regularly, she said, "Well, with her record and yours, I'm sure we'll get into mischief whether we like it or not."

I suggested that we spend the holidays in London.

"That would be fabulous, since I'm not sure I've ever done that. We've always gone away. My mother finds it such a bother."

When we ended the call, for the first time in a very long time, some of the knots that riddled my muscles felt like they were working their way loose. While I would be closer to Des, it would be incredible to be closer to my friends. There was the added bonus that I wouldn't have to see Faith Clarkson on a regular basis.

# Chapter Five

**BETWEEN CARRYING ON** with my regular tasks at work and building the new team, I was swamped. I had been gone so much that my roommate Taylor had to come to my office just to see me.

Plunking down in my guest chair, a cloud of her favorite perfume settling around her, she said, "If I wasn't so envious of your moving to London, I'd almost care about the way the old battle-axe has been working you. Look at you! You're skin and bones, and not in the I-want-to-be-America's-Next-Top-Model-kind of way."

It was true: over the last three months, I had lost quite a bit of weight, and there were ginormous bags under my eyes. Normally I would have been excited about shedding a few pounds. These days, there was rarely time to sit down and eat. When I did, my stomach couldn't handle much.

In general, my grooming had hit an all-time low, a very noticeable and not good thing in New York City. I leaned back in my chair and used a couple of pencils to hold back the hair that kept falling into my eyes.

"Well, the good news is that I've saved all kinds of money and will be able to afford a fabulous wardrobe in England," I bragged gently. I knew that Taylor would love to be part of the team moving to London and the new subsidiary.

"What am I going to do without you?"

"Well, on the good news front, I won't really be moving out for a while, since your mother wants me in both places at the same time for the first few months. The bad news is that you'll just have to come visit me in London or finally marry Marcus." I picked up my cup of coffee and took a big gulp.

Sidestepping my last comment, she said, "Is that all you consume these days? You need a break and some decent food. I have a great idea! Easter is just around the corner, and my family is going to the Hamptons. Why don't you come along? It will be much more fun with you there. My parents are arriving late, leaving early, and the house is big enough you'll only have to see her at one or two meals." By the time she took a breath, the tone of her voice had gone from energetic to begging.

I felt deep creases in my forehead where my eyebrows squinched together. I had been to her family events before, and they were just a tad tense. The *only* silver lining, other than Taylor, was that her boyfriend Marcus would be there. He was hilarious, a fact that drove Faith Clarkson to madness. Okay, there was another silver lining.

"You know the only reason you want me to come is that your mother will give Marcus a break and send all her nasty glares my way. No, thanks. I would rather stay home and eat my chocolate bunny all by myself," I declined ungraciously.

Taylor laughed. "That's only partly true. However, and this is a great however, Marcus is bringing his friend Liam with him. He's drop-dead gorgeous and, with all the trauma of the last few months, I thought you might enjoy a harmless weekend of flirting."

Sitting up in my chair a little taller and pulling a pencil out of my hair, I said with enthusiasm, "Well, now you have my attention! Tell me all about this Liam."

In short, it turned out that Liam was from Ireland and worked as a graphic designer for some technology company in Dublin. Currently he was in New York on an extended business trip; something having to do with high-end Irish fashion designers in the U.S.

"Are you sure he isn't gay? He's good-looking, a graphic designer, and interested in fashion?" I asked, pointing out the salient facts.

"Of course he isn't gay! He's researching the stuff, not wearing it." She laughed. "Why would I fix you up with someone who's gay? It'd be a waste of both your time! Charlotte, he really is nice, and he would feel less like a third wheel if you came. We could go out on a double date this weekend, then you can decide for yourself if you think Liam's charms are enough to make you put up with my mother for a whole weekend."

"For real?" I contemplated the pros and cons for a few seconds. "Oh, all right! Set things up for Saturday, if you can. He'd better be as good-looking as you say he is! I don't really care if he's nice. I'm just looking for sex!" I waggled my eyebrows up and down, causing her to laugh.

Before we could continue, the phone rang. In the outer office, I heard Evelle answer in a quiet voice. My phone soon buzzed with the announcement that I had an overseas phone call.

Taylor jumped up from her chair. "You'd better get back to it. I'll let you know about Saturday." The door closed softly behind her.

I took a deep breath and picked up the phone. "Charlotte Young speaking," I said in my most professional voice.

"Darling, it's Tiziana! How are you? Tell me, do you know yet when you plan to arrive in London?"

I relaxed again into the cozy comfort of my chair and settled in for a long chat with her. "There's a high probability that I'll be in London sometime in early August. The planning is going surprisingly well. But since all I've done is work, it *should* be going well. With any luck, I'll tie up all my loose ends here by the holidays and then live there on a permanent basis."

She squealed as I filled her in, and we chatted excitedly about my new life. I asked her if she could make it to London for Christmas and New Year's, letting her know that Marian and Kathleen had tentatively agreed.

"Well, darling, that's one of the reasons I'm calling. I have some news!" she trilled dramatically.

"Don't tell me, you and Gianni are getting married at long last!" I guessed, my voice full of delight. I sat upright in my chair.

"I *am* getting married, but darling, not to Gianni! I've met a very delightful man who loves me very much. Gianni is wonderful, but when I met this other person, I just couldn't stop thinking of him. Once I realized how important he had become to me, I told Gianni. Gianni was disappointed, of course, but he'll be fine! He'll meet someone else soon," she managed to say all this in one long breath.

"What? Who? Tell me!" I sputtered, confused but delighted at the knowledge that my friend was truly happy. All I could hear was the lilting rapid fire of Italian in the background. Due to the time difference, it was the end of the workday in Italy. "Where are you calling me from?"

"I'm calling from the office. Everyone is saying 'ciao' before they leave. Charlotte, I know you're terribly busy at work. But we're hoping that all our friends can meet together in Saint-Tropez in August, the first week. The wedding itself will be in the afternoon on December 31. You know my mother, she would like it to be in the summer, but we don't want to wait until next year, and there's no way we can arrange a wedding in just a few months. Every church in Italy has been reserved for the last year. Besides, what a lovely way to start the New Year!" Tiziana paused only briefly to draw breath before going on to describe the details.

While listening to the preparations being made for the wedding, I flipped through my calendar. Depressed, I couldn't see how I could take a vacation in August, just four short months away.

I broke the news. "I can promise you that I'll be at the wedding, but I really can't imagine getting time to go to Saint-Tropez, especially at the beginning of August. The new offices in London are scheduled to be up and running by the end of September. Perhaps if things are going well, I could come to Italy for a few days at the end of August. I can't promise anything."

Obviously disappointed but understanding, she assured me, "Oh, bella! It won't be the same without you. But don't worry, darling! I know you'll do what you can."

It suddenly occurred to me. "Tiziana, have you told Hillary, Kathleen, and Marian? I've spoken to them recently, and I know that they were all planning on coming to London for the holidays."

A brief silence followed, and I could hear more Italian salutations in the background. "I spent the day calling them. They're all available to come to the wedding. If you are," she replied a bit hesitantly.

That sounded very odd to me, adding a new knot to the group already living in my stomach. "What does their attending have to do with me?" I asked suspiciously.

After a long pause and a deep sigh, she said, "Well, darling, you see, Des Bannerman will be at the wedding."

I sat in silence. Flabbergasted, I was trying to figure out how this could make sense. To what world had I been transported that not only had a celebrity filed a restraining order against me, but said celebrity was now attending the wedding of my closest friend? None of this was making sense.

"Tiziana, why would Des Bannerman be at your wedding?" I dreaded the answer, dreaded what this could bring into my life.

I heard the gnawing of her teeth on her fingernail. "Well, darling, the man who I'm marrying is Ted."

"Ted who?" burst out of me.

"Ted Blackwell, darling. Des's friend. The one we met in the casino in Chamonix."

"Oh! *That* Ted." I'd completely forgotten all about him. Clearly Tiziana hadn't!

Quickly rushing into a rehearsed monologue, she said, "Naturally, Ted will help sort all of this out. After how hurt and angry you were, Marian, Hillary, and Kathleen decided that they would spend the holidays with you if you didn't want to come to the wedding."

I sat stupefied. Sides were already being drawn!

I stayed calm, up to a point. "First, with regards to Mr. Bannerman, my hurt and anger aren't in the past tense! They're still very much a part of the here and now. After telling you how my life has been since I returned to work, how could you expect that all was forgotten?"

My anger rising, I continued, "I don't even know what I did, but, because of some delusional belief on his part that all women want to have sex with him, on top of everything else, now I can't attend your wedding! It isn't whether I want to or not. It's whether I *can* or not! God! His ego is unbelievable! He probably didn't spare a moment's thought considering how his ludicrous fantasies might affect anyone. I can't explain how embarrassing it has been to explain this to my family and friends. Every day I walk into this office and have to deal with someone looking at me funny! My boss is furious and making my life hell!" By then, my anger was at a fever pitch, and I found myself standing up, gripping the phone and shouting at Tiziana.

"*Shush, shush!* I'm so sorry, darling. I've put off this call as long as possible. I didn't want to be the one to cause you any more unhappiness," she said in a soothing voice, doing her best to comfort me. "Please! Ted will speak with him. I'm sure there was a misunderstanding, and as soon as he realizes that he made a terrible mistake, he'll be begging you for forgiveness."

"His ego is too large for him to contemplate that he's made a mistake. Ted will be wasting his time. Why hasn't he talked to him before now? Anyway, why does Des Bannerman have to be at the wedding?" I ranted in a very ugly tone.

After a lengthy pause, she cleared her throat and rushed into her explanation. "Well, you see, he'll be Ted's best man. They've been friends for years, and it's only natural that Ted would want Des at his wedding."

My mind reeled. I truly couldn't take this all in. How does one absorb the fact that one of the celebrity gods atop Mt. Famous has become a normal character in everyday conversation? How does someone like Des Bannerman become a part of the background of weddings, holidays, and vacations?

And then, *bam!* Right between the eyes, I realized it. "You've seen him, Des Bannerman, since we were in France, haven't you?"

It was now very quiet in Italy. "Yes," was the whispered reply.

\* \* \*

It was Saturday morning, and I'd been looking forward to my first day off in months. Sleep was all I'd wanted. Instead, the phone rang repeatedly.

It wasn't the first time I had heard all this, it was the third!

The general outline:

The phone rings.

The answering machine picks it up, and Taylor's happy voice inquires if the caller would like to leave a message.

An anxious voice asks for me.

I ignore the anxious voice.

The voice apologizes for not having told me that she knew about Tiziana and Ted (and, consequently, Des).

The voice assures me that Ted will sort things out with Des.

The caller asks me to call back.

I hadn't called any of them. In addition to the fact that Tiziana was marrying Des Bannerman's best friend, I'd absorbed the fact that Marian, Hillary, and Kathleen had all known that Tiziana was involved with Ted.

Taylor, hearing Kathleen leave her message, candidly suggested that I was behaving like a spoiled brat and ought to be happy for my friend. After a lengthy tirade from me about what it was like to have been used and abused by Des and the press and *then* left in the dark by my friends, she didn't approach the subject again. I spent the remainder of the morning lying listlessly on the sofa, huddled under an enormous pink fluffy blanket, my armor against the world.

At some point in the morning, Taylor reminded me of my date with Liam that evening. "I'm not going! I'm not in a flirty mood. My nasty mood would put a serious damper on the evening."

"Well, too bad for you. I've told him you'll be there, and I'm not about to tell him that you can't make it because you'd rather mope around like a three-year-old who lost her favorite toy." She grabbed my hand, trying to pull me off the sofa.

"Ouch! What are you doing?" I asked while trying to pry her talons from my flesh.

"You look like crap! Your roots need touching up, your eyebrows need a wax, your nails need a manicure, and who knows what state your legs are in! We're going out and making you look like a woman again!"

"Well, that was just rude!" I dragged myself in the direction of the bathroom.

One shower later, I pulled my coat on, knowing she was right, but I wasn't about to admit it to her. If I did that, she might ask me why I was behaving like a toddler, and I didn't want to talk about "it" anymore.

"You're lucky I didn't mention the state of your upper lip," she said with a smile when we reached the salon. I nudged her hard with my elbow and then submitted to the frivolous indulgence of body maintenance.

After spending an amazing amount of time and money on my appearance, I had to admit that the world seemed a better place, and I wouldn't mind a little light flirtation.

"Don't worry, once you lay your eyes on Liam, you'll be up for more than flirtation," she assured me.

"What makes you think he's going to be all that interested?"

"I told him that you were stunningly beautiful, but way too short to be a supermodel."

I gasped at her description of me. "He's going to be really disappointed! If he finishes his first drink and bolts out of the bar, it will be you who'll be paying the bill while I drown my sorrows in martinis." I laughed.

My height was always a part of every conversation whenever I met someone new. My lack of verticality used to really bother me, but now I see it as an excellent excuse to buy expensive, beautiful, high-heeled shoes. My collection was massive.

She gestured at me, pointing head to toe. "He's not going to be disappointed. You're beautiful! What's not to like? You're thin and curvy, which is totally unfair. You have curly hair, which looks gorgeous even when you don't shower for days! You have what I call elusive beauty; quirky exotic, low maintenance, great bones."

"You're great for my ego! Thanks! I appreciate all that you've done today. Sorry I've been such a cow!" I admitted.

Since we had an hour until the date would officially begin, she suggested we open a bottle of wine. She brought me a glass, which I held up to let the afternoon light filter through it. I had taken a few sips of the wine when my taste buds reminded me of the last time I'd had a glass of Beaujolais.

"The last time I had a glass of red wine was the night Tiziana cooked dinner in Chamonix. The paparazzi had just published the first set of pictures of me with Des Bannerman. Sorry, but my taste for it is gone." I took my glass to the kitchen and returned with another filled with Chardonnay.

We had never discussed the particulars of my encounters with Des. I'd been too angry when I first returned, and most of my friends learned that, if they wished to remain on speaking terms with me, we weren't discussing it.

Taylor commented, as she examined her manicure, "I'm not sure I picked the right color. I had my nails painted pink to compliment my dress, but the pink is too pink. What do you think?"

I shook my head to clear the images of Des as I looked at her. "Other than the fact that you sound like Dr. Seuss, you're being a very good friend by not asking about my fifteen minutes of fame. If you want, you can ask me questions."

"Really? You are finally ready to answer questions? A day of beauty and a date with Liam was all it took? If I'd known that, I would have dragged you to the salon months ago."

She drilled me thoroughly about my foray into stardom. We were laughing pretty hard about Des wearing tighty-whities when we realized we had just enough time to freshen our lipstick.

"Thanks, Taylor. It really helped a lot to talk about it. I'd actually forgotten that there were things that I liked about the bastard," I said as I walked to my bedroom. I leaned on the door after I pushed it shut and laughed to myself. There really had been several hilarious moments. For the first time in months, I was really relaxed, happy, and looking forward to meeting someone.

\* \* \*

"Wow! Did you see him? He's gorgeous!" I gushed at Taylor. Marcus and Liam were in the living room while Taylor and I got drinks for the four of us. "Do you think he likes me?"

"Charlotte's in love!" Taylor teased.

"No, but I could be!" I said as I headed out of the kitchen with a Jameson and ginger ale for him and some wine for me.

"Just don't overdo it and say or do something you'll regret," she warned me.

When we returned to the living room, Liam complimented us on our apartment. While it was a relatively small space, we'd worked hard to make it look elegant and homey at the same time.

"Thanks! We thought about hiring a decorator but decided, between the two of us, we had enough estrogen to pull it off," I joked.

Marcus decided to yank Taylor's chain a bit. "Well, what they *aren't* going to tell you is that they stole most of this stuff from Taylor's parents' houses. They had to! Otherwise they couldn't afford their shoes."

Taylor gave Marcus a look that would have made a lesser man run for the hills.

"We didn't steal! They were redecorating. We were recycling! Besides, they're free to have whatever they want back at any time!" She let herself be baited.

"Yes, but they've never been invited here, have they?" Marcus teased some more.

"No, but that isn't because of the furniture. I just don't think this space is big enough for my mother's ego," she responded.

After another round of drinks and our gabbing up a storm, we headed out to my favorite restaurant in the Meatpacking District, Restaurant Florent. It's a quirky little restaurant that serves French food. While the food is great, I really go for the ambiance.

Earlier, when Taylor and I were discussing where to go, I'd suggested it. "Isn't it a little 'not too much'?"

"Well, I like it, and if he wants to get to know me, he might as well find out what kind of places I like to go to. Since this is my blind date, I should get to decide. See, it doesn't really matter where you and Marcus want to go!" I got just lippy enough for her to realize I was messing with her.

Times like those I missed having Marian around. She would have entered the boxing ring with the enthusiasm of Mohammed Ali. We'd go a few rounds, swinging hard and taking head shots, but always in good fun. Not so with most people.

"Well then, Restaurant Florent it is," Taylor'd acquiesced, her tone full of quiet superiority.

No jab.

Upon arriving at our destination, Liam's reaction to the restaurant was perfect. "This is brilliant! I love it. Do you come here often? Is the food any good? Because, I'm ravenous."

"Well, I love it, and the food is excellent!" I rejoiced and glanced at Taylor to give her an "I told you so" smile.

While studying the menu, I found I'd lost my ability to read. That was a good sign. Generally it meant that I was attracted to my date and had other things on my mind. Fortunately, I'd eaten there enough that I could wing it.

Liam asked, "Do you recommend anything in particular?"

I leaned into him to look at the menu with him, but that proved too huge a distraction, so, in the end, I just made random suggestions. All I was aware of was the heat of his body and the delicious way he smelled. God, he was gorgeous. His wavy black hair just begged to be rumpled.

I tilted my head up to look at him, and he quickly moved back a bit, looking like he'd been caught with his hand in the cookie jar. "Your hair smells incredible."

If I were six inches taller, we'd have been nose to nose. Instead, we locked eyes, and my dark brown eyes were in complete contrast to his clear green peepers.

"You have the longest hair of anyone I've ever sat next to. I thought only mythical creatures could grow something so beautiful," he continued.

Feeling tongue-tied and giddy, I managed, "I love the lemon ginger shampoo from L'Occitane."

"I think I'll need to buy some," he said simply, but the glow in his eyes and gentle smile on his lips spoke volumes.

My brain went into overdrive, wondering what he meant by that. *Did he just like the shampoo? Was it an invitation to move in? Slow down!* I thought to myself.

Our quiet little tête-à-tête was broken by Marcus and Taylor. "Should we order a bottle of wine, or would you rather have a cocktail?"

Eventually we decided to order two different bottles of wine. My only request was that it wasn't Beaujolais, at which point Taylor gave me a little smile.

After agreeing to the blind date, I'd dashed off a quick email to Taylor asking that she and Marcus not bring up the whole debacle with Des Bannerman. There was a fair chance that Liam already knew, but if he didn't, I didn't want to spend the evening discussing it.

A bottle of Cabernet and another of Chardonnay were brought to the table, and, after all the song and dance was performed, we accepted them as our chosen two.

Liam was pouring wine into my glass when he said, "So, I have one little question to ask you." Between his physical appearance and gorgeous voice, he could have asked me to dance the Macarena on the table, and I would have been happy to comply.

"What's that?" I inquired and held my breath.

"Do you really 'recycle' furniture so that you can support your shoe habit?"

"Absolutely, and I'm not ashamed to say so!"

He laughed, then looked down at my feet under the table and softly added, "Sexy shoes." I blushed and had no idea what to say, so I picked up my wine glass and took a gulp. Knowing that he "liked" my shoes made me feel quite warm. I fanned myself with the wine list and giggled up at him.

We made it through dinner with much teasing and blushing. Marcus and Taylor let us have a few quiet moments, but, for the most part, we were a boisterous quartet enjoying the night.

"What should we do now?" Liam asked as we exited the restaurant.

"Well, do you feel like going to a club? Our *employer* is hosting a party for our latest and greatest client at the Bourgeois Pig in the East Village. We could mingle, drink, and see which celebrities Yvette has managed to entice to the party," Taylor offered as an option. It wasn't my first choice, but when Liam and Marcus seemed interested, I went along with the group.

The four of us piled into a cab and gave the driver the name of the club. We swerved, veered, careened, and eventually screeched to a stop near the club.

"Bloody hell! We're lucky to have made it alive," Liam exclaimed once he was on the pavement. The three of us laughed; we'd become immune to the terrors of riding in a Manhattan cab.

"I take it cab rides in Ireland are a lot more sedate than in New York City," I mused.

"Our cabbies tend to be a little less aggressive and a lot more entertaining," Liam replied, as he watched the cab zoom off with another fare.

"If you spend much time in the city, you'll get used to it."

"I'm not sure I want to," he said, a hint of lingering fear in his voice.

Taylor had made her way toward the entry, and, since it was already close to midnight, the line to get in was fairly long.

The young, beautiful, and well-dressed were lounging out front, trying to look bored rather than eager. Taylor was well known to the bouncer, since Faith Clarkson & Co. had used the Bourgeois Pig many times before. Vince, a handsome Italian-American with muscles to spare, let us past the velvet ropes. In we went.

The room was bustling with scantily-dressed women serving the cocktails for which the club was known, the Bordello Special and the Gogol Bordello. Seeing the fruity cocktails, Liam raised an eyebrow and inquired whether there were other, more manly beverages to be found.

"I'll take you to the bar," I offered, "and you can look at the menu. It's huge. I'm sure you'll find something you like."

"Well, that I've already done. I'd follow you anywhere, and, if it leads me to a lager, I'll be the happiest man on Earth," he said, taking my hand. Looking up and surveying the situation, he said, "Seeing as you're a wee bitty thing, I'd better go in front. You're too short for the barman to see." He smiled down at me, tightened his grip on my hand, and leaned down. "I'm very glad that it was me and not someone else who was sent here. I'd hate to think of you holding Edele's hand."

"Me, too," I replied with a laugh.

"Off to find nourishment," he declared, and so we went.

A few beers and much palavering later, I excused myself from Liam's well-maintained side and made my way to the ladies' room. I was finishing up in the stall when the outer door opened.

"Did you see him? I swear that has to be Des Bannerman. Who else could it be?" asked the unknown voice.

Instantly, my hands started to shake so badly I could barely organize my clothes.

The two women continued to chat about Des as they fixed their makeup. "He really is gorgeous. Did you get close enough to see those blue eyes? You know that movie he was in a few years ago, *Deadly Blue?* Do you think it was because of his eyes? I wonder if he's alone."

"Mental giants!" I muttered to myself. At the time of that film, I had loved Des Bannerman. While he was doing the promos for *Deadly Blue,* every TV talk show host had asked him that question. I thought about his interview with Dallin Jones, on *The Late Show.* Obviously tired of the question, he had appeared on *The Late Show* wearing brown contacts. David made a great show of using his pen to strike a question off the list. "Guess I won't be asking that," he'd quipped. Des's broad grin had filled the camera when it zoomed in on him.

Shaking off the past, I finally gathered enough courage to exit the stall and approach the sink. Looking at myself in the mirror, I saw what I feared. Instead of the happy, relaxed, and flirty person who had entered, I saw a scared, pale, fragile-looking creature staring back at me.

I pulled my cell from my purse and dialed Taylor's number. "Hello?" came her voice above all the background noise from the club.

"Come to the restroom, NOW!" My two companions were clearly used to odd things, because they didn't stop applying their lip gloss when I shouted into the phone.

Moments later, Taylor appeared, and the two women exited. Perhaps they were afraid, after all. "Listen, those two women who just left said that Des Bannerman is here. What am I going to do?" I asked frantically. "I can't be here if he is!" And I don't want Liam to see me get arrested. If he finds out, he's going to think that I'm some kind of freakazoid stalker."

Taylor wet down paper towels with cold water, passed them to me, and ordered I put them on my cheeks. "First of all, relax! I'll scout around, find Yvette, and ask if he's here. If he is, we'll just leave. I'll think of some excuse." She squeezed my hands and tried to convey that all would be right in the world. "Just calm down. I'll be right back, and then we'll know what to do."

She finally returned with a big, fake smile on her face. "Okay, he is in fact here. He's across the room from Marcus and Liam. Fortunately, it's pretty dark out there. So, why don't we discreetly leave?"

I nodded, because I was too nervous to speak. I took one more look in the mirror. I'd used the time Taylor was doing reconnaissance to powder my nose and fix my lipstick. I nodded again, giving the go-ahead.

As we opened the door, Liam was standing just outside. "Is everything okay? You've been gone quite a while. I thought perhaps you were trying to run out on me by shimmying away through the kitchen," he said with a smile.

Shocked to see him, and added to the current circumstances, my brain fritzed. Thankfully, Taylor took over. "No, of course not! There's always a line. How about we go get Marcus and head back to our place for coffee?"

Liam looked back and forth between Taylor and me. I could tell he sensed that something had happened. "Why don't you wait for us out front, and I'll go get Marcus?" he offered, giving my hand a squeeze. I'd never felt so much relief and returned the gesture to convey my gratitude. He gave me another reassuring look before leaning down and planting a kiss on my cheek.

"Right then, we'll meet you out front," he said softly, and off he went.

"Get me the hell out of here!" I hissed to Taylor. We walked as far away from where Des had last been sighted as possible. I kept my head down. It was one of the few times in my life I'd actually been grateful for being the height of an Oompa Loompa.

"We're almost there," Taylor reported. I fixed my eyes on the back of her heels and kept walking.

Suddenly, there was a lot of jostling beside me, and, out of reflex, I glanced up to see what was happening. There, among the multitudes of female party-goers was *Deadly Blue* himself. I saw a flicker of recognition.

"Crap! Move!" I ordered, and Taylor picked up the pace. She had to, since I was shoving her from behind. We rushed to the entrance, much like rats scurrying through a maze. I registered commotion behind me.

"Charlotte! Stop!" called a familiar British voice. Not anxious to find out what he wanted, I kept scurrying. Suddenly, we burst out onto the sidewalk. I had the sensation similar to when you burst through the surface of water. Cool, fresh, reviving air. We'd made it through the maze but, instead of cheese at the end, we had our freedom.

Or so I thought. Until I heard, "Charlotte, please stop."

Taylor took the matter in hand. "Charlotte, just keep walking. If anything comes of this, I'll testify that you did your best to avoid him and that he approached you repeatedly." I trotted away on my stilettos.

A hand caught my shoulder. "Bloody hell, Charlotte! Stop!"

The same hand swung me around. It all happened so fast. One minute I was in escape mode, and the next I was spinning on dangerously high heels, and then I was grabbing for anything to stop me from falling. I reached out a hand to the nearest thing, which turned out to be Des Bannerman and, more specifically, Des Bannerman's cheek. I looked up and attempted to register several bewildering sights.

First, I was face to face with Des. His hair was styled very much as it had been in *Last Saturday*: spiky, topsy-turvy, disheveled. His eyes were beseeching, expressing pain. Second, I realized he had let go of me and was holding a hand to his face, which was smudged with blood. The red contrasted to his tailored black shirt. I guessed that explained the pained look. Third, he was speaking, and my brain worked hard to sort out the words. "Clearly, I was wrong," he said.

Then, he turned his back to me and walked away. Having found a handkerchief in his back pocket, he unfolded it and pressed it to his cheek. He returned to the group waiting out front of the Bourgeois Pig.

My brain processed his words. "Clearly, I was wrong." Had Ted managed to talk to him at long last? Had he been willing to hear me out? As I mulled this over, Taylor grabbed my hand and led me down the sidewalk.

"Was that Des Bannerman?" Liam asked when we approached him and Marcus, whom I'd forgotten all about.

"No, no it wasn't. Just an old friend saying hello," Taylor improvised.

"Amazing! They look quite alike. I heard he was in town. It would be fascinating to see them side by side," Liam continued.

Still freaking out, I heard myself say, "No, just an old friend named Will. From college. Let's go get that coffee!"

Taylor persuaded Liam to let her teach him how to hail a cab. He indignantly defended his abilities but followed her anyway. While they were waving and whistling, now halfway in the street, Marcus asked, "What happened?"

"I'll explain later." I wondered when I would be able to call Tiziana and see what she knew.

Liam, having no luck with hailing a cab, left it to Taylor. Returning to us, he said, "She's right! I don't know how. I'm willing to learn tomorrow. Go help your girl, mate!"

Marcus went to help Taylor, giving Liam a chance to ask again, "Are you sure you're all right? You're as white as a Scotsman in winter!"

"I'm fine. I just got a bit overheated. The fresh air feels good." I hoped I sounded convincing. I regretted the lie immediately.

Liam looked down at my shoes and asked, "Can you actually walk in those things?" When I assured him I was quite adept, he invited me to stroll a few blocks.

"We're going to walk a few blocks. We'll meet you back at the flat," Liam called to Taylor and Marcus. Taylor, who had been huddled up against Marcus, whispering in his ear, waved and promised to see us there.

Liam stuck his hands in his coat pockets, seemingly content to wander quietly. We occasionally stopped to look in a window or watch a street performer. I could feel my shoulders relax and my stomach quit churning. Liam also seemed to sense me returning to my former self and asked, "Would it be all right if I were to hold your hand?"

I smiled up at him. "With pleasure." I said, offering my hand to him.

There was no point in ruining the rest of the evening by worrying about Des. I figured that, if he was going to call the police, they'd be at the apartment when we arrived. If not that night, I hoped they wouldn't show up at work; Faith Clarkson would fire me for sure.

Eventually we sought the comfort of a cab and headed back to my apartment. I was relieved to find only Marcus and Taylor cuddled up on the sofa when we returned.

"There's some coffee for you! You'll find the whiskey next to the mugs if you'd like a little drop," Taylor called out as we headed straight into the kitchen. Despite having calmed down quite a bit, I poured two cups of coffee and added a large slug of whiskey to my cup, hoping it would help settle my nerves.

"There's almost as much whiskey in there as an Irish pub. Want to switch?" Liam proffered his more lightly doctored cup.

"No, it's fine! Really? Can you put too much whiskey in?"

"Then you won't think terrible things about me if I add just a drop more?" Liam asked, a grin on his face.

"Pour away!"

We spent an hour sipping coffee and chatting, while, in the deep recesses of my brain, I couldn't help but wonder what was going to come from having scratched one of the most famous cheeks in the world. When Liam announced he ought to go, Marcus offered to share a cab with him.

While Marcus and Taylor said their goodbyes in the kitchen, we stood quietly talking at the door. Liam leaned down and said, "This evening was a very pleasant surprise! It was a lovely to meet you, Charlotte."

"Likewise," I whispered. Between the hefty drop of whiskey and the sensation of his thumb strumming my cheek, I was all giggly and goofy again.

"I have a solid week ahead of me, but I'd like to give you a call," he said, his eyes questioning. I gave a happy nod. He kissed my cheek, then buried his face in my hair and took a deep breath. "You're glorious!"

Marcus and Taylor appeared, leaving us to say our final goodbye. Once they were gone, we reconvened to the living room. Unfortunately, it wasn't so that we could replay the state of my love life.

Sitting on the sofa with my head in my hands, I moaned.

"What exactly happened?" Taylor asked.

I told her about Des having grabbed my shoulder and throwing me off balance. "I swear to all that is holy, I didn't mean to hurt him. I just reached out to stop myself from falling and managed to collide with his face. Then, of all things, he said, 'Clearly, I was wrong.' What does *that* mean? Oh god, what's going to happen now? I'm going to be hauled before the courts for violating the restraining order and get charged with assault! Des's never going to let me go to Tiziana's wedding. Let's not forget that Liam will find out about my supposed affair with Des and all the lies I told him tonight!"

"I don't know, sweetie. What time is it in Italy?"

Looking at the clock I said, "9 a.m. I can't call her. It's Sunday morning."

"Well, then, go to bed while the whiskey's still in your system. It'll help you fall asleep. Call her when you wake up. She might know more by then anyway."

We stumbled to our respective bedrooms, Taylor continuing to comfort me. "We'll worry about this when we have to. Remember, you have me as a witness, and I know that you were trying to get out of there. I'll also testify that he grabbed you, not the other way around."

While drifting off to sleep, several thoughts went through my mind. Des Bannerman was unbelievably arrogant, and there would be some form of backlash, of that I was certain. I couldn't handle whiskey (my head was already pounding). And maybe I'd met a wonderful candidate for Prince Charming. Eventually, I fell asleep with the vision of Liam in my head and Taylor's reassuring words ringing in my ears.

* * *

Come Monday morning, I stared moodily at the computer screen, reading *Page Six*, looking for anything regarding Des Bannerman. Fortunately, nothing was to be found.

The phone in the outer office rang, and soon Evelle passed the call through. "Charlotte Young speaking." Liam's very sexy voice wished me good morning. The day took a serious turn for the better.

"How did you get my number?" I felt shocked but, more importantly, flattered.

Chuckling, he said, "While you're a mysterious woman, I didn't consume so much alcohol that I forgot where you worked or what your name was. It was fairly simple."

"Oh." I was sure I sounded quite intelligent.

Still laughing, Liam continued, "I wish I could have dazzled you with my James Bond secret agent skills, but they weren't needed."

His banter soon had me relaxed, and we talked about life and the universe for a little while; nothing serious or provoking, just light-hearted conversation, which I desperately needed.

"I have meetings lined up day and night for the next few days. May I call again, since I can't take you out on the town?" he asked as we were saying our goodbyes.

Smiling into the phone, I said yes and told him I was looking forward to it.

For the next three days, we developed a pattern of his calling at 9 a.m. and then again around 4:30 p.m. I found the phone to be a pleasant way to get to know someone. Liam proved to be a very easy person to talk to. Within just a few days, I felt that we knew each other's life histories reasonably well—a remarkable difference from all the men I'd met since moving to New York, most of whom were interested in having one-sided conversations that only involved, "I like this, I do that, I went there, and I know them."

The wonder of new romance was a bit tainted, however, with the ever-present fear of a telephone call from Mead, Jameson, and Kelly.

A few nights later, I was ensconced on the sofa eating Kung Pao chicken straight out of the take-out carton, watching TV, when a promo for *The Tonight Show* flashed on the screen. My brain went numb as a disembodied voice announced the night's guests. One was a girl with big, blonde hair and the other, Des Bannerman.

My fear factor amplified. "Taylor," I shouted several times as I sat frozen in place.

She finally darted out of the bathroom with a towel clasped to the front of her dripping body, a razor in the other hand. "What? What's wrong? Are you all right?" She searched the vicinity for signs of danger.

I pointed mindlessly to the screen, which was showing a commercial for Viagra. "Des Bannerman is going to be on *The Tonight Show*. He's going to have a big scratch on his face. He's going to tell everyone that the psychotic woman whom he has a restraining order against scratched his face outside a bar! What if he says my name?" I tugged a blanket over my head, wailing like a banshee, trying to protect myself from whatever torture Des Bannerman chose to inflict.

"Don't worry. He won't mention your name. Hang on, I'll be right back." With enormous patience, she dripped her way back to the bathroom.

A minute later, she returned, wrapped in a fluffy bathrobe, her hair swept up in a towel. She pressed my fingers around a glass of whiskey and helped me get prepared. "Have a sip! No, take a bigger one," she demanded when I returned the glass no sooner than I'd taken it. I noted she was having a glass as well. She saw me looking at her glass. "You nearly killed me. When I heard you screaming while I was in the shower, I didn't know if we were both about to be raped or you were bleeding to death. My god! I've never been so scared in my life."

"Sorry!" I choked. I'd taken a huge gulp of whiskey, which left me breathless after it hit the back of my throat.

We watched the host's opening monologue in complete silence. It might have been funny, but I just couldn't hear a word he said over the pounding of my heart. I barely registered the audience laughing. After interviewing a breathless Heidi Montag, the host, Jimmy Fallon, announced his next guest. "As you all know, our next guest is one of my favorites. A man whose honesty and integrity can't be doubted by anyone who reads the tabloids. Ladies and gentlemen, the divine Des Bannerman." The applause was deafening.

Out he walked. It was worse than I feared. From just below his left eye to his jaw line, there were three noticeable stripes. There was a definite pause in the applause as the audience registered the scratches. Jimmy walked over and pretended to box with Des, who faked a blow to the chin. The audience continued clapping.

"For the love of God and all that is holy, could they just get on with the interview?" I asked Taylor, anxious for the besmirching of my character to be over.

Jimmy escorted Des to the chair next to his desk. The two men chatted and laughed as they walked the fifteen or so feet from the flapping curtain to the guest chair. After the audience settled down, the question finally came. "So, what happened? Did Colin Farrell pick another fight with you?"

Des chuckled and then winced, gently touching the left side of his face. "No, no, worse than that, I'm afraid. I was in New York City over the weekend, attending a rather posh event. I'm dead honest when I tell you that one of the guests had a leopard draped around her shoulders. I know you all know to whom I refer, so please don't ask me to name names. So, to continue, there I am, innocently attempting a new dance move, when this maniacal leopard sprang off her shoulders and viciously attacked me. Needless to say, I wrestled the ferocious beast to the floor. Only after which a rather muscle-ridden bouncer managed to locate a tranquilizer gun and subdue the animal." Des then reached over and took a sip from a cup. After putting it back down, he looked Heidi Montag squarely in the eye and said, "I just want you to know that while I bear no hard feelings, your people will be receiving a letter from my lawyers regarding the doctor's fees and the expenses for plastic surgery!" Jimmy was really laughing hard while Heidi looked stunned, and the audience applauded wildly.

"By the way," Des said, continuing his conversation with Heidi in a conspiratorial tone, "do you recommend your plastic surgeon? The work he's performed on you is barely detectable!" By now, Des had moved in close enough to scrutinize her for surgical scars. Much more laughing ensued on Jimmy's part, especially when Heidi turned crimson.

Des waited for a dip in the laughter and then turned his attention to Jimmy. "I'd stay out of her dressing room, if I were you, mate!" Des suggested, while rubbing his forefinger against his nose. Jimmy was now in hysterics, and even Heidi was laughing. The audience applauded, appreciating Des's humor. To be fair, he was in rare form.

"We'll be right back," Jimmy announced through gasps of air, and a commercial for Des Bannerman's new movie flashed onto the screen.

"What does that mean?" I said out loud. My head filled with visions of lawyers and police officers appearing at my door, and me in hysterics. By now the heels of my hands were pressed into my eye sockets and I was emitting a bit of a wail.

"Well, to be honest, it went better than I thought it would. He didn't mention any of the details. In fact, he seemed to be in a fairly good mood about it. Listen, Charlotte, he must understand that it was an accident. Don't worry about it. I bet Tiziana will be calling you soon and it will be okay."

I was still sitting with my head in my hands, praying to evaporate.

"Go to bed and get some rest. You'll feel better in the morning, I promise!" Taylor attempted to reassure me yet again. I felt her hand pat me on the head and then, a few seconds later, her bedroom door closed.

After sitting on the sofa for another few minutes, I realized I was sleepy, probably from the whiskey and emotional strain. Giving up on making any sense of it all, I stumbled to my bed and hoped Taylor was right. About everything.

\* \* \*

When the alarm rang the next morning, my first realization was that my mouth was dry and my tongue was stuck to the roof of my mouth. The second realization was that I had a pounding headache. It wasn't the whiskey, I decided; it was from the restless dreams I'd had all night.

Most of them had something to do with being chased by leopards and Des Bannerman's laughter.

I stumbled to the kitchen for a glass of water. "How are you doing?" Taylor asked. She was sitting at the table drinking juice and reading the paper.

"Fine, I'm fine. It will all be fine." I stumbled out of the kitchen, heading toward the bathroom. "At least work will keep me busy until the police arrive," I added.

*   *   *

Finally Friday arrived, and with it no signs of the police. Sitting at my desk, I sorted through piles of papers, email, and phone messages. Still nothing from Tiziana. I contemplated calling her, but the rational part of me had long since decided that she was busy with work and wedding planning. No doubt she would call when she could. The less rational side of me wondered if she wasn't calling because she didn't want to be the bearer of bad news. In the end, I decided to get on with the mountain of work I had to accomplish before I could leave for the weekend.

After we'd talked on the phone all week, this was the night I was finally going to see Liam. Our first solo date. We were supposed to drive with Taylor and Marcus to the Clarkson Estate Saturday morning.

While chatting on the phone yesterday, I had mentioned that I was glad that Easter weekend had arrived.

"Me, too! I just love decorating Easter baskets, egg hunts, and buying a new bonnet!" Liam had teased.

"Great! Perhaps we could go shopping for bonnets after work! We could meet in the accessories department at Bloomingdales around 7:30?" I'd suggested.

"Let me look at my schedule. *Hmm*, I have a manicure at 11:00, a fashion shoot at 1:30, and drinks with a columnist from *Cosmo* at 6:00. I think I can make it to Bloomingdales by 8:00. Would that be too late? Or will all the good chapeaux be gone?"

I laughed at the thought of him in a bonnet. "I'm sure only the best ones will be left! 8:00 it is. You'd better get going or you'll miss your manicure!" I'd said once I'd realized the time.

PROSECCO & PAPARAZZI 9 1

"Don't be ridiculous. I'm not having a manicure. I'll leave that to the fairer sex. I'm meeting with a fashion editor from *Vogue* while she has her nails done. It was the only time she could squeeze me in. I think she was a bit surprised when I said I'd join her there."

Impressed with his commitment to his job, I'd said, "Good luck! I'll see you at 8:00."

After wishing me a great day, he'd hung up.

Staring out my office window, I realized that in most respects, it had been a fabulous spring. I prayed that that was an indicator of things to come. For months I had been on edge, and the winter gloom hadn't helped. However, the snow had melted, the faint hint of green could be seen on trees, and the air was fresh. Gloom was behind us, and before me was a weekend at the Clarkson Estate in the Hamptons with a gorgeous Irishman. It was just what I needed.

I cheerfully spent the remainder of the day in meetings. Several of our staff members were seeking positions at the new office. The time had come to approach Faith Clarkson about transferring employees from New York to London. All the divisions were sending representatives to London to interview candidates in June. Now that I had met Liam, I was happy that a power-hungry member of my group was interviewing the candidates I'd chosen.

By the end of the day, I was feeling good about our progress and called down to Faith Clarkson's administrative assistant's desk. "Ms. Clarkson's office. This is Jill Grey speaking." She had the same frosty attitude as our leader. To be fair, she was almost as capable as Faith Clarkson at running the company.

"This is Charlotte Young. I need to make an appointment with Ms. Clarkson for next week," I said with all the authority I could muster. After looking at both calendars, we agreed on an early morning meeting on Wednesday.

# Chapter Six

**WITH THAT LAST BIT** of work complete, I dashed home to put on a very girly dress designed by Bethany Halvorsen. Bethany was an old friend who had moved to New York with the hope of becoming a model. While she was absolutely beautiful, she had been only moderately successful. Fortunately, she had a natural flair for designing clothes. She would chop and sew her own designs when she couldn't afford to buy anything in boutiques. Using the connections she made while modeling, she found financial backers. Now, years later, she was able to hold her head high in the fashion world, and I benefited by having a few originals sewn for me every year.

I was finishing up my makeup in front of the bathroom mirror and deciding what to do with my hair when Taylor walked through the front door.

"How are you?" I called out.

"Fine and dandy! Marcus and I are ordering food. Do you want some?" I came out of the bathroom with my hair loose and slipped into my Kate Spade shoes.

"Where are you going?" she inquired with a big smile.

"No more third wheel for me. I have a hot date with an Irishman to buy Easter bonnets!" I grinned back at her.

"Well, stay away from the ones in Chinatown. You might end up with a live animal on it!" She disappeared into the kitchen.

I went back to the bathroom to figure out what to do with my hair. I was twiddling it when Taylor came to chat with me, bringing two glasses of wine.

Sipping from her glass and leaning against the doorframe, she asked, "Have you talked with Liam about Des yet?" All week she had been encouraging me to come clean. She thought it would make me feel better. I knew it wouldn't.

"I hate my hair. There's too much of it." I grimaced at the tangled mess.

"Cut it off! Quit changing the subject," she replied brusquely while I tugged a comb through it.

"I should! But then I'd have a puffball on top of my head. I'm not changing the subject, I'm ignoring it." I put down the straightening iron I used to smooth out the curly mess and took a sip of wine. "It's way too early in the relationship to bring up personal problems and drama. I really like Liam, and I don't want to scare him off."

"Well, what if he's figured out it was you in all those tabloid photos and that Des is your friend 'Will'? Don't you think he's going to think you have more to hide by not telling him?"

I pondered her comments while taking another sip from my glass. Then I offered the best explanation I could. "You have a great point, actually. I'm still trying to figure out exactly why it bugs me so much. I'm sure this doesn't apply to you, but, in high school I wasn't Miss Popularity. In fact, quite the opposite. I have the same feeling. It's like being in high school and the really hot guy randomly starts talking to you. It feels suspicious and wonderful at the same time. Suddenly you're cool, people invite you to their parties, and you're swamped with popularity. Then, the really hot guy abandons you for someone else, and you're back to being a dork. I don't care about the fame. I just don't like being dismissed without knowing why. There's just this lingering shock… I thought I was past all this stuff, but really, it's just made me question my ability to judge people and situations."

In a rare display of affection, Taylor gave me a hug and said, "I'm sorry. I know you're hurt. I'm sorry you were a dork! I won't say another word on the subject." A huge promise, coming from one of the most opinionated people I know. And I appreciated her effort in trying to understand my feelings. Especially when I couldn't understand them myself.

"You'd better get going!" Taylor prompted me.

Jolted out of my thoughts, I grabbed my bag and said, "Don't wait up!" with a lustful grin on my face.

"Tell me all about it tomorrow," she said as I closed the door.

I flagged down a cab and made it to Bloomingdales with two minutes to spare. I was casually wandering through the hat department when a sexy voice said near my ear, "Would you care to try this bonnet?" Before I could turn around, a hat made from an Easter basket bedecked with ribbon, flowers, bunnies, and ducks was offered over my shoulder.

"Where did you find this?" I asked Liam as I turned around.

When I plopped the hat on my head, he laughed out loud. I found a mirror on one of the counters and arranged the ribbons to add to the flair. While I was fiddling, he offered to put the hat back in the bag he was holding in his hand.

"You're not really going to wear that, are you?" he asked dubiously.

"Of course I am, and thank you for such a lovely hat," I replied in mock sincerity.

"Well, I'm not sure lovely applies, but if you're determined to wear it, I'll happily defend your honor!"

He took my hand, and we wandered through the hat department for a few minutes. The looks I received from customers and employees were a mixture of shock and horror. We laughed so hard, it was starting to be painful.

"Take it off! I can't take it any longer!" he begged.

Regretfully, I gave in, and he restored my bonnet to its bag. Then, with determination, he started to walk toward the store entrance, pulling me by the hand.

"We haven't found your hat yet," I reminded him. "We can't leave."

"Not to worry. No one will notice me anyway, once you put yours on. Let's go find food and drink. I'm famished." He continued to pull me through the door.

We wandered around and soon settled on a bar for an evening of wine, food, and song. I'd never been before, so I took in the atmosphere, which was quite busy and noisy, and hoped the food was as good as the atmosphere.

"How did your day go? Let me have a look at your nails," I said, grabbing his hand.

"I had a pedicure instead. Would you care to see my toes?" He reached down to untie his shoe.

"Thanks, but I'll take you up on your offer later. I'm pretty sure you have to have shoes on to get service here."

"Later it is!" he said, and gave me a very sexy smile.

The rest of the evening was spent in easy, happy banter. I flirted outrageously and was rewarded with his undivided attention. Somehow food and drinks arrived and disappeared, people came and went, and eventually the once noisy and chaotic club turned into a deserted room.

"We'd better get you home so you can pack!" he announced.

"I'd rather not go. Wouldn't you rather just make up an excuse and spend the weekend here?"

"The obvious answer is yes. But then, you wouldn't have a fancy Easter dinner to wear your new bonnet to. Not to mention, Taylor and Marcus would never speak to either of us again."

"Fine," I whined. "If I have to!"

We took a cab back to my apartment. He walked me to the door and, with my heart racing, gave me the single most seductive, delicious, "you are mine" kiss that I'd ever received.

"Would you like to come in?" I asked a bit breathlessly.

"You just want to have a peek at my toes!" he teased.

"You've caught me!" In fact, he had.

\* \* \*

I woke up with the most incredible sense of well-being, delighted in the feel of every hair, bone, and muscle of Liam as they pressed up against me. Lying still, I watched the dusky purple shadows on the bedroom wall fade with the rising sun.

Liam began to stir in his sleep. His body stretched long, while his hands ran over me. Then he pulled me tightly to him while I turned gelatinous, trying to meld into him. "That was the best sleep I've had in years," he murmured into my hair as his hands trailed down my back. Looking up at him, I saw warmth and tenderness in his eyes. I reached my lips up to his, wanting to convey my desire for him.

The sun had glided higher into the morning sky by the time we presented ourselves to Taylor. She was sitting in the living room, cradling a cup of coffee in her hands, staring out the window at the city. "Morning," she greeted us. *Bless her!* She didn't give us funny looks, make any comments, or ask any questions.

"Morning to you," Liam responded first, a grin on his face. "Out with it! I know you're dying to say something, so, just get it over with!" Getting up, Taylor walked to the kitchen to refill her coffee cup. "What are you talking about? If I were to comment every time Charlotte had a man spend the night, every morning would be awkward." Walking toward the bathroom, she continued, "It's my job to make sure that nothing gets stolen during the night!" she added as she shut the door.

Liam wrapped me in his arms, looked me straight in the eyes, and very seriously asked, "Who were you planning on having over tonight? It's going to be awfully crowded in your bed."

"Well, my options are you, Marcus, and Mr. Clarkson. Taylor would kill me, and Ms. Clarkson would fire me. So, I guess, for tonight, it'll be just you." I sighed in disappointment.

Laughing, Liam planted his lips against mine. "I like it. You do cruel well."

"Thanks, I think." I was breathless from a mouth-devouring kiss.

"No! Thank *you* for an extraordinary evening… and morning. Much as I hate to say it, I'd better be going."

After a few lingering kisses at the door, he left to pack his weekend bag. I stared in my closet, trying to figure out what could be sexy, casual, and professional. Mixing a weekend with Liam and Faith Clarkson could prove trying on many levels. I decided to leave the sexy end of things to my lingerie drawer. When I'd packed my overnight bag, I sat on the oversized chair in my room, chewing on my finger and thinking about Liam.

"Come out of there," Taylor called after knocking on the door.

*Time to face the music,* I thought to myself.

She had set her weekend bag near the front door when I entered the room. "I know what you were doing in there!"

Getting myself a cup of coffee first, I walked back to her. "What?"

"You were sitting in there over-analyzing everything! I have just one question."

"Just one?" I asked, surprised. I set about eating part of an apple.

"He's unbelievable. He does this thing where he holds your hands behind your back to keep balance while you're…"

Putting her hand up and looking at me with a very stern face, Taylor interrupted me mid-sentence. "Stop! I don't want to know the details.

Besides, Marcus knows that trick, everyone does. No, what I want to know is did you tell him about Des?"

"Oh! The answer is no, I didn't. But not for the reasons you think. We just had a great night. We chatted about all kinds of wonderful things, drank wine, and ate great food. It was perfect, and the whole Des Bannerman thing just slipped my mind." Picking at some apple stuck between my front teeth, I said, "If you must know, I was thinking about Liam and whether it was truly possible to fall for someone after just a few dates."

"Really? Wow, things are moving along. That's wonderful. About the Des thing, I wouldn't keep putting it off," she said sagely. "The longer you do, the harder it will be."

I nodded at her then went to my room to get my bag and placed it next to hers. She had gone into the bathroom to check her makeup one last time. I joined her to brush my teeth, primp my hair, and apply lipstick. Looking at her in the mirror, I added, "He really is spectacular, you know!"

Her reflection smiled at me. "He really is."

The drive to the Hamptons was great fun. The combination of completely inappropriate jokes about Americans and Irish, Liam's hand resting on my thigh, and the springtime scenery caused the time to fly by.

"Charlotte, do you think Faith Clarkson is going to allow us to share a room?" Liam asked quietly in my ear.

A pleasant tingling surged through my body and a flush rose to my cheeks when Taylor answered, "She's rather straight-laced, but, if you were to explain to her that you're a horny bastard who has finally found someone who'll have sex with you, I'm sure she'll understand!"

Liam flushed just a bit. "Well, I may be a horny bastard, but, from what Marcus tells me, he has to put something in your mouth to drown out the screaming!"

Things went downhill from there.

As we approached East Hampton, Liam asked if anyone minded hitting the shops on Main Street for a bit. Taylor turned around and looked at him. "Are you sure you aren't gay?"

Before Liam could respond, I looked Taylor in the eye. "I can assure you, he isn't." Looking at him, I said, "She does have a point, though.

Since when does a manly Irishman want to hit the shops of East Hampton?"

While stroking my knee with his thumb, he explained, "I did a little research knowing we were coming here, and I want to drop in on a few shops. Not shopping, business. Sorry to mix work with pleasure! I can probably do everything I need in an hour."

"Take all the time you need. I've never wandered through the shops out here and would love to. Do you two mind?"

"Not me. Marcus?" Taylor asked.

"I'm sure I can find something to do while you three go on your shopping spree," Marcus relented, infamous for his lack of fondness for shopping.

"Maybe you can find something to stifle Taylor's screams!" I offered.

"Well, now, that could be fun. Do they have sex shops in the Hamptons?" Marcus asked. Impersonating a wealthy, matronly woman entering a sex shop, Marcus kept us in stitches the rest of the ride.

We managed to find a parking spot near a lovely looking restaurant named Matto. The inside was beautiful, a romantic beach scene. My stomach started to growl like a wild beast at the sight of it.

"I need to feed her!" Liam announced to the hostess at the front door. "She needs to keep her energy up for tonight!" Her dark brown, perfectly groomed eyebrows shot up, and she said in a very monotone voice, "Follow me, please." While she walked ahead of us, I followed, burning with embarrassment.

Once we were comfortably seated and the menus had been dispersed, Liam quietly said to me, "You Americans are certainly a puritanical lot. You turned bright red, and that woman never looked at us again. You could just as easily be performing ballet this evening as giving a blow job." I was no longer bright red, I was now crimson. Liam sniggered and leaned over to give me a kiss on my forehead. "Don't worry, no one heard that."

Lunch proceeded in a respectful and dignified manner. Somewhere along the way, I became preoccupied with my thoughts. *What did Liam think? Were we just having sex? Had this just been some entertainment for the few months he was in New York? Did he have any of the feelings I did? Was it ridiculous to let myself get involved with him? Should I keep a tighter rein on my emotions? How do you ask these questions after two dates? (Granted, one ended with us having sex.)*

Two weeks before, I hadn't known this man, and now I was talking fellatio with him in public. Without realizing it, I finished my pasta and merlot, and the mood had changed from flirtatious and light to something more serious.

"Well, I say we get this shopping expedition underway!" Taylor announced after we had turned down the offer of dessert. "Where do you want to go, Charlotte?" Her tone seemed to evoke the earlier mood of the day.

"I don't really know. I just thought I'd wander and have a look. I'd like to get a bottle of wine or two for dinner this evening. I think we drove past a wine shop," I answered, hoping my lighthearted tone didn't seem forced.

"I saw a bookstore that I think I'll go hang out in until you're ready," Marcus remarked.

"Oh, so is bookstore the code word for sex shop in the Hamptons?" I asked Marcus.

"I don't know. You could ask Martha Stewart when you run into her at the wine store." He seemed relaxed enough.

"How much time do you want, Liam?" I asked without looking him in the eyes.

"How about we wander down the street and see if anything looks promising? I'll need an hour at most. I could give you a call on your cells and let you know..." When he answered, his tone was carefully neutral.

In front of the restaurant, Marcus and Taylor went their separate ways, leaving Liam and me alone. He reached out and took my hand. I looked down at his and felt its warmth. "Let's walk this way," he suggested. We walked the short distance to a wooden bench nestled between two arching trees. When we sat down, I sat farther away from him than he wanted, so he slid closer to me, putting his arm on the back of the bench and resting his hand on my shoulder.

While twiddling with the silk fabric of my dress, he gazed at the bustle on the street. "This reminds me a bit of shopping on High Street in Dublin, where I grew up. Saturday is always a busy day. I love the energy of the weekend. Saturday is electric and then Sunday is so lazy." I found myself relaxing as I listened to the lilt of his voice and the description of his home. He told me about his parents and three brothers, and I found myself laughing at his stories.

"Your poor mother. The four of you must have been horrible!" I remarked after a particularly outrageous story involving a soccer ball, a muddy field, and a group of girls.

"Don't feel sorry for her. One slap from her and you'd never doubt who was in charge!" The twinkle in his eye suggested that he respected his mother and found it all amusing. It was endearing.

Without warning, those laughing eyes turned serious; his look became quite intense and his hands held mine a little tighter. "You don't know, Charlotte, but I'm thirty-six years old. Not to be bragging, but I've had enough relationships to know when a woman is questioning something. I'm not entirely certain what I said or did to make you go all quiet and sit as far away from me as you could. But I hope this helps." He looked at me more intensely, without any nerves. "I really like you. I think that after we get to know each other a bit better, I could more than really like you. I want to hold your hand, talk to you for hours, and see if we want the same things out of life. I'm not going to attempt to deny that when the image of your bare skin next to mine flashed across my brain, the blood left my head, and I said idiotic things." In humor, he added, "By the way, it's likely to happen again!" Back to being more serious, he added, "The only question I have is, what do you want?"

As he began, I'd felt awkward but by the time he was finished, I was mesmerized. Of course I wanted someone who knew me, loved me, and couldn't keep his hands off me. Giving way to brutal honesty, I said, "I want the same things. I was sitting in the restaurant wondering all kinds of things. Truth is, I just haven't had that many relationships, and I still find certain conversations awkward. Thanks for being so honest! It really makes me more comfortable." I put my hand to his cheek. He lowered his head, giving me another heart-stopping kiss.

Through the warmth that infused me, I suddenly realized that a large part of what was bothering me was that I was busy falling for someone and hadn't told my closest friends. Why was that? Tiziana hadn't been able to tell me about falling in love with Ted, all because of Des. My excuse was that I'd been behaving like a six-year-old. I finally absorbed that Tiziana had been trying to spare my feelings.

I was so lost in my thoughts that I only came back to the present when he unfurled his arm from around me and tilted my head so that he could look at me. One look at his beautiful green eyes and I was a puddle. Tears gushed from my eyes, and I felt awful. I was pulled into the safe embrace of Liam's arms, and my face burrowed into his chest. He murmured words of comfort and rested his cheek against my hair. When my tears had been shed, I stayed there breathing in his warmth, aftershave, laundry detergent, and deodorant until I'd regained complete control of myself. I dug a tissue from my purse, mopped my face and blew my nose.

With what had to be a blotchy face and a red nose, I peeked at him with a wavering smile. His hand was holding mine, and his thumb slid across the skin on the back of my hand. I took a deep breath to calm myself and confessed, "I really like you. You've been nothing but very kind and… real… with me. I've had so much going on with work that I've been ignoring other areas of my life altogether. I need to sort out a few things, and then I'll feel much better."

With a squeeze of his hand, Liam let mine go. His smile was warm and polite. *Wait! Polite wasn't good.* I didn't like looking at him and not seeing affection for me in his eyes. *Indifference wasn't good.* Before my brain could put words and action together, he stood up and took a step away. "I'll give you time to think, to try to sort things out. I'll just go pop in to a few shops and see if there's anyone I can talk to. I'll give a call in a bit and see if you're ready to leave." Then he walked away.

I sat on the bench for a few more minutes, realizing that I should have talked to him. Taylor was right. If I had told him about Des, I could have told him about being angry at Tiziana. My guess was that what I said had been horribly misunderstood. Fortunately, I had two days to try to undo the confusion. I scanned the street and saw people peering into storefronts, looking for inspiration.

"Well, it isn't every day a gorgeous, available, successful Irishman offers himself up. Do something!" I muttered to myself.

# Chapter Seven

**WE MET BACK** at the car close to an hour later. Loaded down with bags, Taylor was quickly the brunt of much teasing by Marcus. "Just Easter goodies!" she said, defending herself.

"You're pathetic," Marcus said as he turned his attention to me. "You only have two bags! What kind of woman are you?"

"The kind who uses discretion!" I replied in defense of my honor. I looked at Liam, hoping for some kind of taunt, but only saw polite neutrality. Hoping to draw him in, I immediately teased Marcus about his search for Martha Stewart and sex toys. The distraction only lasted as long as it took us all to pile back into the car.

If during the remaining drive to the Clarkson Estate, Marcus and Taylor noticed that Liam and I were subdued and sitting farther apart, neither of them let on. It was a relief to see the gate to the drive and an even greater relief to get out of the car.

At the massive forest green front door, we were met by the friendly man I'd met the last time I'd come to the Hamptons with Taylor. "Hello, Jeff, how are you? You look great!" Taylor said, greeting him as she gave him a hug. Marcus shook Jeff's hand.

"Who's Jeff?" Liam asked me quietly.

"Jeff runs the house for the Clarksons. I wouldn't call him a butler. I'm not sure that would be politically correct. He's great. He makes everything run like clockwork."

Taylor reintroduced me to Jeff, and Liam stepped forward and introduced himself as a friend of Marcus's. The lack of communication earlier was making itself known. I was becoming more and more insignificant to Liam by the minute. Taylor shot me a confused look, and I replied with a small shake of my head. "Later," I mouthed.

Liam's eyebrows shot heavenward when Jeff's very southern drawl became more evident. "Won't you all have a cocktail on the back veranda? I have the bar stocked and some appetizers waiting. Your mother called to let you know that they'll be arriving just before dinner," he said as he led us into the house. "Now, don't worry about your bags. I'll take them up for you," Jeff added over his shoulder as we walked through the foyer and down the wide hallway to the rear of the house.

Having provided us with our beverages and something to munch on, Jeff was off in a flash.

"I need to get me a Jeff!" Marcus announced. "Wouldn't it be great to show up at home, have a drink waiting, house cleaned, dinner cooking, and laundry done? How do you make that happen?"

The three of them debated which was the best path to take to end up in the Clarksons' enviable position. I quietly listened to the friendly exchange while I sipped my glass of icy-cold white wine. When I'd finished, I excused myself.

I went to the kitchen to find Jeff, who was preparing dinner. "Jeff, I hate to trouble you, but I need to make a long-distance call to Europe. Is there somewhere private I can go?"

I was led to a gorgeous sunroom on the west side of the house decorated in dark mahogany furniture with bright fabrics. Glorious tropical plants filled the room. I found a chaise and tucked up in a corner beneath the canopy of a huge banana plant after Jeff left. It was 4:30 in New York, so it would be 10:30 in Italy. Who knew if Tiziana would be home on a Saturday night?

The phone rang twice before a male answered the phone. At first, I was startled, but then I realized I had heard the voice before. It was Ted.

"Hello, this is Charlotte Young. May I speak with Tiziana, please?" I didn't want to slight Ted. I just didn't know him well enough to start chatting with him.

"Sure! Just a minute," he answered happily.

The phone clattered as it was set down and then there was chatting in a distant room, and footsteps approached the phone. "Charlotte?" Tiziana asked with concern in her voice.

"Hi, Tiziana," I said with guilt.

"Charlotte, how are you? Are you all right?" she asked, rushing.

"I'm fine, Tiziana. How are you?"

"Bella, I'm fine, but not. Life with Ted is perfetto, but everything... no."

Not really knowing where to start, I took the coward's way out and asked, "How are the wedding plans coming along?"

She regaled me with stories about planning hell. And we had a few good laughs at her mother's expense. I gasped when she alluded to how much things cost.

"Well, if you weren't inviting most of Europe, it wouldn't be quite so expensive," I teased when she told me how many people she planned to invite. It seemed that anyone and everyone were being invited to this wedding.

Finally, I said, "Tiziana, I'm sorry. I've spent so much time and energy being angry at Des that it has only just occurred to me that all this has to be hard on you. I've missed out on so much. I'll try, I really will, to let it go. So, please! Tell me how you and Ted came to be in the first place." I thought it would help us both if we got entirely caught up, and there was so much I didn't know.

"Well, darling, it happened so fast. After we met at the casino, I gave Ted my phone number. I felt guilty because of Gianni, but I was so compelled by Ted. He called me several times while we were in Chamonix. When things with Des became so complicated, it seemed better to keep my phone calls with Ted to myself. It wasn't until I returned to Italy and found him waiting on my doorstep that I realized how serious he was. He spent the next few weeks in Rome. We had so many romantic dinners, spent hours walking all over the city. When he went home, I felt dead inside. Fortunately, when he went back to England, he felt the same. He asked me to come visit him. I told him I couldn't do that until I had confessed everything to Gianni."

"Wow. How did Gianni take it?"

"Yes, of course, Gianni was destroyed. I felt terrible. No, I still do. Anyway, I got on the next possible plane to London and spent three days there. They were the most passionate three days of my life." She laughed at the pleasant memories.

"When did he propose?"

"When we were in Chamonix, only I didn't know he was serious. He had just helped us ski out of the clouds while Des was helping you. I thought he was teasing me! It wasn't until I was in England and he proposed again that he confessed that he had been serious the first time," she explained. Finally the subject returned to me. "How about you, bella? How are you? Will you come to Saint-Tropez?"

"Well, things are pretty much the same in that department. I'll have to let you know at the last minute, I'm afraid. Is that okay?"

"Of course, you can just show up at the last minute, you know that."

Then I launched into telling her about my literal run-in with Des. "It was so weird, Tiziana. He said, 'Clearly, I was wrong.' I have no idea what he meant. I was just relieved the police didn't show up and arrest me."

"I have to admit that I haven't talk to Ted about this lately. Des made it clear that he didn't want the issue to come between them. I can only assume that if Ted hasn't said anything, he doesn't know anything," she replied, sadly.

"I wonder what Ted thinks of me," I dared to say.

"Oh, bella, he thinks very highly of you. He knows that you're a smart and capable woman. Obviously, I've already told him about the situation from my perspective," she said, soothing me and my ego. Trying to get the conversation to a lighter plane, she continued with a giggle, "For the future, I suggest you begin by talking to your manicurist about how she's styling your nails."

"That's for sure!" I laughed. Not quite able to let it go, I returned to the previous topic. "I literally hate the thought that, with Des in your life, I can't just show up. That everything has to be carefully planned. I've read and reread the documents, and I don't see any way that he and I can be in the same place."

Tiziana reverted to her soothing tone with her familiar purr. "Bella, please don't worry. Ted will talk to Des. It will all be resolved, and this won't be a problem. I'm sure, by the wedding, we'll be laughing about this. Remember that I love you, too, and I'm not going to let someone, even Ted's best friend, cause us problems."

Restored by her confidence, I declared, "Okay! Enough about him. I want to tell you about someone I've met!"

"How gorgeous. Tell me all about him," Her voice was full of happiness. For the next twenty minutes, I rambled on about Liam, told her everything from how gorgeous he was, to how concerned I was about falling for someone who lived far away and about my possibly having blown it this afternoon. "It sounds like a very familiar story to me. I understand why you're worried. You know what helped me? Do you remember that movie you dragged me to, *The Bridges of Madison County*? In it there is a line, something like, 'This kind of certainty comes but once a lifetime.' You need to let your heart lead once in a while." She wore her passionate Italian heart on her sleeve.

"You're right!" Suddenly I heard talking and heels clicking at the front entry. "Listen, Tiziana, I need to go. I'm at a friend's home for Easter, and her family has just arrived. I really am glad you were home. Thanks for being such a great friend. I love you. Say hello to Ted, and I'll call sometime this week, okay?"

"Okay, bella. Ciao for now. Listen, if Ted talks to Des, I'll give you a call."

I sat for a minute, quietly taking in the conversation with Tiziana. My body and soul were in less turmoil. There would never be enough words to describe how grateful I was for my friends, and I was enormously relieved that I had called her. Whether things with Des Bannerman ever got resolved or not, I couldn't let him affect our friendship. He would have to learn to deal with me.

Leaving the quiet sanctuary of the sunroom, I found Taylor, Marcus, and the rest of her family sprawled on the veranda. A drink in everyone's hand, the party was in full swing. "Oh, hello, Charlotte. Taylor mentioned you would be here," Faith Clarkson said with all the warmth of the Atlantic Ocean crashing on the sand a few hundred yards away.

"Hello, Ms. Clarkson, Mr. Clarkson. I hope your drive was pleasant," I greeted them as I looked around for Liam.

Taylor and Marcus finally bailed me out. "Let's go down to the beach and find Liam. I'm sure he'd like to join us for a drink."

"Oh, I'll go! Your parents have just arrived. I'd be happy to!" I offered, leaping out of my chair.

"My, aren't we eager," Ms. Clarkson commented coolly.

Certain that this was some kind of leading statement, I decided to go in search of Liam before she could sense my present vulnerability or all hell would break loose.

I heard Taylor in the retreating distance remind her mother of her manners as I walked down the worn wooden boardwalk to the beach.

Where the water gently rolled up to the white sand, I looked for sand dollars and shells while searching the horizon for Liam. After walking for twenty minutes, I turned around, thinking to search the other direction. I raised my hand when I saw that he was no more than one hundred feet away, then walked quickly in his direction.

"Hey," I said when we had just a few feet between us.

"Hey," he answered.

"The Clarksons have arrived, and the party is in full swing. There's just enough time to get back to the house to change before dinner."

"Back we go, then." We slowly wandered back. The breaking waves kept us company as we took turns picking up pebbles, shells, and sea glass. While he didn't hold my hand, steal a kiss, or declare undying love, his body language slowly became more relaxed. By the time we were approaching the boardwalk, he'd warmed up enough to give me a smile that reached his eyes.

"Here we are!" I announced unnecessarily. He nodded and followed me down the path.

The veranda was empty except for Taylor's brother, Thomas. I made the necessary introductions. "Hi, Thomas, this is Liam Molloy. Liam, this is Thomas Clarkson." Upon finding out that everyone had already started getting ready for dinner, I excused myself. "I need a bath. I'll see you two later."

Deeply immersed in foamy water, I observed steam billowing in the air and beads of water running down the white tiled walls. I drowsily opened an eye when the bathroom door opened.

"Hi," I said. Liam looked quite surprised, but his expression quickly changed to something far more sensual.

"Hi!" he said back.

"Sorry, I'm not finished. My bags somehow ended up elsewhere, and I had to have Jeff find them for me."

"Did you? Well, I, for one, am disappointed you won't be having dinner in the bath!" He tugged off the layers of clothes that hid his well-muscled body and climbed into the tub without hesitation. After moving my feet so they could rest on his thighs, he reached for the body wash.

His slippery fingers began to massage the arch of one foot and then the other, leaving me utterly relaxed. As his strong hands slid up and down the length of my legs, I briefly wondered if we'd be late for dinner. That thought fled as a great wave of water rushed over my shoulders; Liam had repositioned us in the tub. He easily maneuvered himself behind me so that his chest pressed against my back.

With half-shut eyes, I watched him pour more glistening drops of soap into his hands. I closed my eyes as his hands came to rest on my shoulders, spending a short time caressing them before slipping downwards to cup my breasts, which had been playing peek-a-boo with the bubbles. He gently tugged at my nipples while I slid one hand behind his neck, drawing his lips to mine. My other hand ran down his hip and thigh, longing to find more.

The heat of his erection burned against my hip. I gently pressed back against it, causing Liam to moan. Deftly, he moved to readjust himself. Heat scorched my back and radiated through me. I was aflame.

"I hope to sweet Jaysus you plan on being merciful!" he whispered into my ear.

"Very merciful!" I responded in a seductive growl I'd never heard myself express before.

While he painted swirly shapes on my belly, his teeth sharply nipped my shoulder. What had been nerves fluttering in my stomach became a deep, burning need. His fingers moved further along, finding my most intimate spot. While he was gently stroking me, a low keening echoed off the walls. The primal sound emanated from me, telling him that I wanted him desperately.

Liam leaned forward and pushed down the lever that allowed the bath water to drain out. Lifting me up gently, I found myself swaying on my feet as he switched the shower on then lowered his mouth to mine.

His kiss took me to places unknown. There was nothing but us and nothing left between us. The kiss alternated between exploring and demanding. A kiss that left me so dizzy I felt faint. Letting us breathe, he ran his lips down my neck while his hands at my ribcage held me tightly against the tile, my body completely at his beck and call.

He was all that: graceful, fluid, sensual. He made me feel utterly womanly. Pressed tightly against me, I felt the length of him, which proved to be too much. His arms slackened their grip when I began to climb him, desperate to wrap my legs around his waist.

I didn't ask, and he didn't hesitate. His hands supported me, squeezing my flesh as I slid into place and enjoyed the slight burning sensation in the tight fit of him inside me. He moaned into my ear, then his lips and tongue explored me as we found our rhythm. I squeezed my legs tighter and tighter, and he pushed deeper and deeper.

I teetered on the edge, biting my lip, drawing blood, hoping to survive until he rushed over the edge into oblivion. When the pace was frantic, I let go and called his name. While I quivered, I felt hot pulses from him flow into me. I called his name again and again.

* * *

When we joined the others, nothing was said. I could only assume from the twinkle in Taylor's eye that she had her guesses as to why we were late and was happy all was well again.

At one point during dinner, I found myself staring at our hands entwined on the white tablecloth. I thought how odd they could look, if viewed clinically. If looked at with the heart, entwined hands could tell the story of a relationship. Stiff and unmoving hands could be the result of boredom; smooth, young skin could represent a certain naiveté, a fledgling romance. My hand wasn't young, wasn't lined, was well-manicured and without jewelry, my hand was warm. Liam's hand was identical to mine. This odd little observation filled me with delight, and I squeezed his hand, wanting to convey my pleasure at his existence.

I was torn out of my romantic reverie when Thomas said, "Did anyone catch Des Bannerman on *The Tonight Show* the other night? He's one funny man. He has these three enormous scratches on his face. I think they're real. He was telling the most hilarious story..." He continued as my panic set in. I could feel my heart rocketing in my chest. I kept my eyes glued to the remains on my plate, though the sight of bits of fish and vegetables made my stomach heave.

With the realization that the conversation had come to a halt, I carefully looked up. Ms. Clarkson was looking at Thomas. Thomas was looking confused. Taylor had stood up. I had missed something important.

"Well, of course, Mother, I would be happy to help Taylor pick out another bottle of wine."

"Um, Charlotte, could you help? This is really your thing," Taylor asked, inviting me to join them. I rose to my wobbly legs and made eye contact with Liam long enough to see a look of concern.

"What the hell is wrong with you?" Taylor berated Thomas as soon as we passed through the door to the wine cellar. She helped me to a chair, then took a clean cloth used to dust wine bottles off a shelf and soaked it in cold water in a nearby sink.

"What did I do?" he asked, defensively.

"Okay, Thomas, we'll go through it slowly... At the holidays, who was on the cover of every tabloid magazine with Des Bannerman? Who has a restraining ordered filed against her? Who is a guest in our home this weekend? Who has a boyfriend sitting in the dining room at present wondering what the hell is going on?" Taylor blasted Thomas with question after question.

During her tirade, she'd handed me the cold, wet cloth, and I pressed it to my face. To his credit, Thomas immediately looked horrified. By the last question, he was looking at me with genuine remorse. "Charlotte! I'm such an idiot. I just completely forgot all about *it*."

I was beginning to feel normal. "Thank you, Thomas... It actually makes me feel better that you'd forgotten. Perhaps there's hope for the rest of the world." I smiled at him.

"How can I help?" Thomas asked.

"Well, other than dropping the subject for now and always, nothing!" I suggested we take some wine back to the dining room.

As we took our seats, Liam searched my eyes to see if all was well, and, seeing that it was, he gave me a lovely smile. "I was just telling Mr. and Ms. Clarkson about having met Des Bannerman. We have a mutual friend, John Chapman. They were at university together. John arranged a few friendly games of football. Good fun! He seemed quite nice. I've always thought it would be interesting to talk to him now, you know, see if he's at all the same bloke."

I took small sips of wine, hoping to relax. Meanwhile, Thomas politely asked a few questions and then adroitly guided the conversation to other topics.

Pleading the need for fresh air, I soon vacated my chair again and found my way to the back veranda. I perched on the boards at the end of the wooden walkway and let the sound of thundering waves soothe my mind and body. The fresh air had a wondrous effect, as well. My thoughts, initially focused on my travails with Des Bannerman, wandered down a more pleasant path. Liam's words this afternoon drifted through my head, *I think that after we get to know each other a bit better. I could more than really like you. I want to hold your hand, have long talks with you, and see if we want the same things out of life...*

"Penny for your thoughts," came Liam's voice from behind me.

"Oh, I was just daydreaming about this afternoon," I admitted.

"Well, I'm glad that's the cause for the smile on your face. Aren't you cold?"

"I was feeling a bit over-heated, I'm fine."

"You did seem to go a bit quiet. Are you well enough now for a cup of tea and some dessert? Or shall I get our coats and we can sit outside a bit longer?"

"We should probably go back in. Maybe we could disappear a bit early, though."

He gave me a lascivious smile. "That sounds like the perfect evening."

Returning to the living room, we ensconced ourselves on a heavenly daybed made of dark, heavy wood, ornately carved. The fabrics for the cushions were various shades and patterns in a dense linen weave. It was slightly in the shadows of the room, leaving me feel quite indulged and very relaxed.

Fortunately, the conversation was light and happy. Liam surveyed everyone to find out what a real American Easter was like. "My god, it's true. For the most part, it's all eggs, chocolate bunnies, egg hunts, and food!" he decried.

"Well, don't forget the bonnets. Bonnets are an important component," I added.

"For a country founded on religious freedom, you're a bunch of heathens! In Ireland, at least we throw in going to church!"

At some point, the elder Clarksons rose to depart to their wing of the house. "Thank you so much for the lovely wines served with dinner, Charlotte," said Mr. Clarkson as they left the room. Not even a glance from Ms. Clarkson.

No sooner had the clicking of Faith Clarkson's heels muffled into silence than Liam grabbed my hand, bade everyone good-night, and guided me from the room. "Was that subtle enough?" he asked me with a grin as we wandered down the hall toward the staircase.

"Oh, I'm sure they have no idea what we're up to," I said, mockingly.

I'd climbed a few stairs when Liam pulled me into his embrace and rested his head near my right ear. "All through dinner, the only thing I could think of was you. The way your body feels wrapped around mine, and the sounds you make."

I took his hand and led him up the stairs to our room. Inside, I pushed him down on the bed and hiked my dress up so that I could straddle him. Resting my weight on my elbows, we were nose to nose. Taking advantage of the situation, I kissed him as fully as I knew how. His response left me dizzy and dazed. At some point, he'd pulled the clips from my hair, which formed a curtain around our heads. He grabbed a handful of hair and took a deep breath. "Amazing," he murmured against my lips.

A few minutes later, we came up for air again, and I threw caution to the wind. In a somewhat timid, breathless voice, I said, "I've always been uncomfortable expressing what I want in bed. It's really important to me that our relationship is different. Tell me what you want." He heaved himself up and held me on his lap. His right hand cupped my chin, as his thumb rhythmically stroked my bottom lip. His eyes bore into me, and I knew it was a look that I would remember all my life. It was soul-piercing; a look that conveyed tenderness and passion.

He burned a kiss on my mouth and then crushed me to him. "I love your honesty and your passion. Thank you for trusting me." His body trembled. "There is one thing that I would like to do right this minute." He pulled away from me as he said this and looked me hesitantly in the eye. "And that is to go to the toilet," came his romantic request as he threw me off his lap and dashed to the bathroom.

"So much for grand declarations," I tittered in mild embarrassment. When he emerged from the bathroom, he reached for me, but I ducked under his arm and said, "My turn."

A few minutes later, hair combed, teeth brushed, I emerged from the bathroom in my finery. Liam was sitting fully-clothed on the side of the bed, reading a text message on his phone. "Do you like it?" I asked, displaying my purchases of the day.

His eyes skipped up to look at me and his expression changing dramatically. He let out a quiet wolf-whistle. "Wow!" was all he said as he tossed his phone aside and reached for me.

"I bought it at Bonne Nuit this afternoon," I explained as he lowered us to the bed, me lying on top of him. I brushed my breasts across his chest as I nuzzled his neck and nipped his ear with my teeth.

"I hope there's a bonjour, aussi!" he growled.

"I'm certain there is." I gasped as his hands danced around the silky fabric, dragging up the bottom of my very short nightgown.

Moments later, as I was helping him out of his clothes and pulling him completely free, he muttered, "Merci."

\* \* \*

The first thing I saw the next morning was my new La Perla ensemble dangling from one of the four posts of the bed. Upon further inspection, I realized it was a post of the footboard. I lifted my head to get oriented and found the beach scene outside our window reflected in the glass of the painting above our headboard. I threw my arm over my eyes to block out the sun and spent an entertaining few minutes reflecting on last night.

I felt an arm snake around me to pull me close, and a voice whispered in my ear, "Are you covering your face in shame? Or does the sight of me make you weak with lust?"

I stretched my body to its full length and let out a sigh deep of contentment. The world was a far, far better place than I had ever known it to be. "Well, considering that we're at the wrong end of the bed, I suppose the answer should be shame. I've been lying here torn between the absolute desire to kiss your birthmark and the need to go to the bathroom," I muttered from the crook of my arm.

"I'll race you!" came the reply as the bed bounced, and I heard him dash to the bathroom. He called from behind the door, "You're no fun."

"That isn't what you said last night," I called back.

When I heard the door reopen, I removed my arm from across my eyes and stared at him as he crossed the room. I gave my best lecherous stare.

"That's a mighty provocative look. Well, at least it would be if you didn't have a giant crease across the middle of your face."

I died a thousand deaths then sat up to look in the glass. There was no crease, and when I looked to meet his gaze, his eyes were full of laughter. Then he shifted his focus to the pile of sheets at my waist. "Give me a minute," I said.

# Chapter Eight

WE MADE IT to the dining room in time for brunch. It was an elegant affair, presided over by Jeff. He handed me a white plate with a silver rabbit embossed in the center. I would have never thought it possible to make a rabbit on a plate look elegant, but it did. Jeff then led us to the buffet, where he pointed out his favorites among the spectacular array of food. I piled my plate high with tasty morsels. At each of the table's place settings was a replica of a different Faberge egg made of colored sugar that must have taken hours to create.

I complimented the Clarksons on their lovely décor. Liam seconded it and asked the crowd, "Where are all the eggs, chocolate bunnies, and bonnets?"

"Oh, we save that for after brunch," said Faith, completely serious. One could only wonder what the afternoon would bring.

After a rather filling meal, Marcus suggested a stroll on the beach to work off some of the calories. Thomas declined, as he was waiting for his girlfriend to arrive, while the Clarksons sat themselves in brightly painted lawn chairs and waved us on.

It was a gorgeous day, brisk enough to require a heavy sweater, but still bright and sunny. We wandered along, very much like we had the day before, only this walk was peaceful. I kept looking at Liam and wondering to what god I owed my eternal thanks. I was studying a piece of aquamarine-colored sea glass when I found myself being swooped up in his arms and twirled about. I felt like a little girl and laughed. "I feel like we ought to be a laundry detergent ad!" I giggled.

He set me back down on my feet, snaked his hands up my sweater, and gave me another kiss that left me feeling dazed and dizzy. "Well, we could make a movie, if you like," he teased.

"Not yet!" I teased back.

His response was just a wide grin.

Breaking apart, we wandered along the water's edge and talked about past Easters, Liam's having been predominantly about food and football and mine about dresses and egg hunts. At some point we perched on a large piece of driftwood and enjoyed its warmth beneath us.

"Can I ask you a question?" Liam asked quietly.

"That sounds ominous, but yes, you may," I replied.

His head was tilted so that he was looking up at me through his eyelashes. "I can hardly believe I'm about to ask, but who were you talking to on the phone yesterday?" he asked with some hesitation.

"Long story, which I'll tell you, but can you tell me why you're asking first?"

"After you had disappeared for quite a while, I thought I would check on you to make sure you were all right. When I found you, you were on the phone in the sunroom. You looked happy and relieved, much happier than I had seen before. After your comment in town, I thought perhaps you were talking to someone significant, perhaps someone from the past..." His final words were almost a whisper, and his eyes carefully focused on the sand between his feet.

I brushed the sand off my hands and reached over to hold his in mine, pulling them onto my lap. Looking up at him, I said reproachfully, "For the record, I'm not in the habit of sleeping around!" I received an apologetic look. Continuing but with my gaze on our clasped hands, I said, "It's a very long story, so I'll try to give you the abridged version. What you know is that I went to Oxford. It was there that I met my gaggle of friends, the four women who to this day know me better than anyone. Until the holidays, we used to talk all the time. Then... life got a bit complicated. I didn't speak for a long while with my best friend of the lot, Tiziana. Yesterday, my moodiness was the result of missing her, realizing that I'd been a terrible friend. She recently became engaged, and I was the last one to find out."

I could feel Liam's eyes boring into the top of my head. Looking up into his beautiful eyes full of questions, I continued, "It's a long story that I'd very much like to save for another time. For now, let's say that our falling out was mostly my fault. She was trying to protect me. Instead of being a grateful friend, I was a real bitch. So, I called her yesterday to talk, to apologize, and to let her know that I'm happy for her. I also wanted to tell her about you." Finally, from him came a smile.

I was trying to decide if that was the time to tell him about Des when he admitted ruefully, "I was miserable yesterday afternoon. If I'd been trying to sell caskets or burial plots, I would have made a fortune! Charlotte, if you ever want to tell the really long version of the story, I'm here. I'm both relieved that you worked things out with your best friend and that your best friend is not another man. While I really liked you before, I like you so much more today." He gave me a lingering kiss that tasted of salt. "Would you like to sit here a bit longer, or go back?" My silent answer was to curl myself up against him, tuck my feet between his thighs, and settle my head against his shoulder.

"Good choice," he said. We sat in companionable silence for quite a while, listening to the gulls and waves. If asked, I couldn't have found the words to describe the sense of peace I felt.

I broke out of a light doze after being splashed by water. Liam's eyes were still closed. Gently, I nudged his shoulder, whispering in his ear with mirth, "*Um*, Liam, the tide is coming in!"

He opened his eyes and yelped, "Feck!" I giggled. It was exactly what Marian would say.

We dashed part of the way down the beach and crossed the final distance by walking on the driftwood. We were a little wet and a lot sandy by the time we made it back.

"What happened to you?" asked Taylor as she saw us walking up the veranda steps.

"Tide," I answered. We hurried along to our room, intending to rinse off and change.

"The Easter egg hunt starts in half an hour!" Taylor called after us. Her cautionary voice caused Liam to give me a lascivious look. I giggled again, shaking my head no.

When we arrived back on the veranda, the Clarkson family was assembled, along with Thomas's girlfriend, Claire Montgomery. Perched on Faith, Taylor, and Claire's heads were beautiful bonnets. They were each holding a basket. Taylor had been serious.

"Charlotte, where's your bonnet?" Faith Clarkson questioned crisply.

"I'm terribly sorry, but I didn't bring one. You ladies look lovely, though," I offered as I extended my hand to Claire, intending to introduce myself and Liam. Except Liam was nowhere to be seen.

"Where did Liam go?" I asked no one in particular.

"I have no idea. He was right behind you one moment and gone the next," Marcus declared.

Soon we heard the clatter of shoes on the hardwood floors announcing Liam's return. "Where'd you go?" I asked, then continued to introduce him to Claire.

"Lovely bonnet," Liam nodded as he greeted her.

Liam quickly turned to me and pulled a hand out from behind his back. In it was a gorgeous hat box. "My mistake, actually, Ms. Clarkson," he explained. He made quite the show of presenting me with the gift. I took the box with great trepidation.

I loved the bonnet that Liam had made earlier but wondered how the elegantly-crowned women would react to one like that. I raised my chin a notch, opening the box to gaze inside. A wide grin crossed my face as I looked up at Liam. "Thank you, Liam," I said excitedly. Inside was a lovely Marc Jacobs creation.

I was given a moment to place it properly on my head before Mr. Clarkson declared, "Let's get this hunt started, shall we?"

Jeff, ever ready, reviewed the rules of the hunt:

1) We hunted in couples

2) We couldn't snatch an egg out from underneath someone's hand

3) No arguing over who got there first

4) The eggs were to be shared evenly at the end

5) There were thirty-two eggs total

"Remember, all eggs will be found in this area only," he said, using his hand to direct our attention to the formal garden at the entry of the house. Liam and I stifled smirks and giggles. We were looking at a quarter-acre of elaborately landscaped land. When Jeff glanced at us, there was carefully veiled humor in his eyes.

Taking us off guard, Jeff rang a small handbell. Off we went in different directions. Taylor, Marcus, and Thomas had the advantage, having done the egg hunt before. Once we found our first egg and had some idea of what we were looking for and how deliberately hidden they were, Liam got serious.

The competition was clearly between the men. Taylor, Claire, and I were pulled, dragged, boosted, and prodded, and not necessarily in the pursuit of eggs.

The hunt lasted twelve minutes. The winners were Claire and Thomas who had found thirteen eggs.

"Thirteen! That's impossible. Clearly you knew where they were hidden. Were you out here sneaking around while Jeff hid them?" Liam accused them good-naturedly.

"Would you like a rematch?" Thomas offered.

"I would," Liam accepted, as did Marcus. That meant that Taylor, Claire, and I would be traipsing through the shrubbery again.

"Ladies, if I might impose, would you please take your men and distract them at the back of the house while I hide the eggs again?" Jeff inquired. I was impressed that he was able to keep a straight face.

We went to the veranda where we'd had cocktails the previous afternoon and gulped down water and mimosas while we waited. The guys really had a go at each other while the rest of us were dumbfounded by their absolute competitive nature.

Round two found us standing inside the main entrance to the house, all eagerly awaiting the ringing of Jeff's bell. With a clang, we were out the door. Liam dragged me in the direction of the hedge that ran the perimeter of the formal garden. A heavenly scent wafted off small, creamy white flowers found among the large, glossy green leaves of the shrub.

"Did you notice that Jeff smelled just like these flowers?" Liam asked. *Ah! That was why we were here.*

"You're part bloodhound!" Looking at the hundreds of plants that made up the hedge, I asked, "So, what's the strategy?"

After telling me to crawl on hands and knees to look for eggs, I looked at him like he was insane. "There's no way I'm doing that. Next year, I'll bring a pair of sweatpants. This year, that will be up to you!"

Already squatting to survey the possibilities, Liam ran a hand up my bare leg, which disappeared at the knee of my pale blue Armani dress. Not distracted, he said, "Sweatpants would be better."

"I won't take that personally," I answered with a laugh. The man was invested.

"Okay, I'll take the hedge. You stick close by and check out all the planters and trees as we pass them." I had to hand it to him: he could scamper along the ground faster than I could survey pots and plants. We found four eggs in no time at all.

Minutes later, I was the keeper of the basket while Liam stood on tip-toe, dislodging egg number seven which had been nestled between the neck and shoulder of the Grecian goddess standing on a knoll, overlooking the pond.

"We'd better get cracking. No pun intended," Liam said excitedly.

"Quick!" I spotted Marcus making a mad dash toward us. Pointing excitedly, I cried, "Look, there's a purple egg the size of a football next to the rock pillars."

Unfortunately, Liam looked for a soccer ball, so we lost that egg to Marcus. There was potential for conflict over the confusion, so I apologized to Liam, and we agreed to use strictly American terminology. All the negotiation was done while I tried to reach an egg on top of an arbor.

"I can't reach it," I squawked, straining my arm almost out of its socket as I leapt up and down trying to find something to grab a hold of.

Putting his hands on my shoulders, Liam gently pushed me aside so he could assess the situation. Pressing a kiss to the top of my head, he said, "Kick your shoes off and stand on my shoulders."

Just as I kicked one Manolo off, a moment of clarity struck. "Are you freaking crazy? I'm not going to shimmy up onto your shoulders. What if I fall?"

The two other teams were approaching quickly. "Look, Charlotte, our combined height has us at a slight disadvantage. If we don't get it now, either Taylor or Claire will. Now, go!"

I realized I still wore my bonnet as I kicked off my shoes. I gently, but quickly, pulled the hat off my head and handed it to Liam. "Careful with it," I said. I was devising a plan when I saw Liam flick the hat to the ground. "We'll talk about that later."

"Stand still!"

The next thing I knew, he was squatting behind me and sticking his head between my legs. Then, with powerful legs, he pressed to his full height, carrying me upwards.

I grabbed the wooden post for stability while Liam shouted encouragement up to me. I hoisted myself to my one foot and then the other, praying the whole time I wouldn't fall and kill myself, or embarrass myself horrendously. I looked down and saw his feet spread apart for stability.

"Okay, I'm going to hold your legs so you're more stable. Quickly now, get that egg!" Liam coached. With his hands up my skirt, holding tight to my legs, I dared to stretch to my full height.

Giving up when they realized that Liam and I had a significant head start, Marcus and Taylor called out encouragement. I felt around and soon the ruby red egg was safely in my hands.

Once back on the ground, Liam kissed the inside of my knee as he backed out from between my legs, then gave my backside a gentle pat. Once the egg was in our basket, he gave me a huge hug, clearly flying high from our circus act.

Marcus called to us, "Now that's what I call a trust exercise! Amazing!"

Back to the business at hand, we did a quick tally. Liam and I had ten eggs, Marcus and Taylor had eleven. Which meant there were eleven out there. Either the eggs were in Thomas and Claire's basket or still to be found. We quickly parted ways.

"It's going to be close," I said to Liam.

"Have you been watching them? Is there anywhere no one's looked yet?" Liam asked me quickly, his Irish accent growing thicker from the excitement. He was standing with his hands on his hips atop the baluster on the landing.

"Liam, get down. What will Ms. And Mr. Clarkson think?" I found myself panicking.

"It's their bloody egg hunt. What did they expect?"

"I dunno. A little decorum, maybe!" I said. "Now get down."

The only reason he got down or, rather, leapt down was because he'd spotted a green egg lying in the rough grass where the lawn met the meadow just beyond the knoll where the statue stood. He swept it up just as Thomas started to run toward it. Marcus slammed into Liam with some force. I found myself wondering if a smashed egg counted. As I jogged over, Marcus sat up while Liam lay on the ground, rubbing his shoulder.

"Sorry, man! Are you all right?" Marcus asked, looking at Liam's grimacing face.

I cried a loud, "*Woo-hoo!*" when Liam looked up triumphantly, gently cradling the egg between his thumb and forefinger. Marcus called him something I couldn't quite hear as he helped Liam to his feet. Liam walked over and placed it in our basket.

Taylor had been watching the whole thing from a little distance. I hoped we were tied with Taylor and Marcus.

It suddenly occurred to me that they had probably followed us. Certain they would hear me, I said loudly, "Liam, they're following us. That can mean only one thing. They've run out of places to look! Cheaters!"

Taylor, having none of it, said, "It isn't cheating. It's called using your brain."

"That's right, you're using our brains. Go use your own," I trash talked her as best as I could.

Fortunately, just then, Thomas and Claire came around the knoll, surprised to find the rest of us there. We needed to find out how many eggs they had found. I snuck a peek into their deep wicker basket.

"Liam, there's one more egg," I whispered into his ear after double-counting their eggs.

"Be seeing you, then," Liam said, as he grabbed my hand and pulled me away. "Where the bloody hell is the last egg?"

"Hang on, I have an idea." Still holding his hand, I pulled him along with me as I ran toward Jeff, who sat in a bright yellow Adirondack chair in the sea of manicured green lawn, reading the paper. He'd been there the entire time we'd been racing around the property.

Looking up at me as we approached, he smiled. That was all. Liam and I searched carefully around his chair. Just as I saw the yellow egg nudged between the chair leg and Jeff's leg, Taylor swooped in and grabbed it.

"Foul! No fair!" I called out. "You followed us again!"

"No way. I found it fair and square," she argued.

"The rules say you can't steal it out from under someone's nose," I countered.

"No! The rule is you can't take it out of their hand," she huffed.

We turned to look at Jeff, who was surrounded at this point by Liam, Marcus, Thomas, Claire, and the Clarksons. Jeff pulled a paper out of his pocket and read, "Rule number two states that you cannot snatch an egg out from underneath someone's hand. Rule number three states, that there is no arguing over who got there first."

I looked at Jeff and said very excitedly while poking my finger in all directions, "You know who was here first, and you know that we spotted the egg first."

Jeff took me in, head to toe. There were grass stains on my feet, leaves sticking out of my hair, my clothes were rumpled, and my shoes and hat were missing. I looked like I had been wrestling. Realizing what I must look like, I burst out laughing.

"You certainly are a feisty little thing! In fairness to all, and since it is Easter, I suggest a rematch!"

There were a few minutes of arguing, but then all relinquished, not coincidentally, just after Jeff suggested another round of cocktails. This time we diverted ourselves on the beach.

Sitting on driftwood logs with legs outstretched, Taylor and I examined our limbs and clothing for wear and tear. "I wish I had pictures of you standing on Liam's shoulders. Never in a million years would I try a stunt like that," Taylor said as she pulled wisteria petals out of my hair.

Nearby, Marcus and Liam stood trash-talking each other good-naturedly. "I say we find twelve eggs in eight minutes," Marcus bragged.

"Jaysus, you only found the eleven you did because you followed us. Need me to teach you anything else, son?" Liam taunted.

Thomas and Claire, shyer and less competitive, stood off to one side, laughing.

Marcus was suggesting a list of issues he could help Liam with when Jeff appeared. Liam walked over and hauled me to my battered feet. I winced just a bit but decided I'd had enough. "I think I'll root from the sidelines. The FEHC is too much for me," I declared.

"Feck?" Liam asked.

"The Federation of Egg Hunters Championship," I translated.

Drawing me in to his embrace, he unabashedly patted my bum while raining kisses down on my hair and face. "Sorry, love. Didn't mean to wear you out so early in the day. Put your feet up while your man goes and defends the family name!"

I laughed out loud as he strutted away, his chest puffed out ridiculously.

"Oh, thank you! Twice was more than enough," Claire owned up.

"Yeah, for me too," Taylor agreed.

From the sidelines, we enjoyed the sight of the men running around the back garden, a much less groomed and wilder habitat.

The environment and lack of female participation added a level of testosterone not yet seen. At one point, Liam tossed his basket aside before slide-tackling Marcus as they spied an egg at the same time. Then, when he spied Thomas pilfering his eggs from the abandoned basket, a friendly round of wrestling took place between the three men.

Eventually, the hunt was over. Some eggs were chipped while others were smashed, but the baskets were mostly uninjured. We convened on the back veranda, and, after a fresh round of cocktails, Liam toasted the American tradition of the Easter egg hunt.

With his glass of dark beer raised high, he said, "For of all the customs and products exported by the Americans, this is one of the few the rest of the world really needs! No disrespect intended, of course."

"Next year, we'll have to add a few rules, I see," said Mr. Clarkson with a smile on his face. While Ms. Clarkson had remained uninvolved, Mr. Clarkson had taken turns cheering each man on. He seemed positively pleased with the evolution of the hunt.

Because Jeff had been busy appeasing the wants of the three younger men, dinner was delayed by an hour. I waited in the great room at the back of the house with the rest while the three men changed for dinner. We sipped wine and watched the sun set. The orange, red, and purple light of the descending orb swirled on the ocean waves. The day was ending with the same perfection with which it had begun.

Once he returned, Liam poured himself a glass of red wine and sat beside me on the sofa. It was similar in style to the furniture in the sunroom, only more formal. The lingering light from the sky, the dark wooden floor, and the sumptuous fabrics blended to make an elegant, soothing space.

"Marvelous!" Liam declared, looking around the room.

"Isn't it beautiful?" I remarked.

"What? No, I was talking about the hunt! It reminded me of Easter at home. That was as much fun as playing football with my brothers!" He laughed.

# Chapter Nine

**AFTER SHARING THE DETAILS** of my romance with Tiziana, she promptly called Marian, Hillary, and Kathleen, filling them in on the news. When I returned to the city, I turned my phone back on, only to be flooded with text messages and voicemails requesting details about Liam.

"Good Lord! He sounds GORGEOUS," Marian said in the voicemail she left. "Jaysus, there aren't any more of those types around here. I've looked high and low, and I swear they're exporting themselves. I see more gorgeous Irishmen in other parts of the world than at home." She asked for more personal details, as only Marian would.

When I eventually chatted with Hillary, she tried to maintain her usual reserved air as she inquired whether Liam had any siblings. I'd already ferreted out that two of his brothers were still up for grabs.

"*Hmmm.* After you've settled in, we really must invite Liam and his brothers to visit," she regally intoned. Then, in a quick shift of tone, said, "Whatever you do, don't invite Marian. She'll be grabbing everyone's bits and pieces. She's rather envious." Continuing on conspiratorially, she added, "She was all in an uproar about how you've met the sexiest man from Ireland when she lives there."

"Too bad for her, thank god for me!" was my childish reply.

When I hadn't heard from Kathleen, I learned from Marian that Kathleen was busy flirting with some distant member of the Danish Royal Family. "How in the world did she meet him?" I asked.

"Who knows? Kathleen has a nose for royalty. Kind of like one of those pigs that roots around, sniffing for truffles. She could sniff out royal blood from miles away. She really needs to go into therapy or have an exorcism. Only little girls dream about marrying princes. Prince Charming might exist, but chances are his crown is a bicycle helmet, his castle is a tiny flat, and his family jewels don't reside in the Tower of London," Marian joked.

It seemed that Tiziana hadn't filled the girls in on my encounter with Des outside the nightclub, or at least they didn't bring it up, for which I was glad. The conversations were about the present, and I was thrilled to have my circle of friends back, grateful to be surrounded by the warmth that filtered its way through the phone lines.

Liam and I talked about them and their questions. He took the intrusion lightheartedly and could tell I'd found the relief I had been searching for. "You're happier, which can only be good for me! I can't wait to meet them. They must be a ballsy group!" He laughed.

Spring had turned to summer and with it, mounting pressure for the launch of the London offices. Liam was under his own share of pressure. The IT company that he worked for had acquired new clients as a result of Liam's hard work in New York, and he became busy coordinating the promotional campaigns for their products in Ireland.

We saw each other as often as possible, and, while there were long hours of pure passion, there was an equal measure of laughter and calm. We definitely needed that to offset the mental exhaustion we both lived with.

My meeting with Faith Clarkson resulted in a number of employees transferring to the London office indefinitely. In addition to me, seven of us were expected to relocate to London in less than four weeks. Since there was much to be done to ensure that we were ready to leave and the new employees were up to speed, I had only a few moments here and there to contemplate any future with Liam.

I was sitting at my desk, reviewing the financial data on my computer screen, when the phone rang. Evelle announced that Tiziana was on the line. Before picking up the phone, I saved my work on the computer and turned my chair to look out my office window. There was still no word from Des's lawyers or news from Ted. While I enjoyed hearing from Tiziana, the conversations always began with a little bit of dread, a voice in the back of my head saying, "maybe this time…"

I picked up the phone, "Hello, Tiziana, how are you?" Phone calls from Tiziana had been lasting longer and longer lately. I knew that I would spend the next fifteen minutes listening to the emotional rant of an Italian woman who was planning an enormous wedding.

"All I can say, Charlotte, is that when it comes time for you to get married, run away. Elope, have a lovely party afterwards, and don't mention any of it to your parents!" was Tiziana's sage advice.

"Well, then, why don't you do that? I can't imagine Ted saying no. What's a few dollars thrown away compared to another five months of wedding planning?" I asked.

"I know we should. The problem is that for me to not get married in the church by our family priest would be like, like, like, well, I don't know what! Be glad you're not an Italian Catholic." She sounded frustrated, her trademark throaty purring replaced with a higher-pitched tone. "Is Liam Catholic? Because if he is, I can't imagine an Irish mother being less of a problem."

"Liam and I have barely talked about anything beyond next week, let alone marriage, so I'm not too worried about his Irish mammy! However, that's a good question. I have no idea what religion he is or whether he is religious, for that matter." I realized that there were some fairly large gaps in my knowledge of him.

I was wondering to myself what he might like to know about me but hadn't asked, when the whole Des Bannerman situation sprang into my mind. Since Marian, Kathleen, Hillary, and I were speaking again, I now had five people nagging me to come clean with Liam. It seemed more important to me right now that we figure out what we were going to do about our immediate future. However, I couldn't even figure out how to approach that, either. For all my skill and savvy in the workplace, my sixteen-year-old self shied away from initiating discussion on what could become an inflammable relationship issue.

"Charlotte, you haven't been listening to me!" Tiziana complained.

"Oh, Tiziana, I'm sorry! I was just thinking of all the things I don't know about Liam."

"Then come to Saint-Tropez, bring your lovely Irishman, and take some time to get to know him," Tiziana entreated, her voice purring again. "Just think of it, the two of you on warm, sandy beaches, lovely blue water, no work, no responsibilities. Just sun, food, wine, and love!"

It was both so appealing and becoming more unlikely by the minute.

"I'm hoping to," came the little white lie, "and thank you for including Liam. I would love to bring him and introduce him to everyone." *Another white lie!* This meant that if Liam and I were to go to Saint-Tropez, sometime in the next four weeks I had to tell him what had happened in Chamonix and outside the Bourgeois Pig. I had lied to him. I had to hope not only that he'd find the Chamonix fiasco entertaining but that he would forgive the lie, as well. It all seemed so impossible and fatigued me to contemplate it.

"Now tell me, what have you and Ted been doing to relax and have fun?" I asked her, and sure enough she allowed herself to be diverted. For the next ten minutes, I listened to stories of house hunting, flying on Ted's private jet, making small talk at charity events, lovely dinners in Rome and London… Her life seemed like a made-for-TV-movie these days… or like the fantasies we had dreamt up in Chamonix, including the one about me and Des Bannerman.

My other line buzzed, and I asked Tiziana to hold on for a moment. I switched over to hear the sound of Faith Clarkson's secretary's voice. The entire transition team was being summoned to yet another meeting. I jotted down the information and switched back to Tiziana. "Hey, Tiziana, I have to go. I have a meeting regarding the London office and have to get all the latest information pulled together. I'm sorry. Can I call you tomorrow?"

"Not to worry, darling. Thank you for listening! It will be lovely to have you near. Ciao, bella."

I spent the next fifty-nine minutes uninterrupted. Just as I was walking out of my office, the phone rang. Evelle answered it, and then announced that Liam was on the phone. I dashed back into my office to take the call in private.

"Liam, I'm on my way to a meeting. Can I call you back later?"

"Meet me for drinks at that little bar near your apartment at 6:30," he suggested. "The one with all the potted plants outside the patio."

"I'll be there," I answered, and then sprinted to the conference room outside of Faith Clarkson's office.

Throughout the meeting, I tried to pay attention to various reports and jotted down notes out of habit. These ongoing meetings weren't only Faith's way of staying on top of issues; they were her way of coping with stress.

Halfway through someone's droning on about computer equipment and office organization, I suddenly realized that my brain was trying to tell me something important. There was *something*. *A tone in Liam's voice that suggested something important was happening.* My heart was pounding and I started to sweat. All the possibilities dashed through my head: happy images, sad images, scary thoughts, sexual fantasies. About one minute of it was all I could take. I took a deep breath and told myself I would face whatever it was head-on. Fortunately, the same person was just wrapping up his report when I came out of my fog.

I made it back to my office just before 6:00. I grabbed my oversized purse and headed to the ladies' lounge. I freshened my makeup, cooled myself down with the help of a cold washcloth, and then set my hair free of its restraints, managing to pile it up in a somewhat sexy fashion.

I arrived at The Spotted Pig with no time to spare. I squeezed my way in between the masses and found Liam sitting on a stool with his back to the bar, sipping a beer. I made my way to him and was rewarded with a very malty kiss. A few of my concerns faded away. "You both look and taste great! Can I have one?" I asked.

Liam turned around, picked up a sweaty glass up from the bar, and handed it to me. "Cheers!" he offered before taking a large guzzle from his glass.

I was beginning to feel a bit iffy but waited for him to fill me in.

"I've put our names down for a table. I got here early enough, so, with any luck, we won't have to wait too long. They gave me one of these contraptions! What does it do?" he asked.

"It flashes and vibrates when the hostess is ready to seat us."

"I'll have to get you one of these when I leave," he said with a grin. I smiled shyly up at him. "Would you like to sit?" He offered me his stool.

"Yes. Otherwise I'll be staring at your belly button the whole time!" I hopped on the stool, happy to have the subject changed.

Standing next to me, he said, "Now we can be eye to eye, lip to lip."

It was warm inside the restaurant, so I took my jacket off to reveal a form-fitting, frilly top. I was rewarded with a kiss to each shoulder before his lips met mine for a quick flirtation.

The people perched on barstools next to us made their way to the front desk after squealing with surprise at their buzzing, flashing box.

"Told you that you needed one!" Liam said as he plunked down on a vacated stool. When the waitress came by, Liam order us each another drink. "This place must be unbearable in August."

"Most of New York becomes unbearable in August," I replied.

It was Liam's turn to squeal when our pager went off. "On second thought, you might not want one. The surprise might kill you before you get to enjoy the benefits," he teased.

Once we were seated on a velvet banquette with our menus, Liam grabbed my hand, and I knew that whatever was on his mind was about to be announced. "Charlotte, I have both good and bad news. The bad news is that I have to head back to Ireland. The good news is that I have until Sunday to wine and dine you—and whatever else you'll let me do." He paused, searching my face. "Don't look like that!" he said seriously.

I had no idea how I looked. I was guessing I looked shocked, confused, and scared. Attempting to inject a lighthearted tone, I replied, "I guess I'm going to need a vibrator of sorts."

"We can pick it out together. Or would you rather it be a surprise?" he asked, trying to make me smile. When my fake smile didn't cut it, he said, "Is it because I'm leaving or because I want to buy you a sex toy?"

Deciding to appear more confident than I felt, I said, "No, no, I'm fine! Bring on the handcuffs and whips." It was about then that we both realized that the waiter was standing at our table, listening to our conversation, having forgotten to ask for our order.

"Two more beers please…," Liam ordered. "The darker the better." The waiter seemed reluctant to leave. When he was finally out of earshot, we laughed hysterically. I wasn't sure if it was the beer or the stress or the combination of the two, but things suddenly seemed bearable.

"So, Sunday," I said.

"Yeah, but don't worry, though. Once you're in London, it will be so easy. It's a short flight between London and Dublin. We can spend most weekends together," Liam said to reassure me. The knowledge that he was that invested in our relationship filled me with a good kind of fear.

"The tough part will be the time in between. We can talk on the phone and Skype, I suppose," Liam continued.

How do you describe the feeling you get when the person looking at you wants you as much as you want them and not just in the sexual way? I felt giddy, I felt honored, I felt safe. I felt like the sexiest woman alive, I felt empowered!

While sipping our new beers, we chatted about what he needed to get done before leaving and when we'd be able to spend time together. "I was wondering if you'd be interested in staying with me at the hotel until I leave. I'd love to have you to myself as much as possible," Liam asked.

"I would love to," I said softly.

Pulling his loosened tie from around his neck, he stuffed it in the pocket of his jacket, which lay on the bench beside him. "I've been dreading this all afternoon. We haven't talked about the future at all. It's amazing how hard these kinds of conversations can be," Liam admitted.

"Well, at first, I was just using you for sex, but, after you brought those two girls to the hotel, I knew you were the guy for me," I replied, having seen the waiter approach our table. At first, Liam looked totally confused, and then, spotting the look on the waiter's startled face, he started to laugh. After the waiter disappeared, we decided we couldn't tell if he was offended or intrigued.

When the waiter returned soon to take our dinner order, we decided he was intrigued and managed to pick out something to eat in between fits of laughter. We were munching our way through dinner while happily chatting about all the benefits of moving back to the U.K. when a funny buzz started to work its way through the restaurant.

Looking around to see what was happening, Liam was the first to figure it out. "Look, it's what's-her-name… the actress from *Star Wars*. You know who I mean. She won a Golden Globe for her role in *The Black Swan*!"

"Natalie Portman? Where is she?" I asked, my head was spinning on my shoulders. "I loved her!"

"She's seated at 7:00." Liam covertly gestured.

"Is she with someone?" I asked.

"Yeah, she is. I just can't see who. There are too many people in the way. Jaysus, some people are standing up and staring at them. You have to feel sorry for celebrities, really. They can't go anywhere and have a moment's peace," Liam continued, all the while looking over his shoulder.

Bitterness reared its ugly head. "Well, if you ask me, it's part of being a celebrity. If you are one, walk out the door and expect to be stared at. If you're a celebrity and you want to be left alone, rent a private room. If you ask me, most of them have maniacal egos." Liam looked at me oddly. He opened his mouth to say something when a voice said, "Hello, Charlotte!"

"Oh crap!" I said out loud, and loudly. I looked up at the man standing beside our table, knowing from his voice that it was Des Bannerman. Of the eight million thoughts that raced through my head, the one that stood out was that his cheek appeared to have healed well.

"Hello," I replied, not knowing what else I was supposed to say or do. I just sat there, staring at my plate, praying for mercy.

When I didn't make a move or say a word, Liam stood up and extended his hand. "Hello, Liam Molloy. We met years ago at a football match in London. John Chapman arranged it," I heard him say, seeing the two men shake hands in my peripheral vision.

"Des Bannerman, pleasure to meet you again," Des said politely.

It really was surreal. I was, from the perspective of the people in the restaurant, a friend of Des Bannerman's. I could hear whispering; people were wondering who Liam and I were. My insides had turned into a quivering mass; sweat was beading down my back. I hadn't a single idea of what to do. I felt trapped. I offered a silent prayer that Des would have mercy and not have me arrested for violating the restraining order in front of Liam. I was so focused on my thoughts that I hadn't realized I had gnawed my lips raw or that the conversation had continued. Not only had it continued, it had been directed at me.

"Charlotte," Liam said gently, trying to gain my attention. His eyes zinged between Des and me.

"Oh, sorry! I was just... Well, yes?" I asked Des, rising to my feet as I spoke. We were now within earshot of each other.

"Let me remind you that I have a restaurant full of witnesses who will testify to the fact that I didn't approach you, that you sought me out," I whispered to him, all the while wearing a smile.

Charmingly, Des inquired, loud enough for Liam to hear, "Charlotte, I was wondering whether we'd have the pleasure of seeing you in Saint-Tropez in August." He wore a full smile as he did his quirky lip-tugging thing.

How could someone so awful be so charming?

"I won't be able to make it, unfortunately. I'm sure you'll have a lovely time, though. I spoke with Tiziana just this morning, and she was telling me all about it," I said loud enough for Liam to hear. Much more quietly, I said, "Are you satisfied? I won't be there, you've won." Des gave me a concerned look.

"Well, I'm sure they're disappointed. I'll hope to see you in December, then," said Des, no doubt warning me off from attending the wedding as well.

"Thank you for stopping by. I see Ms. Portman looking this way. Perhaps you'd like to rejoin her?" I had an edge to my voice.

"Yes, well, it was nice to meet you again, Liam. And, as always, a pleasure to see you, Charlotte. Enjoy your meal." Des waved as he turned toward his table.

"Excuse me," I said to Liam a few moments later. I fled to the bathroom at a dignified pace. Once safely inside the cubicle, I sat down and took inventory of my body. I was sweating profusely, devolving into a quivering mass again. Feeling absolutely confused, I sat until the fear left me and the sweat dried.

The most pressing thought on my mind was, "Why hadn't I told Liam about this ridiculous situation?"

The moment of truth had arrived.

Leaving the cubicle, I used a wet paper towel to wipe myself down as I muttered, "I need a shower!" I tidied up what was left of my makeup, and, with shaking hands, I brushed out my hair before pinning it up with some hairclips from my purse. I skeptically surveyed myself and decided it would have to do.

With my hand on the door, I took in a deep breath, squared my shoulders, exhaled, and walked at a dignified pace back to the table. I saw faces swivel toward me. After I sat down at the table, Liam took one look at me and suggested we pay the bill. I surveyed him. In his eyes there was a hint of concern. "That would be really great," I said quietly.

I didn't know exactly what I was going to say, but, in that moment, I knew that I was deeply in love with Liam Molloy.

We walked to my apartment building hand in hand in silence. I dashed a few looks at him, wondering what his thoughts were. For the moment, he seemed content to look in windows, at people, the sidewalk—everywhere but at me. I couldn't blame him. His brain must be firing a thousand questions. At this point, the obvious thing to do was to answer any questions he asked honestly.

"Would you like to pack a bag and come back to the hotel tonight? Or would you rather stay home?" Liam asked, once we were standing outside front my door.

"I'll quickly pack an overnight bag and come back for more tomorrow. Okay?" I answered over-anxiously.

"Perfect," he said quietly with a soft smile.

Within an hour we were sitting in his hotel room, and I was sipping water I'd taken from the mini-bar, lost in thought. Liam was on the phone to room service, ordering what he thought we'd need to make it through the evening.

"Would you mind if I had a shower?" I asked, deferring bravery.

"That's fine, but there's a fabulous tub in there. You might like to check it out," he said calmly, as if nothing unusual had happened. Taking my hand, he led me to the cavernous bathroom.

"Wow, look at the size of this place. It's huge. I could go swimming in here," I exclaimed. Continuing more quietly, I added, "I really would love a bath." I needed to hide and sort out my thoughts.

Liam started to fill the tub. "I think there's some form of bubble bath here, if you'd like," he said, pointing to the basket on the bathroom counter. I picked out a citrus-scented version and dribbled some in under the running water. Then he disappeared to the other room.

Once the tub was half-full, I shed my clothes and poked a toe into the water. *A little hot, perfect!* I submerged myself while Liam wandered around the hotel room, doing who knew what. My mind wandered down various paths but kept returning to wishing like hell that I'd taken everyone's advice and told him at the beginning. Then it would have been funny and weird, not weird and bad.

True to their word, room service knocked at the door twenty minutes later. I heard muffled voices in the outer room and then the silence returned. I was contemplating my evacuation from the tub when the bathroom door opened.

Careful not to slip on the wet floor, Liam maneuvered the room service cart next to the tub. It was loaded with desserts, a bottle of sparkling water, two glasses, and a bottle of white wine. He left momentarily, returned in his birthday suit, and then stepped into the water. "Eat this," he ordered, handing me a forkful of dense chocolate cake. It contained marvelous healing powers. "What do you think we ought to do before I leave?" he asked softly, licking the remnants of the last bite of chocolate cake from my lips.

"I'm pretty happy right here." My response slid on the back of a lazy sigh.

*  *  *

A long while later, we lay in bed, limbs entwined. Liam's hand was tangled in my hair, stroking my head. I looked up into his beautiful green eyes and said, "I love you." I was fearless.

"I love you, too," he replied.

It was as if we had said it a million times, it was so comfortable. I folded into him and fell into a peaceful sleep.

*  *  *

At work the next day, I immediately had a conference call with Marian, Kathleen, and Hillary. Quickly, I filled them in on meeting Des Bannerman outside the nightclub, including my accidentally scratching his cheek and finished with the prior night's encounter.

"That was you? The tabloids in Britain were full of trash talk... *Brynn Attacks Des After Finding Him with a Prostitute*... You know, that kind of thing," Marian filled me in.

"Don't tell me stuff like that. It's bad enough to know I did it! Did you see him on *The Tonight Show*?" I asked.

"Who watches *The Tonight Show*? I like the other fella, older guy. What's his name?" Marian asked.

"Dallin Jones," I answered.

"Yes, well, if we're done discussing talk shows, what do you think he's up to?" Hillary asked, sensibly.

"I have no idea. I can't ask Tiziana to sort this out. I'm sure the last thing she needs is a day-by-day accounting of my restraining order violations. That and the fact that it puts her in an awkward situation."

"Well, at least Liam was there. What did he do when Des Bannerman casually strolled over and started chatting you up?" Marian wondered.

"Well, it's actually hard to describe, because I was busy trying not to throw up. Half of my brain was trying to figure out how to flee, and the other half was trying to figure out what Des was up to. Liam made small talk with him while I was paralyzed with fear. Then Des asked me if I was going to Saint-Tropez. I haven't even told Liam about Saint-Tropez. After he went back to his table, I rushed to the bathroom and tried to regroup." I tried to finish the narration on a humorous note.

"What did Liam do when you came back?" Hillary asked.

I described how gentle and kind he'd been. "He still hasn't asked a single question. I tried to tell him, but I just wasn't brave enough. What if he hates me for lying? If the shoe was on the other foot, I would have been asking questions the second we were alone."

We'd been on the phone long enough that we all needed to get on with work. Everyone demanded that I call them the instant something happened.

*　*　*

Over the next few days, life took the pleasant pattern of waking up early enough to have a leisurely morning, dashing off to work with a phone call or two from Liam during the day, and then evenings spent at various restaurants throughout the city. The late evenings were passionate, romantic, and perfect.

Perfect except for the lingering issue of my relationship with Des Bannerman.

The summer heat was driving diners to sit at outdoor cafés. After wandering past many crowded nightspots looking for dinner, Liam and I decided on the Blue Water Grill. I was drinking a lovely combination of prosecco, lemon juice, and crème de cassis—a Prosecco Royale— while Liam sipped his favorite beer when the heat really turned up.

"Charlotte, I'm leaving in two days, and there's something I would like to know." He spoke calmly, adjusting the cocktail napkin as he spoke.

Sensing that the moment had arrived, I snatched up my own napkin and began torturing it. "Ask away!" I said with a lightness I was far from feeling.

"Charlotte, what was Des Bannerman talking about the other night? What's happening in Saint-Tropez? Why would you both be there? And now that we're talking about it, how do you know Des Bannerman?" He remained calm.

"Liam, can we go back to the hotel now?" I asked, shredding the napkin into a million pieces.

"Charlotte, I was hoping that you would tell me on your own. If you aren't ready, that's fine, but you don't have to distract me by having sex with me. You could just say you aren't ready to talk about it," he answered, with a hint of humor in his voice.

"No, Liam. We need a computer for me to explain it to you. My laptop is at the hotel," I explained.

"Oh, right. Sorry," he said a little stiffly.

Half an hour later, we were sitting at the desk in the hotel room. I was connected to the Internet and searched for "Des Bannerman Chamonix France December." Several links to newspapers and tabloids popped up. I clicked on the *Daily Mail* website and slid the laptop toward him. He scrolled down the pictures on the right side of the screen, slowly looking at them and reading the captions. An eternity passed, and then he turned to look at me with his right hand covering his mouth. "That's you?"

"Yes," I answered. The laughter that followed was both a relief and an annoyance.

"I can't believe it!" Liam said for the umpteenth time. His eyes flickered between me and the computer screen, saying, "Wow," before returning to scrolling through articles that were full of lurid innuendo. I was torn between wanting to explain everything and wanting to run out of the room, never to be seen again.

After finishing the mini-bar vodka bottles, I finally worked up enough courage to face the music. Reaching over, I pushed the lid of the laptop down. Liam's gaze remained focused on the air where the screen had once been, his hands limply resting on the chair armrests. We sat in silence for a moment, and then suddenly both of Liam's eyebrows shot up, his face showing signs that he had returned to the present. I knew that the time for full disclosure had arrived.

"Okay… So you're the girl in all the photographs. This certainly explains how you know Des Bannerman," Liam quickly reviewed.

I got up off the bed and wandered the room. I heard chuckling coming from behind me.

A bit peeved that he found humor in this, I said a bit huffily, "Well, I'm glad you think it's funny."

"I'm sure it wasn't funny at the time, but you don't seem to be the kind of person to stay angry. Besides, nobody believes these things. Not to be unkind, but has anyone asked you if you're the woman in the pictures with Des Bannerman in the last three months?" Liam asked, his voice still holding traces of laughter.

Perching on the edge of the bed with my head resting in my hands, I quietly contemplated his question. "No, no one has asked me in the last three months. However, that doesn't mean that there weren't repercussions or that it's all over. When it happens to you, it's a bit traumatic. The photographers and paparazzi were a walk in the park compared to what happened afterwards."

"What happened afterwards?" Liam asked more seriously, finally recognizing that there was more to this than a photo of me pointing at Des's underpants.

Taking a deep breath, I found myself telling Liam the whole embarrassing story, starting with my crush on Des Bannerman and how we had searched high and low for him in Chamonix. When I described using Tiziana as bait, he interrupted, "That's a real friend. I'd like to see her in action."

"Yes, well, back to the story." Continuing with the saga as I paced around the hotel room, I reached the part about being served the restraining order. He listened intently with no more interruptions.

"Then, when I returned to work after the holidays, I had to deal with Faith Clarkson. You've met her. You have some sense of what she's like. She wanted me to recruit Des and all his buddies as clients. And if that wasn't enough, I had to deal with phone calls from my parents, my sisters, friends. It was awful." Gesturing to the computer, I asked, "How would you like to be known as the guy who threw himself under Angelina Jolie?"

"Well, that's a stupid question. No man minds being known for that!" Liam quipped. When I took a breath to speak, he raised a hand and said, "Hang on! I'm trying to put all this together. Tiziana helped you to meet Des Bannerman by flirting with Des's mate Ted. Now, Tiziana is engaged to be married to Ted. You've had a row with her, from which you've just made up, and now Des Bannerman appears on the scene talking about Saint-Tropez."

"Yes," I said.

His eyes implored me to fill in the rest of the details.

"So… he filed a restraining order against me while I was still in Chamonix! Before you ask me why, I have no idea. I was stunned. If I had received it two days earlier, I would have understood. At that point, I probably seemed like a stalker. But just before the pictures were taken of me lying under him in the snow, we'd been having this great conversation. Marian had told him I had a crush on him, but I had assured him I knew he was in love with Brynn Roberts, and it had been fun talking with him. He said he had enjoyed talking with me, that he liked my candor. I'm positive at that point he believed me and that it was all just friendly."

"So, you've no idea why he went to such lengths?" Liam asked. It wasn't necessarily doubt I heard in his voice, but I did hear something wanting.

"Trust me when I say that I've scoured my brain looking for anything that I could have said or done. I keep coming up with nothing," I said. Looking at Liam, I realized now was the time to confess.

Pulling up a chair to sit beside him, I owned up. "The restraining order requires no contact of any kind, and I have to stay five hundred feet away from him. It *was* Des Bannerman we ran into on our first date, outside the Bourgeois Pig." I told him the story from beginning to end: the women in the bathroom and my scratching Des's face. I sighed when I finished, taking a long look at him. He seemed amazingly calm, so I continued. "When you asked me if that was Des, I just panicked! I was still freaking out inside, wondering when the police or more lawyers were going to show up. How could I tell you all this on our first date? I didn't want you to think I was a nutcase."

"So what do you suppose was behind him coming to the table at the restaurant?" Liam asked me, now seeming as confused as me. "I still don't get the Saint-Tropez thing either," he added.

"I have no idea why he came to the table at the restaurant. Probably to get me to leave! I tell you, his ego is of gargantuan proportions. He just decided he doesn't like me and turned my life into hell. As for Saint-Tropez, Tiziana and Ted are throwing an engagement party for themselves there, and because of Des, I can't go, and I probably won't be able to go the wedding, either, because he's Ted's best man!" I finished in a rush.

"Truly bizarre!" Liam responded.

At some point I said, "I'm sorry. I only made it worse."

I received a soft kiss on the top of my head. "Don't worry. I understand, really I do."

Liam pulled me down beside him on the bed. I curled into his side while he stared at the ceiling for a while. Worn out from the conversation and months of dread and drama, I had almost fallen asleep when Liam said, "It's unfortunate that Ted and Tiziana are in the middle of all this, but I have to believe that, if she's the friend you think she is, it'll all get sorted out. She wouldn't have invited you to Saint-Tropez otherwise."

"I suppose. It may be too much to hope for, but can we talk about something else? I'm really tired of talking about Des Bannerman. I might actually hate him."

"Let me see if I can distract you." His fingers gently tilted my lips to his, and, with that kiss, the passion that followed was a quiet passion. The kind that builds a fortress around you, a harbor, a safe place.

Later, once all our energy had been spent, Liam spooned me, molding his body to mine after arranging blankets and pillows to create the perfect nest. With his right hand trailing up and down my hip, he whispered in my ear, "I love you."

"I love you," I squeaked between tears and sniffles. Finally, I had shed all secrets and fears, and Liam loved me. What more could there be?

My tears were finally from joy.

# Chapter Ten

**WE DECIDED TO SPEND** Liam's last day in New York City sightseeing; our first stop was a tourist shop so that he could take home a few tacky presents for his family.

He bought a shirt that said *Yank my Doodle, It's a Dandy* for his father.

"I really have to meet your dad someday," I replied when he held the shirt up. Never in a million years would I buy a shirt like that for my father.

"He'll wear it down to the pub on Saturday night just to mortify my mam," he said, admiration in his voice.

Our next stop was the Metropolitan Museum of Art. "The place is enormous, how are we to see it all?" Liam asked me.

"My strategy when I come here is to pick an artist, genre, theme, or color."

"Sounds perfect. Why don't we look only at paintings that have blue in them?" Liam teased.

"Well, you'll have to narrow it down. Do you mean cerulean, teal, peacock blue, Dutch blue, Wedgewood blue, or baby blue?" I asked, as seriously as possible.

"Cerulean." He took my hand and led me down one of the many long corridors; we ended up in the Drawing and Prints Gallery. "There must be some cerulean in here!"

I leaned toward him and asked quietly, "Only one question—what does cerulean look like?"

Liam chuckled as he threw his arm around my shoulder. "*Hmmm*, it lies somewhere between cyan and blue. Not azure or sky blue, though. Definitely on the green side of blue." He was matter-of-fact as his head swiveled around the room.

Suddenly, a gong reverberated in my head, shocking me for a moment. This man was a graphic artist. Of course he would know what cerulean was. Quickly, the conversation with Tiziana about what I did or didn't know about Liam came back to me. As we got a closer look at the pieces occupying the walls, I took the opportunity to learn a little more about him. While we wandered, he vaguely explained the skills necessary to be a graphic artist.

Although he did not seem to be very interested in discussing it, he was very interested in finding our subject matter. We wandered the galleries for a few hours; Liam had many "Ah-ha!" moments, pointing out all the cerulean. By then I was an expert.

Finally, we left the museum in search of food. "How about grabbing something from a vendor in the park?" I suggested as we walked down the wide stone steps outside the Met.

We bought loads of food from various vendors as we wandered through Central Park, making our way to the north end of the lake to the Loeb Boathouse. After renting a row boat, we spent all afternoon munching and paddling around the lake.

"Do you suppose all Saturdays could be this glorious?" I inquired through a mouth stuffed with pretzel covered in mustard.

"I have no idea what you just said! You have mustard all over your mouth and bits of food sprayed everywhere. I think you've become entirely too comfortable around me. If you start scratching your arse, I'm taking you back to shore!" Liam teased.

The image of that caused me to laugh so hard that I started to choke. Putting down the paddles in the bottom of the boat, he handed me a bottle of water. When my coughing fit subsided, he used a paper napkin to dab at my mouth. "Disgusting," he said with a smile. He gave me a quick kiss, licked his lips, and announced, "Now, show your breeding. Be dignified while I demonstrate my manly rowing skills. Just wave to your public, madam!"

Exhausted from our action-packed day, we both just wanted to lie down and relax for a while, "Do you suppose we could call Taylor and Marcus and delay dinner a bit?" Liam asked as we walked into his suite.

"Fine with me. But you have to call. Marcus is your friend."

"Coward!" I threw myself onto the bed and he tossed me the remote control for the TV before going to get his phone.

I responded, "I think I've clearly established that."

He glanced over his shoulder at me. "My dream woman is not a coward. Don't forget it."

After a minute, Liam reported, "Faith made a reservation at the Grand Central Oyster Bar for 9:00. Is that okay? Good Lord, my arms are already sore!" He collapsed beside me.

I continued flipping channels and nodded, secretly pleased that he hadn't assumed control of the remote. Finally, I landed on one showing old films, and we watched Fred Astaire and Ginger Rogers expend energy dancing across the screen while we lay like sloths on the massive bed.

Promptly at 9:00 we met Marcus and Taylor at the Grand Central Oyster Bar. "What a great place," Liam shouted over the noise. The atmosphere was infused with the history and flavor of New York City that had seeped into its walls. It was cavernous and lively. People sat at tables and counters; waiters hustled and bustled with trays of food. It was the kind of place that you moved to New York City for.

"I don't think I've seen this many bricks before. That's saying a lot, considering where I'm from. How many do you think there are?" Liam asked as he glanced around the massive space, taking it all in.

The huge space was a group of rooms joined by arching walls and glass windows. Most of the space was built of brick, with wood paneling on the walls. The arches were outlined in white lights, and the ambient light was warm and inviting. On the ceiling above us was a massive circular chandelier. It too twinkled with white light.

The waiter passed out hand-written menus then hovered in the background. We quickly ordered a round of Guinnesses, in tribute to Liam, and an assortment of oysters from the raw bar. The waiter left the menus but was gone with a flash.

"I love it here! I really do. This is fabulous. When you come to Dublin, I have somewhere like this I want to take you. Nothing quite as huge, mind you. But if you like this, you'll love the Saddle Room."

The delivery of our beer and oysters caused a pause in the conversation. No sooner had the waiter whooshed away than Marcus laughed. "How funny is that? Aphrodisiacs served in a place called the Saddle Room. Are there private dining rooms? Or do you have to eat in public?" Liam got it immediately, of course. It took Taylor and me a moment longer. She whacked his arm and made a few disparaging comments about his less-than-gentlemanly behavior.

Ignoring her objections, he went on to add, "The images that wander through one's mind. I can just imagine some woman slurping down oysters, straddling a saddle, doing who knows what. Then in teeters some little old woman saying, 'I'll have me some of that!'"

When Marcus and Liam had explored all possible permutations of the saddle and oyster, Taylor quietly said, "Gives a whole new meaning to 'saddle sore'!"

Thankfully the waiter returned, putting a pause on the rude humor, and asked for our order. We ordered another round of drinks, a beer brewed on Long Island.

"Would you prefer something instead of the oysters? Perhaps some chowder?" the waiter asked, seeing our appetizer tray sitting largely untouched in the center of the table. We all rushed to assure him that we were enjoying them, they were superb, and all the etceteras. This, of course, set off another round of laughter.

A few hours and several thousand calories later, I moaned, "I'm full to the gills."

"Do oysters have gills?" Taylor asked with a straight face.

"I'm pretty sure they're nothing *but* muscles and gills," Marcus replied nonchalantly.

Interrupting what I was certain was going to be another round of juvenile humor, I declared, "I have something gigantic to announce."

"If you bring that up, you can't comment on my behavior anymore!" Marcus spoke quickly, getting a rib full of Taylor's elbow.

When I interpreted his innuendo, I gave him my best "you're an idiot" look.

"What? What?" Taylor asked, having moved to the edge of her chair, her eyes wide with excitement and a huge smile on her face. I realized at once that she was expecting the announcement of something much more life-altering than what I was about to share.

"Calm down! I just wanted to tell you that Liam knows all about Des Bannerman," I said evenly. The look on Taylor's face changed from super-excited to very pleased.

"Well, did you think she was a stalker?" Taylor asked seriously.

Looking at me with a blank face, Liam finished the last of his beer before answering. "I have to admit there were a few moments of doubt.

I mean, there was the initial bit of stalking, and she did savagely attack him." After a few more minutes of teasing, Liam finally concluded, "Nah! He's a prat! I'm going with ego-maniacal. But of course I have to say that, or she won't sleep with me tonight, and that would be dreadful, since I'm leaving tomorrow."

Not waiting for a response from me, Taylor announced, "I completely forgot. I'm so sorry. Well, we'll let you go so you can have some time to yourselves!" She jumped up from her chair and gave Liam a kiss on the cheek. "Thanks for spending part of your last night out with us. We'll miss you!"

Marcus whispered something into Liam's ear that caused them both to burst out laughing.

"All right, all right, enough of that," I said, pulling my man away. "I don't even want to know what that was about."

Taylor gave me a hug goodbye and said, "We'll keep you busy for the next few days, don't worry. I'll see you at home."

My eyes brimmed with tears, but I was determined not to cry before Liam had left. "Maybe we can watch *Far and Away!*" I knew Liam hated that movie.

"Not Tom Cruise and that dreadful Irish accent. If you watch that, I'll never feed you oysters again," Liam pronounced, pulling me from Taylor's side.

"Seriously, take good care of Marcus. He'd be shite without you," he said to Taylor, while quickly giving her another hug. "Look after her for me," he whispered, just loud enough for me to hear.

"Will do," she said, smiling into my watery eyes.

I whined a few minutes later as we ambled down the street, moaning about the amount of food I had consumed.

"I told you not to have the tart and the sorbet," Liam replied, showing no pity.

"It isn't just my stomach that hurts. Imagine how my poor feet feel, now that I've added ten pounds to the balls of my feet." I was teetering on four-inch Bottega Veneta heels.

Looking down at my feet briefly, he quickly hailed a cab.

I sighed. "If you could solve all my problems that simply, I'd love you forever." It was pure heaven to be off my feet.

"Why do you insist on wearing shoes like that?" he asked.

"Well, if you were barely five feet tall and wanted to look like a woman instead of a girl, what kind of shoes would you wear?"

"I've no idea! I'm just glad you're a woman!"

\* \* \*

The following morning, I woke up to a finger lazily drawing patterns on my back. "Yesterday was the second best day of my life," I said.

"Would you like me to make today the best?" Liam suggested, scooting right up against me, his finger dancing along my stomach and thighs.

"Give it your best shot," I said, rolling over to face him. "And take your time."

\* \* \*

A long while later, struggling against Liam, who was pressing me facedown into the mattress, I pushed hair out of my eyes and struggled for air. I managed to flop onto my back beside him. While I waited for my blood supply and nervous system to return to normal, I used the sheet to wipe the sweat from us both.

The sex had been fantastic. Liam had introduced me to some new experiences, leaving me to wonder if it was to burn the touch and taste of each other on our senses or if he was just more adventurous than I'd ever had the courage to be.

Liam looking at me self-satisfied and asked, "So is today the best day of your life?"

"No," I replied without compassion for his ego. "Parts of me burn while others have put 'Out of Order' signs up."

Laughing hard, he offered, "Let me kiss them better!"

Quickly stretching one arm across my breasts and cupping my crotch with my other hand, I giggled. "Oh no you don't."

Not giving up, he nuzzled at my neck, trailing fingers lightly down my side. "I know of a few other places I can explore that will make your toes curl from pleasure," he said as he pulled me onto my side, hooking a leg over my knees.

Beating gently against his chest, I begged, "Stop! Please, stop. For the love of god. You're insatiable today."

"True, but a drought is about to come." He pulled me closer, pinning my arm between us. His hand cupped my bum, massaging it, causing me to rock against him. A growl from somewhere deep in his chest quietly rolled out of him.

It was hard to resist him, but, drought or not, we'd been in bed for ten hours and had sex four times. I pled mercy. "I'll call. We'll have the most amazing phone sex ever."

That caught his attention. "Will we, now? You have hidden talents."

"No more hidden than any others. I'm a quick study, though. What I can't learn from YouTube and the Internet, I'm sure you can teach me," I said, my face pressed against his chest. I was too embarrassed to let him see me.

Sensing I was at the outer limits of my comfort zone, he took pity on me. "Tell me then," Liam asked, settling back against the headboard, "what has been the best day of your life?"

Continuing my mean streak, I said, "I dunno, I'll tell you when it happens."

He looked disappointed. "I thought you were going to say, the day I met you. Something far more romantic than that."

"Well, the day I met you was fabulous. The first night you stayed over was perfect, and every day since has been more incredible than I could have ever dreamt. And though my parts are sore, last night was incredible," I summarized. "There are a few days that I could imagine to be a little more perfect, though," I said honestly.

"Me, too," Liam answered softly.

Liam pulled me in his arms and kissed me fiercely. "Charlotte, there will be many, many days as wonderful as these. There may even be a few tough ones, but trust me, we have many incredible days coming to us. I don't think we should make any decisions today, only because there are so many changes happening in both our lives. When the dust has settled, we'll talk about all the days that lie ahead of us. I may be flying back to Ireland, but Charlotte, you must know that I'll love you wherever I am."

As a tear slid off my cheek, I managed a nod. "I know," I said in a tremulous voice. "I know it's all going to be fine. You're right, there's so much going on, and it would be best to get through the next few months first, before thinking about anything else. I'm just so sad. New York just won't be as magical without you."

He kissed my eyelids and murmured comforting words in my hair while I cried the rest of my tears. When I had cried the last, he put the corner of the sheet in my hand for me to dry my face on. "Feeling better?"

"Yes and no, but mostly yes. I'll be fine. You'll be fine. It will all be as it should," I said, wishing for a Kleenex.

"I'll get you a tissue," Liam offered, reading my mind.

He dashed to the bathroom and was back in a flash. Handing me the box and perching on the side of the bed, he said quietly, "I hate to do this, but I have to start packing. Would you like to have a bath while I get it done?"

"I'd love to." He went to the bathroom and turned on the water for me. While he was gone, I called room service to order coffee and then dug out some clean clothes from the drawer.

While the tub was filling, I pulled all my clothes from closets and drawers and stuffed the lot into my bags. Liam announced the tub was full as he came out freshly shaved. I gave him a kiss on his smooth cheek and went in, telling him, "I ordered coffee." As I dipped my toe in the tub, I realized that no corner of my life would be the same.

Why is that, when you want time to linger, it speeds up? In no time at all, we found ourselves standing in the lobby of the hotel, Liam signing the bill. Our bags stood side by side. To the entire world it seemed that we were traveling together. I drifted away, thinking of places Liam and I might go. The image popped into my head of us standing on the Bridge of Sighs in Venice, the most romantic place on Earth.

Tucking the image away for future thought, I came back to reality when he led me to a quiet corner in the lobby, the summer sun streaming through the window. "I know this sounds odd, but I'd really like you to go home. I feel sad at the thought of you leaving the airport on your own. Go home, and let Taylor distract you," Liam said. The look on his face gave me no room to disagree.

"Okay," I agreed. "The truth is, I feel sad thinking of leaving the airport by myself."

There wasn't really anything left to do but hail a cab and say goodbye. We lingered a few minutes in our quiet corner. Between kisses, goodbyes, and reminders of how it wouldn't be long before we were back together, the parting grew emotional, and I found myself needing to breathe calmly. At last I pulled myself from him, pushed my shoulders back, looked him straight in the eye, and said calmly, "See ya'."

"Bye. I'll call you when I get home," he said very matter-of-factly.

With that, the concierge whistled for a cab. My bags were loaded, and, with a quick kiss, I was gone.

# Chapter Eleven

**AFTER HAVING COMPLETED** the mundane task of unloading my suitcases and sorting laundry, I hunkered down on the leather sofa in an old sundress with my hair knotted on top of my head. While perched in front of the TV, I sipped a glass of iced tea and flipped through the channels, finally finding a sappy movie of the kind that are inevitably aired on Sunday afternoons. I was crying at the death of the leading lady when Taylor walked in the door.

"You're already here? When did you get home? What are you watching?" Taylor asked anxiously as she crossed the room. Glancing at the screen, she looked at me with disgust, grabbed the remote control, and turned off the television.

"What are you, a masochist? Who watches a movie designed to make them hysterical on the day their boyfriend leaves? Why not at least watch something romantic or funny?" She gave me a pathetic look.

After sizing me up, I was ordered into something presentable and told to get ready for an evening out. "Make sure you wash your face. You look like a raccoon." She continued to order me about, even though I repeatedly moaned that I didn't want to go out. "Too bad," was her response.

An hour later, we arrived at one of the latest and greatest trendy bars in Manhattan. I was perched on a shiny chrome barstool at a glass-topped bar sipping on a brutally cold gin and tonic, trying to pretend I was happy, when Taylor smiled and waved to someone. The next minute, I was gasping at the faces of Marian, Kathleen, and Hillary.

"Oh my god! How perfect is this?" I gushed in amazement. It was hard to take in such an unexpected surprise.

"Well, we couldn't leave the mopping up to just one poor woman," Marian responded. She glanced around the room. "Where in the name of Jaysus is the waiter? We'll be needing a few bottles to sort this one out," she pronounced as she took in my pathetic state.

While I dreaded the state my head would be in in the morning, I was speechless with delight.

"Now, isn't this better than an iced tea and some sad movie?" Taylor asked. The lot of them reproached me, wondering how I could be so cliché. Just about then, my phone rang.

"Just a minute," I shouted over the friendly harassing.

"Hello?"

"Ciao, bella, how are you?" It was Tiziana! After a minute of chatting, she apologized for not being there and advised, "Don't let Marian dance on any tables. You know her legs aren't her best asset! Take care of yourself. Remember to drink lots of water." We hung up with the promise to talk tomorrow.

Miraculously, a waiter arrived to tell us that a table had opened up and took our cocktail orders. Marian, in a low-cut, figure-hugging green dress, leaned into him while perched on her own chrome barstool, batting her big green eyes, and said, "Bring us two bottles of the best white wine you have, and don't stop until you close!"

"Certainly," he said, maintaining eye contact.

After he left, she said, "He had to be gay! There isn't a straight man alive that can resist this dress." Clearly Marian knew what her best assets were.

"Well, then, tell us all about him. Get it out of your system! Bring it on," Kathleen demanded.

Since I'd barely spoken with her since the trip to France, she knew the least about Liam. I rambled on and on about how wonderful he was, how kind and handsome. After a few return trips from the waiter, I segued into how sexy he was, how perfect his bum fit into my hand, how gorgeous he was. At some point we sat hunched over my cell phone so the girls could see pictures of Liam.

After passing the phone between themselves, Marian lamented, "How the feck is it that she met him here, this fine Irish boy? God's truth, there aren't any like this left in Ireland. I'd know. I've been actively searching for years!" She returned the wine glass to her lips.

Hillary, having just drained her own glass, suggested, "Have her take you out. Clearly she knows where to look. Did you see those arms?

That chest?" Hillary was referring to a picture I had taken of Liam while he was rowing us around the lake in Central Park. I felt quite smug.

"Okay, Kathleen, spill it. Rumor has it that you're trying to woo a certain Danish prince or something," I said as I returned my cell phone to my purse.

"Well, he's only a distant relation to the Danish royal family. He's 278th in line for the throne, or something like that. While he may not have the same raw manliness that Liam has, he has his own appeal. He's elegant and refined!" And with that, Kathleen whipped out *her* phone and proceeded to show us pictures of Frederick.

"Frederick? What kind of name is that? There isn't anything masculine about that. Wasn't that the name of the fat one on *The Flintstones*?" Marian teased.

"Are you saying Liam isn't elegant and refined?" I challenged Kathleen. I felt very Tammy Wynette-ish (*Stand by Your Man* and all that).

I looked to Taylor to defend Liam's refinement. She gave me a look that clearly stated she wanted to be left out of this competition. As Kathleen and I were comparing our men digitally, I heard Taylor shout to the passing waiter, "Two more bottles, please!" I looked at her with a grin. This was far better than sitting at home, crying my eyes out.

At some waning hour, closer to morning than night and more than a little tipsy, we stumbled to the curb to hail cabs. While we stood there, I had the sudden realization that I had never asked how they came to be in New York or where they were staying. I was surprised to find out they were staying at the very hotel Liam had just vacated.

"How amazing is that?" I said when I found out, swaying with the summer breeze.

"Well, not really at all, considering Liam arranged all this!" Hillary said.

"He did? When?" I asked in wonderment, still swaying. "Isn't he wonderful?"

"While I hate to break up this party, I'm going to get her home and into bed so she's at least somewhat sober when she goes to work in the morning," Taylor issued, taking command. "We'll see you all at 6:30 tomorrow night or in fifteen hours, at our apartment, for drinks? We can sort out where we'd like to go then, okay?" We managed to get everyone into their respective cabs and tell the drivers where we were going.

"Isn't he wonderful?" I asked Taylor, my head resting on her shoulder.

"Yes, he really is," she answered.

"I'm so lucky!"

"Yes, you are."

"I don't feel very well!" I yelped.

"Stop the cab!" Taylor shouted. We stopped, barely in time.

I returned to the car after having left an indelicate deposit of wine and appetizers in the gutter. "I'm so glad Liam didn't see that."

"I'm sorry I did," Taylor answered.

*   *   *

I'd no sooner closed my eyes than the voice of Anita Ward wailed out of my phone, "You can ring my be-e-ell/Ring my bell!/Ring it, ring it!" I truly struggled to sit up in bed. I hadn't been in it long enough for the walls to stand still and the floor to quit spinning.

"Liam, how are you? You made it home all right?" I asked, knowing it was him. We secretly shared a love for all things disco. It had been a moment of pure bliss when I found that out. More than once we had danced around the apartment or hotel to blaring disco.

"I'm fine. I got in to work hours ago but thought I'd better let you sober up a bit before giving you a call," he said very quietly, having sensed the fragility of my head.

I managed to recline on the pillows, my elbow thrown across my eyes to shield them from the sun's piercing rays. I didn't think I had ever noticed how bright the sun truly was. Well, that was what a couple of bottles of wine would do for you: rearrange your views of the universe.

"Oh, Liam! Thank you so much for suggesting to the girls they come over. I was moping around when Taylor forced me to go to some new bar and was about to call it a night when all of a sudden Hillary, Marian, and Kathleen showed up. I couldn't believe it. But god, Liam, we got so drunk. Marian was ordering two bottles of wine at a time."

"I'm glad you enjoyed the night out. It was actually Taylor who did all the work. I hadn't any idea how to get ahold of them. Thank her. So, how's your head?"

"Well, my head is pounding, the room is spinning, and I honestly don't remember getting into bed. That was only about three hours ago.

Oh, Liam, I think I might have compared the size of your manly parts to Kathleen's boyfriend's!"

"Well, did you have pictures to compare these parts or was it just guesstimating?" he laughed softly.

"Thank god, no pictures were involved, of that particular part at least. I did show them loads of pictures of you, though. They all agreed that you were the most gorgeous man in the world," I said quietly, to prevent my head from exploding.

After a prolonged lapse in conversation, Liam quietly said, "Listen, love, I'm going to ring off now and let you have a little bit of a doze before you need to get up and go to work. When should I call you?"

"I feel so dreadful. My head is spinning. I could sleep all day. I'm so glad you got home safely. I really do miss you, despite what it sounds like. Oh shit, I'm supposed to be in a meeting all afternoon. Can you give me a call at lunchtime? 1:00?" I wondered how in the world I could go to work in this state.

"I'll call you then. I love you. Feel well!" Liam wished me warmly.

"I love you, too. I will survive!" I declared in my best Gloria Gaynor impression.

*　*　*

At exactly 1:00, Liam called to say hello. Still in the state between hangover and recovery, I picked the phone up mid-way through the first ring. "I don't know what possessed me to think I could consume that much alcohol. I should know better than to try to keep up with Marian!" I whispered.

"I thought, after we hung up this morning, I might need to call in the local priest to give you last rites! You sound less drunk and well into your hangover. Don't worry, soon you'll feel much better." Liam laughed quietly.

"Trust me, I've had moments of doubt all day. Even now, I can't stomach the thought of anything more than a cracker and ginger ale." Changing the subject, I asked, "Anyway, enough of my stupidity, how are you? How's work? Have you seen your family, friends? Did your plants die in your absence?"

"Work is work, although it's nice to see the lads. I had lunch with my parents today. I didn't have any plants, so I don't have their deaths on my hands. I'm going out with a few people tomorrow night." Liam answered all my questions. What he didn't do was tell me whether he had mentioned me to parents, friends, workmates, or the milkman, for that matter. I stewed on it for just a moment and then shook it off, realizing I was borrowing complication and trouble, of which I needed no more.

"How was lunch?" I inquired, trying to imagine what it would be like to sit around the table with Liam and his parents.

After talking for a few minutes about this and that, he exclaimed, "Oh, I forgot! My dad loved his shirt. I haven't seen him laugh that hard in years. My mam said there was no way she'd go anywhere with him wearing it. I told her that's why I bought it, so he could go down to the pub with me more often. She said she was glad it was me he'd be going out with, as she didn't want anyone to think she'd be yanking his doodle, whether it was dandy or not." That made it harder for me to imagine dining with the Molloys.

"Did your mother like her book?" I asked. Liam had bought her a book on the original design and history of Central Park. She, apparently, was an avid gardener.

"She did. Give her a few days to look at it, and she'll have my dad outside with the spade, digging up the garden!" Liam replied, lightness in his voice.

After talking quite a bit longer, it was time to go to my afternoon meeting. "Listen, Liam, I have to go. I need a few minutes to get myself ready for my meeting. All the different divisions are getting together to make sure the transition team is ready to head to London. Now that you're there, I'm ready to get this show on the road."

"All right then, I'll let you go. Be a good girl tonight! Maybe only a bottle of gin and tonic?" he suggested.

"Oh Lord! I'd forgotten all about that. Well, it won't be like last night. My body would shut down if I were to do that two nights in a row," I replied, wincing at the thought.

"Reminds me of Saturday night. Best to take a day off between intense rounds of self-indulgence. Don't do your body any harm. I have plans for it!"

Blushing to the roots of my hair at the mention of our last night together, I was glad he couldn't see me. "I'll call you tomorrow, 6:00 your time. Maybe I'll have an arrival date to report," I said hopefully.

"Oh, and Charlotte, my parents can't wait to meet you."

I beamed throughout the entire afternoon meeting.

* * *

Later, once we had all met up at our apartment, the consensus was to see if there were any tickets to be had for a Broadway show on Tuesday. Wednesday would be for a shopping extravaganza, leaving that night for more drinking and eating debauchery. Kathleen and Marian were leaving New York on Thursday morning, Hillary on Saturday.

Set in motion, the week went off without a hitch. A constant headache from all the frivolity was the chief complaint. Taylor joined us for the Wednesday night outing. When we arrived at the Hotel Chelsea bar Serena, upon seeing Kathleen, Marian, and Hillary's outfits for the evening, Taylor remarked, "How do you keep up with them?"

Though tasteful, their dresses were quite revealing. "This is one of the things I love about them. They revel in being women! They dress up for themselves and truly don't care if anyone looks, but they like to look good if someone does," I answered.

Kathleen sat there in a plunging, form-fitting halter dress the color of a tangerine with strategic beading. It looked quite nice with her golden tan, long highlighted blonde tresses, and strappy summer sandals. Marian had on a purchase from Barney's. She wore a black knee-length dress that appeared to be held closed by a single crystal button between her breasts. Every time she moved, she bared a different patch of almost translucent flesh. Hillary was wearing a sleeveless white silk collared dress that was paired with silver sandals and jewelry. Her style was cool, elegant, and fuss-free.

"Don't worry, we look gorgeous, too," I said, sensing Taylor having a moment of self-doubt.

"I do not! I feel overdressed, literally. Compared to them, I might as well be dressed like a nun. I have an urge to go in the bathroom and hack off parts of my dress."

"Well, I think you look stunning. Just don't sit next to Marian! Next to her, you *will* look like a nun," I added, seeing the long length of Marian's exposed leg.

Seated at a corner table, the banquette was a plush, black velvet affair with colorful throw cushions. The dangling ceiling lights glowed in warm hues. We were gingerly sipping our cocktails when Hillary asked in her drawn-out, nasally way, "Charlotte, when are you going to tell Liam all about Des Bannerman and this dreadful situation?" The side conversation between Kathleen, Marian, and Taylor came to a halt. Marian fixed her remarkably green eyes on the situation.

"I can't believe I forgot to tell you! I told him. The whole sordid story! He thought it was all hilarious, at first. Once I told him all about the restraining order and how it was affecting my spending time with Tiziana and Ted, he was supportive and really kind."

"Well, shite! There goes my hope of him leaving you for me. I thought once he found out you were stalking Des Bannerman, he'd be done with you!" Marian interjected.

"He's perfect for you. He knows you had a crush on Des Bannerman, and he's still willing to take you seriously," Kathleen chimed in.

Once the gory details of the conversation had been covered, it was unanimously decided that: 1) Des Bannerman was a prick of gigantic proportion; 2) the girls needed another round of drinks; 3) Liam was a god personified, because who else could be that good looking and kind at once?; and 4) to hell with the gigantic prick, I should go to Saint-Tropez!

"Well, fortunately for me and Tiziana, that's out of the question. I'll have just arrived in the U.K., and I'll have too much to do. I have a gorgeous boyfriend waiting to take me out on the town, I have my new work group to sort out, and, most importantly, Tiziana's nuptials should be devoid of negative drama. I'm not going!"

Volleys of cowardice and booing were directed at me.

Fortunately, the waiter arrived just in time to take the drink orders, and conversation returned to the subject of finding a man for Marian. "How about your Marcus, Taylor? Call him up and have him join us!" Kathleen suggested.

Before answering, Taylor candidly glanced at Marian's dress and then her own. "Oh, no! Marcus couldn't handle all of you. He's a gentle soul and would be horribly scarred for the rest of his life." She laughed.

A few cocktails later, we ventured forth and arrived at the Bryant Park Hotel to have dinner at Koi. While most of us had looked forward to sushi, Marian was not having any part of it. "How can a restaurant that's so elegantly appointed, so serene, so refined, serve raw, cold fish?" Marian complained.

"Elegantly appointed?" Hillary scoffed. "I didn't even know you knew those words could be combined!"

"Yikes," Taylor whispered under her breath to me. "Is this okay, or has all the imbibing turned them nasty?"

Waving off Taylor's concern, I said, "Oh, they're fine. This is normal for them."

Sure enough, the evening passed without a hitch, and Hillary even managed to convince Marian to try a bite of fresh water eel by telling her it was egg. I hastily handed over the bottle of sake once Marian found out the truth.

# Chapter Twelve

**TWO WEEKS LATER**, I was settling into a business class seat aboard a British Airways flight when a long sigh escaped from me. The months of meetings, planning, and interviewing were finally at an end. In six short hours, I'd be stepping onto British soil, and the second half of the project would begin. Another sigh followed.

In between having spent the last weekend with my family and then packing, there hadn't been any real time to chat with Liam.

"Are you okay?" Taylor asked. Faith Clarkson had decided to send Taylor to London for a few months to help out with the settling in. I was glad there would be a friendly face at work.

"I'm fine. Just looking forward to all this being over. It's been constant stress for the last seven months, and I could do with a little bit of normal," was my exhausted answer.

Chewing on ice, Taylor commiserated, "You and me both. My mother has been driving me crazy. A little time away from her doesn't hurt my feelings. You have no idea what it's like to be her daughter." She took a deep gulp from the cocktail glass that the flight attendant had placed in her hand.

I drank down the Crown Royal and ginger ale I had requested upon boarding the plane. Before meeting Liam I had never had it, but it provided the double benefit of relieving stress and reminding me of the taste of him. "No, that's not something that I could imagine! If I were you, I would have taken a position at the London branch. I know you love New York, and Marcus is there, but I just think it would be really good for you to do your own thing and not worry about the specter of your mother."

"Well, it isn't too late. My plan is to discreetly see where the holes are in the plan and see if anything interests me. Marcus and I talked about it, and he knows it would be better for me to get out from under my mother's thumb."

I felt my jaw drop. "You never mentioned any of this. I would love it! Don't worry, if you want to stay, we'll find a way to make it happen. Someone will know of a job Marcus can't refuse."

The flight attendant had returned to take the empty glasses along with our dinner orders. For the next few hours, conversation turned to less pressing matters. Stabbing a fork into her salad, Taylor said, "It's really nice of Hillary to let me stay with her as well. Are you sure she has enough room?"

In between bites of slightly rubbery chicken cordon bleu, I explained, "She comes off a bit stuffy, but she's great fun. You just have to get used to her dry sense of humor. She has enough room for you, me, herself, and a couple dozen other people, which will come in handy when Marcus and Liam come to visit."

Our conversation strayed through myriad topics, and, after a massive yawn, I settled down for a couple hours of sleep.

"Great idea. We don't want you looking too worn out when you step off the plane," Taylor teased.

In what seemed like a moment, the flight attendant was gently waking us from our nap. We peeled the eye masks back, sat up, and used the warm face cloths offered to us. As soon as it was possible, I dashed to the tiny bathroom facility to reapply my makeup, brush my teeth, and regain control of my hair. After a few attempts to confine the copious tresses in a professional-looking chignon, I slid the final hair clip into place.

Upon returning to my chair, I noticed that the flight attendant had tidied everything up.

Taylor, who was fussing with her carry-on, asked, "Are you ready?"

"Abso-bleedin'-lutely!" I squeaked in excitement. Moments later, the wheels touched down on the tarmac.

Butterflies were swarming in my midsection, and I could feel the beads of perspiration just waiting to ooze out of my pores. "Don't be ridiculous, it's all going to be fine. He loves you!" I said to myself, as giddy and nervous as a schoolgirl.

Like sheep, we made our way through customs and baggage claim, finally heading for the doors that separated the International Flight Lounge from the rest of the airport. Taking a deep breath and tugging down my pale blue suit jacket, I let out a deep breath and said, "Here we go."

No sooner had we pushed the door open than Liam strode up to us with confidence. He politely greeted Taylor with a peck to the check and then said, "Excuse me."

Wrapping me in his arms, he kissed me thoroughly and said, "My god, you're beautiful." He took my face in his hands, holding me close for another long moment, and then turned his attention to us both. "Welcome to London, ladies." My butterflies flitted away.

Once stowed safely in a taxi, Liam gave the driver Hillary's address. While he was talking to the cabbie, Taylor quietly said, "Was the stress worth it?"

I replied through the enormous grin on my face, "Abso-bleedin'-lutely!"

*   *   *

At last, the cabbie pulled up in front of Hillary's house in Chelsea. It was distinctly Victorian architecture: large, square, and symmetrical, with clean lines. "Even her house matches her," Taylor said after a quick glance out the window. Liam paid the cabbie while we got out. No sooner had we put our fashionably-clad feet on the sidewalk than the front door opened. Hillary, dressed in a tailored white skirt and blouse, offered warm, welcoming hugs.

Once Liam had divested the cab's trunk of our luggage, he stretched out his hand to Hillary. "You must be Hillary. I'm very pleased to meet you."

Hillary gave him a heartfelt smile, squeezed his hand firmly, and replied, "You, as well." Looking at Charlotte and Taylor, she said, "I'm thrilled to have the company. I hope the chintz doesn't put you off." The last bit was tacked on in an unusually self-deprecating way. Hillary appeared to be lightening up.

The cabbie and Liam struggled to get the luggage into the house while we quietly gossiped about Liam. "Marian is going to wet herself when she meets him. He's absolutely lovely! I'm not one to comment, but Charlotte, I just have to say, have you looked at his arse?" That comment coming from Hillary left us all shaking in hysterics.

"It's a thing of beauty, isn't it?" I agreed as we appreciated it from a distance. Feeling us staring at him, Liam turned around to find the three of us suddenly discussing the surrounding architecture.

Once safely inside Hillary's house, we were given the tour, received room assignments, and then took our beverages of choice to sit outside in the back garden. It was the end of July and a perfect summer day. Blue sky, green grass, and flowers stretched around the garden border. We talked about the flight, the last few weeks in New York, and the upcoming months when we'd be setting up the new London office.

After lazing around there for a good, long while, Hillary suggested lunch. "There's a terrific place on Brompton Road called Aubaine. Lovely French food, pastries to die for."

"I'm in!" Taylor announced. She had a passion for pastries.

Not long after, we stood in front of the restaurant, admiring its décor through large glass windows that stretched along the street front. The interior exuded an elegant balance between rustic and contemporary. The heavenly scent of bread wafted out into the summer air, and my stomach began to make unbelievable noises.

"Quick, we'd better get food into her before she's useless to me later," Liam announced. Hillary's eyebrows shot heavenwards, and Taylor giggled.

We roamed in front of the boulangerie, admiring the baguettes and pastries. After waiting fifteen minutes for a table, all four of us were climbing the walls, made ravenous by the sights and smells. By the time we were finally seated and handed menus, we were in a state of desperation. "My god, does it get any better than this?" Taylor gasped. "This is what England is supposed to be like. I can't tell you how excited I am!" I decided it was a combination of starvation and freedom from her mother that made Taylor seem nutty. Liam looked at me questioningly. I shrugged my shoulders and gave him a "roll with it" look.

We all studied the menu with great care. Unable to take it anymore, I slapped down the menu and gnawed on a breadstick from the basket that had recently been placed on the table. I moaned and groaned with each bite.

Taylor peered at me from over her menu. "What are you doing? If you don't quit making those sounds, we're going to get thrown out."

Liam leaned over and growled into my ear, "If you keep eating that breadstick like that, I'm going to be forced to throw your skirt up over your head right here. Show a little mercy! Eat your food, and think of a reasonable excuse for us to go our separate ways. As charming as Hillary and Taylor are, I want you, alone!"

The meal was dutifully ordered and truly appreciated. Due to hunger and the lunchtime crowd, lingering wasn't really an option. Liam paid for lunch, and we thanked him profusely for having rescued us several times that day. As we arrived back at the house in Chelsea, Hillary and Taylor solved my problem.

"I'm sorry to run off on you so soon, but I have a few things I really must take care of this afternoon," Hillary announced as we passed through the front door of the house. "You won't mind, though. I'm sure you're knackered. A lovely nap will do you wonders."

"That sounds wonderful," Taylor announced.

A few minutes later, Hillary was out the door, and Taylor was about to head up the stairs to her room. She said over her ascending shoulder, "Whatever you do, make sure you're here for dinner. I like Hillary, but I don't want to be left alone with her on my first night." Liam and I made small talk until we heard her bedroom door shut.

Liam grabbed my hand and started to drag me toward the front door. "Where are we going?" I asked.

"Somewhere that, when I make you scream, no one will come bursting through the door!" Happily, I followed him into the afternoon sunshine.

*   *   *

The bleating of the alarm clock woke me from a deep and dreamless sleep, and, through the open curtain, I could see that the sun was beginning to drop toward the horizon. My brain was muddled. Struggling to put an end to the noise, I rolled over to find the clock, but instead looked into deep green eyes. Liam reached over me to turn off the alarm.

"Hey!" I whispered.

"Hey, yourself. Do you feel better?" Liam's voice was soft and velvety.

"I feel absolutely perfect, just a little tired." I tried to smother a yawn. "What time is it?"

"It's 6:00. We have enough time to have a shower and get back to Hillary's. That is, if that's what you want to do." Liam pushed my hair off my shoulder and onto the pillow.

"It isn't really what I *want* to do. I want to stay under the blankets, order room service, and go back to sleep. Unfortunately, I promised Taylor I wouldn't leave her alone with Hillary tonight. But don't worry, things will be more settled soon, and then I can come and go as I please," I explained between kisses.

"I hope we don't see the people who are in the next room. These walls are paper thin. I wasn't really expecting that much screaming. You've lived up to the reputation of Americans being loud!"

Blushing red as a beet, I pressed my face against his chest and said, "It's either move to a hotel with thicker walls or don't do that thing with your tongue. I can't be held responsible for my behavior under those conditions."

Pulling me even closer, Liam nibbled my ears. "Well, then, I guess I'll be looking for a different hotel tomorrow."

Groaning and pushing gently against his chest, I said, "Okay, you're going to have to quit that for now, or else Taylor will be pissed because we'll be very late. Shower with me?"

"Absolutely. I never miss an opportunity to lather up breasts!" Liam swung his legs over the edge of the bed and, moving toward the bathroom, gave me a full view of his backside. Looking at it, I knew it was a backside I would never grow tired of admiring.

# Chapter Thirteen

**THE FIRST WEEK** at Faith Clarkson International's London offices was a hectic one. The managing director was relying heavily on the team from Faith Clarkson New York.

Taylor and I came and went at odd hours of the day, rarely seeing Hillary. Working for the Institute of Philanthropy, Hillary kept odd hours herself. We made a habit of having a nightcap at the end of the day, before stumbling to our respective bedrooms.

After staying in London for two days, Liam returned to Ireland with the promise of coming back for the weekend. In the end, it looked as if it would be a working weekend for me.

Sitting in the back garden on a teak chaise, watching the sunset, I said, "I just want to do nothing. I've been chasing my tail for months. What was I thinking? I'm going to have to call Liam and let him know." I spoke into my glass, sipping the remnants of the sangria Hillary had made.

"Another?" Hillary asked, reaching for the pitcher of ruby red liquid and citrus slices.

"Thanks, but no. I'd better call Liam before it gets much later." I felt like a six-year-old who'd been denied her favorite toy. "Depending on what he says, I might have another when I come back!" I called out to her as I went into the house to use the phone.

The sitting room looked like the cover of the British arm of *Homes and Garden*. Once there, I cozied myself up in a chair, tucked my feet underneath me, and dialed Liam's phone number with dread.

"Hello! My god, am I looking forward to the weekend. What's the plan for shedding ourselves of your roommates and our clothes?" Liam asked.

After a lengthy conversation, mostly comprised of me whining about work, we decided that Liam would still come for the weekend but bring his younger brother, Michael. The two Molloys would find entertainment during the day and then, on Saturday night, we would all go out.

As we were hanging up, I daringly said, "I've been discreetly researching hotels known for soundproofed rooms."

Liam chuckled. "Look for one that comes equipped with toys, as well."

My confidence fled me. Shocked, I was stumped for what to say so I went with, "Oh, I forgot. Marcus will be here this weekend. Taylor told me this afternoon. It will be fun."

Certain that I had just personified the uptight-American stereotype, my guess was confirmed when I heard Liam laughing on the other end, "Are you suggesting a foursome?" I sat in dead silence, not knowing what to say.

His deep voice now soothing, Liam said, "We'll work on your phone sex skills. We can practice this weekend." At my continued silence he added, "I love you, truly, madly, deeply, you silly woman."

"I love you, too," I said before quickly hanging up. My cheeks flamed in mortification.

Walking to the back garden, I saw that Taylor had made it home. "A glass for me as well, please," I said as Hillary poured her a sangria. Taylor looked dead on her feet. "How was the rest of your day?"

"Work, work, and more work. I can't believe how much work. My mother had damned well better give us all excellent bonuses, pay raises, extended vacations, and a thank-you gift. I'm exhausted, and it's only day number four." Happy to sit back and listen to Taylor whine, Hillary and I sipped our drinks. "Well, enough of that, what have you been doing all day, Hillary? Saving the world from starvation?" Taylor asked, not unkindly.

Hillary, who had been quietly listening and staring off into the night sky, turned her head and remarked, "Oh, nothing so noble today. Just a little shopping trip and travel planning."

"Where are you going?" Taylor asked.

Sitting perfectly still, my breath caught in my throat, and my quickly-recovered peace evaporated in the evening air. Taylor cast a quick glance in my direction as she put two and two together. "Charlotte, I'm so sorry! I completely forgot. Would you like to talk about it?"

"I certainly think we should," Hillary interjected. "I think you should be going to the tanning salon and buying a ticket to Saint-Tropez.

Charlotte, this is all so ridiculous. Tiziana is terribly disappointed. You really must go."

"First of all, in case you haven't noticed, I'm so swamped with work I couldn't imagine going, even without the other issue. Secondly, the other issue will be there, and I don't wish to deal with *it*. So, no, I'm not going."

Taylor looked anxiously at both of us, not sure what to say.

"Charlotte, Tiziana is getting married only once. It isn't just a trip to the beach. This means the world to her. You know Tiziana better than all of us. How could you possibly put five hundred feet first? We'll help you. It won't be perfectly simple, but it won't be the challenge you think. If you'd be willing," Hillary added.

Changing the subject, I said, "So, it turns out that Liam is coming this weekend after all, and he'd like to bring his younger brother Michael with him. Are you available to go out on the town with us on Saturday night?"

"Oh, and Marcus will be here, too. He and I will stay at a hotel," Taylor offered.

"We have plenty of room. No one needs to stay at a hotel. It might be snug around the breakfast table, but I'm all for it," Hillary replied enthusiastically, letting the subject be changed.

The rest of the evening was pleasantly spent planning the weekend's events. Eventually, Hillary announced she was off to bed. "I want to look my best!" she declared as she left us to ourselves.

"I'm sure not a single hair on her head has ever been out of place," Taylor remarked when she was out of hearing range.

"Well, let's see if Michael can muss it up," I giggled, all thoughts of Saint-Tropez having drifted from my mind.

\*　\*　\*

Friday morning found me sorting through a mountain of paper. Pressing the heels of my hands to my eyes, I contemplated for the thousandth time if taking this job had been the craziest thing I'd ever done. While making a mental pro and con list, the telephone began to ring—the European version: *ring, ring,* pause, *ring, ring,* pause. "Where the hell is what's-her-name?" I muttered, trying to find the phone among the stacks of paper.

"Hello? Charlotte Young's office," I finally answered after five rings, rubbing my knee that had banged into the drawer.

"Charlotte, it's me. Tiziana!"

Hearing her familiar voice brought a smile to my face. Relaxing back into my chair, I said, "Tiziana, how are you? Thanks so much for calling. I'm sorry! I've been so busy, I haven't had a chance."

"Well, you can make it up to me. We're flying into London for the weekend. I'm dying to see you, so I told Ted that we must come. While I flatter myself that he's indulging me, I think he's desperate to get away from my mother."

"Oh, Tiziana. Fabulous! You can meet Liam. He's coming for the weekend. This is perfect. What a great weekend. We're going to have a full house. Liam's bringing his brother Michael, and Taylor's boyfriend Marcus will be here as well."

"Perhaps we can all meet at the Waldorf Hilton for cocktails? There's a nice cocktail bar."

"That sounds decadent and fabulous. Let me check in with Taylor and Hillary, and I'll give you a call. Where are you staying?"

"Call me on my cell. Ted is having his house renovated before he puts it on the market. It's in Chelsea. Not too far from Hillary's, actually." Moments later, we were buried in conversation regarding wedding plans. A voice on her end returned us to our current life, beckoning us back to reality.

After leaving messages for Hillary, Taylor, and Liam, there was no choice but to return to the mountain of work. At least I was a much happier person.

* * *

"Happy" was insufficient to describe my emotions when Liam walked across the airport terminal on Friday at 4:30. He dropped his bag at his feet and swept me up in his arms, giving me a spine-tingling kiss. "I'll never get tired of kissing you," I breathed into his mouth. "You're gorgeous!"

"Ahem!" The sound came from not too far away. I spun around on my magenta stiletto heels to see an amazingly attractive man who looked quite a bit like Liam, wearing a grin.

"You must be Michael. I'm so happy to meet you… and embarrassed." A rosy blush bloomed from my neck and reached the tips of my ears.

"I am. No need to be. You must be Tiziana. I'm happy to meet the lady who has captured my brother's attention. Lovely to meet you," Michael said while giving me a brief but warm hug.

Confusion must have swept across my face, because Liam jumped to the rescue. "Very funny, Michael! Charlotte knows not to believe a word you say. And what's with the interruption? The number of times I've had to stand around whilst Michael here has dallied with the ladies is uncountable," Liam bantered. He picked up the bag at his feet, and the three of us trooped out of the airport to a cabbie waiting patiently in line.

"Tiziana, huh?" I asked Liam quietly.

"You can't expect me not to repeat your description of her! Especially when we're about to meet her. She sounds like someone you have to be prepared for," Liam teased.

"I expect so," I said softly.

Once we were sitting inside the cab, Michael asked, "Are you sure Hillary has enough room? I really don't mind holing up somewhere. I have a friend or two I can go to."

"Hillary is delighted to have you come to stay. Actually, this is turning out to be quite the weekend. Did you get my message?" The last part was intended for Liam.

"I did. I told Michael about the Waldorf. We've each packed a clean shirt, and we'll be on our best behavior, so we won't shame you," Liam replied, continuing to tease me.

"I've even brought some clean socks as well," Michael added. The playful banter continued all the way to Chelsea.

Down the street from Hillary's house, Michael pointed to a hoard of people on the sidewalk. "Look at that. I wonder what it's all about." We pressed our faces against the window while the cabbie slowly maneuvered around the crowd. "Jaysus, it's Des Bannerman and Brynn Roberts coming out of that house!"

The cabbie suddenly took on the air of a tour guide, telling Michael, "Des Bannerman lives in Chelsea, though I've been told he owns seven or eight houses in the area."

My brain couldn't take it all in, and I felt the color drain from my face as the cabbie prattled on about Des and Brynn. Liam whispered something in my ear, but my brain was still busy absorbing that I was living a few doors down from the bane of my existence.

Somehow, we made it out of the cab and through introductions. I had shown Michael to a bedroom off the sitting room before giving in and collapsing onto the chair in the dining room, pressing my hands to my eyes and moaning.

"What's wrong? What happened?" Hillary asked Liam in alarm. "You didn't do anything, did you?"

"No. Absolutely not! Charlotte just found out that Des Bannerman lives in the same part of London as you," Liam replied, defending himself.

"Oh, dear, Charlotte." She immediately calmed down and then offered the British cure-all. "Would you like a cup of tea?"

"No! I'd like a glass of wine. Make it large and cold." I rubbed my temples, dug my fingers into my hair, and let my eyes scurry around the room. I could sense Liam staring at me, wondering what he ought to say. Hillary quickly returned with a glass of Chardonnay for me and a beer for him. I gulped it down and then began to cross-examine Hillary while pacing the floor, hoping for answers before Michael appeared.

"Did you know that Des Bannerman lived in Chelsea? Of course you did, but why didn't you tell me? Unbelievable!"

In a calm voice, Hillary commanded, "Charlotte, calm down! Yes, I did know that Des Bannerman lives in Chelsea. Chelsea is big enough for the two of you. I've lived here all my life and have only seen him a handful of times. Secondly, you can't continue to run and hide like you've done something wrong. You're always saying that you want to know what happened. Well, maybe now is your chance. If you meet him on the street, you can ask, even if you have to shout from five hundred feet away. I hear Michael coming. Liam, perhaps now would be a good time to take Charlotte upstairs so she can freshen up. I'll look after Michael. Take your time." She finished with a smile.

Upstairs in my room, we sat side by side on the bed, Liam's eyes reflecting his concern. Taking my hands in his, he said, "Charlotte, Hillary's right. You were bound to meet at some point. Isn't it time to just let it go? Face the bastard, do something, but don't let him ruin a beautiful weekend or another day of your life."

Letting out a deep, cleansing breath, I said, "I'm fine, not great, but fine. I think it was mostly the surprise. How is it you go from never laying eyes on someone to their just popping up unexpectedly in your life?"

Liam gently pushed stray hairs back from my face, and then pulled me to him. After blowing out a ragged breath, he gently kissed my dewy eyes, and drew away, saying, "I don't know what to say other than I believe that, when the moment arrives, you'll handle it. Maybe not perfectly, but at least it will all be over."

Pushing myself to my feet, I said, "I'm going to go wash my face, fix my makeup, and quit thinking about the fucker. You can unpack or go rescue Michael." With resolve and my shoulders back, I left the bedroom to restore my makeup and inner calm.

Liam called, "That's my girl." That put a smile on my face.

Not too much later, we joined the party. "Great to see you," Marcus said to Liam after finishing off a bite-sized something or other.

"I see you've met my little brother Michael," Liam remarked, as he bent down to give Taylor a kiss hello.

In a quiet voice, Taylor said, "Well done! I would never have believed it possible, but I think Hillary is all atwitter!"

Stealing a quick glance over his shoulder, we saw Hillary dabbing imaginary food from her chin and Michael brushing his finger across Hillary's jawline in friendly assistance. Hillary looked ready to swoon.

Liam chuckled and replied softly, "Just wait! She might even warm up to normal body temperature by the time the evening's over." We laughed at the possibilities, and when Hillary looked up to see the four of us gazing at her, she blushed.

"May miracles never cease," I whispered.

\* \* \*

The following morning, we ladies whined as the men pushed our professionally-clad bottoms out the door and into the waiting cab.

"Have a nice day!" Marcus and Liam called playfully, still unshaved and motley-looking.

By that evening, Taylor and I were worn out and in desperate need of being prompted to leave the house for a night on the town. The men didn't look too much better; they seemed to have been dragged backwards through a hedge.

"*Phew*, go sit over there! Where have you been?" Taylor asked Marcus when he leaned over to give her a kiss.

"I've been doing manly men stuff! I've been thrashed to the ground, had my ear bitten, and been chased to the point of exhaustion," he explained.

"Michael has a few friends who live in London, so we met up with them for a game of football, *er*, soccer." Wrinkling my nose at his potent odor, I couldn't resist the kiss Liam gave me after he explained.

Rubbing his unshaven cheek with my hand and looking into his beautiful green eyes, I felt more enthusiastic about the evening. It slid through my mind that, after a few more months, we could start thinking beyond a few days at a time, and that thought was exhilarating.

Hillary, prepared as always, walked into the sitting room with a tray holding a variety of beverages and bowls of snacks. Wearing the hand-painted dress she had worn to a charity event that afternoon, she was the image of sophistication and wealth. All eyes followed her as she circulated the room, ending up in front of Michael. "Would you like a glass of beer?"

Michael took it appreciatively and remarked, "Hillary, I don't think I've ever had such a lovely serving wench in all my life." I held my breath, Taylor gasped, and the men quietly chuckled. We all waited to see how she would respond.

"I'll be right back with refills," was all she said, as she left the room with a rosy hue to her skin and a smile on her face.

"Careful there, brother," Liam warned playfully. "Too many more of those comments and you'll have us all sleeping on the pavement. Being that we're in Chelsea, I can't see the neighbors putting up with that for very long."

"She handled that rather well, didn't she? Maybe you lot don't know her as well as you think," Michael responded, his voice indicating he was as surprised as the rest of us.

"Trust me, I know her well, very well," I said loudly enough for everyone. "And I've never seen her let anyone get away with a comment like that." For Liam's ears only, I said, "I sure hope this doesn't end ugly."

Hillary returned with more liquid refreshment, and the group happily chattered away. Eventually, the late afternoon party gave way to the evening's preparations.

"It's a shame we aren't at a hotel," Liam complained when we returned to the room.

"Why's that?" I asked, a little worried, surveying my wardrobe for a suitable dress for the Waldorf Hilton.

Liam lifted a handful of hair so that he could gently nip at my shoulder. "Because I'd love to take a long, hot bath with you and do absolutely nothing."

Shivers ran through my body. I turned to wrap my arms around his shoulders. "That does sound fabulous. Next weekend, we'll find a hotel to hide away in." I rubbed against him suggestively.

"Not next weekend, I'm afraid," Liam answered and withdrew my arms from around him. He looked serious.

"Why? What's happening next weekend?" I asked nervously.

Liam began to dig through his bag for his clothes and his bathroom kit. He was clearly trying to avoid looking at me. My stomach flopped while I quietly waited for his answer. Finally looking up, he said nervously, "Well, my mother and father would like to meet you. So I thought you could come to Dublin next weekend."

"Oh!" I distracted myself by preparing for the evening while I pondered the enormity of this. Liam seemed happy to follow suit.

Because there were so many of us, we took two cabs to the Waldorf. Taylor and Marcus went off by themselves, leaving the rest of us to cozy up in the back of the other. Hillary pointed out the sights of London as we drove past St. James's Park, Buckingham Palace, and Pall Mall. "Covent Gardens isn't too far from the Waldorf, if we feel like heading over there later," Hillary explained, continuing on. She was clearly nervous at being in such close proximity to Michael.

While Hillary described the history of the Waldorf, Liam quietly said, "She does realize we've all been to London before, doesn't she?"

"I think she's just nervous. I have to say, I really didn't expect Michael to make such an impact on her. Do you think he's interested or just having fun?"

"I really don't know. Michael hasn't said anything, but then again, he wouldn't. Even though we've evolved to the point where we can send our women off to work, we don't meet for tea and biscuits and share our feelings with each other," he gently teased.

"I just hope she doesn't get hopeful without any reason to. I'm sure Michael is a nice guy and will be a perfect gentleman."

My attention was diverted when Michael started to talk about a transvestite club near Covent Gardens that he had stumbled upon. Not sure what Hillary's response would be, I was thrilled to see the Waldorf. "Look, there's the hotel. I'm so excited to see Tiziana! It seems like forever since we were in Chamonix together."

The cabbie pulled up in front of the hotel; Taylor and Marcus were waiting for us. Together we ventured inside, Hillary leading the way to the Homage Bar. The contemporary décor was in sharp contrast to the exterior façade. Tiziana and Ted weren't there yet, so we gathered at a table away from the bar.

The drinks were just being delivered when Marcus and Michael said in unison, "Wow!" Looking up to see what they were staring at, we followed their gaze to the beautiful woman entering the room.

"Tiziana!" I shrieked, jumping up to greet her.

"Wow," said Liam, rising to his feet.

Tiziana rushed over. Her cleavage seemed to nearly spill out of her low-cut dress. "Bella, look how beautiful you are! You look so happy." She greeted me with kisses. "You remember Ted!" she added, once she released me from her embrace.

"Of course. How are you?" I replied more sedately, giving Ted a brotherly hug. Liam had approached us and was immediately introduced.

"Now I can see the reason for Charlotte's smile. I'm so happy to meet you!" Tiziana purred to Liam, giving him hugs and kisses, too.

Tiziana then introduced Ted to Liam. "You're a very lucky man. Congratulations on your wedding," Liam replied, shaking hands with Ted.

"Don't I know it? Thanks!" he said with a huge smile and a pat on Liam's back.

As they walked back to the group, Liam teased Charlotte, "You might have mentioned that Ted, was *the* Ted Blackwell."

"Does that change anything?"

Liam didn't want to admit that it did, so he shook his head no, letting the subject drop.

At the table, introductions were made all around. Michael and Marcus were clearly having a hard time keeping their train of thought. They seemed to be mesmerized by Tiziana's shimmering silver gown.

"Don't worry! You'll recover," Ted told them quietly, with a snigger. Embarrassed at having been caught, once the two men refocused on the group, the penny dropped. Almost simultaneously, both men suddenly recognizing Ted for who he was, an international business mogul responsible for generating thousands of jobs worldwide. The men at the table exchanged stunned looks, and then decided to play it cool.

Ted called the waiter over and ordered champagne for everyone. There was much ceremony around the delivery of the sterling silver ice buckets and chilled champagne. The bottles were expertly opened, glasses were filled, and Ted rose to make a toast. "To my gorgeous Tiziana and her beautiful friends. Oh, and of course to the men, as well! We look forward to many such occasions." We all called our thanks and raised our glasses in tribute before letting the bubbly fluid trickle down our throats.

The champagne continued to flow freely as the women in the group happily entertained the men with tales from when we first met through to our encounter with Ted at the casino. I was so thrilled to be there, in the moment, that even thoughts of Des Bannerman couldn't take the smile from my face.

Ted took over. "I'm sure you can appreciate the situation. I'd gone to Chamonix to visit an old friend and play cards. We were well into our third round of drinks and had lost several hands of blackjack when suddenly two delightful women accosted us. Charlotte here passed herself off as an expert at the game, giving us all kinds of advice. I was so dazzled by Tiziana that I couldn't focus. In the end, I couldn't tell you if Charlotte's advice was any good. All I know is that I lost a hell of a lot of money that night." Everyone laughed, most wondering what a hell of a lot of money was to him.

"I didn't know you were an expert at blackjack," Liam said to me, drawing the group's attention.

"I read *Blackjack for Dummies* when I found out there was a casino in Chamonix. You'll notice that it was Ted who lost his money. I never lost a dollar of mine." I smirked.

Soon after, I made my excuses and went in search of the restrooms. I was soon joined by a few others, and we chatted while unnecessarily fussing and primping. Upon returning, I saw that Liam and Ted were standing apart from Michael and Marcus, looking somewhat serious. Hoping nothing had happened, I walked over to them and said, "What are you two discussing, a trip to Monaco? I can lend you my book."

Ted quickly replied with a smile, "No, no! I wish, but no. We were just talking. Tiziana made me promise that I would make sure Liam was on the up and up and not another gigolo trying to spend your millions."

"Ah, well, now he knows I have millions. I'd been keeping that from him. Don't let any more of my secrets out of the bag." I laughed, sliding an arm around Liam's waist and relaxing. All seemed well.

Just then, Tiziana and Hillary walked over, bags and wraps in hand. "What's next? Where are we off to now?"

"Ted and I booked a table at Scott's, if that sounds appealing. If not, we can go elsewhere. Have you been there? They serve the most delicious food. There's an oyster bar, and I know how much you love oysters!" Tiziana replied, teasing me.

"Well, if there are oysters involved, I'm all for it," Liam replied with a leering grin.

Marcus called from just a few feet away, "Oysters? Did I hear someone mention oysters? If there's a saddle involved, I'm definitely in."

Ted and Tiziana exchanged a confused look while Taylor and I laughed. "Never mind," I said to everyone else. "It isn't worth explaining."

Tiziana, Liam and I waited for Ted in front the restaurant, the others safely stowed in a cab and heading toward Scott's. When Ted pulled up, Liam let out a whistle and remarked, "Wow, I don't think I've ever been in one of these!"

"Would you like to drive?" Ted offered, keys dangling from his hand.

"Ah, I don't think I would know how," Liam said, laughing and waving off the keys.

The four of us climbed into his 1938 Morgan 4/4. "Isn't it lovely? To be so free, on a summer evening, the air warm?" Tiziana hummed over her shoulder, her fingers stretching toward the evening's stars.

Liam asked just loud enough to be heard over the roar of the engine, "Does she always talk like that?"

"Do you mean the purring or the drama?" I asked quietly, nuzzling his neck to muffle my voice.

"Bella, you see! The summer night just begs for romance," Tiziana trilled again, seeing our heads together. She laid her head back and gazed at the night sky. "So lovely."

"I have my answer about the drama and the purr!" Liam chuckled. "She is unique."

"Yes, she is." I leaned forward to give Tiziana a kiss on the back of her head and heard her throaty laughter.

Liam and I realized that Scott's was in Chelsea when we arrived just a block away from Hillary's house. Ted dropped us off at the restaurant and set out to find a parking spot with Liam's help. We joined the rest of the group standing under the canopy.

Michael held the door open for us all to enter. Tiziana made her way to the elegantly dressed man who was charged with the responsibility of seating guests.

"Hello! Is the private room available tonight?" she asked.

Eyeing her décolletage discreetly, he gulped and replied, "I'm afraid not this evening, madame. I apologize for the inconvenience. We're booked quite full. I would be happy to call Bam-Bou or Le Caprice and inquire if there is seating available." He was truly an accommodating fellow.

"Not to worry, darling. We have a reservation. I think I see our tables now." Tiziana pointed to a large empty space at the back of the room.

"Oh, are you Mr. Blackwell's party?" He seemed relieved to be able to seat our group.

"Yes, we are," Tiziana confirmed with a dazzling smile.

Taylor elbowed Marcus and Michael. "Would you please put your tongues back in your mouths? On behalf of all mere mortal women, we acknowledge she's beautiful. But if you guys keep this up, those of you who are mere mortal men won't be getting laid tonight!" Tongues back in their mouths, once again looking contrite, Marcus and Michael took up the rear as the maître d' lead us to our tables.

We didn't have to wait too long until Liam and Ted joined us. It turned out that they had parked the car at Hillary's and walked back to the restaurant. "Lovely night. A shame not to enjoy a few more moments of fresh air," Ted remarked.

Just then, the maître d' who had greeted us at the door approached the table. "Sir, may we begin?"

"Charlotte, since you're unable to join us in Saint-Tropez, I thought we would bring the party to you!" Ted explained. No sooner said than an extravagant tropical centerpiece was placed on the table; at the same time, a waiter appeared with a tray of spectacularly beautiful cocktails. After he had presented mine with a flourish, I asked the waiter about the pale pink concoction.

"A fresh hibiscus blossom is placed gently in the glass. Then a touch of syrup made from hibiscus flowers with a subtle rhubarb flavor is added. The glass is then filled with a perfectly chilled, delightfully dry sparkling wine picked by our hostess—an Italian prosecco." Tiziana, who had followed the waiter's explanation, earned an air kiss from me. Years earlier, Tiziana had introduced me to prosecco, and it had become a favorite. If on a menu, I ordered it.

The tables were soon cluttered with assorted dishes that were both beautiful and tasty. Halfway through the meal, Ted announced that the men were to pick up their drinks and plates and switch places with someone else.

A moment later, Ted set down beside me. "I'm indeed a lucky man, Charlotte. I have the pleasure of sitting next to the second loveliest woman in the room."

Dismissing his compliment, I said, "Ted, you're very kind. It's easy to feel beautiful in such a glamorous place." Our exchange paused momentarily for the waiters to clear away debris. I held on tightly to my cocktail, knowing without a doubt that I would need it.

"So, now an opportunity to get to know each other. Other than your blackjack skills, Tiziana tells me you have many talents."

I suddenly found myself suspicious. I searched my brain for something witty or intelligent to say. Glancing around the table quickly, my eyes found Liam, who was laughing at something Taylor and Marcus were debating. I was on my own. I glanced back at Ted and found him studying me. Grasping for something, I said, "Work! Right now there's an endless supply of work. That's where most of my talents are focused these days. I'm somewhat surprised that Taylor and I were able to get away tonight."

"I've heard Faith Clarkson can be a real ball-breaker." For Ted to know who Faith Clarkson was surprised me, quite frankly. I'd thought they were fish in very different ponds.

"Lucky for me, I don't have any balls," I stammered.

"I don't know. Tiziana tells me you can be quite tenacious," he said with a smile. I found myself wondering if he had a point to any of this and what the hell Tiziana's comment was supposed to mean.

Giving myself time to understand the much-too-subtle subplot to this conversation, I stuck with a familiar topic. "When I need to be, I suppose. The new office is coming together, thanks to all hands on deck."

There was a moment of prolonged silence while Ted assessed me. "So, coming to Saint-Tropez for a week on the boat is really out of the question then?"

Surprised, I said, "I want to come! Of course I do. However, Ms. Clarkson would be extremely unimpressed with me if I took any vacation before the winter holidays."

"I wouldn't dream of asking you to do less than you should. I just thought that, if other issues were preventing you, we could make it work." I was surprised by his comment.

Taking a deep breath and not knowing what else to say, I looked at him calmly. "You must have a big boat!"

"It's big enough," Ted said, nonchalant.

Game-playing time was over, if that was what we were doing. "I respect the fact that Des is your friend and best man." I paused briefly to take a deep breath and regain my slipping composure. "The main reason I'm not coming is work. But if it weren't, I don't see any way around the restraining order. Instead of asking me about this, I suggest you ask Des Bannerman. I am and always have been in the dark."

"It's as good a time as any to tell you that I've tried. Des doesn't want to talk about it with me. He doesn't want Tiziana and me caught in the middle." With that, a look of frustration crossed Ted's face. "Too late for that." He blew out a long breath. "I know you won't believe me, but he's a decent man."

"We'll have to agree to disagree on his decency. I don't want any more conflict, so I won't take any risks. Now, if you'll excuse me, I need to find the ladies." With all the poise I could muster, since my legs were rubbery due to nerves and several glasses of alcohol, I rose to my Lulu Guinness-shod feet and walked away from the table.

Shortly thereafter, I heard a faint knocking on the restroom door. Liam called, "Charlotte, are you in there?" Just as he was walking away, I stepped out.

"Hello, gorgeous," I said.

With a deep, throaty laugh, he wrapped his arms around my waist and drew me into him. "Darling, are you aware that you've just stepped out of the men's loo?" Drawing in a quick breath, I turned around to see the writing on the door. "Didn't you notice the difference?"

Blushing, I giggled, "No. I'm guessing I need to move on to water and coffee."

Liam kissed the top of my head, murmuring into my ear, "Not to be ungrateful, but can we get out of here soon? I'm glad to have had the chance to meet Tiziana and Ted and to see Marcus, but what I would really like now is some time alone with you."

"I think that would be fabulous. Why don't we go bow out as gracefully as possible?" I gave Liam's dimpled chin a quick kiss.

When we returned to the dining room, the group was deep in conversation. The men were having a lively discussion about Sunday's soccer match between two rival teams, while the girls were laughing hysterically about the evening that Ted and Tiziana's families finally met. I sat quietly in the circle of Liam's arms and downed several large glasses of water, feeling quite content.

Conversation soon turned to what was next on the agenda. Tiziana was yawning discreetly behind her hand, giving Ted the perfect opportunity to end their evening.

"I think we'll head home, too," Liam said.

Taylor, Marcus, Michael, and Hillary decided to venture out to find some late, late night entertainment.

Since Ted had parked the car at Hillary's, we walked home with them. Liam firmly wrapped an arm around me as I walked beside Tiziana. By the time we had arrived, plans had been made to meet up the next day.

Ted opened the car door for Tiziana. Before she climbed in, she embraced me and kissed my cheek. In my ear, she whispered, "He meant well, bella."

"It's okay," I whispered back.

After one last goodbye, Liam swooped me up into his arms and said, "Thank god! Any chance we'll have the house to ourselves all night?"

"I doubt it! On the other hand, everyone else will be too occupied to wonder what we're doing." I wriggled seductively against him and dropped kisses all over his neck.

"Where the bloody hell are the keys?" Liam asked as I fished them out of my purse, dropping them into his waiting hands. He soon shooed me up the stairs, him fast on my heels.

\*   \*   \*

I came out of the fog of sleep to the sound of a something soft hitting the wall and Hillary laughing uncontrollably. Night had given way to day, and sunlight was bouncing off the robin's-egg-blue walls of my boudoir.

Liam drew me to him and, while stroking a particularly sensitive part of my body, said, "Well, as long as everyone else is making a lot of noise, we might as well, too!"

Quite a while later, the group convened in the kitchen for toast, eggs, coffee, and aspirin. After leaving Scott's to take in some nightlife, it turned out that the four had enjoyed several more drinks at various clubs around London.

While I was buttering toast and trying to avoid looking at them, I said to Hillary, "I hope you don't mind, but I've invited Tiziana and Ted over for dinner and to watch the soccer game."

A giggle preceded her answer. "No, that's great! What fun. I'll pick up some things, shall I?" Hillary was the consummate hostess.

"Nope, I'll go. They won't be here until later, so there isn't a rush." I popped the toast into my mouth.

After breakfast and some tidying up, I announced, "I'm going to have a shower and then go to the grocery store." Dashing up the stairs for a moment's peace and quiet, I'd just managed to sort out the bedroom and my thoughts when Liam joined me.

"Do you think it's safe for me to take a shower with you?"

"Absolutely."

We were steaming and sudsing when I finally gave in and whispered, "Well, what's going on?"

Liam lathered my foot and calf before telling me, "He really likes her. He seems to think they're on the same page."

"What does that mean?" I persisted.

"Charlotte, ease up. They'll sort it out." Liam sounded somewhat gruff.

Leaning my head against the tile, I relaxed and muttered, "Oh, fine! I suppose they will. No offense to anyone, and even though I hoped for it, I never thought they would hook up so quickly."

As we were getting dressed, there was a sharp rap on the door. "Oiy! Hurry up in there!" Michael called.

"Well, if Michael's going to be around, it makes it easier to leave on the weekends," I pointed out.

\* \* \*

While walking to the shops, Liam asked me about my conversation with Ted. I gave a brief, lighthearted synopsis as I sorted through an array of salad vegetables. Liam watched and listened closely and then said in a slightly annoyed voice, "He asked me if I thought it would be a good idea to talk to you. I told him that you'd let him know if it was or wasn't. All he mentioned to me was that they'd like for us to come to Saint-Tropez, but I didn't have any idea he was going to talk to you last night."

"He didn't mean anything by it. They're getting married, and he wants her to be happy. You have to respect that," I said distractedly as I chose some cuts of steak. Having indicated my selections to the man behind the meat counter, I rose onto my toes and gave Liam a kiss. "I'm fine. Really!"

Each carrying bags in both hands, we meandered through the streets of Chelsea. It was a beautiful Sunday afternoon, and the population was out in full force. We stopped from time to time to give our hands a break and make up for not having had any time alone. After a particularly breath-catching kiss, Liam announced, "Next weekend, be prepared to spend the entire weekend in bed. There will be no one to interrupt me having my way with you."

"No one but your parents, that is!" I laughed.

"Oh, Christ! Will I ever get you all to myself? We haven't been alone in over five weeks," he complained.

"Well, I'm sorry that you feel deprived," I said with a note of confusion. If anyone had been going at it like bunnies, it was us.

Reading my mind, he said, "It isn't sex. It's just hanging out without other people. We don't even really know what it's like to just have a lie in, read the paper, and watch telly together." He kissed away my frown.

"I have to admit, I'm really looking forward to seeing your apartment and all the places familiar to you. I don't really have any idea what your world is really like."

I lost my breath when he said with complete candor, "Charlotte, *you're* my world. You know exactly what it looks like."

After carefully putting down my grocery bags, I declared myself by throwing both arms around him and kissing him fiercely on the lips. "I love you."

# Chapter Fourteen

**IT WAS A BEAST** of a mountain to climb, but soon people got down to the real business of Faith Clarkson International.

One evening, stumbling home earlier than any in previous weeks, I found Hillary and Taylor talking about Michael being a decent guy. He had called Hillary that afternoon to thank her for putting him up over the prior weekend. She reported that the rest of the conversation had been light and fun, but that not a word had been said about whether they'd see each other again.

"You should have asked him," Taylor said casually.

Hillary looked at her with one eyebrow raised. "Really? You think so? I've never asked a man out, and it isn't likely to happen. If it was just a weekend fling, I'd rather find out by never hearing from him again."

Taylor took another shot. "Doesn't that sound antiquated?"

"Perhaps. I'm fine with that."

Feeling more and more anxious about meeting Liam's parents on the coming weekend, I stayed out of the conversation. I didn't want to relay anything about Michael back to Hillary. Besides, I figured that my friends would make a big deal out of it and envisioned Hillary marching me to the shops with the sole purpose of finding a "meet the parents" outfit. Her idea of an appropriate outfit and mine were different, and I didn't need the additional hassle.

* * *

I was scheduled to fly out at 5:00 on Friday afternoon, so my fear that Faith Clarkson would call, requesting an end-of-week update, kept me at work later than usual on Thursday night. "Coward," I muttered to myself as I crept into the dark house, tiptoed up the stairs, and quietly packed a bag for the weekend. I would send Taylor and Hillary an email in the morning, taking the easy way out.

The next day, I was just about to leave for the airport when the phone rang. I heard Samantha in the outer office answer, "Faith Clarkson International, Charlotte Young's office. How may I help you?" I chewed my lip and quickly sorted through my bag for all the necessary documents and forms. Samantha put the call through. "Ms. Young, Mr. Molloy is on the line."

Immediately, I released my lip from its tortuous clamp and picked up the phone. "Liam, hello. I was just leaving. Is everything all right?"

"Everything is just fine. I was calling to make sure that meeting my parents hadn't frightened you off. My mother is planning a dinner for tomorrow. I thought I'd better warn you." He sounded a bit anxious.

"I'm still coming, don't worry. I'll see you in less than two hours. I gotta go!"

"Bye," I heard Liam say as the phone landed in its cradle.

Sure enough, two hours later, the Aer Lingus flight landed on Irish soil. During the flight, I grew quite nervous, and my stomach kept somersaulting. We had spent most of our relationship in my environment, and now it was time to see what Liam was like on his own turf. There were still plenty of things for us to learn about each other. What if we discovered something that changed everything? What if Liam's parents didn't like me? What if he had disgusting habits? Or what if *my* habits were disgusting?

"Okay, Charlotte, buck up! Don't go predicting doom. Everything has gone better than expected so far. Things are going to be just fine," I said to myself, discreetly glancing around to see if anyone sitting near me had overheard. Fortunately, the fellow who'd sat next to me was already getting his suitcase down from the overhead compartment.

Stepping off the plane into the airport, I was immediately struck by how warm it was. It was a gorgeous evening. I slipped off my jacket and unbuttoned one more button of my shirt, hoping to look a little more feminine and a little less like a bank officer. Since I had packed secretly the night before, I had been so worried about it being found out that I had forgotten to pack a summer dress in my carry-on bag. Instead of being all girly and smelling like summer flowers, I was wearing a suit and smelled like I needed a shower.

After leaving the arrival area and venturing into the airport, I looked for Liam. There was no sign of him but there was a news agent not too far from the gate. I went over to buy some gum and look at the souvenirs while I waited. Flipping through a book, I heard my name being called. I turned around and saw Liam jogging through the airport, head and shoulders above most people. The sight of him took my breath away. When he finally reached me, I was all atwitter.

After coming up for a breath from his kiss, he said, "Welcome to Ireland."

"Now, that's my kind of welcome," I replied, still standing on my tip-toes to get another kiss.

"Well, I have a much more personal welcome waiting for you back at my flat." He ran his hands up and down my back as he nibbled my neck. "God, you smell wonderful."

"You're desperate! I need a shower." I laughed.

"I am desperate! Let's get you home and get you naked. I have water and soap at your disposal." He took my bag in one hand and my hand in the other.

The prospect of a weekend alone with Liam filled me with buoyancy. All earlier feelings of doubt and concern were obliterated. Instead, with hands tightly clasped and the world our own, we walked out to the parking lot, where Liam steered me toward his car... a very flashy black sports car. It stopped me in my tracks.

After putting my bag in the trunk, he shut the trunk of the car and saw me standing there. "A bit much, isn't it?"

"Well, not if you like that sort of thing, no!" I tried to keep my voice neutral. "Maybe it's because I don't own a car and have no idea what I would buy."

"It isn't mine. I drive a horse and buggy, usually, but the horse went lame, and I didn't have time to buy a new one. We can go shopping for one tomorrow if you like." Liam grinned. I laughed at the image and adjusted my perspective to include a blingy car, full of bells and whistles.

Once we were driving through the streets of Dublin, my appreciation for the car grew. When I admitted to liking the car, Liam asked, "Want to drive?"

"God, no!" I responded immediately.

He played tour guide while I took in the scenery. Suddenly taking a sharp left, we soon came to a stop in front of a brick building. Most of the doors were neutral colors, but one was painted turquoise with a dark blue portico. "Too much?" Liam asked again.

"Well, not if you like that sort of thing, no!" I repeated, with a laugh.

Within moments of arriving at his flat, I stood naked under the spray of a hot shower. I heard the phone ring, then Liam said, "Hello? Yes, she's here. Yes, she made it safely. No, we'll come over tomorrow. Yes. Yes. Yes. Right, then, see you tomorrow. God bless." Seconds later, he was standing in the steamy spray.

"Your mother?"

"Yes, and if she calls again, I'll turn off the ringer. She'll invent an excuse to come and meet you." Liam had exasperation in his voice.

Trying to suppress my concern at his mother showing up unannounced, I asked, "Where does she live?"

"Fortunately, almost an hour away, not to worry." He must have seen the fear in my eyes.

The stress began to drain away with the hot water. Liam's welcome was very gracious. After all of me had been lathered and rinsed, he wrapped me in fluffy towels and rubbed me down. He even attempted to comb my hair.

"How do you manage this every day?" he asked in despair, surrendering the large-toothed comb.

"I'll worry about it later." My body was a bundle of tingling nerve endings. After anchoring my hair in a messy bun, I took his hand and received a quick tour of the house, all the while wondering where his bedroom was.

When we entered it, I took in the dark wood flooring, the contemporary furniture, and the colorful duvet on the bed. This room seemed like Liam: inviting, warm, and edgy—but in a good way. I closed the door and dropped my towel. He was by my side, taking me in his arms without a moment's hesitation.

Though it was hardly the first time we had made love, it was unique. It was the first time we had been alone in one of our own apartments. Liam's essence enveloped us in an intimate cocoon. As he hovered above me, his caresses were tender and lingering, his words soft and promising. I felt too inhibited to speak such words, but I took his body to mine and wrapped myself tightly around him, hoping that all that I felt for him infused him.

Much later, when our breathing became hushed and the sunset washed the walls with orange and red, we both lay stunned by the experience. We could see it in each other's eyes.

*  *  *

Waking with a start, I was confused by the darkness and unfamiliar surroundings. "Liam," I whispered. His side of the bed was empty but warm. The clock on the bedside table said 10:08. Not knowing where my bag had gone, I groped around for my discarded towel and, wrapping it around me, went in search of Liam.

I followed the soft glow of light that bounced off the walls, down the stairs, and into the kitchen at the back of the house. The kitchen was galley-style, with a worn wooden table and chairs on the back wall, beneath a massive window that looked out to the garden. Liam was sitting naked on a chair, his back to the window, staring down at his shapely feet. He hadn't heard me enter.

"I'm not sure we'll make it. I'll take her for a bite to eat and then, if it isn't too late, we'll stop by," Liam said into the phone, then listened. "All right, then. Cheers, thanks for calling. Yep, we'll see you then." At that point, he looked up and saw me standing in the doorway wearing a towel.

He set down the phone as he walked toward me. "You're amazing," he said, taking me in his arms.

"You are, too. I feel all drifty, like this is a dream, that it can't be real." I softly twined my fingers into his hair and pushed my body more firmly against his. The movement caused the towel to slip to the floor. His nakedness against me, he growled softly as his fingers began exploring me again. He flicked off the kitchen lights, and we slid onto the table. "Is this thing sturdy enough?"

"I don't know, but if it isn't, we'll go shopping for one of those, too." He licked my neck.

*  *  *

Much, much later, I hated to bring up such banal issues as hunger, but I was starving. "Would you like to make something to eat?"

I felt his body laugh before I heard the sound.

"I was going to take you to this lovely restaurant just down the road, but I don't think I can bear going back out into the world. Do you mind? Can we order take-away? I can have anything from Chinese to fish and chips here in ten minutes."

"Chinese it is," I replied.

After eating from the boxes at the kitchen table, I tapped its surface and said, "Nice table."

"I'm growing fonder of it myself," Liam replied, stuffing the last bite of garlic chicken in his mouth.

\* \* \*

The next morning, I opened my eyes to see that the day was bright and sunny. It was Liam climbing back into bed that woke me.

"Good morning," I murmured, my voice slightly husky from sleep.

"Good morning to you," he said, before giving me a gentle kiss on the lips. When I rolled over, innocently brushing my leg against his groin, he whimpered in pain and carefully readjusted himself. "I can't believe I'm about to say this. Charlotte, as much as I love you, as much as I long for you, please don't do anything remotely sexy or sexual."

That fully woke me. My eyes opened wide and I suppressed a big smile. "Wow, I've never heard that before."

"Well, I think it was the four times in six hours that did me in." He chuckled. "I haven't done that since I was…" A pause while he mulled it over. "Well, ever."

"I'm beginning to see what you mean. Or should I say *feel* what you mean? I'm not sure I can walk normally today. What's your mother going to think when we walk in bow-legged, stiff, and sore?" I asked, chuckling at the vision in my head.

"Well, I don't know what she'll say, but my Dad will say, 'Well done, lad.'"

Rising up onto an elbow to see the clock, I was shocked at the time and gasped. "There's barely enough time to get ready. How long does it take to get there?"

"Don't worry. No one in my family is ever on time. We're supposed to be there for 1:00. We've loads of time. If we get there before 1:30, my mother will be putting things to right and get annoyed." He pulled me down to his chest and ran a hand up and down my back.

Giving into it, I collapsed onto him. "*Mmm*, that feels good," I mumbled into his hairy chest. "I could lie here all day. I have to say, I've been really looking forward to this. No one about, no demands. It's wonderful to just lie here and relax."

He continued his back rub and I wriggled in enjoyment. "Okay, you're going to have to stop that. It's playing havoc with my nether regions." He swung his legs over the edge of the bed and pulled out a pair of brightly-colored boxers from the dresser drawer. "My back is sore!" He flexed from side to side before straightening up. "Would you like something to eat? I have some bread for toast and jam, or I can go down to the shops and get something more substantial, if you'd like. I had thought of stopping for a few things last night, but I was a desperate man."

Turning around, he saw me laying on my back, watching him, an amused look on my face. "What?" he asked.

"I'm just trying to put the pieces together. The flashy car, the bright blue front door, the yellow boxers with pink stripes. I thought of you as a much more conservative person. It's interesting."

Sensing that I was more in the mood to talk than have a big breakfast, Liam climbed back into bed and rested his back against the headboard, pulling the white sheet up over his legs. "Well, there's bound to be a few surprises. I love color, always have. I wanted to be a proper artist, but, since I wanted the flashy car, I realized I needed to make a better living than selling a few paintings at the Saturday market."

"Now that you have the flashy car, have you thought of doing something else, or do you like your job? Have you ever thought of leaving Dublin?"

"Well, lately, I've been thinking of taking a trip to Saint-Tropez." It took the briefest moment for his words to penetrate my thoughts.

"What?" I shot straight up in bed. The sheet fell down around my waist; I must have looked like a rumpled Lady Godiva.

"I was going to talk to you about it later, but later seems to be now. I really believe that we should go to Saint-Tropez. I know that time is short and that you have a great deal going on at work, but I think it's time for the past to belong to the past. Let's go to Saint-Tropez and confront the bastard. Tell Des Bannerman what you really think about him. Whatever happens, I'll love you still." He was holding on to my hands and kept eye contact with me the whole time he was speaking.

"I don't know! What if it all goes wrong? What if I end up in jail? What if we ruin Tiziana's party?"

"Charlotte, answer this one question. Other than talking to him, is there any other way of putting this business to rest and letting it belong to the past?"

Leaning back against the pillows and drawing the sheet up around my chest, I chewed my bottom lip for a minute. "No, I suppose not."

"Then I say we go. If you end up in jail, I'll bail you out or hire the best lawyer. We'll do the right thing and apologize, if it comes to it, but really, so what? Everything isn't about Tiziana. She'll still be marrying the man she loves. You have a right to be happy, too. You have the right to not have this thing hanging over your head. Even if we were to find out that you *had* done something, wouldn't it be better to know what it was?"

"I suppose so," I answered nervously.

"Things are slowing down a bit at work, right?" I nodded. "Well, then, maybe Ms. Clarkson, Faith, will let you have a long weekend. We don't have to go for the whole time."

"I suppose so." He looked at me expectantly. "Can I think about this? I need to think about it. We need to get ready to go to your parents'. Can we talk about it more tonight?" Clearly I needed his patience.

"Of course. I'm just glad you're even considering it. I thought you'd say no and that would be that."

*  *  *

An hour later, we pulled up in front of a flower shop just down the street. I jumped out of the car and dashed into the store to buy flowers for Mrs. Molloy. Re-emerging moments later with a brightly-colored bouquet, Liam reassured me, "She'll love them," before I could ask.

We zoomed down the byways of County Dublin, heading south with the Atlantic Ocean on my left. "So, where are we heading?"

"My parents live in a village called Enniskerry. They haven't been there very long. They moved there after my father retired. It's quiet and pretty with plenty to keep them happy. You'll like it. Very touristy, right off a postcard." Liam seemed happy and relaxed.

After driving for quite some time down a windy country road flanked by shrubs and briars, our flashy car came to a stop outside a golden cottage. The roof was steeply pitched, with two gabled windows peeking out and a chimney pot covered in soot. The trim was painted bright white. Out front, flowers of every color and kind were randomly planted. It was the quintessential cottage.

I was enchanted. "Oh, Liam, you're right! I love it. It's right out of a fairy tale. Don't you wish you'd grown up here?" I gushed.

He came around to my side of the car and opened the door. "It is pretty, but, to a teenage boy, living in Dublin was much preferable. We'll drive past the house I grew up in at some point." He tugged me out of the car.

"Hold on a minute, I haven't taken my seatbelt off!"

Liam apologized and we both laughed. "I guess I'm a bit nervous."

"What do you have to be nervous about? I'm the one being looked over. I'm about to wet my pants."

He leaned down and gave me a thorough kiss. "You'll love them, they'll love you, and if even if they don't fall madly in love with you, I have. It'll be fine. I'm more worried that my mother will bore you endlessly with stories of my ill-spent youth."

"Well, from my perspective, that would be great! I've already seen you in action at the Easter egg hunt. I can only imagine the trouble you've gotten yourself into." I laughed at the memory of his pushing Marcus headfirst into the hedge at the Clarksons.

Squeezing my hand, he dragged me away from the car, my hand releasing the handle at the last moment. "It's easy for you. I didn't make you meet my parents. My father would hate you!"

Over his shoulder, he shot me a surprised look. "I'm kidding!" We both started laughing so hard, we had to stop to catch our breath and settle down.

Wiping the smudged mascara from my eyes and running a hand nervously down my throat, I gave Liam a look that said, "I'm ready!" He then knocked with a few quick raps, then opened the front door and shouted to no one in particular, "Hello?"

There was no immediate answer, so Liam led me in and was heading down the hall toward the back of the house when we heard a call from above, "Hello. We'll be right there."

Liam showed me to the sitting room. In an antique glass cabinet next to the fireplace were pictures and trophies belonging to Liam and his brothers. He entertained me with a few stories while we waited for his parents.

"See, I told you that the Irish are always late. We were twenty minutes late, and they still aren't ready," Liam said quietly.

Just then, Mr. and Mrs. Molloy bustled into the little sitting room. Mr. Molloy walked forward and took my hand.

Though it was a little damp, his hand was warm and firm. Immediately, I took to the twinkle in his eyes. Liam said, "Charlotte, these are my parents, Eamonn and Niamh Molloy. Mam and Dad, this is Charlotte."

Liam's mother stepped forward. "Charlotte, it's so very nice to meet you. We've heard what a lovely girl you are."

I handed her the flowers. "These are for you. Thank you so much for inviting me, Mrs. and Mr. Molloy."

Still holding my hand, Liam's father gave it a gentle squeeze. "Enough of all that. Now, let's relax and get to know one another. You can start by calling us Eamonn and Niamh."

As we followed them to the back of the house, Liam's parents gave us a brief tour of the garden. "Wicklow is famous for its gardens," Eamonn was explaining when Liam intervened, offering to get the drinks. Eamonn ordered a glass of beer; Niamh was having white wine. I decided to have the same as her.

I felt a moment's trepidation as Liam retreated to the house, leaving me alone with them. It must have shown, because his father leaned toward me and said, "Don't worry, he's coming back." Surprised by his comment, I let out a laugh.

The afternoon was spent lazily chatting. Eamonn, a retired truck driver for a frozen food company, managed to coerce my family history from me. "So, your father owns a hardware store. I bet he really appreciates your sister's husband taking an interest," he said.

"Poor Dad, he was cursed with three girls who couldn't remember a wrench from a hammer. He was thrilled when my sister, Grace, married her husband Paul. Paul loves the store. Their son, Stephen, loves the store almost as much, and he's only seven. They have a daughter, as well. Isabella. She's as girly as they come. Perhaps she'll be as bad as the three of us were."

"What about your other sister then? What does she do? Is she married?" Liam asked.

"What, don't you know about her family?" Niamh asked, full of curiosity. "Haven't you met them?"

"Oh, they live in Maine. We haven't had a chance to go there yet. Someday soon, maybe. My other sister, Laura, lives in the same town as the rest of my family. I doubt she'll ever get married. She's been with someone a long time, but they seem happy enough with how things are." I hoped that wouldn't put them off. I started asking plenty of my own questions about Liam and his brothers.

Eamonn clearly enjoyed telling stories of his children's adventurous youth. There seemed to be story after story of mischief and injury. Liam, growing more uncomfortable with each tale, intervened. "I don't think we need to tell Charlotte *all* our family secrets, Dad. She'll think we're a bunch of hoodlums."

"Well, they still mess about with each other," Niamh added before heading into the kitchen to see about dinner. She brushed aside our offers of help, saying, "Not to worry, Eamonn will help. Come on, old man!" He happily followed behind her, listening to her instructions with half an ear.

"Your parents are really nice. I like them. I hope they don't read anything into why you haven't met my family. It didn't seem like a good idea to tell them that we barely have enough time to have sex, let alone go out in public," I said once they were out of earshot.

Liam got up and dragged his chair beside me. Leaning over, he looked down and said, "From here, I can see straight down your dress and appreciate a very sexy purple bra."

Teasing, I said, "I take it that your boy parts aren't in pain anymore?" I inhaled sharply as Liam quickly ran a finger over my nipple.

"I'm ready and able to satisfy your carnal needs, madam." His hand ran up my thigh, under my dress. "I had told some friends we'd meet up with them for drinks tonight, but I don't know if we'll make it."

Craning my neck for signs of life, I asked, "Can your parents see us?"

"We'll hear them before we see them. It's okay," he whispered against my lips. "Besides, they know what I was like as a teenager."

I didn't have an opportunity to find out what that meant, because Eamonn called from the house, "Ready then? Dinner is served."

I took a deep breath, rearranged my clothes, and asked, "Do I look okay?"

"Perfect."

Dinner was a tasty affair. Liam's parents went to quite a bit of effort, which really touched me. Afterwards, we chatted pleasantly for a while before Liam announced that it was time to go. Niamh and Eamonn walked us out.

"Don't kill yourselves," she said, looking at the flashy car with trepidation.

Chuckling, Liam hugged and kissed his mother and assured her all would be well. I gave Liam's parents hugs goodbye and thanked them for the wonderful meal and lovely day.

After Liam helped me into the car and climbed in himself, I said, "Your parents are very nice people." I waved goodbye to them.

We talked about the day as we drove. Surprising me, Liam pulled over to the wide canopied shoulder of the road. The moon was straight ahead. "What? Is something wrong?"

"Undo your seatbelt," he said. In no time at all, his seat was reclined, and I was straddling his lap.

"I've never known parents to be an aphrodisiac before," I said as I released his bottom lip from my teeth.

"I've never wanted anyone so much that even talking about my parents didn't turn me off." Liam sucked in his breath as I unbuttoned his shirt and ran my tongue across his nipples. After a minute, he lifted me up, took my breast in his mouth, and slid a hand between my legs. An absolutely delectable warmth coursed through me, and I felt waves of heat roll through my body. More than ready, I slid down his shaft and took him deep within me.

"Are you sure?" I asked when the grunt he released sounded more like pain than pleasure.

"No, it hurts like bloody hell, but if you quit, I might die." He held my hips firmly and guided our rhythm.

A few moments later, we collapsed into each other. Finally dredging energy from somewhere, Liam opened the windows further, letting in the evening air and the twittering sounds of bugs and birds. Quietly, I rested on him. He cradled me, one hand stroking my bare bottom, the other brushing feathery strokes up my side. Both of us were content in the silence.

"Liam, let's do it," I said, breaking the silence a few minutes later.

"I think I need a few more minutes," he responded, "and perhaps some ointment."

"Not that!" I laughed, lightly thumping his chest. "I want to go to Saint-Tropez. You're right. I think it's time to take the bull by the horns and get this all sorted out. I'll talk with Faith Clarkson when I get back to London."

Taking my head in his hands, he gently kissed my lips. "Are you sure?"

"Abso-fucking-lutely!"

"Such language!" He pretended to be shocked.

"I blame it on the car."

"I'll have to say thank you to the salesman at the dealership."

With a "plock" I unstuck myself from him and threw myself back into my seat. Flipping my hair over my shoulders, I rested against the car door with my feet in his lap. "Oh, so you'd like it if I talked dirty?" I inquired.

"I can't imagine a man alive who wouldn't." He tugged up his pants and put the car seat in its usual position, giving me a lecherous grin.

Instead of meeting anyone for drinks or touring his old stomping grounds, we spent the rest of our time together alone, answering many forgotten questions and exploring each other's thoughts on life, the world, and what we wanted in the future. Oddly, the trip to Saint-Tropez was completely forgotten.

# Chapter Fifteen

**RISING VERY EARLY** on Monday morning to catch the 6:00 a.m. flight to London was painful. Liam gently nudged me awake and helped pack my overnight bag while I showered and got ready for work. Then we were off to the airport.

"In case I forgot to say thank you before, thank you." I threw my arms around him, pressing my head against his chest.

"For what?" he asked, his face buried in my hair.

"For everything… The times you've come to London and had to get up at the crack of dawn to get to work, helping me to take life a whole lot less seriously, for encouraging me to go to Saint-Tropez. We're going to have to do something about living in two different countries. I don't care how close they are!"

The final announcement for boarding my flight was called. Giving me a thorough kiss, he said, "In due time!"

Three hours later, sitting at my desk, I stared at the computer screen, trying to figure out how to get from London to Saint-Tropez. While it was tempting to ask Hillary for help, I didn't want to answer questions about whether I planned to confront Des Bannerman or not.

An hour later, I sent an email to Liam to see if it was possible for him to fly from London on the thirtieth of July and return on the third of August. Tiziana's party included a weekend, which let me feel slightly less nervous about asking for the time off. I literally debated with myself as to whether or not I should add a day, in case I needed to get bailed out of jail. I decided to live on the edge and deal with things as they came. Over the prior few weeks, I had come to realize that the pre-emptive strategy I had felt compelled to take all these months was doing me far more harm than good. I was going to try the I-let-the-chips-fall-where-they-may attitude.

Instantly, Liam replied that his schedule was clear. So I booked two tickets on Ryan Air and forwarded the reservation information to him, including his ticket for arriving in London on Wednesday.

*  *  *

The trip was just three days away. I had two days to find a holiday wardrobe, tell Tiziana and Ted we were coming, and deal with work. Three days was more than enough time to work into a panic. Nerves were truly setting in when I received an email from Liam.

> *To: 'Charlotte Young'*
> *From: 'Liam Molloy'*
> *Subject: Breathe In and Out*
>
> *Hey Gorgeous,*
>
> *Don't panic. Going to Saint-Tropez is smart. I'll be there every step of the way. I love you.*
>
> *Liam*

Having gone this far, I sent an email to my assistant, Samantha, and to Human Resources, to notify them that I would be gone for three days. Settling into work for a minute here and there, I knew I wouldn't be able to really focus until I heard from Faith Clarkson. She would immediately be informed of my request. Eventually, an email did arrive from Human Resources, stating that my request had been duly noted and approved.

Not long after, an email from Faith Clarkson arrived.

> *To: 'Charlotte Young'*
> *From: 'Faith Clarkson'*
> *CC: 'Human Resources, London Branch'*
> *Subject: Work-related travel*

*Charlotte,*

*I am assuming that this is somehow work-related. I will expect
a full report on your return.*

*FC*

Staring at the monitor for a few minutes, I decided to let Faith believe it was work-related. For eight months, I had worked day and night, almost seven days a week. I needed to go to Saint-Tropez and get resolution. If I had to delay the truth or even lie, I was willing to. "There are other jobs," I told myself while sifting through a spreadsheet on the screen in front of me, hoping the worst-case scenario wouldn't occur.

Realizing I wasn't seeing the numbers in front of me, I quickly called Hillary and Taylor, leaving messages for both of them to meet me at Saint Hill Couture Boutique at 5:00 sharp. It would mean leaving work way too early, but, between the lack of focus and the little time I had to spare, I was prepared to walk out the door at a reasonable hour and come back afterwards if necessary.

Knowing I was leaving early made it a bit easier to commit myself to what remained of the day. Suddenly it was 4:30, and there was just enough time to call Liam.

"Hello?" came Liam's voice across the distance.

"Hi, it's me. I'm just calling so you can wish me luck."

"Good luck! For what?"

"I'm going shopping for a few special items for this weekend. I want you to be the envy of every man there!"

"Ah! The ultimate revenge! Looking drop-dead gorgeous and making Des Bannerman regret his behavior for the rest of his life." He laughed.

"Yes, well, that too!"

"I'm glad. That's the perfect attitude. As for me, I get to see you naked, so I'm happy either way." He laughed again. "Have a great night. While you're out shopping, I'll be explaining to an angry mob why they didn't get to meet you over the weekend. I'm not sure who needs more luck, you or me."

"Well, before they lynch you, let them know that I'll be back very soon, and we can all have a drink then. Tell them we'll buy! That should stop the hostilities." I stuffed my oversized bag full of work files and my cell phone.

Just before hanging up, I promised to call to say goodnight.

The phone rang the second I put it down. It was Liam. "Hey, really quickly! I meant to ask, what did Tiziana say when you told her we were coming?"

"I completely forgot to tell her. I'll have to give her a call. I'll let you know later. Thanks for the reminder." I laughed at myself for having overlooked a pretty important issue.

Moments later, I ran for the elevator, calling instructions to my assistant as I left. "Tell anyone who calls that I'll call back first thing tomorrow morning. I'm on my way out. See you tomorrow." Samantha's eyebrows shot straight up, since I had never left at such an early hour.

I took a cab to Saint Hill Couture Boutique and used the privacy to call Tiziana. The phone rang three times before her familiar voice purred hello.

"Tiziana, it's me, Charlotte. I'm calling to let you know that Liam and I will be able to come this weekend after all. Well, if that still works for you." Now that the plans were in motion and I was telling Tiziana, my voice was full of happiness.

There was the briefest, almost undetectable, pause before Tiziana enthusiastically responded, "Bella, of course! Now my party is perfect. I'm so happy! I'll have a room prepared especially for you. Is Liam coming? We have so much to celebrate!"

"Yes, Liam is coming. Are you sure this boat is big enough for all of us?"

"*The Sophia* is eccellente. Hillary, Marian, and Kathleen are coming, and Ted will have a few friends, as well. What a wonderful party." She sounded happy. "Oh, just a minute, darling. Let me tell Ted—he just walked in."

There was muffled talking in the background, then Tiziana returned. "He's very happy you and Liam can come after all, bella. He asked me to find out your flight arrangements."

She took down our flight information and then happily chatted away about the upcoming festivities. There seemed to be ample fun-in-the-sun time and a few dressy events. I had never heard her happier and was deeply appreciative that she had found someone special.

"I'm sorry, but I need to go. The cab just arrived at the shops, and I have tons to buy. It will be so nice for us all to be together. I'll see you on Thursday."

"Bella, I'm thrilled too. Hillary has all the details. We'll see you when you get there."

I leaned over the seat and paid the driver before jumping out. Casting a quick glance through the shop windows, I sighed in relief that I was the first to arrive. I needed a few moments to compose my thoughts and some answers before Hillary and Taylor arrived.

Upon entering, a blonde goddess approached with just the right amount of obsequiousness and sincerity. "Welcome! I'll give you a few minutes to take a look. Please let me know when you're ready."

Having no real idea where to shop or what was needed for the weekend, it was great to have a chance to look around. Just a moment later, I realized all the dresses were wedding dresses. No sooner had that dawned on me than the bell over the door jingled, and in rushed a moment of street noise.

Looking over my shoulder, I saw Hillary enter, giving me an expectant look. I realized instantly what she was thinking, and it was wrong! Had she called Tiziana? Something in Tiziana's voice had sounded a bit off.

Just then, Taylor entered the store. She took one look around and the smile on her face built to epic proportions.

Walking over to them, in order not to be overheard by the blonde goddess, I whispered, "It isn't what you think. Let's get out of here." Turning around, I thanked the confused employee profusely and whisked everyone out the door.

Once on the sidewalk and away from the door, Hillary pulled me by the elbow and forced us all to stop. "You disappear to Dublin for the weekend, leaving Taylor and me to wonder if something was happening, good or bad. Then you return and invite us to a wedding dress shop, only to tell us you've made a mistake? Charlotte! Did Liam propose? Are you having second thoughts?"

Seeing the confusion in their eyes, I felt a bit guilty and blurted out, "No, he didn't propose. Liam and I are going to Saint-Tropez, and I need something to wear. I saw the shop the other day. It looked like the right place from the outside. Sorry."

The two women looked at me, a bit stunned. "You're going?" Taylor asked. "Will Des Bannerman be there?"

Standing aside to let some people pass, I answered, "I am and I don't know."

Hillary became the Queen of Belgravia and took control of the situation. "Well, then we need to get over to Sloane Street. There are some decent shops there. We only have a few hours, but we can probably get you sorted out with a few things. Honestly, Charlotte, leaving this to the last minute! You won't be able to have anything fitted." With that, she raised her hand elegantly and flagged down a cabbie.

A few hours later, we had toured the ins and outs of Alberta Ferretti, Anya Hindmarch, Marni, La Perla, and Fendi. Pushing away Hillary, who was holding up yet another cocktail dress for my inspection, I whined from exhaustion. "I'm not trying anything else on tonight. I'll come back tomorrow, but, for now, I'm finished. I'm also starving. Let's go find food."

Taylor was with me. "I'm a native New Yorker, the child of a woman whose only concern is image. I'm a woman who has been and always will be a slave to fashion, but Hillary, you're killing me. I'm done. I need food, a drink, and, most importantly, a place to sit down."

Dripping with disappointment, Hillary handed the gown back to the salesperson, asking her to hold it until tomorrow and assuring her we would return.

Minutes later, the three of us were ensconced in comfy chairs in the Langtry at the Cadogan Hotel. I was famished to a point of desperation and ordered an array of finger foods for the table. It wasn't until we had consumed quite a bit of food and finished one glass of wine with another on its way that civil discourse was approached.

"Can you believe that Lillie Langtry lived here? I'm not sure that even Tiziana could have held a candle to her," Taylor remarked, taking in the marble fireplace, red velvet cushions, and chandeliers.

Finally returning to the evening's earlier confusion, Hillary remarked, "I have to admit, of us all, Tiziana was the last one who I thought would get married. She seemed disinterested to me. She seems happy, though. Ted appears to be a pleasant man."

"Well, I've only met her very briefly and have to admit that I'm surprised! She's just so 'va-va-voom.' However, it isn't like Ted is the average guy. Life will be plenty extraordinary, I'm sure," Taylor added.

I chuckled and nodded in agreement. "Life for her does seem to exist on a different plane. Speaking of planes, Tiziana said we're staying on a boat. I'm supposed to get the information from you," I said to Hillary.

Raising a glass of chilled champagne to her lips, Hillary took a small sip before remarking, "Boat? Trust Tiziana to call it a boat. It's 635 feet long. *The Sophia* has a helipad, eighteen cabins, a crew of thirty-six, and endless luxuries! I'll give you the information when we get home." She took another taste of champagne before asking, "But what finally convinced you?"

"Well, it was Liam, actually. He encouraged me and, after we talked about it some more, I decided to hell with it. The hard part was getting Faith Clarkson to agree to me taking time off. Of course, she's expecting something in return. Anyway, I really need to come face to face with Mr. Bannerman, get things out in the open, and deal with it!" I raised a hand to stop Hillary from interrupting. "Don't worry, I'm not going just to pick a fight. I'll be as discreet and diplomatic as possible. But you have to admit, short of an event having something to do with Tiziana and Ted, I'm not likely to run into Des Bannerman. If I don't do it now, I won't be able to go to the wedding, and that feels terrible." I averted my eyes, bright with tears. The platinum and gold sling-backs of my Prada sandals sparkled in the warm light.

Once under control, I drained my glass, and said, "Ladies, if you're ready, it's time to go home. I have a busy day of work and shopping ahead of me tomorrow. Are you available for another round? I still need one more dress and some beachwear."

Grumbling disparaging comments, both Taylor and Hillary committed to more frantic shopping. "Don't forget, you need an engagement present, too," Hillary added as we exited the lovely Edwardian building. I made a silent note to myself that I wasn't going to worry about that. What could they possibly need or want that I could find in the next twenty-four hours?

* * *

By the time Liam's plane landed on Wednesday evening, I was seriously regretting the decision to go to Saint-Tropez. Very little real work had been accomplished and guilt had settled in.

Fortunately, Liam had a righteous speech prepared, which lit a fire under my sense of injustice. Soon, I was willing to face a firing squad and Faith Clarkson, for a shot at redemption.

"While I have no idea how much all your finery has cost, and please don't tell me, I have to say you've made excellent choices." He was closely examining a lacey lilac chemise I was wearing. "I can't wait to see what else you've got in those bags." He lifted the gown over my head and threw it onto a chair. A very satisfied and primal look crossed his face. "That's my favorite outfit," he added before lying down on top of me.

# Chapter Sixteen

**WE STAYED AT A HOTEL** near Stansted Airport, since we had a very early departure. We woke up in time to nibble on toast and jam in bed. While we ate, I shared my excitement with Liam about the boat.

"It's *how* long?" he asked, when I had described the eighteen cabins and helipad.

I bit into another piece of toast. "Hillary says 635 feet. It must be huge!"

"How much money does Ted have?" There was a bit of awe in his voice.

"I have no idea. All I know is that I've never looked forward to being on a boat this much." I imagined myself lounging on the deck with a fruity cocktail in hand.

"Well, if we don't quit daydreaming, we'll miss the plane and possibly the boat. Get a move on it." He gave me a nudge with his toe. Looking at the clock, I put my cup and plate back on the tray and dashed for the shower.

As soon as we arrived at the airport, we checked in and then headed toward the departure gate. Liam browsed at a newsstand while I went in search of the restrooms.

I found him looking out the window at the tarmac. A sleek Learjet with its nose pointed in the opposite direction gleamed in the sunshine. "Nice plane!"

"Yes, it is. I would imagine Ted has one of those, as well."

"Do you have plane envy?" I teased.

"Not at all. We all know it isn't the size, but how you use it. My plane is bound for the south of France, soon to be full of people filled with joie de vivre. His plane is parked in a hangar, empty and useless."

Laughing at his innuendo, I tugged him away from the window. "Let's go find out if they're loading your plane yet."

We didn't have long to wait before we boarded our flight from London to the Marseille Provence Airport. Caught up in my excitement, and diverted by Liam, the four hour flight felt as though no sooner had *his* plane ascended than the pilot announced our descent. We surveyed the brilliant blue sea and colorful stucco buildings that were scattered down the blue-green hills, forming a boundary between sea and land. The sight was spectacular.

A few rows back, a little boy yelled, "Wow, look at that boat." Peering out the window, it wasn't hard to figure out which boat he was referring to. A sleek, white yacht with a red stripe dominated the harbor below; next to it, the smaller, more colorful boats bobbed like fishing lures in the water.

Finally, with luggage in hand, we stepped out into the heat and bright sunshine of southern France. In front of the airport, Liam asked, "Now what?"

"Tiziana sent an email saying a driver would meet us here, so look for someone looking for us."

After a moment or two, a voice thick with French sophistication said, "Mademoiselle Young?"

"Yes. I mean, *oui*," I replied with much less elegance. Choosing to ignore Liam's chuckle, I said more assertively, "Yes, I'm Miss Young."

"How delightful. My name is Maurice Girard. I'm Monsieur Blackwell's driver. I'm to drive you to the airport, where the helicopter will take you to Saint-Tropez."

While Liam and I processed what Monsieur Girard had just said, a flurry of French was directed at two teenaged boys, and our bags were stowed into the back of a shiny black limousine.

I said "Merci" when Maurice opened the door for Liam and me. We scooched in and were immediately enveloped in the luxury of wealth.

"Not my style, but it'll do. So, do you have any idea what's happening?" Liam asked with a confused smile.

"No! When I told Tiziana the flight plans, she said she would sort everything out. Honestly, all I did was Google the closest airport to Saint-Tropez. I was so busy, I didn't think beyond that. I don't even know how far away it is. I just thought we would get a map at the car rental. Oh no! I have a car rented. I'll have to call and cancel." I dug through my purse to find my phone.

He gave me a quick kiss while I dialed. "Well, you know what they say, when in Rome, do as the Romans." Stretching his legs out in front of him, he poured us each a glass of prosecco and then proceeded to twiddle with all the buttons and knobs. I silently toasted Tiziana, thanking her for treating us to one of this year's best proseccos, Bisol.

When I got off the phone, I drained my glass and began to wonder how smart this trip was. Not much planning had gone into it, and a whole lot of trouble could come of it.

Liam refilled my glass. "Don't worry. One snafu. Who knew we'd need a helicopter and not a rental car?"

"Tiziana!" I replied without hesitation.

"Maybe she thought you would enjoy a helicopter ride."

"Who knows? This feels so weird! If someone had told me a year ago that I'd be in a limo on my way to hitch a ride on a helicopter to board a yacht in Saint-Tropez with *the most incredible* Irishman, I would have thought that they or I was on drugs."

\* \* \*

Just over an hour later, we touched ground once again. "God! I never want to ride one of these things again." My voice was wobbly, and the stress and alcohol hadn't agreed with me so I'd been queasy every windswept moment of the flight.

"It's all over now! Just a short drive to the harbor."

Walking across the tarmac, still escorted by the limousine driver Monsieur Girard, Liam said in a startled voice, "Would you look at that?"

"What?"

"There!" He pointed to what appeared to be the same Learjet we had seen at Stansted Airport, rolling to a stop off in the distance.

"Plane envy? Darling, not only is your plane bigger, it's faster!"

"Well, not *too* fast, I hope!" Liam glanced at me with a sexy smolder.

I was feeling quite overwhelmed. Between nerves at seeing Des, helicopters, and leaving a mountain of work behind, I was more than happy to sit quietly while Monsieur Girard made his way through the maze of one-way streets and arrived at Port de Saint-Tropez. There, an enormous, sleek white yacht with a blue stripe floated, bobbing beautifully on the sea. The yacht we'd seen in Marseille was miniscule in comparison.

The moment the car stopped, my door was whipped open, and I was in Tiziana's arms. I took in the deep-throated giggle, the scent of sunscreen, and perfume.

"Come on, bella, get out. We've been waiting all day for you to arrive. We're all so excited." She hauled me out of the car.

While welcoming me with a hug and a kiss, Ted said, "My god, she's been like a little girl all morning. Just staring out the window, waiting for her friend to come play."

Ted went to give Monsieur Girard a hand with the luggage while Tiziana gave Liam a dose of her Italian exuberance.

There was only a moment to digest the scene. My weariness melted as my heart filled with joy that these people were a part of my life. In all my dreams, I could never have imagined anything as rich as the colors, smells, and sounds of that moment.

But then, with a horrible screech—the kind that you get if you drag your nails across a chalkboard—the scene turned sour.

Another limo pulled up beside ours and out stepped a long, shapely leg, followed by the curvaceous body and beautiful face of Gemma Newley, Des Bannerman's longtime friend and one-time lover, according to the tabloids.

Ted quickly went over to greet her. Casting me an apologetic look, Tiziana joined him and exchanged air-kisses with her. I felt no surprise when Des Bannerman emerged a moment later. Feeling Liam's warmth beside me, I realized how cold I had become.

"This just keeps getting more and more surreal!" he said.

"It certainly does," I replied.

Not knowing what else to do, I stood frozen in place. Tiziana rushed back over to us with a big smile painted on her face and quietly said, "Bella, take that terrible look off your face. Everything is fine. I promised you that Ted would handle things. Liam, let's take Charlotte to the boat."

"What happened to Brynn Roberts?" I asked, too curious for my own good.

Tiziana smiled and pointed at something in the distance. "Last minute cancellation!"

My smile became genuine. Brynn would have made my life hell. After a few steps, I felt the butterflies settle and my heart slow down. I swallowed a deep breath and threw my shoulders back. Looking Liam in the eyes, I announced, "What the fuck! Let's do what we came here for."

He sniggered and patted my bum with a grin. "Exactly! Don't let that bastard get to you. Remember, you came here to get answers and make him regret being such an arse." Tiziana diplomatically didn't join in and let herself be diverted by the decadent surroundings.

The pep talk did the trick. Deciding to initiate the first move, I slowed us all to a stop and turned to wait for the others to catch up with us. When they did, Tiziana re-introduced Liam to Des, and both of us to Gemma. She'd skillfully overlooked any connection between Des and me.

Gemma, with a sly grin, said, "Charlotte, I believe you've met Des."

"Yes, I have." Instead of shaking Des's hand or kicking him in the balls, I coolly returned my attention to Tiziana and Ted, saying, "I don't know about you, but I could use a drink."

With that, our entourage paraded toward the yacht. A passel of men with suitcases and a gaggle of paparazzi brought up the rear. Many gawkers watched us as we passed.

With a toss of his head toward Ted and Des, Liam whispered to us, "I bet they're wondering who the hell those *other* people are." Tiziana and I laughed until we cried. I squeezed Liam's hand, needing to say thank you, knowing that I wouldn't make it without him.

On board, the crew took the suitcases to our cabins, and Ted directed us to the outside bar at the back of the boat.

"We'll be pulling out in just a few minutes, once the crew has us settled," he said over his shoulder as he opened a bottle of Silvano Follador prosecco. I barely registered the dry, crisp Italian wine as it slid over my tongue.

I was still absorbing the fact that I was politely sipping prosecco less than twenty feet from the man from whom I wanted retribution. Suddenly, I heard the sound of a virtual cattle stampede and barely managed to pass my glass to Liam before being assaulted by Hillary, Marian, and Kathleen.

Tiziana joined in, and we danced around and hugged and talked all at once. The hugging and dancing moved in Liam's direction, and he was quickly absorbed into the mass, giving himself over to their enthusiasm— another reason why I loved the man.

I overheard Ted explaining the connection between the five of us to Gemma and Des, while Tiziana talked a mile a minute about all her plans. Quickly, I glanced in Des's direction. Much to my surprise, he was looking at us with what could only be described as kindness. A moment later, he looked away and replied to a comment Gemma had made.

The rest of the day was a complete indulgence. First, Liam and I disappeared down to our cabin and changed into bathing suits.

Once back on deck, we found Des putting up with questions from Marian and Kathleen. When Marian produced a camera, I heard Des deadpan, "I'll let you have your picture. But if it makes it to the tabloids, I've had it. My career will be in ruins. I haven't seen the inside of a gym in, well… months! What do you think, Gemma? Dare I risk it?"

While Gemma reassured him that he looked fine, she gave him a final once-over before adding, "Mind you, next to Hugh Grant, you look positively flabby!" She roared with laughter.

"Bitch! He's never seen the inside of the gym, I'm sure. I should know better than to ask for support from you, you bloody cow! I'm going to leak to the media that you've had a breast lift, a tummy tuck, and one of those new facelifts. Maybe I'll add a bum lift and liposuction, as well!" Their banter continued for a few minutes as Marian and Kathleen laughed along with them.

After the laughter died down, Gemma declared, "I've had enough of this abuse. I'm going to converse with more civilized people." She picked her glass up and wandered toward us. Liam and I sat with Hillary, Tiziana, and Ted.

I stared at her from behind my sunglasses and quietly said to Liam, "Her legs are as long as I am tall!"

"I can measure, if you like," he happily offered.

"Get near her legs and you're going overboard," I said with a smile as she drew near.

She joined us as we lounged in the sun and managed to engage Hillary in conversation, who, until that moment, had remained her usual aloof self. Gemma and Hillary found they had various social and charity activities in common. From listening to their conversation, it was clear that they had been in the same circles for quite some time but had never met.

"And what about you, Liam? What line of work are you in?" Gemma asked. I listened to the two of them talk for a bit, but, between the sun and the sparkling wine, the conversation became a comfortable buzz in the background. My thoughts turned to Des and what I should make of the current situation. I was fantasizing about him admitting to being an egomaniacal horse's ass when I became aware that the conversation was directed at me.

"Charlotte! Lost in thought?" Hillary prompted me.

"Oh, sorry, I was just daydreaming. What did I miss?"

"Gemma was wondering what you made of the media circus over the holidays," Liam responded, a hint of concern in his voice.

I quickly dashed a look at Des, thankful to see him firmly engaged in a conversation with Marian and Kathleen.

"Oh, don't worry! He's really quite reasonable!" Gemma said, observing my glance.

"Well, reasonable I wouldn't know about. As for the media circus, there's nothing in the world that would induce me to go through that again. It was awful. All the innuendo and lies."

"Well, I think you handled it remarkably well. From what I've heard, it was all a misunderstanding," Gemma replied, as she shot Ted and Tiziana a quick glance.

Realizing the second group was coming over to join us in the sun, I hoped she would drop the subject. Fortunately, Tiziana was a formidable opponent in the attention-seeking department.

"Darlings, we need to decide what we'd like to do for dinner. The chef is prepared to make us a lovely meal, or, if you prefer, we can find some delightful place in Saint-Tropez!"

My brain was so busy thinking about Gemma's comment that I let the others decide what we would do.

Tiziana announced, "I'll tell Monsieur Lambert that we'll be in the dining room at 9:00. That should give us enough time to pamper ourselves and have a cocktail on the upper deck. The sunset is spectacular from up there."

I decided to retreat to a quiet place to think. "I'll see you all in a while. I'm going to go have a dip in the tub." I tied an aqua blue sarong around my hips and picked up my bag.

Before leaving, I gently squeezed Liam's shoulder and gave him a reassuring smile.

Tiziana said, "Charlotte, I'll walk with you.

After stepping through the heavy double doors, we entered the coolness of the yacht's interior. She started to talk as soon as they shut, her voice conveying her anxiety. "Bella, are you all right? Don't worry, everything is going well. Everyone seems to be having a lovely time."

Walking down the marble spiral staircase that was awash in the pure light of the Mediterranean coast, I answered honestly, "I'm assuming Ted has talked to him, and that a truce has been called since we are onboard?" Tiziana nodded. "He hasn't said a word to me. I need to think about what I would say if he did."

At this point, we were walking down a wood-paneled corridor to the guest cabins. We stopped in front mine.

"Yes, well, let's hope it goes smoothly." Her voice was anxious.

"Tiziana, it's okay! No one wants to ruin your special party. We're here to celebrate your beautiful life and lovely wedding." I felt guiltier by the minute; my being there might cause regret. I knew she had to return to her guest. "Listen, the strangest thing happened. Gemma was talking to me about what happened in Chamonix. She said she'd heard it was all a misunderstanding. Do you know what she means?"

Another flitter of concern wrinkled what had been her smooth brow. She shook her head no. "Perhaps Ted talked to her. He knows Gemma from long before, when she and Des were dating. I can ask him."

"No, don't! Like I said, it's all okay."

With her usual enthusiasm, Tiziana threw her arms around me and kissed my check. "Thank you, bella. I'd better go speak to the chef. Put on something colorful and sexy. We want to dazzle them tonight!"

I vowed to positively sizzle.

"Ciao!" She released my arm and floated in the direction of what must have been the ship's kitchen.

Entering my room, I threw my bag on a chair upholstered in a brightly colored fabric. I crossed the room and lay down on the bed. My brain raced, wondering what Gemma Newley knew. While lying there thinking, the day's heat and excitement took hold, and I fell asleep trying to decide how I was going to find out.

I woke with a start when Liam gently nudged me out of a deep sleep. I quickly noted he had a bath towel wrapped around his hips. He leaned over and gave me a gentle kiss while I inhaled the smell of soap and cologne.

"Hello, Sleeping Beauty!" he said, smiling down at me.

"*Mmm*, that makes you my prince," I said in a sleepy whisper.

I looked around the room, taking in my semi-naked boyfriend and then the clock. I sighed, "I'd better get a move on it. I promised Tiziana I would sizzle tonight."

"You always sizzle!" He pulled me to my feet and snaked his arms around me, wearing only a delicious grin on his face, the towel having fallen to the floor. I let myself be distracted for a few minutes. It was only when I felt my knees buckle that I returned to the present.

I gently pushed Liam away and headed to the bathroom. He teased me about a wasted stiffy while I twizzled the water taps of the shower.

Warm water ran over my head and down my body. I was on autopilot when a soapy hand began to lather me. Suds and bubbles trailed over my breasts and across my belly, then dripped to the juncture of my legs, where I felt a warm flutter ignite. I moaned my appreciation and leaned back against him.

He slid his hands upwards. "Just to help you sizzle."

"God, you're good." I whimpered.

Impossibly, less than an hour later, I was showered, fluffed, and dressed in a snug-fitting midnight blue off-the-shoulder dress. My feet were adorned with strappy silver sandals. I'd spent a lot of time getting my hair piled on top of my head, a few curls cascading down.

Just as Liam and I joined the group, I said quietly in his ear, "I don't have any underwear on."

His hand trailed down my backside and he slapped my bum.

"Who's sizzling now?" I asked over my shoulder into his green, smoldering eyes.

Just then, Ted said, "Charlotte, you look like Aphrodite." I took a cosmopolitan from him and accepted a kiss on the cheek.

"She's mine!" Liam said good-naturedly. He pointed to Tiziana. "*That* one's yours!"

She beamed a smile that dazzled Ted. He gripped his chest and staggered to her side. "Kiss me!" he demanded.

After they shared a kiss, he turned to the assembled group and raised his glass. "To the ladies! We men endeavor to deserve you. To the men! It's my hope that you're as happy as I am." We all raised our glasses cheerfully, and the evening celebration was underway.

We watched the sun descend into the Mediterranean, looking for the last flash of color on the calm sea's surface. For a brief moment, we stood silent in our appreciation. Once the last flash of light was gone, the burst of a thousand twinkly lights lit the boat up. We all "*oooed*" our appreciation and the chatter became lively once more.

It wasn't until after dinner and we had returned to the deck that my mind wandered back to what Gemma had said earlier.

I stood at the rail, wondering what to do, wishing I had talked to Liam about this instead of falling asleep. I felt a presence beside me and looked to my left to see Des leaning on the railing, cocktail in hand, staring out at the water. My heart did a flip, and my mouth went dry. Too late to talk to Liam now, I thought.

The silence between us was like a third person. My mind raced through the many things I had wanted to say, but no coherent thought made its way to my tongue. He leaned his left elbow on the rail, swiveling his body toward me. Oddly, my brain registered that he had a healthy glow from the sun. He tried to break the silence, starting and stopping a few times, a frown across his face.

"Charlotte, or perhaps I should say Ms. Young, although that seems frightfully formal given the party atmosphere." He looked at me through his eyelashes. "Well, then, I know this is awkward for us all, but I think it best for Ted and Tiziana if we manage to get through this." He let out a deep breath and ran his hands through his hair. "Look, I want to say, you know, bygones should be bygones and all that." Then he held his hand out, as if a handshake would make everything better.

My mind reeled in confusion as I stared at his hand. The opportunity I had been waiting for had presented itself, yet I felt more confused than angry. I didn't know what I wanted to say. A quick thought flittered through; perhaps not everything needed to be said that night. In the midst of my confusion, I did figure out that, while I didn't know where to start, complete absolution in the form of a handshake wasn't happening.

Suddenly Frank Sinatra flooded the airwaves, and Liam appeared out of the darkness. "Charlotte, I need to dance with you!"

He then registered Des's proffered hand and looked at me. The two men studied each other. I looked back at Des, waiting to see if there was more explanation to come. A heartbeat or two passed before my brain accepted there wasn't. I took Liam's hand and let myself be led away, calmed by the crooning of "Fly Me to the Moon."

As the melody clung to the dark, Liam asked, "What was that all about?"

I relaxed and leaned into his body. Taking a deep breath of his scent, I looked up at him. "The hell if I know!"

We twirled around the deck of the ship to "Something Stupid." By the end, we were singing together, *"Then I go and spoil it all by saying something stupid like I love you!"*

"Hey, you two! Men are in short supply. Pass them along!" Marian called from a few feet away. I laughed and relinquished Liam to her. He gave me a frightened look as she dragged him away.

"Be gentle with him!" She stuck her tongue out at me and then led him further away, dancing an exaggerated version of the cha-ha-cha to "Girl from Ipanema."

I found safety at the bar and perched myself on a stool. I watched Ted dance with Kathleen. Somehow Des had managed to get Hillary on her feet. Tiziana settled down next to me, breathless.

Finally, she purred, "What a perfect night! I wonder if I can get a few of the crew to come and dance! Tomorrow will be better when the rest of the guests have arrived."

"Well, I'm sure Hillary would just love to foxtrot with the fellow who's cleaning the toilets," I replied dryly.

"Have you seen him? He's rather gorgeous." She giggled.

When the next song began, Ted exchanged Kathleen for Tiziana. She and her laughter disappeared into the twinkling darkness as they danced to "Summer Wind."

Kathleen buzzed in my ear, "What was going on with you and Des? I saw him talking to you. I couldn't tell if you were going to punch him in the nose, or what. I was glad when Liam headed over there." She sipped a fruity pink cocktail from a martini glass while waiting for my answer.

Before I could speak, we were joined by Gemma, who had been a short distance away, speaking on a cell phone. "Sorry, ladies! That was my husband. He'll be meeting us in Saint-Tropez in time for tomorrow afternoon's fun and games. So, what are we talking about?"

I poked a finger to the dance floor. "Figuring out which one to rescue."

Gemma smirked. "I say we let them fend for themselves. We rescue them too often and ruin their chance to become men."

We stayed at the sidelines and talked about the wedding plans. Gemma, having recently survived two nuptial ceremonies, was the expert in the group. "Well, I loved each ceremony for different reasons, but at the end of the day, I would have been just as happy to fly to Las Vegas."

We continued to keep track of who was dancing with whom. Finally, the men grew tired and decided to rescue themselves. "You see, one more step toward manhood," Gemma whispered into my ear as they extracted themselves from the dance floor and moved toward the bar.

Everyone settled into the chairs scattered about the deck. I was flanked by Marian and Liam. Somehow Des ended up farthest away, leaving me more than a bit relieved because we could only avoid each other so long.

Tiziana and Ted kept us entertained with stories of her exuberant mother's demands regarding the wedding. "I keep telling her, 'Mama, please, no more,' but you know my mama! The only thing we're missing is the log." We all looked at each other for an explanation, Ted the most perplexed.

"What? Did I forget to mention the log? You've never heard of the log? Okay, okay, let me explain! It's a very old tradition, and maybe some people still do it. It's when a couple getting married use a *sega a mano* to cut the log." While she explained, her arm moved back and forth. Seeing our continued confusion, she added, "You know, the thing you cut wood with, with the little sharp points?"

"A handsaw!" Kathleen called out excitedly.

"Yes, yes, a saw! So the bride and groom saw the log to represent partnership. I told her, 'No, Mama! The only log I want to get near is of another nature!'" She gave Ted a loaded look.

Marian and the men sang a rousing chorus of, "I'm a lumber jack and I'm okay" by Monty Python.

Liam moved his arm from the back of my chair, took my hand in his, and brushed it discreetly across his lap. I felt his arousal. Heat radiated off him.

"Let's go before I leave a wet spot," I said into his ear.

Quickly standing up, with me in front, I gave the girls a kiss goodnight and waved to the men. Liam and I made our way to our room, him carrying the shoes that I had kicked off earlier.

Once the door closed, he pushed me up against the wall and said, "Do me a favor?"

"Anything," I answered, breathless as a result of his one hand sliding up my thigh and the other kneading my breast.

"Fuck me," he said with his lips pressed against my mouth.

"Oh, so the dirty talk commences?" I stroked the length of him through his trousers.

\*   \*   \*

Later, when he had some strength back, he held his weight on his forearms. Through his heavy breathing, I heard, "Well, I think we've taken this to a new level."

"What level is that?" While gasping for breath, I was a bit embarrassed at having proven myself naturally gifted in the saucier art of talking dirty.

He grinned at me lewdly. "Well, we've made love, had phone sex, and now we're having dirty sex."

I tucked my face into his neck. "That was all with me! For such a delinquent youth, you must have talked dirtier to a woman than that."

Prying my face out of the crook of his shoulder, he wore a broad grin. "True, but never to someone I've loved. It didn't seem right. But I'm sensing there's a lot of potential here."

"I draw the line at bondage, three-ways, and toys that induce pain. However, I'm willing to negotiate on a few of those."

He put on his thickest Irish brogue. "You're a wee little pervert, aren't you?"

"Yes, I am."

He looked very pleased, maybe because of his newfound potential or the increased signs of life in his nether region.

After an hour of exploring new territory, I was lying on the floor, rubbing my shoulders. Liam threw himself on the bed, looking very satisfied.

"How am I going to hide the carpet burns?" I asked with a grimace.

"Tell them it's sunburn." He hopped into the bathroom and returned with a bottle of aloe, gently massaging it onto my damaged skin.

The combination of a long day of travel, sun, and strenuous hanky-panky suddenly washed over me, and I could feel myself collapsing into his massage.

Kissing the top of my head, he rolled me onto my back and lifted me onto the big bed. While we were snuggling, he whispered, "So, do you think he comes in peace?"

"I've no idea. I guess. He just said something about 'bygones should be bygones' and stuck out his hand like a handshake could fix everything."

"I've got a joke for you," Liam said suddenly, changing the topic.

"I don't want to hear it if it rhymes with body parts."

"A young couple gets married and they have sex in every room in the house. Time passes, they have kids, and then the only sex they have is bedroom sex. More time passes, and then all they have is hallway sex." The images flitted through my head as he told me the joke.

"Hallway sex?" I asked, not getting it.

He chuckled. "When they pass each other in the hallway, they say, 'Fuck you.'"

"That's terrible! Funny, but terrible."

Pulling me against him, he tucked the crisp white sheet up around my shoulders and wrapped an arm firmly around me. "I love to hear you laugh. I'm absolutely exhausted; I need sleep. Goodnight." He kissed my abused shoulders.

"Goodnight." As I stared at the moon over the water, I drifted into the deepest, dreamless sleep I could remember.

\*    \*    \*

The next day was planned to the fullest. We were to be in Saint-Tropez at Capitainerie du Port just after breakfast to pick up a few more guests.

"Who?" Marian grilled Tiziana with determination, while tearing into a large, flaky croissant, her coffee steaming away on the table.

Coyly, Tiziana looked around the table and said, "My brothers, Alessandro and Paolo, and Gemma's husband Colin, as well as a lovely gentleman by the name of Michael Molloy."

Hillary placed her silverware down with a clatter, glancing quickly at me and Liam. I shrugged my shoulders to let her know I hadn't a clue. She looked a little nervous, a little excited.

Tiziana jumped up to give Hillary a quick kiss on the cheek. "So you see, we'll all have someone to dance with tonight!"

Liam, clearly happy to have his brother included, rose to give Tiziana a kiss. "I love these people." She giggled and hugged him back.

"Well, if that's all it takes, I love these people!" Marian joined in, grabbing Des's face and planted one on his lips. It was his turn to drop his silverware with a clatter.

"Blimey," was his reply when Marian let him go. Inwardly I cringed, wondering what lawsuit she'd be saddled with.

Liam plopped back down into his chair with a very satisfied smile. He threw his arm across my shoulders and gave one a squeeze.

"Ouch!" I yelped.

"Sorry!" His smile quickly turned to one of concern. "I forgot."

Tiziana asked, "Bella, what's wrong?"

"Sunburn…" I mumbled into my coffee cup, feeling a healthy blush rise from the tips of my toes to the top of my head. I was inundated with remedies when the only one I needed was to be left alone to suffer my embarrassment in peace.

It was a very jubilant group that glided into the harbor. Having quickly become accustomed to the luxury yacht, it wasn't until we reached the dock's edge and saw all the staring faces that we remembered the glamorous life we were living.

Kathleen was one of the first off the ship. Dressed in a white cutout bathing suit and bright yellow sarong, she said with a smile, "I'm going to take a look at the other dinghies."

"She's off to find Prince Charming or Prince Harry, or Prince, for that matter," Marian said as we watched her long, willowy body flutter down the ramp and disappear among the yachts.

"Yup! Has she met Tiziana's brothers before?" I asked.

"I don't know. Why?" Marian asked, her voice curious.

"Oh, you'll see."

In a repeat of the day before, two limousines arrived and out of each stepped two elegant men. Gemma had walked down to meet one, giving her attention to a tall, dark, and handsome man known to all for his place in cinematic history. Hillary stood beside me at the rail and gazed at the other tall, dark, and handsome man who was looking about, a bit overwhelmed.

"Go rescue him," I whispered to her. Somehow, Hillary managed to sedately bolt down the ramp.

In her typical fashion, Tiziana descended upon the second limo with gusto, pulling open a door and dragging her brothers out, hugging them close. Liam and I watched with affectionate amusement, listening to the Italian lyricism float its way toward us.

Marian poked me in the side, pointing to the slips where the boats were moored. Kathleen was drifting back toward Tiziana.

Laughing, I said to Marian, "I'd go stake my claim if I were you."

With no dignity to spare, she raced to Tiziana's side to beg for introductions.

"It's going to be quite an adventure!" Liam observed.

"Poor boys, they'll never be the same!"

"We never are." Liam patted my bum.

I gave him a wry glance and said, "Thanks for remembering my shoulders this time. Next time you forget, I'm going to announce what a pervert you are!"

He gave my bum a much firmer swat and said with a laugh, "You do, and I'll tell them all about your bondage fantasies."

"I specifically said no bondage!" I hoped he'd heard me and was just teasing.

Liam scoffed. "They'll never believe you, not with friction burns on your shoulders and bite marks on my chest." Since the crowd was walking up the gang plank, all I could do was concede this round to him.

After everyone had climbed aboard, luggage and introductions were sorted out. Gathering on the rear deck, we all toasted the newly arrived guests as the boat quietly maneuvered out of the harbor. Everyone fanned out around the deck, nattering to whoever sat next to them. I did notice that Kathleen and Marian had quartered themselves near Paolo and Alessandro. I sipped my grapefruit juice and smiled.

Liam's eyes followed mine. "Poor bastards! Little do they know that in three days' time they'll be hiding in the shadows, hands over their worn-out wee bits, praying the rosary."

"Probably!" They really did have their work cut out for them.

Liam surprised me a short while later by handing me a life jacket and leading me to a lower deck where a jet ski bobbed on the water, waiting for us.

"Do you know how to drive one of these things?" I asked, hopefully disguising my concern.

Tugging at the straps of my jacket, he made sure it was snug. "Well, one of the lads showed me. How hard can it be?"

I was flooded with doubt. Before I say so, I heard the sound of Hillary's voice and Michael's laughter. I turned to see them suited up in life jackets, as well.

"Well, at least we'll have help if you crash!" I said.

"Or they can bring our bodies back!" Liam wasn't going to let me back out, that was clear.

Michael offered Hillary the same assurance of his driving skills. "I'm not completely convinced, are you?" she asked me after taking a moment to assess the situation.

"I'm not convinced at all." But, seeing Liam's disappointed face, I added enthusiastically, "But what the heck?"

He stretched his long leg over the seat and got comfortably seated, studying the dials and buttons. "Come on." He held a hand out to help me climb on.

"Have I mentioned I'm short?" I could not see how I was supposed to clear the distance from the edge of the boat to the seat of the jet ski.

The next thing I knew I was dangling in the air as Michael passed me to Liam. "Okay, well, that was humiliating!" I grumbled.

Michael looked at Hillary, and she said with an absolute lack of humor, "Not on your life."

We slowly chugged away, and, with a backwards glance, I saw Hillary much more gracefully climb on behind Michael. We floated at a safe distance, and, once Michael and Hillary were ready, Liam gave Michael a thumbs up, and we burst forward.

After riding between waves and jumping over the crests of swells for about a half hour, Liam stopped the engine and said over his shoulder, "Want to drive?"

With trepidation, I agreed to try. Liam jumped into the water, I scooted forward, and he climbed back on. He patiently explained what to do, and I gave it a tentative go. Michael and Hillary watched and laughed when Liam and I puttered along quite slowly at first.

I quickly accelerated and turned the jet ski in time to spray a wide arch of water on them, leaving both Hillary and Michael gasping.

"Why, you little daredevil! You didn't tell me you already knew what to do," Liam shouted in my ear over the roar of the engine.

I shouted back, "Well, that will teach you to be presumptuous!"

Michael and Hillary soon caught up, and we chased each other around for quite some time. I felt Liam motion to Michael, and then told me to follow him. Soon, we were floating in the shallow waters of a quiet bay.

Before I could ask any questions, he said, "One of the crew told me." From a storage compartment in the back, he took out a waterproof bag and handed it to me. I carried it to shore while he drove the jet ski onto the beach. Michael and Hillary repeated our performance once I was safely on shore.

In no time at all, we were having a lovely little picnic.

With a full stomach, the sun helped induce drowsiness. Dozing with my head on Liam's chest, I felt completely spent. "Liam?" I whispered, not knowing if he was awake.

"Yes?" he whispered back, stroking my hair back from my face.

"I wish we could stay here forever." I rolled over to look into his beautiful eyes.

He smiled at me. "Coward!"

I sat upright. "That wasn't what I was expecting."

"Don't forget half the reason we're here."

Bannerman! "Well, you certainly know how to kill a perfect afternoon," I grumped.

"Not kill so much as sour." Michael and Hillary, returning from a walk on the beach, arrived back in time to hear the last part of the conversation and wanted to know what was sour. It turned out that neither Liam nor Hillary had told Michael about my situation with Des Bannerman. The range of emotions that crossed his face was like watching my life over the last year accelerated into fifteen seconds. "Wow," he said, once caught up.

After agreeing that the current situation was strange at best, I was peppered with questions about my next move. Fortunately, Michael's support helped temper Hillary's "etiquette at all cost."

"Really, you think I should?" I asked them again about the strategy we devised, as I perched on the back of the jet ski and we headed back to the boat. There were three resounding yeses.

Upon returning to the boat, we were greeted by a fairly worn-out group. They had spent the afternoon playing in the water where the boat had been anchored. An enormous water trampoline was tethered to the anchor line. We joined them for a drink and an hour of lounging in the sun before Tiziana called out in alarm, "What time is it?" After a handful of people replied, "6:32," she announced, "Dinner will be at a little restaurant on the beach tonight at 8:00. Hurry!" And with that she disappeared.

Shortly thereafter, we all drifted to our cabins to do the necessary ablutions. As always, it seemed, the moment we were alone, we were ready for each other.

Ten minutes after arriving in our room, Liam threw himself off me, both of us sated. I quickly threw myself on the length of him, wanting to feel him beneath me.

"Pleased as I am with your belief in my virility, I fear the development of a callus." He flinched as he responded to my enthusiasm.

"And you were worried about Alessandro and Paolo!" I lowered my head to his worn-out appendage.

"No! No!" Liam grabbed my head gently. There was laughter in his voice. Feeling me slide upwards, he sighed in relief, causing both of us to laugh. Instead, we took a shower.

We made it in time to watch the sunset. Most of the others were already there, with their beverage of choice in hand.

"What would you like, madam?" inquired a crew member.

"A glass of prosecco, please," I answered.

"A beer for me," Liam requested.

"Where the hell have you been? We thought you were going to miss dinner," Michael said as he made his way toward us from across the deck.

All eyes focused on us. "Being the gentleman that I am, I won't answer that!" Liam responded loudly, the glint in his eye tattle-telling. When Michael had reached his side, Liam added much more quietly, "What do you do when your willy gets worn out?"

A roar of laughter burst out of Michael, causing everyone on deck to look our way again. Wiping his smile away, he boasted equally as quietly, "While that has never happened to me, I believe that's why the good Lord has given you other body parts!"

Thankfully, the only other ears nearby were Hillary's, and she matched my deepening shade of pink. "We'll have to develop thicker skin if we plan to spend time with these two," I offered, hoping to soothe her.

"Oh, don't be taken in! She might be all prim and proper on the outside. Behind closed doors, well, that's another matter altogether," Michael said quietly in my ear.

My eyebrows shot straight up, disappearing into my hairline.

"I see what you mean," Hillary said to me even more quietly, but there was a twinkle in her eye when she looked at him.

Liam slapped Michael on the back good-naturedly. "All right then, best manners. These fine people aren't ready for the likes of us, and we don't want to find ourselves put ashore on some nameless island."

Michael turned the conversation in the direction of my having recently met his parents. Following Hillary's gasp, he announced, "They loved you! Thought you were perfect for Liam." I was in the middle of saying, "I'm glad," when he interrupted me and said, "They were a bit worried about what kind of woman you are when you let Liam put his hand up your dress in the garden!"

Horror overcame me. "They saw that? I can never face them again. Liam!" I whacked his arm.

Both Molloys laughed at my pain. Liam offered me a comforting hug, saying, "Don't worry, they were young once. How on earth do you think they ended up with all of us?"

Not certain that I could handle more Molloy banter, I finished my drink. "I'm going to find more civilized conversation and another drink."

Hillary joined me, drilling me about meeting Liam's parents as we walked the short distance to the bar. My gaze found Des Bannerman, who was talking to Tiziana's brothers and Kathleen. I wondered if it would ever seem normal to have him among my circle of friends. My thoughts changed to dinner when Tiziana announced it was time to go on shore.

# Chapter Seventeen

**I WOKE WITH** a pounding headache. Liam's getting out of bed brought me unwillingly to consciousness. Through bleary eyes, I watched him make his way to the bathroom. It was intolerable to think about the night before. The only word that came to mind was hedonistic. I closed my eyes, letting sleep overtake me again.

When he returned, he sat on the edge of the bed with his head in his hands. In a strangled whisper, I asked, "How are you?" A grunt was his answer. All I could think was, *At least he can grunt.* The words "aspirin" and "water" made their way into my dulled consciousness. He must have felt my nod, because he slowly shuffled to the bathroom and returned with both. I managed to take them without nausea overtaking me. We collapsed back into bed, and sleep rapturously overtook us once again.

Hours later, I awoke to find my head was improving, and I could move without fear of vomiting. Liam was still asleep, so I decided to take a shower and see if it would return me to some semblance of normal.

Afterwards, I donned a bathing suit and quietly made my way up to the sun deck to sleep some more of last night off under the sun. I found myself joining Hillary, Gemma, Colin, and Des. They all looked at me vaguely, and no one spoke. I took that as my cue to join the group, just not to speak, which was fine by me. The less charitable side of me hoped Des Bannerman was suffering more than the rest of us.

By early afternoon, everyone had made it to the deck and was returning to normal levels of vivacity. Fruit juice and water were still the beverages of the day. Nothing more than fruit and breadsticks passed anyone's lips.

I knew what was on everyone's mind, but they were all too afraid to ask. Bravely, I ventured forth. "Tiziana, what are the plans for tonight?" I was proven correct when groans came from all corners of the sun deck.

Very quietly for her, she said, "I have the most perfect plan for this evening! A light dinner, perhaps we could play cards or dance a little under the stars!" Collective sighs of relief followed. "However, tomorrow you all need to be back to normal. We have a day at the beach planned!" I heard a few acknowledging grunts.

The evening meal was buffet style, featuring delicately prepared seafood. Quiet music played, and a few couples stole dances in the shadows.

It was while Liam and I quietly rocked in circles under the evening stars that we heard the group reliving the previous night. "Couldn't we just forget last night? I'm only just beginning to feel the will to live," I murmured. Liam said nothing and continued to soothe me by rocking to the tempo of the music.

When the song finished, he ushered me toward the doors that led to the cabins below. I saw a few newly-formed couples swaying in the moonlight as we passed. Taunts of being party poopers were called out. Liam gave a few ripe remarks and waved a hand.

I was ready for bed and sitting in a lilac silk wrapper brushing my hair out when he asked, "Do you feel like watching television?" I nodded, pleased to do something mindless and low-key.

Seeing me glance at his nether regions, he laughed. "I'm afraid my willy is out of action. I'm embarrassed to admit it, but there you have it."

I took pity, reciting all the remedies people had offered me earlier for the sunburn on my shoulders. "How about aloe, a tea bath, cucumber slices, or ice?"

He laughed as he searched for the remote control. "If you don't mind, I wanted to catch the news to see who won today's football games. My brothers and I have standing bets, and I want to see how much I've won or lost." I picked up a book and started to read while he switched channels.

At some point, he stumbled on *A Man About Town*, a British period piece. "Sorry, but this is too good to pass up." He quickly bounced off the bed and into the hall.

"Des!" he shouted. Moments passed, and a few cabin doors opened.

"Yes?" Des asked in a confused voice as he stepped into the hall, wearing a pair of cotton shorts and a shirt.

"You can see what you looked like when you visited a gym on channel 431," Liam taunted.

Chuckling broke out as Marian called, "I'd like to see his six- or two-pack in my room!" A loud but frightened "ha-ha" from Des echoed down the hall before all doors were shut.

* * *

Tiziana was true to her word. The next day, two small boats were packed up with everything one might possibly need for a day at the beach: umbrellas, towels, coolers full of food and drinks, tables, chairs, colorful tablecloths, and vases of flowers. Even a tent was stowed on board to create a makeshift kitchen.

"Wow!" Michael said when we landed at the beach. We were a bit dazzled by the idyllic scene.

"It's perfect!" Tiziana clapped her hands in glee. She had carefully planned it all and was very pleased with how it turned out. She grabbed Ted's face between her hands and kissed him soundly.

We couldn't have been a more startling contrast from the day before, everyone laughing and running about.

"Has it always been like this with Tiziana?" Ted asked, as he threw himself next to me under a bright blue umbrella.

"Oh, yes! It takes years to build up the stamina, and even now I falter from time to time. But don't worry, you have the inside track. You might need to get a personal trainer, though!"

Liam joined us and asked if we wanted to take a dip in the ocean. In happy agreement, we rushed out into the bubbling surf with wild abandon. It felt glorious to have the cool water wash up around me. I dove under an incoming wave and treaded water behind the break, watching the group on the beach play volleyball. Liam and Ted joined me, asking if I liked the game. "God, no! I hate volleyball!" I spouted a mouthful of saltwater out like a fountain.

"How can you hate volleyball?" Liam asked me.

"When you're barely five feet tall and the ball comes barreling down at you at a million miles an hour, it's pretty easy to hate it."

"Put that way, I see your disadvantage." Liam laughed and gave me a salty kiss.

"Yuck, I'm leaving you lovebirds alone." My suspicion was that he wanted to go claim a kiss from Tiziana. She was dangerously close to spilling out of her skimpy pumpkin-orange-and-gold bikini while serving the volleyball. Watching him embrace her, I couldn't help but wonder how their future would unfold. Was this a glimpse into their daily life?

Before I could ponder further, Liam kissed me before suggesting we bodysurf to shore. I was much less elegant than Liam and ended up with about five pounds of sand deposited in my bathing suit bottom. Seeing me, he laughed. "You look like you're wearing a nappy."

"Well, get your laughs now, cause someday it might be your job to change my diapers."

He shot me a horrified look before setting off to play volleyball. Once again, I perched under the umbrella on a blanket.

"So, will there be another wedding in the not-too-distant future?" Hillary asked, apparently having overheard us while seeking refuge from the sun.

I just smiled and slurped on an orange-and-pineapple-juice concoction. She tried a few more tactics to wrangle information out of me, but as nothing was forthcoming, she resigned herself to talking about nothing in particular. We watched the others flex their physical and verbal muscles.

"For such a successful and educated group, there sure is a lot of trash talk going on," I observed.

"*Hmm*," was Hillary's only reply.

"Almost time for lunch. Anyone need a quick dip?" Tiziana called out after receiving a signal from the chef. Everyone playing volleyball joined her, splashing into the water.

By the time they had cooled down and dried off, the crew had set up a buffet of salads, antipasti, white fish terrine, and mounds of exotic fruits. We all sat down at the tables to fine white china plates heaped with delicious morsels. Having recovered fully, I took a sip of icy cold prosecco. My taste buds were quite happy. I looked up from my plate to see Des sitting across from me. He gave me a dubious smile, as if to say, "Sorry, but here I am."

While eating my lunch, I wondered what would happen when we got off the boat. Was the restraining order reinstated? The biggest weight on my mind was how and when I would get answers to my many questions.

Liam, tipping more prosecco into my glass, brought me out of my thoughts. I pushed my empty plate back, apparently having made my way through the mound while deep in thought and sipped more wine.

Tuning into the conversation, a volleyball rematch was being discussed after an afternoon siesta.

The crew was tidying up our luncheon inside the tented area that housed the kitchen. We called *merci beaucoup* as we took our spots in the shade. I unfolded my hair in order to return some order to it.

"My god! Look at your hair!" Gemma exclaimed. All eyes turned to me.

"Wow, you're a trichophiliac's dream come true," Des replied. All eyes turned to him.

"A what?" Gemma asked in an astonished voice.

"A trichophiliac is a person who has a fetish for long hair, like the Thin Man in *Charlie's Angels*," he answered matter-of-factly.

I quickly said to him, "I can't imagine you watching a *Charlie's Angels* movie."

"Well, there you are. I'm the same as the next man. Call me a pervert, but I quite enjoy watching a sexy woman with a powerful motorbike between her legs or jogging down the beach in a teeny tiny bikini, or, for that matter, grinding her perfectly shaped bottom straight at the camera. Yes, I'm quite enraptured."

All the men raised their glasses in a silent toast.

Gemma explained to the group, "Des has a real thing for movie trivia. Recite a line, name a song, or ask what actor was in any movie. A walking encyclopedia!"

I felt several pairs of eyes land on me. Marian pointed square at my chest. "Her, too! That's bloody amazing."

Unexpectedly, Des was still stuck on trichophilia, saying more to himself than anyone, "I remember once seeing a woman with hair very much like yours. It was years ago, I can't really remember where."

I could see Marian about to respond, so I waved her off.

"Was that was you? At Oxford?" he asked.

My response was immediate. "Yes, probably." *A reference to our last conversation in Chamonix at last.*

Ted, wanting to be the peacekeeper, tried to lighten the mood. "It's all the drink. His memory is crap!"

"Well, mine isn't. He lives in a world that lets him play judge and jury, ignorant of the wreckage he leaves behind," I said, holding my ground.

A variety of emotions rolled across Des's face. Finally, he said angrily, "Charlotte, I don't know what you're playing at, but if you're suggesting you're without fault in this, you—"

Gemma interjected in a calm, quiet voice, "No one wants to forget why we're here. You two clearly need to sort this out, and soon, but not now, not here." To the rest, she said, "How about that game of volleyball?" People were only too happy to escape and be diverted. Well, maybe not Marian. She was always up for a fight.

The rest organized themselves into two teams as they walked to the volleyball net, leaving the three of us standing under a colorful awning. In that moment, it seemed necessary to stay put. "I'm all ears!" I taunted Des.

"You can screw this up for Ted and Tiziana all by yourself," he said angrily, as he reached down to pick up his towel.

"That's your style. You can't handle actual confrontation, so you have someone else do it for you. That way you can be misunderstood or wronged and not worry about anyone but yourself." I spoke much more calmly than I felt.

His eyes glared at me and then slid to Liam, where they lingered. "You, Charlotte, are full of shit. You can pretend to be innocent, but I know you're not." Then he was gone.

Reaching down for a hair clip and my hat, I said, "I'm going for a walk. Alone." Liam didn't follow.

I headed into the sun at a fairly good pace for quite a while. I had long since slowed down when I heard my name called.

It was Hillary, the only one who would dare ignore my request to be alone. I slowed my pace so she could catch up. When she did, we wandered quietly for quite some distance before she spoke. "So, any progress?"

"Nope, just confusion. Tiziana must hate me." I sighed regretfully.

"Tiziana doesn't hate you. She had to expect that you and Des might have it out. As you said, if not now, when?" She was surprisingly patient with my breach of etiquette.

I abruptly stopped and turned to face her. "Shit! Has the reprieve from the restraining order been revoked? You know, that's what finally provoked me, his fucking selective memory." And then I cried out of pure frustration. My head was pounding from the tears and sun. "Suppose we should head back?"

With her arm around my shoulders, she pulled me close for a tight hug. "Only if you're ready."

"Well, we can't wait for that!"

Taking our time returning to give me a little longer to collect myself, we examined sea shells and bits of sea glass along the way.

After a little prompting, I managed to learn that things were going quite well with Michael. "Well, I have to admit, the Molloy charm is hard to resist. I don't even know him, but he's the only man I've ever met that I want to throw caution to the wind for."

"How do you feel about that?" I knew it couldn't be easy for Hillary to let herself be out of control.

"Perfectly fine, most of the time."

We had reached the beach where the party had been. The scene had transformed into a clean-up crew. I found the object of my desire helping to stow kitchen equipment back into the boat.

"Hello, gorgeous!" he called out to me, waving at Hillary. "We were all worn out, so one boat with half the gear and half the party has returned. The other boat is coming back for us. There won't be any room on this one." Hillary ambled away, giving him the chance to ask, "All right?"

"Other than worried about Tiziana, I'm fine."

*  *  *

When we returned to the yacht, there was no one to be seen.

The sun was still high in the sky when I woke up to the rapping of knuckles on the cabin door. Surveying the room, I saw discarded clothes and towels strewn about. I quickly found a robe on the back of the bathroom door and shrugged into it before opening the door slightly. A crew member stood in the corridor.

"Madam, I have an urgent message for you." I took the piece of paper he held and thanked him. Does one tip in such circumstances? I might be floating on a fancy boat, but I clearly lacked the experience necessary to pass myself off as one of the truly wealthy.

I sat down on a chair by the window and opened the envelope. It was from Taylor. She needed me to call. "Can't be good," I said to myself.

Searching the room, I found my cell phone plugged into its charger. Going into the bathroom, I stood near the open window, hoping for satellite reception. When I turned the phone on, I saw that there were three messages from her. I gave her a call.

\*     \*     \*

"Liam, I need you to wake up," I whispered into his ear. I felt his body move, knowing he was making the supreme effort to wake up. I ran my fingers through his hair and over his back while I waited. Finally, his eyes opened and he stretched.

"What is it?" he asked, sitting up, running his hands over his face.

"Taylor called. Faith Clarkson is arriving in London tomorrow. She's expecting me to be in my office Monday morning. I'm sorry, but I'm going to have to head back tomorrow as early as possible. I should have realized she'd do this." My feelings were jumbled.

He was suddenly wide awake now. "Don't worry, I'm sure Tiziana and Ted will understand. We can have them take us back to Saint-Tropez, and we'll get it all sorted out. Let me get dressed, and we'll go find them." He was off the bed, dredging through the drawers, looking for something appropriate to put on.

Wrapping my arms around his waist, I pressed my forehead against his back. "I feel so bad! This afternoon's meltdown and now this. Tiziana will be so disappointed. Des will have won. Regardless, I'm sure you can stay."

He turned around in the circle of my arms and pulled me tightly against him. "Des didn't win. You'll have your chance another time. As for me, I'm only here because you are. If you have to leave, I can come back to London with you and fly back home. If I work Monday, I can head to London on Thursday night and take another long weekend. What do you think?"

My answer was a grateful kiss. "Thank you."

He twirled me away. "You'd better get ready."

Liam set about getting our stuff a bit more organized while I dressed for the evening and prepared myself for Tiziana's disappointment.

# Chapter Eighteen

FACING THE WORST-CASE scenario, we found Tiziana and Ted chatting with Des in the lounge. If Liam hadn't shoved me into the room, I doubt I would have had entered.

"Bella, what's happened? Did you break the bed?" she laughed nervously, clearly doing her part to keep the situation light. The guilt I had felt on the beach was now enormous. It seemed like she was prepared for more confrontation because of me.

Not glancing at Des or Ted, I answered her. "Taylor called. Faith Clarkson is on her way to London and is expecting to see me at my desk Monday morning. I'm afraid I'll need to head home as soon as possible."

Her smile turned into a frown. "Bella? If it's about this afternoon, we were just talking, and I think, between the heat and overindulgences, everyone was worn out." She sounded hopeful.

"Oh, Tiziana, if I could, I would stay. But I really do need to be in London tomorrow. You know what life has been like." I had admitted to myself while I was changing that I was glad to be leaving. Des appeared to be without remorse. I couldn't imagine remaining on the boat without exploding. Who knew that Faith Clarkson's demanding nature would prove serendipitous?

Ted stepped forward. "Don't worry, Charlotte. I'll arrange everything. We appreciate that you were able to be here at all. We'll miss you." I hugged him then her, thanking them profusely for their generosity. Liam did the same, and then followed me when we left to continue packing. We would see them shortly for cocktails and dinner, anyway.

On the way to our cabin, I grumbled, "I should have expected this from Faith." My mind began to inventory what I had brought with me and where I'd last seen it. "Damn! I meant to grab my book. I left it in the lounge."

"I'll get it," Liam offered, concern in his eyes.

Shaking my head, I said, "No, it's fine. Tiziana and Ted are there. I'm still drained from this afternoon. I don't have it in me to pick another fight."

When I returned, only Des was there. Half of the reason I was on this boat was sitting in the room by himself. Knowing there was too much to cover and too little time to do it, I took a deep breath of resignation and crossed the room to where my book sat on a side table.

Seeing me, he waited silently until I'd picked it up then surprised me by speaking. "You might find this hard to believe, but I'm glad you're back. This isn't the ideal opportunity, but, if I may, I'd like to speak with you privately."

Having come this far, I couldn't imagine there was too much more to lose. I sank into a leather armchair and dug my nails into it, my stomach churning away. "Yes, fine, right. What is it you'd like to say?"

"Well…" He tugged at his bottom lip, then began again. "Obviously, it's about everything. Tiziana, Ted, this afternoon, and the wedding. It's been awkward as hell, but I think we need to clear the air, for all our sakes." All in all, I was impressed how calm he was, given this afternoon's blow-up.

Shocked into silence, my brain couldn't put all of this together. I wanted to ask the right questions in a dignified way, to show that I was intelligent and rational, but I felt tongue-tied.

He reached right in and took the bull by the horns. "First, I'd like to say that I'm very confused. The person I met in Chamonix and spent time with here doesn't match up with the person who kept calling my house day and night. Or who sent that unusual gift."

We sat staring at one another, while my brain tried to sort out what he had said. Ted, Tiziana, and Liam entered the room, clearly anxious.

"Charlotte, Ted has it all fixed up," Liam said, offering a diversion. He moved to my side, while Ted and Tiziana stood slightly apart from the rest of us.

"Are you all right?" Liam asked me quietly. I nodded, my eyes still on Des, still unable to speak.

Liam, clearly worried, jumped in. "Right! Whatever has happened in the past, let's get it out in the open."

Tiziana and Ted took a few steps forward at the same time. I held up my hand, signaling everyone to settle down.

Ignoring them, I looked at Des and said, "Wait, wait, *wait*! What are you *talking* about? What phone calls? What odd gift?" Everyone was quiet, including Des.

While processing my question, incredulity crossed his face. "Do you really want to go into the details, now?" His eyes shifted from me to Liam. I nodded affirmatively.

"I received more than fifteen phone calls from your cell phone over a two-day period. You sent me a pair of…" At this juncture, he waved his hand in circles at my waistline. "A pair of your underpants. Tiny ones, at that. To top it off, they were sprayed with perfume. What about the letter asking me to meet you at the casino for cocktails? How can you possibly deny this? You kept showing up everywhere. It was great fun to begin with. You were a nice, normal person with a great sense of humor, and then all of a sudden you were just there, everywhere." He looked almost as drained as I felt.

I was shocked as he recited my sins. Once he finished, I crumpled back into the chair. I felt Liam move to stand beside me then reach down and take my hand.

Ted and Tiziana took another step forward. "Listen, Des, perhaps now isn't the time," he suggested, rather forcefully. *Why wouldn't he?* It was *his* boat and *his* party, plus *his* fiancée was falling apart. I took a better look at her and registered that she was taking all this rather hard. My heart went out to her. This certainly wasn't how she anticipated the weekend going.

"Ted, if it's all the same to you, I would rather get this over with now. There will never be a good time, and there may never be another time. Perhaps you and Tiziana should leave." I nodded toward her. My voice was slightly wobbly, but my resolve complete. I had faced harder things, surely.

Tiziana let out a deep sigh, shook her head no, and began to pace while wringing her hands. Ted watched her with confusion on his face.

"Bella," Tiziana started to say. Her voice faltered when she heard others approaching. Ted quickly crossed the room and quietly spoke to those outside. After shutting the door behind him, he returned to Tiziana's side. We were now isolated and uninterruptable.

Kneeling on the floor before my chair, she looked up at me with her big doe eyes, her makeup carefully overdone. Tears slid down her cheeks. My brain was searching for answers.

She looked over her shoulder at Des and took a deep breath. "Des, it wasn't Charlotte. It was me. It was a huge, horrible misunderstanding." Quickly, her eyes flashed to Ted and then shifted back to rest on mine. "Bella, let me explain. It was a simple mistake. At the casino, Ted gave me the phone number where he was staying—with Des. When we got home from the casino, I called him, but I felt so guilty about Gianni, I hung up. You know what falling in love can be like, torturous at times. I can't remember how many times I called and hung up. It wasn't until I got up in the morning that I realized I had your phone. Remember when we came home from the casino? We both put our bags and phones on the table by the door. Our cell phones were almost identical, and somehow I picked up the wrong one.

"Finally, I got the courage to call Ted. Afterwards, I realized I had the wrong phone, so I put it next to your purse. Then the next night was the night I stayed in and the rest of you went into Chamonix. While the rest of you were getting ready to go into town, I decided to call Ted again. I had forgotten to charge my phone, so when I saw yours, I used it. It didn't seem like a big deal. I think it might have been the snowstorm, but we kept getting disconnected, so we kept calling each other back." She took a breather here, and directed her full attention to Ted. "When I found out you were leaving, I decided to send you a souvenir."

After a moment's pause and a search for some understanding in my eyes, Tiziana rose to her feet, stiffly. Her hands shook as she raised them to her face. Pushing back her long, black hair, she tried to cool her flushed skin. We all sat and stared at her silently. "I'm so embarrassed. I never thought I would be explaining this to most of you, and definitely not all at once."

She paced the room, trying to figure out what to say. "It was only after the restraining order was delivered that I began to wonder if this could be my fault. I wanted to tell Ted right away, but he never mentioned the package I had delivered to him, and I was too embarrassed to ask. I thought perhaps it was too risqué for him." She looked up at him. Her cheeks were deep red and a faint smile crossed her lips. "After Gianni and I were officially over, things with Ted moved quickly. We were so swept up. I did ask Ted to talk to Des, hoping that with time it would all be resolved, simply, quietly." She finished in a whisper.

I looked at Des. He was looking at Tiziana, stunned, his mouth opening and closing like a guppy. My brain was trying to absorb what she'd said. I looked at Liam and saw compassion in his eyes, for whom I wasn't sure. Ted had taken Tiziana into his arms and murmured quietly in her ear.

We remained silent for a minute or two. Finally, Des cleared his throat, looking completely uncomfortable. He looked at me and said with sincerity, "I don't know what to say, other than I'm genuinely sorry." He looked at Tiziana as he stood to go. "Brynn received the package. We knew it came from the chalet you'd rented, since it was the same address you gave the chauffeur when we dropped you off the night we met. I never told Ted about the package. There didn't seem to be any reason to."

My brain was functioning enough to let me know that he was about to leave and that I had things to say. That I was worthy of respect, not just pity.

"Wait!" I almost shouted. "I'd like for you to stay." I stood and wiped my hands on my dress, as if the action would smooth away the emotional upheaval we were all feeling. I looked at Tiziana, who had left the safety of Ted's embrace. I said, "A million thoughts ran through my mind. The most prevalent one is that you'd hoped it would quietly go away. I've had to endure a restraining order being filed against me which, to the best of my knowledge, could follow me forever. I've had to explain this to my family and friends. I've had to deal with the open hostility of my employer. I've had to work every hour of the day and night to prove myself to her. I've had to endure whispering from co-workers and strangers. I've had to crawl out of a bar, and I've spent months hoping that there wouldn't be more legal problems to follow. I've been hurt, confused, humiliated, and questioned my own judgment, all because you hoped it would go away quietly. I came here, risking the wrath of my boss, because of our friendship. It broke my heart to think I couldn't come to your wedding. To me, a little embarrassment is worth friendship. Finding this all out, here and now, like this... You're selfish."

I turned and looked at Des. He seemed about to say something but thought better of it. "I'm sorry for having judged you so harshly. I don't know you and you didn't deserve it."

I turned to Ted and said, "I'd like to leave sooner rather than later, and if you could make that happen, I would appreciate it."

With that, I turned on my heel, walked out the sitting room, passed our group of friends and family who were hovering in the corridors, and entered my room. I sat down on the chair by the window and cried.

# Chapter Nineteen

**A FEW HOURS LATER**, the boat anchored at the dock in Saint-Tropez. Liam and I made a quiet exit. A private car awaited us; our belongings were stowed in the trunk.

Just before we stepped into the car, Ted hugged me and said, "Please call her. She's devastated."

I kissed him on the cheek and said, "Me too." I received another quick hug before he and Liam shook hands. I heard them speaking quietly while I arranged myself in the car.

It turned out that Ted had been quite generous. The driver of the elegant black Mercedes whisked us to a private airport. We were flown back to London in Ted's private jet. I patted Liam's knee as he took in all the finery and assured him that I still loved his toys more.

"I don't know, I think you're making a big mistake," he said.

Not entirely convinced I understood what he was referring to, I didn't respond and allowed myself to be lulled into sleep by the hum of the jet and the coziness of the reclined seat. The strain of the preceding few hours had worn me out.

No sooner had we landed and exited the plane than my phone rang. It was Taylor letting me know her mother was in town. "Not to worry, Liam and I are here in London. We'll be home in an hour or so."

Surprised and confused, she asked me an array of questions. Instead of answering them, I only asked, "Where is she staying?" I was certain I couldn't face Faith Clarkson anytime sooner than I had to. "Oh, okay, see you then." Once I reassured Liam that she was staying at the Savoy, he relaxed, too.

It was strange, returning to Hillary's house. I imagined my friends floating on the Mediterranean, trying to soothe Tiziana. Taylor wanted to hear all the gossip. Liam did his best to be entertaining, but, sensing that something was amiss, she took herself off to bed. Not long after, we did the same.

Liam curled himself around me, his hand skimming my skin from shoulder to knee, dropping kisses wherever they landed. "I'm sorry. I know it all seems childish. Just don't forget that, in the past Tiziana, has been a true friend," he whispered into my ear.

I rolled over. "I know. I just feel drained. Not just from what happened on the boat, but the whole eight months." I wrapped my arms around his neck and inhaled his scent, letting myself drift away. I felt him gently move us into a more comfortable position and fell into a deep sleep.

The next day, we slept in, made and ate a huge breakfast, and lazed around. The surroundings and privacy felt quite luxurious, since Taylor had taken herself out for the morning. I suggested that it might be better for me to go to Ireland for the weekend instead of him returning to London.

"Coward! You just don't want to hear what Hillary has to say about Des, Tiziana, or the rest of the trip," he said, knowing she was due back at the end of the week.

"First, I don't think you want our first fight to be about this! You're calling the wrong person a coward. I just thought that having another weekend alone would be wonderful, but if you'd rather be here with Hillary, Taylor, and whomever else, that's just fine!" I was perhaps a little too harsh for a person claiming not to want a fight.

After leaving him at the airport, I deposited myself at my desk and prepared for my meeting with Faith the next day.

I was relieved to find out that nothing significant had occurred in my absence and felt quite ready to deal with the devil. The transition team had done well. The new offices were up and running at almost one-hundred percent. A huge gala was in the planning, and celebrities on both sides of the Atlantic had been invited.

*Let the celebrity pandering begin!*

I decided to take the Tube home, not having ridden it since my return to London. The clatter of shoes against the stairs, noise ricocheting off the tile walls, and the faint smell of diesel pulled me back in time. Memories from what seemed a lifetime ago, when Hillary, Marian, Kathleen, Tiziana, and I were eager graduate students.

I was pulled out of my reverie by the train's arrival at Knightsbridge. I decided to walk the rest of the way, since it was a beautiful evening. I took out my cell phone and called Taylor. Fortunately, she was free, so we decided to meet at Covent Gardens to find some dinner.

When we finally settled in at Bertorelli Restaurant, she told me all about her day with her mother. Her crumpled light gray linen suit bore the signs of the day's struggles.

"Good luck tomorrow, that's all I can say. Lord, she's foul when she's tired. I'm not sure I can show my face at the Savoy ever again. Everyone who works there along with the guests were on pins and needles by the time we finished tea. Can you believe she sent the tea back with instructions on how to make it properly?" She tipped back her large glass of red wine, drained it, and then grabbed a waiter by the sleeve to beg for another.

"Certainly, madam," he said, but he appeared to be wondering if he ought to.

She briefly rested her head on the back of the burgundy leather chair and stared up at the ceiling. The frown melted off her face as the serene surroundings and wine took effect. Having taken a moment to regroup, she leaned forward. "Okay, spill it, sister! It must have been a doozy of a trip!"

Impatiently, she waited while I finished my glass of wine and nibbled my way through a breadstick. Reluctantly at first, I recounted everything including the confrontation between Des and me then Tiziana's confession, ending with my request to get off the boat as soon as possible. She sat silently, listening to the whole story without interruption. I was just finishing up when our main courses appeared. The waiter seemed relieved to see her glass still half-full.

After he deposited our meals before us with a *buon appetito*, she let out a quiet whistle. "Wow, poor Tiziana! How embarrassing." When I failed to echo her concern, she said, "Look, I know it hasn't been easy for you, but surely you can see how silly this is. She must have been humiliated to have to tell you what had happened in front of Des and Liam. I'd rather spend another day with my mother at the Savoy than witness that train wreck. I suppose it might have been funny if it had been just the two of you."

"Trust me, it was never going to be funny. She knew all that time that she could have been responsible for the restraining order, and yet she didn't tell me. I would never have done that to her." I stabbed at a bite of tagliatelle and pumpkin.

"Look, she lives in Italy, and you lived in New York. She probably had no idea how much all this had affected you, personally and professionally. She wasn't around to see people pointing fingers and hearing the gossip. Unless you had told her, how could she have known? You didn't talk to her for a couple months! And when you called her, she didn't hold a grudge. Listen! You know how self-absorbed people falling in love can be! Take yourself, for example!"

I was so busy contemplating what she had said that it took a full minute for the last part to sink in. "What do you mean?" I clattered my fork onto my plate.

"Marcus and I have decided to call it quits." She pushed back her plate and downed her second glass of wine, all while keeping an eye out for our roving waiter.

"What? Why? When did this all happen?" *My God, I had been completely self-absorbed.*

The waiter had seen Taylor's subtle wave and came to take her order. He cleared our dinner plates and asked if we'd like anything besides another glass of wine. I ordered strawberry gelato, and Taylor ordered some kind of chocolate truffle cake—a sure sign of a broken heart.

"It has nothing to do with love. We love each other very much. It's distance. I'm here, he's in New York. We could fly back and forth, but for how long? I need to be here, I need the opportunities that being here will give me. It was a hard and horrible decision, but we both think it's for the best. Don't look at me like that. It's hard enough. You'll make me cry, and I don't want to. I want to eat my chocolate dessert and enjoy a night out." Tears rolled down her cheeks and her voice got higher and squeakier.

It was on the tip of my tongue to say that Liam and I had done just that. We lived in different countries. We were prepared to fly back and forth. But her question was a good one. How long could this continue? I shook my head clear. I didn't need something else to contemplate.

Changing topics dramatically, I distracted her with stories about the boat, about Kathleen sashaying around the harbor in Saint-Tropez looking for her prince, of Marian and Kathleen exhausting Alessandro and Paolo, and Hillary's cool, aloof exterior crumbling when near Michael.

Reluctantly, we got ready to leave. Outside Bertorelli's, we breathed in the London night air, listening to the buzz of people and traffic. We made it only a few blocks before we gave in and hailed a taxi. Between the wine and the events of the last few days, we were both exhausted. We decided to head straight to bed. It would take all our strength to deal with Faith Clarkson.

\* \* \*

The next few days proved to be the longest of my life. I didn't have time to worry about Tiziana, Taylor, Marcus, or anyone else. It was every man, woman, or child for themselves when Faith Clarkson was around. Liam had left messages, but I hadn't found time to call back.

Every nook and cranny of the facilities had been inspected. Every employee interviewed, every document read. The only thing she hadn't done was comment on the toilet paper. Well, she had remarked on its stiffness but hadn't demanded we find a replacement. What a difference one week could make!

I was summoned to Faith's office at the end of the day on Wednesday. Taylor and I ran into each other on our way there.

"Now what? I wish she would just go home. Not only am I being flogged for what still needs to be done, she's been anything but motherly about Marcus and me splitting up. I can't wait to see her back." Taylor, who was clearly irritated, took her mood out on the hair that insisted on falling into her eyes by shoving it back aggressively.

I put an arm around her and gave her a squeeze. "Don't worry. As soon as she's safely on a plane and in the air, you and I are taking a break! Maybe we can take a long weekend somewhere." I really needed to get a hold of Liam. I hoped he hadn't booked a ticket yet.

Arriving in the conference room, the bane of our existence ignored us as she stacked papers into piles then shuffled them into folders then into a briefcase. She looked cool as a cucumber, literally. She was wearing a soft green sheath dress and jacket, her blonde hair perfectly in place, her makeup without a smudge.

"Ladies, go home and pack a suitcase or two. We're leaving on the 9:00 plane to New York tomorrow morning. I've already notified your groups. Your staff will carry on without you for a while." She finally lifted her demon eyes to us before returning to shuffling papers fast and furiously. Secretly, I was hoping she'd get a paper cut that became infected.

"What? Mother, really. There's too much work to be done here. Why do you need us to go to New York?" I certainly didn't have the nerve to ask that.

"Taylor, when your employer tells you to get on a plane, you get on a plane. I'm only answering you because you're my daughter. A few issues still need resolving, and I need to head home. Therefore, you'll accompany me, we'll sort them out in New York, and then you can return. That is all!"

It was obvious the conversation was over. Without uttering another word, we turned around and walked out of the office, different emotions on each of our faces. Taylor was elated, and I was irritated.

"This is so good. This means she respects my opinion and needs my help," she giggled, like a school girl.

"Well, this is completely annoying. I have a life. Liam is expecting to see me this weekend *and* I have a massive amount of work to do here." I was angry.

We dashed back to our offices and packed up what documents we thought we might need for the next however-long. Taylor stopped by my office as I was placing my laptop into its bag.

"Ready?"

"I guess!" Without a backwards glance, I walked out of my office, flipped off the light switch, and shut the door.

We had barely walked in our front door when the bell rang. Taylor hopped to answer it, struggling to take one shoe off while she carried the other.

I rummaged in the fridge, looking for something to eat. There wasn't anything all that spectacular to be found. A wedge of cheese, some cherries, milk, and what appeared to be a very despondent tomato, all wrinkled and splotchy. I stuffed a chunk of cheese into my mouth and peeked around the corner to see what was going on.

I saw incredulity on Taylor's face. Gemma Newley was standing in the foyer, looking as stunning as a film star should, in a deep blue, tailored halter dress. The sun and surf of the last week had agreed with her.

"Gemma! Hello, how are you?" I dashed forward to give her a kiss, hoping I didn't smell like musty cheese. Taylor looked a bit dazzled, but when I made the introductions, she managed to pull it together and offer a normal greeting.

Leading the way to the terrace out back, I left them to search for glasses and a bottle of white wine. When I returned and everyone had a drink, we talked for a short while before Taylor graciously excused herself.

As soon as we were alone, Gemma said in her straightforward fashion, "Tiziana was devastated when you left. We didn't see her until the next afternoon, and I'm sure that was only at Ted's cajoling."

*I should have brought another bottle of wine,* I noted to myself as I gulped the air in my glass. She continued, "Des would only say that the two of you had a falling out over what happened in Chamonix. As you undoubtedly know, I have experience in forgiving someone who has hurt and humiliated me. Des wasn't very discreet with his indiscretions. But when the person who did the hurting is genuinely sorry, you must forgive them. She loves you!"

I was having enough difficulty absorbing the fact that I was returning to New York the next day for an indefinite amount of time. So the fact that Gemma Newley was sitting in the back garden pleading Tiziana's cause seemed like a hallucination. Finding my voice, I told her as succinctly as possible all that had happened since my return to London.

"I know it sounds terrible, but I really don't have time to deal with this right now. My being in Saint-Tropez was a fluke, a gift from the gods. Then I got a call saying I had to return to London just before things with Tiziana blew up. Now I have to explain to Liam that I'm going to New York for god knows how long. My brain hurts from all of this. I haven't even begun to figure out how I feel about anything. I'm just running right now, trying to keep all the balls in the air."

"Well, it must be a bit much!"

We sat in silence for a moment. Clearly, Gemma was invested in Des or Ted or both, so I confided, "You probably understand better than most, it isn't pleasant to be caught up in the public eye. Especially when you don't want to be. It's not like I had any idea what it would be like. At least when you're a celebrity, you have experience with billions of flashbulbs and lies. What hurt me the most was being on the receiving end of everyone's judgment, including Des's. I wasn't given the opportunity to ask questions, explain my side, or say how I felt. I just had to live with it."

She nodded, understanding. "Look, he's open to talking to you. He's become a very decent person. Call him and sort it out. Then call Tiziana. She needs you to forgive her." With this, she gave my hand a quick squeeze, and I followed her as she walked to the front door. We gave each other air kisses, and then she disappeared into the evening.

While I stuffed clothes into suitcases, Taylor hovered in the doorway, asking for a recap. I gave her some details as I tried to figure out how much to pack. I glanced at my watch and saw it was getting quite late. I still needed to call Liam.

I dashed down the hardwood staircase and into the unlit sitting room to call him, kicking the door shut behind me. After a few rings, his voicemail kicked in. "Liam, it's Charlotte. I'm sorry I haven't called. I received your messages. Faith has us running in circles. Call me when you get this."

I sat in the oversized chintz armchair for just a moment and looked out the window. The streetlights reflected off cars passing by and lit the way for a few couples taking late-night strolls. *Why are other people's lives so calm, so easy?* I found myself wondering.

After I had had enough of pondering the mysteries of life, I took the phone upstairs and stuffed toiletries into a bag. Taylor and I shouted back and forth down the hallway about our unexpected visit from Gemma and what to do about Des. I was so thankful Hillary wasn't here. She wouldn't appreciate our noise and confusion.

Eventually, the phone rang. "Hello!" I said anxiously.

"Hello, gorgeous. How is everything? You sound exhausted," Liam asked.

*Phew, his broody glance a few days before was forgotten.* Apparently, he wasn't a person to harbor anger. I filled him in on all the details: my sudden trip to New York, Gemma Newley showing up, Taylor and Marcus's break-up, and the grueling three days I'd had.

"That's a hell of a few days. How long will you be gone?" Silence hovered between us when I told him I had no idea.

"Liam, I'm so sorry. I don't want to go. We'll make it work, I promise. I don't want to end up like Marcus and Taylor." Another prolonged silence. I felt more and more anxious.

"We won't. That's the last thing to worry about. I was just wondering what we could do to help them. Maybe you could encourage her to see him while you're there. I don't know if that's a good idea, if they're determined to end things, though." I loved him all the more for thinking about this and simultaneously felt a whole lot better about our situation. The same thought had rushed through my head a few hours before, but I was afraid to approach Taylor with it.

"What about Des? Are you going to call him?"

"I suppose I should. I'd like to know the state of the restraining order. I'd love to believe it's over. I guess it will have to wait until I get back. I'm sure all my time in New York will be taken up with work." I took a deep breath and blew it out. The chaos was still swirling around in my normally well-ordered mind, and I was struggling to find the silver lining. "It all seems overwhelming right now. I just want to go to New York and get that finished up. The quicker I can get that sorted out, the sooner I can come back, see you, and start to figure all the *other* stuff out."

Pointedly, we changed the subject for a few minutes to catch me up on Liam's life over the last few days. "Well, it certainly hasn't been as exciting as yours!"

"Just hang out with me, and I can promise you all the excitement and chaos life has to offer!"

"I was talking about Faith Clarkson, you eejit! Look, we're in agreement that your life's pathetic. You live in a tip, you have no friends, and your job is complete crap and unchallenging…"

I should have known I would have my pity party all by myself.

Chuckling, I promised to call when I got settled in New York and then said goodbye. I felt weepy at the thought of not knowing how long I'd be gone.

While I got ready for bed, I found myself thinking about Liam's comments and Gemma's advice. Did I dare contact Des? He had acknowledged my innocence, and I had apologized for my presumptions about him and his enormous ego. As I threw myself into bed, I found myself grateful to be returning to New York and escaping England, with all those questioning eyes. I needed time to think. I just needed a few quiet hours to myself to figure out what the next step was.

# Chapter Twenty

**SITTING IN TRAFFIC** on a Friday night in New York City during the summer was generally hideous. Having left the cooler and less humid climes of London just over a week before, I was grateful to be sitting in the air conditioned town car provided by Faith Clarkson International. I was finally on my way to talk to Des Bannerman regarding the insanity of the last eight, almost nine, months; my stomach churned with excitement and dread. If nothing else, I was sure we would mutually agree to conduct ourselves in a fashion that wouldn't put us on the covers of tabloids.

Edging toward the Metropolitan Museum of Art, I told the driver, "I'll get out and walk from here." I walked at a brisk pace, shaking off the melancholy I'd felt while sitting in the car, ruminating about the past. Looking at my watch, I saw that it was 8:47. I had thirteen minutes to get to the museum, find *The Block* by Romare Bearden, and come face to face with Des. I also had to pray that my new Fendi sandals were actually meant to be walked in.

Moving through the crowded sidewalk was much more pleasant than observing the hustle and bustle through the car window. The evening was warm. Golden light ricocheted off windows and through leaves on the trees to cast shadows on the cityscape. The smell of a recent summer shower lingered in the air. Groups of people milled around on the terraces in front of the museum.

Climbing the steps, I felt sweat trickle down my back and registered my sweaty palms. I quickly glanced at my watch and saw that I had eight minutes—hopefully enough time to speak with the necessary person, do a quick mop-down, find the painting, and then meet Des. The last two words seemed fatal.

Months' worth of uncertainty, hurt feelings, and anger were parked inside of me. "Just be yourself, get the answers you want," I said firmly to myself. "Don't let your emotions get the best of you." My foot rolled over and I cursed the Fendis. "They should be called O-ffen-sive," I continued to myself, but immediately felt remorse when I saw a scuffmark on the soft buff-colored leather.

Upon entering the museum, I found the concierge. Taylor had taken the necessary measures with the museum to allow Des to view the painting in privacy. The museum was expecting a representative of Faith Clarkson to join him. After my ID was handed over, my briefcase was discreetly searched.

Calmly, the bushy-browed man said, "You'll find Mr. Pan waiting for you in the correct gallery. Would you like Mr. Williams to escort you?"

I accepted the offer of an escort and down the hall we trudged. *Trudged* because Mr. Williams was in no hurry and didn't seem to sense my need to get this over and done with. As we wandered the halls of the Met, he kindly pointed out popular attractions, restrooms, maps, historical facts, the color of the sky in a painting (not cerulean…)—whatever seemed to drift through his mind.

My nerves were stretched thin and my chest felt tight. Under my breath, I chanted, "Breathe in through your nose, out through your mouth." I felt my pulse slow and my shoulders drop; my stomach no longer seemed to quake.

"Here we are, Miss," Mr. Williams informed me as we stopped outside a spacious room that housed the painting. I took a Kleenex from my briefcase, dabbed at my face, smoothed my straightened hair, and used the side of my finger to scrub any lipstick from my teeth. Mr. Williams, having stayed to observe my preparations, remarked, "You look just fine, young lady." His kind words lifted my heart and put a big smile on my face.

"Thank you, Mr. Williams. Wish me luck!" I felt a surge of confidence that I hadn't felt in a very long time skip across my psyche.

"I'll wait out here, in the hall. Call if you need anything."

I took a deep breath and walked at what I hoped was a normal pace toward the man viewing *The Block*. He wore dark denim jeans and a fitted navy blue linen shirt. His outfit reminded me of the one he wore in one of his recent movies. About five feet behind him, I came to a stop.

I took a final deep breath to calm myself and spoke his name. He turned from the painting. "Ms. Young, Charlotte. I see you've made it." He was calm, which I took as a good sign.

"Not a surprise, then!"

"Not really. I do know whom you work for. Now that we're here, thank you for providing the opportunity for me to come to the museum. I rarely find the time to do such things. Odd, really, considering how much travelling I do. Would you like to sit or wander?" He pointed to both the bench in front of the painting and the room around us.

"Moving would be best." I was sure I exposed my anxiety.

"Moving it is." He kindly extended his arm to suggest a direction. "I hope the use of Mr. Pan didn't confuse you. It's for Peter Pan, really. It's silly, but I rather like the idea of using cartoon names. It was Julia Roberts's idea. She often uses a princess's name to hide from the press."

"*Notting Hill.*"

Smiling at me, he walked slowly about the room, his eyes taking in the artwork. "So, Ms. Young, what are we doing here?"

"Well, if I were to follow Taylor Clarkson's plan, I would be selling you on the finer points of using Faith Clarkson's services. But, since meeting you, nothing has gone according to plan, so why start now?" I had humor in my voice as I stopped to face him. His blue eyes slowly lifted to mine. The thought ran through my mind that I had seen many of his personal mannerisms in his movies and wondered where real life stopped and make-believe began. "I want to know what the state of the restraining order is." I was proud of my calm, straightforward manner.

Folding his arms in front of his chest, he looked me squarely in the eye. "Right! Well, let me just start by saying that the whole revelation was truly dramatic. I had no idea real life could be that way. Ah, let me take that back. I have had my own moments bandied about the press for over a decade." He paused briefly, his eyes glazed over, giving the impression he was reliving another moment. I only had to wait shortly, before he continued speaking. "In any case, after hearing Tiziana's confession followed by your trouncing and then being assaulted by Marian, Kathleen, and Hillary the night you left, I think I have a much better understanding of the world, egotism, honesty, true love, and one more thing… which right now seems to escapes me. So, I returned to England the next day, called my lawyers, and had all the formal details dealt with. I didn't know you were in New York until seeing you at The Volstead yesterday. Which explained, perhaps, why the legal papers couldn't be delivered to your London address. Yesterday afternoon I asked my lawyers to arrange a meeting with you, but apparently there was only an answering machine. Frankly, I just want the whole thing over with." He nodded with a swipe of his hand through his hair.

That was it. It was over. It was very anticlimactic. I stood looking at him and waited for the sadness to retreat, the knots in my stomach to unfurl. I waited for it to all go away. But it didn't. Realizing now was not the time to try and unravel this mystery, I did the next best thing.

"Thank you. Taylor Clarkson is also my housemate. She was terrified when she saw Mead, Jameson, and Kelly on the caller ID yesterday. Right now she's probably waiting for a phone call from the police station. I'd better give her a call. After that, would you like to go to the Gordon Ramsey opening dinner?"

Surprisingly, he said, "He comes across as a bloody prick. I'd rather not, actually. Do you know anywhere that serves good seafood?"

"I have a few suggestions, just a minute," *How bizarre life could be? One minute you were having the weight of the world lifted off your shoulders, and the next you were going out for seafood.* Honestly, there was no point in trying figure out what normal was.

He roamed around the room while I made a reassuring call to Taylor. I blatantly disregarded the fact that I had been instructed to turn my cell phone off by the many museum docents and signs. And I ignored Mr. Williams, who was glaring at me.

"Are you in jail?" she asked instead of saying hello.

"No! He had his lawyers formally request the restraining order be withdrawn just after I left Saint-Tropez. So, it's all over. I'll fill you in on the details when I get home. As odd as it may seem, we're going out to dinner."

Between her gasps and questions she said, "Well, you'd better give Liam a call as soon as possible. He called just after you left, and I told him what you're up to."

"All right, thanks." As the guard approached me, I preemptively apologized. "It was a life or death situation."

Neutrally, he said, "It always is." I walked over to Des. His hands were stuffed in his jacket pockets while he stared at a pastoral painting.

"I don't understand this kind of bucolic art. Ready?" I nodded and we were escorted through the empty corridors of the museum. At the entrance, we extended our thanks to Mr. Williams and the concierge.

"Right, now, where the bloody hell is the car?" He glanced about the busy streets.

"I'm sorry, I'm not quite ready. I just couldn't handle Mr. Williams's wrath. One more phone call, I'm afraid. Liam wants me to call."

"No worries. If I were in his shoes, I'd want to know that the love of my life wasn't in the tabloids or jail." He grinned.

I moved away a short distance and called across the miles of choppy gray water. Liam snapped the phone up halfway through the first ring. I reassured him that all was fine and that Des had withdrawn the restraining order.

Liam let out a breath. "Well, that's a massive relief. How do you feel?"

I was touched by his concern. While I knew that he loved me and would have bailed me out of jail, I had never stopped to think about how this might be affecting him. "I feel great. Thanks for being on my side! I wouldn't have done it without you. Well, not quite so soon. Do you mind if I fill you in on the details later? I've asked Des to dinner, just to finish clearing the air. I'll have more to tell you then. Should I call tonight or wait until tomorrow morning?"

"Whenever, I don't mind." With that, we said our goodbyes.

Then, as if it were the most natural experience in the world, Des and I walked down the steps and into the summer evening. I walked without fear and began to feel elated. As we approached the curb, a black town car with tinted windows pulled up. "Your car, I presume," I said. It all sounded James Bond-y.

"Yes, someone from Faith Clarkson International set this all up!" Des teased.

We slid inside and settled ourselves on the soft buff leather. Returning to the task at hand, I asked Des if there were any restrictions on where we could go and received the green light to select anyplace that had good food. I asked the driver to take us to the Grand Central Oyster Bar.

As we slowly pulled into traffic, he turned to face me, then surprised me by gently taking my hand and looking into my eyes.

*Good Lord, what is this*? In alarm, my thoughts banged around my head.

Seeing my fear, he quickly said, "I've suddenly remembered what else your friends enlightened me on—friendship. Yes, that was it! Charlotte, what are you going to do about Tiziana? She's in misery. By the way, you look terrible in whatever you call that neutral-colored businesslike affair. I much prefer the scarlet frock you were wearing last time I saw you."

He let me change the subject entirely. As we drove from Central Park, down Fifth Avenue, I pointed out the sights along the way. "I've been in New York City before," he said kindly. I stopped the dialogue and laughed, remembering Hillary acting as tour guide when Liam and Michael had come to London.

The driver pulled up to the curb and let us out. The hustle on the street left us anonymous, at least so far as I could tell. A beautiful quality of the Grand Central Oyster Bar was that it was vast, noisy, and busy. So, while a few women did go gaga over Des while we waited to be seated, we were mostly left to ourselves.

"My god, look at this menu. It's fabulous. So American! Too many choices! That's the benefit of going to hoity-toity restaurants—they offer some form of a special menu and all decisions have been made." Des perused the sheet in his hands. Quickly, he looked up from the menu. "Before you even say it, I know the word 'special' in this case offends you!" Looking back down at the menu, he muttered as he searched through the list. A fleet of waitresses arrived at our table to take our order; well, his, really. He politely looked up, smiled, then glanced back down and tugged on his lip. This was becoming a familiar sight.

"Ready?" he asked me a minute later.

"Yes." I gave my order, not certain that I would end up with my crab Caesar order, given how distracted the waitresses were, staring at Des.

When he spoke, they jumped to life. "Yes! First, a bottle of the champagne. Then, we'll start with an order of the fried oysters and poached mussels. For my main course, I would like the pan-roasted lobster."

Once we were alone, I took the opportunity to make a deeply-rooted complaint. "This is exactly the problem. This is how the whole mess came about. They don't even have champagne on the menu and yet you ordered it. Where are they going to get it? Why do you think you're entitled to order something not on the menu?"

He tugged at the cuffs of his shirtsleeves and then folded his arms on the table in front of him. Leaning toward me, he replied, "First of all, I'm not evil. I've been here before. In fact, the kindly gentleman who ran the place let me know that there's a stash of the stuff. So I doubt anyone is being asked to rush out to purchase a bottle or two. Secondly, I don't think I'm entitled to *anything* special! Some celebrities do, and they make the rest of us look like spoiled brats. To be fair, at times I take advantage of it. Trust me when I say that, at times, it's very hard not to. You, yourself, do it. You didn't think twice about asking the blokes on the boat to bring you cocktails or schlep picnic baskets to and fro. In my defense, I would say that, for the most part, I'm reasonable." He sat back in his chair, waiting for my retort.

"Oh!" I said, but because Taylor and Marcus had just entered the restaurant. They looked nervous and were standing a healthy distance from each other; with any luck, it was a start.

Des followed my eyes. "Friends of yours?" I filled him in on the superficial details.

We watched them get settled in. A waitress hovered nearby, discreetly staring at Des. I quickly called her over. "Could you please send a bottle of champagne to that couple over there?" I carefully pointed out Taylor and Marcus.

"Certainly. Would you like anything else, Mr. Bannerman?"

He looked startled. "No, that's all, thanks."

As she walked away, he laughed at me. "You see, we all do it from time to time. You had no compunction about using your connections to get what you wanted. I say, what's wrong with that? The restaurant has sold two bottles of champagne, four customers are happy, everyone wins."

I let myself be teased into agreeing with him but made clear it was okay only in circumstances where everyone won. "You know, in a non-romantic way, you broke my heart. I've seen most of your films, and I just assumed that you were this really likeable guy. Then, after chatting with you at the casino, I really liked you, in a platonic, non-sexual way. I felt really hurt and confused."

"Well, now you know that in real life I'm an arrogant prick." He smiled even when I didn't laugh, then reached across the table and took my hand. "Sorry! I do understand, and for that I feel awful. Now, could we please move forward? I'm dying to try the mussels." The appetizers arrived and the bottle of champagne was ceremoniously uncorked.

I heard another 'pop' a minute later and looked up to see Marcus and Taylor raise their glasses to us. I raised mine in salute, and Des very kindly joined in.

While I ate I realized just how thoroughly stress had affected my life. Food hadn't tasted this good in quite some time. From his happy hums and sighs, I assumed Des was enjoying his as well. While we ate we talked about everything from my move to London to Des's new film. While we were discussing the merits of working with someone like Olivia Wilde versus Keira Knightley, Taylor and Marcus came over to the table. Des stood up to shake Marcus's hand and gave Taylor a quick squeeze on the shoulder. They didn't linger, but Taylor gave me a happy grin.

Marcus bent over to kiss my cheek and said in my ear loud enough for Des to hear, "Careful, no more tabloid photos!" I whacked his arm and sent them on their way hand in hand.

I quietly clapped my hands. "Oh, I'm so happy. I hope it works out."

"No more dilly-dallying! Let's talk about the wedding. What are we going to do?" Des said before taking a sip of his coffee.

"What do you mean? What needs to be done?"

"Haven't you spoken to Marian, Kathleen, or Hillary? *Anyone?*" A serious look crossed his face, and his forehead creased with frown lines.

The waitress approached, asking if there was anything else Des might like. I intruded on her thoughts by requesting the bill.

"I'll pay," I offered when she left.

"The hell you will. Faith Clarkson is paying." This thrilled me to no end.

Various waitresses purged the table very slowly, halting any personal conversation. When the bill was paid, using my corporate credit card, I suggested we skedaddle.

When we were back in the car, I asked, "What's happened with Tiziana and Ted?"

Des quickly filled me in. While I was up to my eyeballs with Faith Clarkson, Tiziana decided to postpone the wedding. She'd told Ted they had become engaged without knowing each other well enough.

Apparently, she was taking her part in mine and Des's situation very seriously.

Ted had been working triple-time trying to convince her that they knew each other more than well enough, and that, while what had happened in Chamonix was embarrassing, it wasn't life-altering for them.

After Des finished explaining, I told him that Tiziana had a superstitious streak in her and that she wouldn't get married with a dark cloud hovering over her head.

"So, then, clear the air." He seemed pleased with the pun he'd made but I made a face and said I'd think about what to do.

"That's it?"

"Yes. For now, that's it."

"Beginnings are scary. Endings are usually sad. But it's the middle that counts the most," Des recited poetically.

"What are you talking about?"

"Think about it!" He pushed his legs out and leaned back into the chair.

I knew better than to think it was simple. He seemed to be making an obvious point but through playing a game. *A game! That was it.*

"Sandra Bullock, *Hope Floats*!"

"How'd you guess so quickly?" He seemed astonished.

"I used my cell phone!" I responded immediately, pulling it from under the briefcase that I had slid strategically onto my lap.

"That's cheating!" Des's voice was full of horror.

"So it is," I responded with no remorse. "In the future, remember that I'm resourceful as well as honest."

"Like a Girl Guide."

"Something like that."

* * *

Not too much later, the town car pulled up in front of my apartment building. "Shall I have the driver walk you up?" Just as I was about to rage against this, he started to laugh. "You're going to take a lot of convincing, aren't you?"

"Yes, I am." I grabbed my briefcase and slid out the door. Then I ducked my head back inside and smiled. "It was surreal but nice."

"*Notting Hill*! What is it with bloody Hugh Grant?"

"I like him!"

Upon entering the apartment, I saw light shining from under Taylor's bedroom door. I was about to knock when I heard Marcus laugh on the other side. Quickly, I redirected myself to my bedroom, closed the door, and turned on the television.

*   *   *

I woke to the ringing of the phone. "Hello," I managed to croak out.

"Hello, my love. How was your date?" Liam teased.

"Hello! I have to whisper, because he's still asleep." Liam belted out a loud laugh. *God, I missed him.* First, I apologized for not calling when I got in, but it had been too late. Then I filled him in on all the details of my conversation with Des.

"So, it's all over. You feel well and truly vindicated?"

After contemplating this for a moment, I announced myself to be completely done with the issue.

"Good. Now, tell me when you're coming home to my bed."

"Oh, that reminds me, Marcus is here, in Taylor's bed! Good news, I hope. We have to find a way to get him to London. I know, if he could find work there, they'd sort it all out and live happily ever after."

"That would be great for us all. In any case, any news on when you'll be back?"

I'd been back in New York for nine days at that point. Faith had run us ragged every day we'd been there and hadn't said a word as to when we could return to London.

"No clue. Chances are she'll tell me an hour before the plane leaves. I'll let you know the moment I know." I switched the subject and told Liam about Tiziana and Ted.

"What are you going to do?"

"Why does everyone think it's *my* job to do something? She owes me an apology."

"I believe she's already apologized, twice." He sounded irritated.

Not wanting to have our first fight over the phone, I quickly changed tactics. It didn't take much effort, and, as a result, we spent the next half hour helping each other start the day in a pleasant way.

After his breathing returned to a normal pace, he proclaimed, "Charlotte, that was spectacular! You've really picked up a knack for phone sex. Even if we manage to live in the same country, we're still going to have phone sex." Then, without missing a beat, he added, "Speaking of phones, call Tiziana."

"I love you, Liam. I have to go."

"Coward."

"Bye." I quickly hung up.

I spent the day running around in circles, doing Faith's bidding, and finally encountering Taylor as she stepped out of her mother's inner sanctum.

"How did it go last night?" I held onto her elbow and dragged her down the hallway.

"God, I love him. What am I going to do?" She sounded confused.

"Beg him to move to London with you. Convince him that you can support the both of you while he looks for a job. Beg your mother to hire him. Whatever it takes."

She stopped in her four-inch-heel tracks, looked me in the eye intently, and then marched back to her mother's office. I walked to my own office with a big smile on my face.

*    *    *

When I got home from work, I found Taylor lounging next to Marcus on the sofa. Her long legs were curled up on his lap. I was about to dash discreetly down the hallway when she jumped up in excitement. "Good news! We're going to London tomorrow, and Marcus is heading over next week!" We jumped up and down together, squealing like little girls.

While sitting next to him, she explained how she had marched into her mother's office and announced that she had more than proven her value to Faith Clarkson International and that she wanted recognition for her work both financially and professionally. She also wanted a permanent position in London. In a complete twist, it turned out that it was Faith's hope that, in making Taylor return to New York, she and Marcus would work things out.

"She told me that just because people thought she was a cold-hearted bitch didn't mean she liked to see her daughter brokenhearted."

Taylor beamed. "So, Marcus has agreed to be a kept man until he can find a job!" We squealed like little girls again.

I gave him a hug and gushed, "Oh, Marcus, I'm so happy. Liam will be thrilled. Oh! I have to call him. He won't mind me waking him up!"

I dashed down the hallway, looked at the clock, and realized it was 1:00 a.m. I dialed Liam's number.

"Hello?" he growled into the phone.

"Hello, yourself. Are you alone?"

He sighed. "No, let me tell the little bitch to get her clothes on and go home." I laughed loudly.

"Guess what? Marcus and Taylor are moving to London. He's willing to be a kept man until he can find a job."

He responded happily to the great news with a *'whoop'* that could have awoken a few neighbors. "What about you? Any news on when you get to come home?"

"Well, I could come back tomorrow, but I need to make a detour to Rome. My plan is to return on the weekend. I'll let you know when I have the flights finalized." I hoped his faith in me had been restored.

"Sounds like an excellent plan. But I'd like you to come to Ireland for the weekend, if you can." He sounded serious.

Assuring him that there was nothing I wanted more, we switched to talking about my trip to Rome, mostly about my being nervous at seeing Tiziana. "Don't be nervous. She'll be thrilled to see you." He was so calming.

# Chapter Twenty-One

**TWELVE SHORT HOURS LATER**, I found myself on a plane heading to Italy. Exhausted, I knew it would take little effort to fall sound asleep. I had run around like a mad woman, packing a few extra suitcases with the clothes I would need for the fall. My hope was that I wouldn't be returning to New York before the holidays. Before leaving for the airport, Taylor and I spoke briefly about packing up the contents of the apartment, but when that became teary, we deferred the discussion until we were in London, where nothing would ever be sad.

I dropped my luggage off at the hotel and quickly freshened up before making a quick call to Liam to let him know where I was and what was happening.

"*Buona fortuna*," he offered.

When I called Tiziana's office, I deduced from her secretary that she had taken an extended leave from work. I then called her parents' home, the only other number I had. With all the drama that can be afforded an Italian mama, her mother told me that her Tiziana was too distraught to work. However, she could strong-arm her into coming over for dinner that evening, if it would be helpful.

I arranged for a car to take me to Tiziana's family house in the Villa Borghese area. There, Alessandro stood sentinel outside the front door, waiting for me. In truth, I suspected he was really taking an opportunity to smoke a cigarette away from his watchful mother's eyes. He kissed me on each cheek and greeted me in broken English while gesticulating wildly. "Ciao, bella! We're most happy you here! Our only hope. Finally, all the drama can stop, and we can get back to making the plans for the wedding."

"Does she know I'm here?"

CELIA KENNEDY

"Sí, and she's very nervous. I'll walk you to her. She's waiting in the *giardino*." He stubbed out the cigarette with the toe of his shoe.

We passed through the beautiful, winding house to an enclosed back garden. Italian cypress and pine trees looked like sculptures against the darkening sky. Warm light from the house glowed on the ancient stone and lit up fragrant flowers in pots scattered around the patio.

The garden seemed to echo Tiziana's sensuality. There she sat beside a table ladened with a jug of water, a bottle of prosecco, two glasses, and what looked like a tray of antipasti. While my brain raced in turmoil, wondering what to say, my stomach registered its complaints at going unfed.

I slowly walked toward her, not really certain what I should say. I looked in her big, brown eyes; they instantly dissolved into tears. "Bella," she managed to say, and then I rushed to her and gave her a hug.

"Silly girl. Postponing your wedding over something so silly. Everything is fine, it's fine." I reached for a napkin that lay on the table and handed it to her to mop her face, then smoothed her hair and continued to murmur comforting words.

# Chapter Twenty-Two

**TWO DAYS LATER,** I landed at the airport in Dublin, a bit weary of travel but thrilled to see Liam. It had taken twelve days, thousands of miles, three countries, and two momentous conversations to get me there. I walked into the arrivals lounge and saw him waiting for me. As before, he descended on me with a sense of hunger and ownership, and I lunged right back at him.

"Been taking the penicillin?" I asked when I came up for air.

"What? Why?"

"'Cause you slept with that floozy, and, after everything that's happened, I don't need any STDs."

While I was speaking, I could see the light dawn in his eyes. "Yes! For good measure, I went to the see the doctor on St. Stephens Street, bared my arse, and took a major dose. So there's nothing to worry about." He pressed his answer against my lips.

When we arrived at his house, he led me straight to the bedroom. "Not to be unkind, but you look like you could use a week's worth of sleep."

"You're just trying to get me out of my clothes."

"Nope! Take off what you need to be comfy. We're taking a nap." He pulled at my shoes and I gratefully gave in.

\* \* \*

I woke up from the much-needed nap and set about adjusting my brain to where I was. The other side of the bed felt cool to the touch. Liam must have been up for a while. Late afternoon light shone on the brick wall opposite the bed, and the shadows cast by the window blinds directed my attention to a bedside table. On it was a lamp and a book. I picked up the latest detective novel by a well-known author and saw two postcards poking out from the same page. One was a black and white photo of New York City's skyline at dusk; the other, a similar photograph of London.

Staring at them, I began to realize how completely the complications of my job and the drama of Des and Tiziana had affected my time with Liam. We had had many great days together, but there had always been background tension.

I had the sudden realization that the sense of sadness I had felt for so long was gone. My stomach held no knots; it was unfurled from its clenched state. Lying in his bed, I felt all the calm and ease with the world that had evaded me for so long.

I had lain there quietly, thinking for some time, when Liam softly walked into the room and realized I was awake. "All right?"

"Perfect."

He pointed to the postcards I held in my hand. "Silly, I know. The first and last thing I see every day."

"Thank you." I sighed. Not trying to stop them, tears welled up in my eyes and slid down my cheeks. He got in bed, pulled the covers up around us, and gathered me to him. A tissue materialized from somewhere, and, while mopping me up, he whispered, "It's been a hell of a few weeks."

"It's been a hell of a year." The remaining deep shudders of stress rippled through me. We clung to each other for quite some time in absolute silence, just still and quiet. I felt peace wash over me.

The silence was finally broken when he said, "I'm hoping you're happy about this... My friends are wanting to meet you this time, so I said we'd meet them down at the pub later. Is that okay?"

"Perfect."

That evening, I found myself in a neighborhood pub surrounded by hordes of people who greeted Liam and me. Michael and his parents showed up at some point, and I found myself sitting at a little table, chatting away with them. It had taken some effort to put aside the fact that they had seen Liam put his hand up my dress. I was relieved that Michael didn't see fit to remind us all.

"Your father and I need to go," Niamh said. "We're getting too old for all of this."

"Speak for yourself, woman!" Eamonn declared.

"Well, I'll be speaking for you. You're the one who'll be useless tomorrow if you stay much longer." She shared Liam's determination in her eyes.

We stayed for another drink and then I, too, had to beg off. I was physically and emotionally finished. Saying our goodbyes, we promised to meet up again soon with several of his friends.

"Great friends," I said while we walked back to his place. "We need to hook Marian and Kathleen up with a few of them. Wouldn't it be great?" Liam rolled his eyes.

*   *   *

The next day, we woke up in the early afternoon. I threw on a soft, drapey cover-up while Liam pulled on sweatpants before going to the kitchen to explore. He was prepared with a load of supplies this time. I was soon throwing eggs and slices of bacon into pans, and he took over making coffee and toast. My stomach rumbled: I was almost faint from the smell of the food for the second time in just a few days.

I sat at the table, gobbling down every morsel on my plate, when Liam brought over the coffee pot to refill my cup. Returning to the table, he watched in amusement as I used a piece of toast to round up remnants of egg. He leaned his chair back on its legs and said, oh-so-casually, "I've been thinking about this for a while now, and, seeing that you're in favor of Marcus being a kept man, how would you feel about it for yourself?"

"Kept men? What are you talking about?" I was completely confused.

He coughed uncomfortably into his fist, looking uncertain. "Charlotte, what I'm saying is this. I want to marry you. Now. Today. I want to eat breakfast with you every day. I don't want to stare at postcards at night and wonder how you are, where you are, what you're doing. I want to stare into your eyes and know. I want to have a home with you. If I were to pack the lot up and move to London, would it bother you if I didn't have a job lined up? Is that a financial option?"

Taking a deep breath, I carried my dishes to the sink, then looked through the window at the street scene below for a moment. "Who would we ask?"

"What do you mean who would we ask?" He was standing right behind me. His hands came to rest on my shoulders, his voice hopeful. He spun me around gently.

"Who would we ask to be witnesses?"

# Chapter Twenty-Three

**THE DAY HAD** finally dawned. It was seven months later than planned, but it was Tiziana and Ted's wedding day.

Liam and I drifted slowly around the dance floor. A wooden platform was in the center of a large, manicured lawn in the center of a garden adjacent to an ancient Italian castle. The perfume of summer flowers hung on humid night air, and the twinkle of the stars above us accentuated the romantic setting Tiziana had created for her wedding.

"You have to hand it to them, they know how to throw a party," Liam whispered loudly in my ear over the band's lead singer, Bono.

I nodded, seeing no real purpose in talking.

Liam led me to a vacant table in a quiet corner of the garden. While I settled into the chair, he ran his lips along my mostly naked shoulder. With a kiss to my cleavage, he said, "Be right back!" and went off in search of cold drinks, leaving me a few minutes of solitude before he returned with what appeared to be beer for him and a large glass of sparkling something for me. Behind him was a familiar crowd.

"My feet are killing me. Next time one of you gets married, remind me to wear sensible shoes," Marian complained.

"You don't get the boy by wearing sensible shoes!" I reminded her.

"True, very true." She sighed, pulling off a golden Versace sandal to massage her foot.

Des dragged up a chair and said to me, "You look heavenly."

"*Notting Hill*," I answered immediately.

Over the prior year, Des had become a familiar face in our crowd. Not only was he the nice guy Gemma claimed him to be, I was genuinely pleased to learn he could take as well as he gave. He had a rather ribald sense of humor. The first time he told a fart joke, I nearly wet myself.

"No, this time I mean it! You do," he repeated kindly.

"Well, that's one way of looking at it. I'm almost as round as I am tall." I plucked the empire waist away from my ever-expanding abdomen.

"She does look heavenly, Des," Ted pitched in, having joined the group. "Like a Grecian goddess! Well done, Liam!"

"I don't remember seeing any drawings of Aphrodite looking like a... Well, whatever. Why is it that men always get the credit? It isn't like his sperm did the job alone!"

Hillary didn't flinch. Clearly being involved with Michael had desensitized her. A year before, the discussion of sperm at a wedding reception would have caused her to go catatonic.

Seeking out her groom, the blushing bride joined us. Tiziana glowed with excitement. She had dressed us all in floor-length gowns in the palest of pale gold, each unique in subtle ways that benefitted our various assets. She herself wore a stunning gown made of Mikado silk designed by an up-and-coming Italian designer. A diamond tiara glimmered from within the confines of her intricately woven hair.

"A summer wedding, isn't it beautiful?" Her voice had a melodious, joyful ring to it. In a more conspiratorial voice, she said, "Don't tell my Mama she was right. I'll never hear the end of it." Clearly sharing her happiness, Ted gave her a long, passionate kiss, which was followed by the appropriate rude remarks from the rest of us.

A waiter, dapperly attired, arrived bearing a tray of cocktails. They looked delicious. I turned sad puppy-eyes to Tiziana. "What are those?"

She looked guilty. "A Sbagliato."

I knew she was keeping her answer short on purpose.

"Which is?" I prompted.

Summoning up all her charm, she draped her arm around my shoulders. "Bella, we'll toast the bambino with these! A combination of prosecco, sweet vermouth, Campari, and an orange twist. Sugar and spice, and everything nice!" I gave her a big smile to let her know she was off the hook.

I gave Liam a glance and ventured my thought. "Since we have you all here, it seems as good a time as any to invite you all to the christening. Since the wedding was a quiet affair, we've decided to pull out all the stops and have a big party. Obviously the exact date is a bit nebulous, close to the end of October. We'll send out invitations when we know."

My abdomen tightened and I felt the flutter of the baby readjusting itself. Reflexively, I put a hand to my belly and used the other to catch Tiziana's hand. "Tiziana, I'd like for you to be the baby's godmother." At this, she jumped up and down, nearly toppling the tiara and hairdo. Marian, Hillary, and Kathleen looked despondent.

"Good Lord, I've married an Irishman! Don't worry! You'll all have your turn!"

"True enough," chorused through the group.

Liam took over. "As for godfather, Des, we'd like to ask you."

Des, who was stuffing his bowtie into his tuxedo jacket pocket, looked up in utter shock. "Seriously? Look, I'm flattered, but let's be realistic. I'll be crap! I'll probably forget all her birthdays, and then, when she's eighteen, I'll take her out for a few drinks. And then, let's face it, I'll probably try to shag her!"

"*About A Boy!*" I shouted.

Keep reading for an excerpt of

Cognac and Couture,

The Passport Series, Book Two

# Cognac and Couture

**"DARLING, COULD YOU** just lean a little further back, lift your left foot just a touch, and make sure your toes are softly pointed?" the celebrated celebrity photographer Jeremy Sutton sang out to Kathleen in a sycophantic voice, just before bellowing to the hairstylist, "For Christ's sake, brush her hair off her forehead and keep it off. I want her hair over her right shoulder, not her left."

A fairly large number of people were attempting to juggle light reflectors, hold down wind barriers, and grapple with styling weapons, while dodging small ocean waves that rushed the beach. Granted, they were in the shallow blue waters, but it was all so ludicrous that Kathleen had to suppress laughing while the makeup artist applied another layer of powder to take the shine off her forehead.

"She's sweating! Someone get a bloody umbrella over here and shade her," the photographer demanded, while he prowled around Kathleen, looking at her through various camera lenses. Lowering the camera from in front of his face, he looked at her and said charmingly, "Darling, you are simply beautiful. For you, there is no bad angle."

Cries of urgency registered in Kathleen's head, just before a wave swept the photographer to his knees. He heroically held his camera over his head, saving his equipment. Once she realized the photographer was fine, she looked where all the commotion was occurring. Two of the wind barriers had blown down the long sandy beach, and several people were chasing after them, hoping to stop them before they crashed into innocent bystanders.

The scene unfolded on Finn's Beach at the southern tip of Bali. To get there, they had had to take a two-minute funicular ride between two steep cliff walls covered in a dense jungle of plants. At the base of the cliffs, a sandy beach rushed into the crystal clear Bali Sea.

The photo shoot was officially a disaster! Kathleen waved to one of the staff hired by *Forbes Magazine*. "Could you drag this under the palapa for me?"

Taking in the general chaos, the darkly tanned employee grabbed the teak lounge chair out of the surf and tugged it into the shade. "Would you care for a drink while you wait?" The man had a dignity discordant to the situation.

Kathleen smiled from beneath the protection of the dark green palm fronds that roofed the palapa. "A tall glass of pineapple juice would be wonderful." Not that she was cruel, but, since it wasn't her turn to clean up a disaster of epic proportions, she sat back and watched the scene with a wide grin.

The soggy photographer made his way to her after directing all of his employees to pack up their equipment. "Truly sorry, love, but it's a bust. The wind is too strong. We'll need to find another location. My assistant has a spot in mind a few miles up the road. Okay?"

"Absolutely fine. How long until we leave?"

"Twenty minutes or so." With that, he was off to confer with his assistant.

Kathleen drained the glass and leaned her head back against the wooden frame of the chaise. She felt a catnap coming on; with nothing more to do than listen to the lapping waves and the clacking of the palm fronds, she let the heat and the soothing melodies pull her into a short sleep.

\* \* \*

When they arrived in the remote and tiny cove of Padang Padang, it was still early in the day. The photo shoot soon attracted the interest of the beachgoers and locals; they quickly set up places to watch from a few hundred yards away. The owners of the small fish cafés on the beach enjoyed a high volume of business.

"Fancy a nosh before we get started?" Jeremy asked Kathleen. "You need a make-over anyway."

*What an ass,* she thought to herself. Not that she was surprised that her makeup and hair needed fixing, but he just was so abrupt and arrogant. The consummate professional, she replied, "The fish smells incredible. I could definitely do with some food."

The two made their way to one of the smallest cafés and ate a quick meal of ikan bakar, grilled fish, and fried noodles. "This is extraordinary," she said after a few bites.

"Try this." Jeremy held a small dish that contained a red sauce.

"What is it?"

"Sambal. Its base is bumbu—a combination of many spices. A bit on the picante side. Tasty though."

Kathleen used her fork to take a small sample. Using her little finger to deliver a sample to her mouth, she felt the fire. "Excellent. A little too hot for me, though." If the photographer realized how much she was sweating through the material of the lightweight business suit chosen for the photo shoot, he'd have a conniption.

While he finished his meal, her eyes swept the crescent-shaped cove, taking in the massive boulders plopped down along the beach randomly by Mother Nature; trees grew out of them at odd angles. The natural beauty of the cove was more rugged than Finn's Beach, which appealed to her.

Jeremy interrupted her thoughts. "This should suit you well."

"How so?"

"A lily among thorns." He tossed money onto the table. "Shall we?"

"Sure."

As they walked back to where the minions wrangled equipment and props, Jeremy called to the stylists, "All right, she's all yours. Get her ready. Someone find her a toothbrush. She's had fish for lunch. A fresh suit, too. She's ripe!"

Kathleen stopped abruptly, kicking up sand. *You're definitely a thorn,* she thought to herself.

*       *       *

Just as the sun began to set on Padang beach, Jeremy called it a wrap. "You know, I think some of these photos with the soft colors of the sun setting will be perfect." He stared at the digital screen of his camera. "Lovely, really lovely."

Kathleen was grateful when one of his quieter assistants offered her a lift. She wouldn't have to listen to Jeremy drone on for the next hour as they drove to their hotel, The Four Seasons Bali at Sayan. The name sounded as gorgeous as the landscape they drove through.

The resort was built on stepped hills amongst lush jungle and rice paddies; it had plunge pools, riverside restaurants, and a spa, all of which called her name. She had perfected the art of being busy while relaxing.

\* \* \*

# About the Author

Celia Kennedy was born on a military base in Wurzburg, Germany. Her parents' penchant for traveling stuck with her: she's lived in and traveled through several countries.

The imagined world has always fascinated Celia. She has studied art history, interior design, landscape architecture, and architecture. Her thirteen-year career at the University of Washington in Seattle ended in 1996. Not wanting to be homeless, she left the academic world and worked as a landscape architect, married the love of her life, became a mom, and served as PTA president and Boy and Girl Scout leader.

Her love of travel, the designed and natural world, friendship, self-discovery, wine, chocolate, AND love are the foundation of her books.

### Celia Kennedy's other work includes:

*Prosecco and Paparazzi, The Passport Series, Book 1*
*Cognac and Couture, The Passport Series, Book 2*
*Venus Rising*
*Sugar, It's Cold Outside (Cupid on The Loose Anthology)*
*April's Fool (Fools Rush In, April Fools' Day Anthology)*
*Meri's Over A Barrel (Girls of Summer Anthology)*
She is currently working on book three in the Passport Series: *Gin Fizz and Grit.*

**To learn more about Celia Kennedy:**

Website: www.celiakennedy.weebly.com
Blog: www.womanreinventsself.blogspot.com
Twitter: https://twitter.com/KennedyCelia
Facebook: https://www.facebook.com/CMKAuthor
Goodreads: https://www.goodreads.com/Celia_Kennedy

# More Great Reads from Booktrope

*Unsettled* by **Alisa Mullen** (Contemporary Romance) American Girl falls for an Irish boy in a summer filled with adventure, wonder, and the unexpected.

*Jeep Tour* by **Gail Ward Olmsted** (Contemporary Romance) The road to romance can get pretty rocky! When her marriage falls apart and she loses her job, Jackie Sullivan decides to start over among the red rocks of Sedona, Arizona. Is she chasing a dream or Rick, the dreamy tour guide she just met?

*Unsettled Spirits* by **Sophie Weeks** (Contemporary Romance) As Sarah grapples with questions of faith, love, and identity, she must learn to embrace not just the spirits of the present, but the haunting pain of the past. Can she accept her past in order to let love in?

*Tumbleweed* by **Heather Huffman** (Contemporary Romance) When a cruel twist of fate threatens her new life in the Ozark Mountains of Missouri, Hailey must choose between rebuilding and fighting for love, or continuing to drift through life like a tumbleweed.

*Tripped Up Love* by **Julie Farley** (Contemporary Romance) When Heather Meadows loses the only man she's ever loved, her perfect, ordinary life is turned upside down. Little does she know that her world is about to be turned upside down again when one wrong step puts her in the path of a new destiny.

Discover more books and learn about our
new approach to publishing at **booktrope.com**.

15498116R00162

Printed in Great Britain
by Amazon